THE EXPERTS PRAISE ROBERT SCOTT

Shattered Innocence

"Robert Scott shows that the Jaycee Dugard story is more compelling and more shocking than the news previously reported. *Shattered Innocence* is a fascinating account of a young girl's abduction by a monster who should never have been free to walk the streets. This is a ground-breaking book."

—*New York Times* bestselling author
Robert K. Tanenbaum

"Robert Scott's book zeroes in on many compelling but unreported aspects of the Jaycee Lee Dugard case. What happened to Jaycee Lee is equal parts fascinating and horrifying, and Robert Scott embraces both to tell this extraordinary story in a fresh way. The result is a fast-paced, informative read."

—**Sue Russell**, award-winning author of *Lethal Intent*

Monster Slayer

"An intriguing look into a gruesome series of crimes, a brutal serial killer and the culture of the Four Corners in which he found his victims."

—*New York Times* bestselling author **Tony Hillerman**

D0822251

Also by Robert Scott

AND
THEN SHE
KILLED HIM

ROBERT
SCOTT

PINNACLE BOOKS
Kensington Publishing Corp.
http://www.kensingtonbooks.com

Some names have been changed to protect the privacy of individuals connected to this story.

PINNACLE BOOKS are published by

Kensington Publishing Corp.
119 West 40th Street
New York, NY 10018

All Kensington Titles, Imprints, and Distributed Lines are available at special quantity discounts for bulk purchases for sales promotions, premiums, fund-raising, and educational or institutional use. Special book excerpts or customized printings can also be created to fit specific needs. For details, write or phone the office of the Kensington special sales manager: Kensington Publishing Corp., 119 West 40th Street, New York, NY 10018, attn: Special Sales Department, Phone: 1-800-221-2647.

Pinnacle and the P logo Reg. U.S. Pat. & TM Off.

ISBN-13: 978-0-7860-2038-6
ISBN-10: 0-7860-2038-5

First Printing: November 2012

10 9 8 7 6 5 4 3

Printed in the United States of America

PROLOGUE

Delta, Colorado, April 30, 2008

Businessman Alan Helmick, age sixty-two, was finally selling his part ownership of a mortgage company in the picturesque Colorado city of Delta. Alan had recently told a friend he wanted to take more time off and "smell the roses." Ever since the death of his first wife, Sharon, from a sudden heart attack, Alan had a new appreciation about the fragility of life. He began to believe that a person had to enjoy himself, as well as work hard at a profession.

Alan's second wife, Miriam, certainly embraced that belief. She, too, had shared her own tragedies. Miriam's daughter, Amy, age twenty-three, had died from an accidental overdose of medication in 2000. Two years after that tragedy, her first husband, Jack, had committed suicide over the loss of their daughter. Now Miriam spent all the time that she could teaching dance lessons in the nearby city of Grand Junction, as well as running a horse-training center, which Alan owned.

On April 30, however, Miriam was not feeling good. She complained of stomach problems; and as Alan finalized the documents at the title company, Miriam kept having to dash off to a restroom in the business complex. Returning to their car in the parking lot, Miriam found Alan already sitting inside the vehicle behind the steering wheel. It was a hot day, and she asked him to pop the back trunk lid so that she could retrieve a pair of sandals from the trunk. She wanted to wear the sandals instead of her tennis shoes. But before Miriam had a chance to grab her sandals, she suddenly felt sick again and rushed off to the ladies' room.

As Alan sat in the car waiting for Miriam to return, the engine of his Buick was running. Suddenly, to his amazement, he noticed a white plume of smoke coming from the rear of the vehicle. At first, he thought it was just normal exhaust fumes, so he turned the vehicle off. But soon the white plume turned darker and became more intense. Alan realized that the rear of the vehicle was on fire. He jumped out of the driver's seat and noticed flames leaping upward.

Alan rushed into the building to try and find a fire extinguisher, but he was unable to find one there. He met Miriam coming out of the restroom and told her the astounding news of what was happening. Miriam scurried down the hall and was able to obtain a large pitcher of water. She ran outside and threw the water on the car fire. Miriam ran back inside the building several times, filled the pitcher with water, ran back out and threw the contents on the fire. Finally, after several trips, the fire went out.

Alan looked at the gas tank area and noticed a cloth-type article sticking out of the gas tank. It suddenly struck him—someone had just tried killing him or Miriam, or both of them, in a car fire.

The next day, May 1, both Alan and Miriam were interviewed by a sergeant at the headquarters of the Delta Police Department (Delta PD). Asked if Alan could think of anyone who might want him dead, Alan could only think of one person, a man named Don. Don was a former vice president of the Olathe State Bank, and Alan had done business with him. Alan discovered that Don was involved in fraud and deception in bank dealings, something Alan despised. Alan's testimony helped send Don to prison.

The Delta PD officer then asked Miriam if she could think of anyone who would want to kill her or Alan. The only name Miriam came up with was a woman named Barbara, but Barbara lived a long distance away, in Gulfport, Mississippi. Miriam had worked at Barbara's dance studio there after the suicide of her first husband. Barbara had accused Miriam of stealing from her, but eventually those charges had been dropped. Miriam also thought that when she started her own dance studio in Grand Junction, Barbara, who owned a dance studio there as well, was angry at the competition.

The investigators kept looking into the car fire, but no one was arrested for the incident. And as May 2008 turned into June, the car fire remained a mystery.

CHAPTER 1

UNANSWERED MESSAGES

Life went on at the Helmicks' extensive home on their sixty-acre ranch in Whitewater, Colorado, after the car fire incident. Alan had been sick all spring, and there were times he couldn't even get out of bed. He felt much better now, however, and was enjoying getting back into his normal routine. Alan was a particularly good golfer, and he looked forward to more rounds on the local golf courses, now that the weather was getting better all the time.

Alan was a local boy, having grown up in Delta. He'd been an outstanding baseball player and all-around athlete. He married his high-school sweetheart, Sharon, eventually raising four children, three girls and one boy. He had lived an almost Horatio Alger–like life, building up a business as a real estate broker from practically nothing. He then branched off into subdivision developments and other business ventures. Alan created a comfortable and secure environment for his family.

All of that came crashing down on New Year's Eve, 2003, when Sharon Helmick unexpectedly died from a massive heart attack. Alan went into a state of shock and deep depression. Alan's son, Alan Jr., later said of this event, "I think that he died that day—a big part of him. He lost my mother, who he'd been with since he was fourteen. His love, his life."

It was only the advent of a newcomer to the area, Miriam Giles, that helped to pull Alan out of his depression. Penny Lyons, a friend who knew them both, later said about Miriam, "She was exhilarating. She was very lively. And she'd match him in his joy of doing the things they liked to do. You get someone to do it with, you can't beat that."

After the car fire incident of April 2008, Miriam also went back to her normal routine of running the dance studio in Grand Junction and especially the task of taking care of the Helmicks' horses. Miriam loved horseback riding, and she did so whenever she could. The Helmicks not only had three horses on their Whitewater property, but also a horse-training facility in the nearby town of Loma. The facility was tucked beneath the red cliffs of Colorado National Monument. This was a quintessential Colorado landscape, with green pastures beneath soaring red rocks. There was a picture-postcard quality to the setting and Miriam loved it.

As far as the dance studio went, it was the reason that Miriam and Alan had met in the first place. After the death of his first wife, Sharon, Alan decided to use some unused credits he had at a local ballroom dance studio in Grand Junction. At the time, Miriam was managing a studio, Amour Danzar, in Grand Junction. It was there that Alan met forty-eight-year-old Miriam Giles, and Alan soon became her student. He was fifty-eight years old at the time.

Penny Lyons, who took dance lessons at the dance studio, agreed with Alan that Miriam was very good at dancing. Penny spoke of Miriam as not only being technically good, but having a lot of flair and style as well. Later, Penny would say of the reason she took dance lessons, "I worked at New Life Chiropractic as an assistant, and I met Miriam and Alan at the studio in December of 2005. The dance studio was on Main Street, down in the lower garden area off of Winery Alley." Penny was very impressed about the way Miriam was able to teach her dance students.

By the time Penny took dance lessons, Alan had become so enraptured with Miriam that he bought her a dance studio, Dance Junction, in downtown Grand Junction. Now Miriam could not only manage a place, but she could tailor it the way she wished.

Penny recalled, "I started with group classes, and there were maybe six to ten people in the group on an average night. A young gentleman named Gabe and a young woman named Vanessa taught us most of the time. But Miriam did as well. And Alan was in one of the groups. He participated a lot. I became pretty addicted to the lessons and began taking them three or four nights a week. The people in the group— we got to know each other quite well, and we became friends.

"There were a couple of dinner parties and stuff out at Miriam and Alan's house, when they got together as a couple. At other times, we would meet at Boomers. Bars weren't really my thing, but I went a few times. There was one night a week where they would do dance lessons at Boomers, and then everyone would just stay and dance.

"There were some times I wasn't interested in the dance lessons, such as salsa, so Miriam and I would just stand outside while she had a smoke, and we'd talk the whole hour. Later, in March 2007, there was a dance recital for me. Some people who take piano lessons, they would do a little piano recital for friends and family. This was my little dance recital, and Alan was my partner. After that, Alan quit coming so often to the dance studio. He and Miriam were getting into horses and horse training. By 2008, they didn't come much at all. A nice young teacher named Luda Miller started teaching me and my brother-in-law with private lessons. Miriam and Alan were mostly doing the horses and just weren't coming into the studio by then."

Miriam did have flair and style, as Penny noted. The one thing she didn't have in the beginning was a yen to go out with Alan on dates. Miriam had a policy of not dating her dance students. But Alan was persistent, and eventually they did go out together. After a while, a romance blossomed, and Lyons later said, "Alan, to her, was like her knight in shining armor. He came into her life and said, 'I want to care about you. And your joy is my goal.'" Perhaps part of it was Alan's realization that Miriam had suffered grievous personal losses of her own, with the suicide of her husband and accidental death of her daughter.

Miriam moved in with Alan in his residence in Delta, a home they shared for a while with his daughter, Wendy, who moved in for a while after her divorce. This was a home that Alan had shared for so many years with wife Sharon and their children. Perhaps to make a break from the past, Miriam began looking at other properties in the area. And because of her love of horses, she took a closer look at the area of Whitewater. A few new homes were sprouting up there on lots with forty, sixty, and even higher acreage. It was a very good locale to have a few horses on the property. And Whitewater was also located between Delta and Grand Junction. Alan still had business interests in Delta, while Miriam managed the dance studio in Grand Junction. In many ways, Whitewater was a good in-between choice as the site for a new home.

In 2006, Alan Helmick bought sixty acres and nice modern 3,200-square-foot house on Siminoe Road in Whitewater. To the east, rising above it all, was Grand Mesa, the largest mesa in the world. The top of Grand Mesa was covered with forest and numerous small lakes, ideal for hunting and fishing. On the east side of Whitewater, East Creek wound its way through an array of colorful red cliffs and cottonwood trees.

Alan and Miriam were married in 2006, and they had a large reception afterward at a Grand Junction convention center. Many of Alan's friends were there, including Bob Cucchetti. Cucchetti had been a friend of Alan's for years, and an accountant as well. As far as Alan taking on a project like Dance Junction, Bob later said, "Oh, it had to be Miriam." Cucchetti thought that Alan would never have opened up a dance studio on his own in a million years, but Alan loved Miriam so much that he bought the dance studio for her.

Alan put his heart into it, as he did all business ventures, and even held a dance competition to showcase the new opening of Dance Junction. Ed Benson, a good friend of Alan's, who watched Miriam and Alan dance at the competition, said, "He was good. I mean very, very good!"

In Alan's world, the business ventures were par for the course, and he always liked having something of that nature going. But the dark cloud lingering in the background about the car fire incident was something else. Why would someone want to start a car fire in the Helmicks' car? Had he been targeted? Had it been just a random prank?

Other than that, life seemed to have taken a turn for a more stable and happier aspect in Alan's life by June. And yet, in the background, there were other troubling incidents in the Helmicks' lives. Especially for Alan's daughters, Kristy and Portia. Kristy lived in Denver, and Portia was in Delta. They both wondered why their father wouldn't call them back after they'd left numerous messages on his cell phone. Was he depressed? Was he angry with them for some reason? Neither one of them knew.

To try and reach their father, both women began leaving phone messages on Miriam's cell phone. On June 4, 2008, Portia left a message at 10:27 A.M.: "Hey, Miriam. It's Portia. I need to talk to my dad. I just got a phone call that I need to relay to him." Portia didn't go into more details than that, other than she seemed distressed at the time.

Kristy, who was planning to visit Alan and Miriam soon in Whitewater, phoned on June 6 at 8:29 P.M. and left a message. "Hey, Miriam. This is Kristy. I've been calling my dad for about a week and a half, and not hearing back. I was just hoping to get ahold of him. If you can, have him call me as soon as you get this. Thanks so much. Bye."

The next day, Kristy left a message once again on Miriam's voice mail at 11:52 A.M.: "Hey, Miriam. I just got your message. Thank you so much for calling me back. I'm just trying to get ahold of my dad. Would you really try to talk to him, if he does know that I'm calling him, and not really calling me back—um, that's what I'm assuming. Thanks."

The next morning, June 8, at nine o'clock, Kristy phoned once again to Miriam's voice mail. "Hi, Miriam. It's Kristy. Sorry to bother you again. I've just been leaving messages with my dad. And I thought I'd try leaving a message with you. I wanted to talk to him just 'cause I'm coming on Thursday. And Alan Jr., he left a weird message. I'm trying to cut him off at the get-go. Because I don't want to do what everybody else does. I'm not interested in housing him or anything. But I wanted to ask what Dad thought. And just talk to him in general and see how he is."

On the morning of June 9, 2008, Portia left another message on voice mail: "Hey, this is Portia. I'm starting to get a complex here. I had a flash that you weren't picking up because of what I said for not picking up for Alan Jr. If you don't want to talk to him, and you guys aren't wanting to talk to me because of that, um, you guys have never not picked up before.

"So maybe somebody could call me back. I have a few things I need to talk to Dad about. I need to know if you guys are coming by tonight, and at what time. I have an appointment tonight. So I was going to see if you guys could come by at that point and watch the kids for about an hour. I have a whole other list of things I've been trying to get ahold of somebody about. So give me a call if you can. Thank you."

Miriam already knew that there was a lot of friction between Alan and his son, Alan Jr. The friction tended to spill over to Alan's daughters as well, when it came to Alan Jr. Miriam's understanding was somewhat vague about the problems between Alan and his son. Alan didn't like talking about it.

All of these phone messages hung in the background as night closed down on the Helmick residence in Whitewater on June 9, 2008. Among the unanswered questions were why Alan wouldn't return Portia and Kristy's phone calls. And what "weird message" had Alan Jr. left for Kristy?

CHAPTER 2

"HE'S ALL BLOODY!"

Miriam left the Whitewater residence sometime around 8:15 A.M. on June 10, 2008, to run a number of errands around the Grand Junction area. Her first stop was Walmart, where she called, via cell phone, horse trainer Sue Boulware and told her that she would be sending her a check that day concerning horse training.

At 9:03 A.M., Miriam phoned Alan from the Walmart parking lot and left a voice message on his cell phone. She said, "Hey, Alan. Love you. Just want to let you know I'm going to Walmart. So, um, thought I'd pick up the groceries there instead of going to City Market. I know you're dropping off your prescription at City Market, but I'm gonna pick up groceries there instead of going two different places. Also, do you want salad this time?

"You didn't really give me a list. You said just buy what I want. But that's not really helping me. I think that's it. If you're gonna meet me for lunch, let's meet at the Chinese buffet. 'Cause I don't think I can do Mexican today. So if you want to meet me at the Chinese buffet—I know you wanted to do Mexican, but, anyway, once you get your car serviced, call me. Let me know. Love ya. Bye."

After being in Walmart for a short time, Miriam went across town to a Safeway store on Horizon Avenue to buy carrots for her horses. Sometime after that, she phoned Alan's cell phone again at 9:57 A.M. and got his voice mail. "Hi, Alan. Haven't heard from you, but I have a question. I know you were gonna clean out the truck. But did you happen to leave that bit in there? We can exchange it. I didn't want to go in there without it. I didn't want to spend my money on such an expensive bit. So if you have it in your truck, will you let me know? Or when we meet for lunch, we'll go by and exchange it. Because we'll be close by the equestrian shop then. So gimme a holler. Love ya. Bye."

From the Safeway store, Miriam journeyed to a City Market in Grand Junction. Around that time, she once again phoned Alan, at 10:27 A.M., and did not speak with him directly, but got his voice mail, instead. Miriam said in a more irritated voice than on the previous calls, "Hey, Alan! You need to turn on your phone! When I went to pick up your prescription, they said you hadn't been by yet. So, are we still gonna be able to meet for lunch? If not . . . well, give me a holler. Thanks. Bye."

Then it was on to Hastings Bookstore to pick up coloring books for Alan's granddaughters. And finally Miriam drove to a Chinese restaurant around 11:00 A.M. By eleven-fifteen, Miriam's next phone call to Alan sounded more worried than irritated. She said, "Gee, Alan! This isn't funny anymore." She said she had been sitting in front of a Chinese restaurant for fifteen minutes, and he was never late. She decided she would just go home at that point. If he was caught up in business somewhere, he should call her when he got home.

Miriam made her way through midtown Grand Junction, and then down the highway to Whitewater. She couldn't bring all of the groceries from the car's trunk into the house at one time, but she did bring her purse in and a few shopping bags. She walked through the laundry room, as usual, from the garage, where she had parked her car, turned a corner, and saw something that made her stop in her tracks. She first glimpsed an overturned wastepaper basket in the kitchen/work desk area. The next thing she saw was Alan's legs on the floor. Miriam quickly turned the corner and saw that Alan was stretched out on his back, neither speaking nor moving at all.

Miriam dropped her purse and bag of items and rushed to Alan's side. He was not only not moving, but he didn't appear to be breathing as well. In a panic, Miriam reached for her cell phone and dialed 911.

An operator at the central emergency command post came on the line:

OPERATOR: This is Arnold. What is your emergency?
MIRIAM: (Sobbing) Somebody . . .
OPERATOR: Hello. Hello!
MIRIAM: (Crying) I came home and . . .
OPERATOR: Ma'am, where are you?
MIRIAM: (She gives him the address, but she is crying so much that he can't understand it.)
OPERATOR: Ma'am, what is your address? (She gives it again, but he gets it wrong.) Ma'am, you need to calm down. What happened?
MIRIAM: My husband is dead!
OPERATOR: I need your address one more time.

Miriam had grown irritated by now, but she spelled out the address once more, very slowly. Still, the operator couldn't get it right. He thought it was "Seminole," and then "Femi-noe." Almost beside herself, Miriam spelled it out again—

S-I-M-I-N-O-E. However, her problems weren't over. The operator couldn't seem to place Siminoe Road and asked what county it was in. She finally got him to understand that Siminoe Road was in Whitewater, Mesa County. She also said that the house had been burglarized.

> OPERATOR: (turning to someone else in the command center) Someone else was there. A wife found her husband dead. (turning back to Miriam) I have to ask you a couple of questions. What's the problem? Tell me exactly what happened.
>
> MIRIAM: He was on the floor. And it was like somebody came in and robbed us. He has blood under his head.
>
> OPERATOR: Okay. Are you with him right now?
>
> MIRIAM: I'm in the hallway.
>
> OPERATOR: How old is he?
>
> MIRIAM: He's sixty-two.

Then, in light of Miriam saying Alan wad dead, the next question must have surprised her.

> OPERATOR: Is he conscious?
>
> MIRIAM: No!
>
> OPERATOR: Is he breathing?
>
> MIRIAM: Nooo!

There was a long discussion between the operator and someone else in the command room. Perhaps they thought Miriam was so rattled that she couldn't judge if her husband was really dead or not. The operator asked if she had seen what had happened. She said that she hadn't. She had just returned home from shopping and found her husband on the kitchen floor.

The next question must have sent Miriam into a tizzy.

The operator asked, "Is there a defibrillator in the house?"

Miriam nearly screamed out, "No!"

Nonetheless, the operator was going to have Miriam try and revive Alan by cardiopulmonary resuscitation (CPR).

OPERATOR: I need you to lay him flat on his back and remove any pillows.

MIRIAM: He is on his back.

OPERATOR: Is there anything in his mouth? (Miriam said there wasn't.) Okay. I need you to place your hand on his forehead and your other hand under his neck and tilt his head back.

MIRIAM: He's all bloody.

OPERATOR: Where is he bleeding from?

MIRIAM: It looks like the back of his head.

The operator talked once again with someone in his office, and then back to Miriam. Despite her insistence that Alan was dead, the operator still began walking her through CPR. He had her do chest compressions, telling her, "Place the heel of your hand on the breastbone in the center of his chest. And then put your other hand on the top of that hand. I need you to push down firmly, two inches, with only the heel of your lower hand touching his chest. Listen carefully. Pump the chest hard and fast, twice per second. You've got to do this four hundred times. That's only three and a half minutes. Tell me as soon as you're done. I'll stay on the phone with you."

Miriam checked in with the 911 operator every so often, and told him it wasn't working. In the background, he could hear her crying. Finally, seven minutes into the call, she got on the phone again and said, "It's not working!"

The operator responded, "Have you done it four hundred times?" She answered that she was still working on it, but it wasn't helping. Then he had her change tactics. The operator said, "I'm going to have you do mouth-to-mouth. With his head tilted back, pinch his nose closed and completely cover his mouth with your mouth. Then blow two regular breaths into the lungs. About one second each. The chest should rise with each breath."

After Miriam did that a few times, he asked her if she had felt any air going out. She answered no. Then she added, "He's cold."

After a short period of that, the operator said, "Okay, I want you to give two breaths and one hundred pumps. Then two breaths and one hundred pumps." Miriam said she would. During this period, the operator asked if anyone else was in the house. Miriam said no. The operator turned to someone in the command center and said, "She says no one else is there. There's blood on the back of his head. She was shopping."

Miriam came on the phone again, stating, "His mouth is full of blood."

The operator replied, "You need to tilt his head to the side and clear out his mouth and nose. Don't hang up. We just need to continue to help him until they get there. You may have to blow through some of the blood."

After a short period, the operator asked Miriam, "You said it looked like someone had been there?"

Miriam answered, "I haven't even gone into the other rooms. I'm in the kitchen and it looks like someone went through the drawers and stuff. His wallet's on the floor."

For the first time, the operator asked, "What's your name?" Miriam answered with her first name. When he asked her last name, she spelled it out for him.

Throughout this whole period of time on the phone, Miriam could be heard, crying in the background. Then she let out a wail, "They're here!"

Perhaps worried about who "they" were, the operator asked, "Don't hang up! Is it an officer?"

Miriam responded that it was. After seventeen minutes and forty seconds of being on the phone with Miriam, the 911 operator said, "Okay, I'm gonna let you go, Miriam."

She sobbed, "Thank you."

He replied, "Okay. Bye."

CHAPTER 3

SCENE OF THE CRIME

On June 10, 2008, Mesa County Sheriff's Office (MCSO) deputy John Brownlee was assisting another deputy on a traffic stop when he heard a message go out from a 911 operator. It was about a man in Whitewater who was "unconscious and bleeding" at his home on Siminoe Road.

Deputy Brownlee left the other officer at the traffic stop and made his way to Whitewater. However, as he recalled later, "I had never been in that subdivision before. I took a left road, instead of a right road, and ended up in back of the residence. One road went down to a barn, and the other to the front of the house. Eventually I got to the front of the house, and the garage door was open. I asked dispatch to run a plate for me to make sure I was at the right residence. I didn't want to walk into somebody's house, where I'm not supposed to be. Dispatch advised me I was at the right residence.

"I went to the front door, opened it, and announced myself. I could hear somebody inside, so I went inside. There was a male lying on his back in the kitchen area and a female kneeling by his left side. Dispatch had advised me that she was doing CPR as I was en route. But when I looked, she was not performing CPR or doing anything. She was just kind of kneeling. She turned around and looked at me, and I gathered she had just gotten off the phone with dispatch.

"The fact she wasn't doing CPR, as she said, was kind of weird to me. I didn't hear her crying or anything else. She did have some tears in her eyes, but she wasn't bawling. She wasn't erratic. She wasn't too highly emotional at that point in time.

"I asked Miriam if there was anybody else in the residence. She stated that she didn't know. I told her I'd be right back, because I wanted to clear the residence to ensure nobody else was in the residence at that point. I was searching for another family member, someone they didn't know, a perpetrator. Just anybody."

Deputy Brownlee didn't find anyone in the house, and he went back to check on the male, who was on the kitchen floor. Brownlee recalled, "I touched Alan, but I did not feel a pulse. Also, he was very cold to the touch. There was a lot of blood at the scene." Brownlee, who had a camera, started taking some photos of the area. The main reason was to show investigators, who might arrive later, exactly how things looked when the first officer arrived on scene. It was even before any paramedics were there. Brownlee knew from experience that paramedics could alter the scene dramatically.

Brownlee did notice about the area around Alan Helmick that "the drawers didn't appear to be the way they would be in the way a normal house is kept. I found that kinda strange. Also, a trash can was tipped over. It struck me as odd, the cabinet drawers being open and the trash can down on the floor."

There was also one more very jarring thing. Deputy Brownlee found a shell casing lying on the floor. He took several photos of it and began to wonder if Alan had been shot. Nothing had been mentioned concerning that by either dispatch or by Miriam.

Brownlee did not ask Miriam about this, but he did note

that there was a little dog in the residence. Not wanting the dog to change the scene inadvertently, Brownlee put the dog in an adjacent room and shut the door. Brownlee noted that the dog never barked at him. He didn't know if that was because Miriam was present or not. Brownlee wondered if the dog had barked if there had been an intruder.

Soon two other deputies arrived—Deputy Pennay and Deputy Quigley. Brownlee asked that Miriam go outside with Deputy Quigley. And when she did so, Miriam left two important items in the house. One was her purse, with almost all the money she had, and the other was her driver's license. As to why Brownlee had Miriam leave the house, he later said, "We try to have as few people as possible in there. We can get footprints and people touching stuff, so we try to keep as many people as we can out of the scene."

And as to why Deputy Brownlee did not allow Miriam to take her purse with her, he related, "Due to evidentiary purposes, we need to include those things that need to stay in the house. Even somebody's purse and their ID. It could be important." Brownlee admitted later that he didn't explain this aspect to Miriam, and he wasn't sure if some other law enforcement officer had later told her why.

Once Miriam was out of the house, Brownlee took more photos of Alan Helmick lying on the floor. Brownlee could see just how much blood was behind Alan's head. Brownlee later described it as "a lot." One thing that was odd to him: If Miriam had been doing CPR, as she claimed, there should have been a lot of blood on her clothing. Brownlee hadn't noticed any blood on Miriam's outfit.

Later that afternoon Josh Vigil, Alan's son-in-law, who was married to Portia, came to the residence and was informed what had happened there. Deputy Brownlee noted about Josh's demeanor, "He was kinda frantic. He was worked up." This was just the opposite of Miriam. She had been teary-eyed, but never "frantic or worked up," as Brownlee put it. Nor was she "catatonic," as Brownlee had often seen other family members in situations like these—an individual so traumatized that he or she couldn't respond to questions or follow orders. Miriam had basically seemed quite calm, answered all of Brownlee's questions in a rational manner, and obeyed every order that he gave without complaint. In some ways, this was odd to Brownlee. She seemed to fit right in the middle of those two extremes. Brownlee thought she was very calm, considering the traumatic event that had just occurred.

CHAPTER 4

"I SAW BLOOD UNDER HIS HEAD."

Around one-thirty that afternoon, Miriam was escorted into an interview room at the Mesa County Sheriff's Office. She was wearing the same pair of blue jeans, striped red T-shirt, and shoes that she had been wearing when she found Alan lying on the floor of their home.

The interview room was very spartan, with no photos or anything on the walls, and a small round table in one corner. Miriam and a blond-haired female detective named Beverly "Bev" Jarrell sat down on chairs near the table. The interview was being videotaped, and off camera in the room, there was a male detective, Danny Norris, sitting on another chair.

Miriam was sniffling a lot, on the verge of tears, so Detective Jarrell handed her a box of Kleenex, which Miriam used throughout the interview. Both Jarrell and Miriam spoke in low, soft voices, as if trying not to awake a sleeping individual.

Jarrell said, "I know this is going to be difficult. What happened when you got up this morning?"

Miriam said that she and Alan got up around the same time; they made coffee and went out to sit on the deck and talked about what they were going to do that day. He had a lot of errands to run, and so did she. Miriam told Jarrell that Alan was self-employed, and she didn't work. Miriam related that Alan had a long list of things to do—one of the activities was to go by a power company in Clifton because of land he wanted to develop. Then he was going to go by Big O Tires in Grand Junction, and he had about ten things on his to-do list.

Jarrell asked if anyone else was there in the morning, and Miriam replied, "No, our son-in-law Josh had already gone to work. He stays with us because he's on call from his job at Halliburton. He left before six A.M. He stays downstairs in, like, a kind of apartment. It has a kitchenette and we hardly ever see him."

Jarrell said, "What's your relationship like with Josh?"

Miriam responded, "It's okay. It's normal. We're not real chatters."

Miriam said that Josh was married to Alan's daughter, Portia, and Portia lived in Delta, about twenty-five miles away. Miriam added that Alan had two other daughters, Kristy, who lived in Seattle, Washington, and Wendy, who lived in Denver. Miriam thought that all three daughters were in their thirties.

Jarrell wanted to know if Miriam had any children, and she said that she did. She had a son named Chris, by a previous marriage. Chris lived in Florida. Getting back to Josh, Miriam said that because of his irregular hours, he might be at the house one or two days a week, or gone for a long time. He was on call when it came to working for Halliburton, so his hours were very erratic.

Jarrell asked if there was any dialogue between Alan and Josh that morning. Miriam said no, and then outlined Alan's morning. She and Alan had discussed their divergent plans for the day, and then he had gone to take a shower. She had gotten into their blue Oldsmobile and had driven off after 8:00 A.M. to do her tasks.

From off camera, Norris asked, "What kind of vehicle does Josh drive?"

Miriam had to think about it, and finally said that it was an older model blue pickup. Alan had sold that used truck to Josh in years past. Miriam added that it was "kind of beat-up."

Getting back to her errands for the day, Miriam said that she had driven to City Market in Orchard Mesa, where she bought two packs of cigarettes and a cold drink. From the parking lot, she had phoned Sue Boulware, who was their horse trainer. With Sue, Miriam discussed Alan's granddaughter's future riding lesson.

Jarrell related, "You seem to be a pretty quiet person."

Miriam admitted that she was.

"Always been that way?"

"Yes," Miriam responded.

"Okay, so you finished talking with Sue. Then what did you do?"

Miriam said that she went to a Walmart to buy shirts—barn shirts, as she called them. These were inexpensive shirts that would get dirty out in the barn. Along the way there, she had called Alan on her cell phone, but he didn't answer, so she left a message. From there she went to buy carrots, because, as she put it, "we needed a really big bag of them, because we feed them to the horses."

Miriam said she bought the bag of carrots at a Safeway on Horizon Avenue in Grand Junction, and then she wanted to get some coloring books for Alan's granddaughters. She drove to a Hastings Bookstore across town and "piddled around in there for about twenty minutes."

Jarrell asked, "Had Alan called you back yet?"

"No," Miriam replied.

"Was that odd?"

"Yes. But I figured he was running a lot of errands, too. Um, he was also planning to go by and see an attorney that was connected with his land deal. It was property that we didn't live on."

"How much property do you have?"

"I don't know. He's trying to split off those parts in front of the house. And he also has a project in Clifton. It's not really—well, they won't allow him to do so until it passes inspection or something. And then we have a lot of groundwater down at the bottom of our property. And he was going to go by and talk—um, he was going to go talk to some group or something about that. Anyway, it was on his list. He had about ten stops to make today."

"You spoke of a daughter coming to visit. Which daughter was that?"

"Kristy from Seattle."

Jarrell asked where Miriam went from Hastings, and she said that she went to a Chinese restaurant on North Avenue. She and Alan were supposed to meet there for lunch. Miriam couldn't remember the exact name, but she thought it was "Great Wall," or something like that.

Jarrell wanted to know how long Miriam waited there for Alan, and Miriam said that she waited until about eleven-fifteen and then drove home. "I wasn't happy that he hadn't called me back."

"Were you upset with him?"

"Not really, upset, but kind of miffed. 'Cause normally, he's Johnny-on-the-spot. I drove down North Avenue, and then onto . . ." She had to think a long time. Finally she admitted, "I'm not good with road names. I just know left and right." Miriam started crying again, then wiped her nose with a Kleenex.

Jarrell asked, "Okay, you're driving to Siminoe Road. What did you see?"

Miriam responded, "Just the same thing as always. Everything was normal. I saw his truck. And I walked inside from the garage, and I saw him on the floor." Now she really started crying.

Finally Jarrell asked, "What happened then?"

Miriam sniffled as she said, "I saw blood under his head. I didn't know what had happened. I kind of shook him, to try and wake him up. Then I called 911. They kept me on the phone a long time. Trying to do CPR. But it didn't work."

Jarrell said, "I'm sorry, but I'm going to have to back you up. I'm going to have to walk you through this. You drive up. What do you do with your car?"

"I opened the garage door and parked my car inside."

"Anything unusual in the garage?"

"No."

"You accessed the house. From the garage?"

"Yes. I took two of my bags from the car and walked in through the door into the laundry room. Through the laundry room, you see a wall, and you have to kind of turn to the right to go into the house. It goes to the kitchen area. I went in there and that's when I saw him on the floor. I dropped my bags and purse on the floor when I saw him."

"Where was Alan?"

"On the kitchen floor. He was lying kind of catty-corner to a desk near the wall."

"And what position was Alan in?"

"He was on his back."

"Describe the position his body was in. How was he lying on the floor?" Then Jarrell said, "I'm a visual person." She handed Miriam a pad and pen, and had her draw a sketch of what she observed. All while she did so, Miriam was sniffling and quietly crying.

Miriam drew an outline of Alan's body as it lay on the kitchen floor. His arms were out by his side, one of them touching a liquor cabinet. Miriam drew the location of his head and feet.

Jarrell asked, "Then what happened?"

"They (the dispatcher) asked me to do CPR."

Jarrell interrupted her, "Did you see any weapons? Anything out of the ordinary?"

"I saw his wallet on the floor." Miriam marked on her sketch where that was located in relation to Alan's body. "And I saw some drawers pulled out."

Jarrell asked, "Did you have any important papers in there?"

"No. The only important papers were in his desk."

"Was his wallet open or closed?"

"It was like a cloth wallet. Not one you carry around in your pocket. More like a travel wallet. It was lying out flat."

"What did he carry in his wallet?"

Miriam thought for a moment and answered, "Credit cards. Fishing license. A card to get into the national parks. And cash."

Jarrell wanted to know how much cash, and Miriam said, "A few hundred dollars. He gave me two hundred dollars today. And he gave me a credit card to use if I needed that. But I didn't need it today."

"What credit cards did he carry?"

Miriam replied that Alan had two credit cards, both of them from Bank of America. He had given her the one with the lower credit amount to use.

Jarrell asked if Alan was the primary holder on both cards, and Miriam said yes. Then she added, "We've been married for two years. And we had a prenup. Everything was in his name."

Jarrell said, "Okay, this prenup . . . I don't know that much about them. Explain to me about it."

"In a nutshell, it said that I didn't have rights to the things he owned before we got married. Those assets went to his kids. I can get it (the prenuptial agreement) if you want. It was my suggestion."

"Your suggestion?"

"Yeah, because his daughters were learning to like me. And I wanted to make sure they knew I loved him and wasn't after his things. They'd just lost their mother a couple of years before."

Jarrell replied, "It had to be very difficult, not only for you, but them also."

Miriam responded, "I think it was good to do. They seemed to have some issues about their mother. They thought I was going to come in and take the china."

CHAPTER 5

"WE HAD A WONDERFUL
LIFE TOGETHER."

Getting Miriam back to what she saw, Jarrell said, "You walk in here, Miriam, and see Alan. Did you see anything missing? Anything out of the ordinary?"

"No. Just drawers that had been opened and a garbage can turned over. My desk is kind of a mess, so I couldn't tell on that."

"Anything missing off of his desk?"

"I didn't look."

Jarrell asked if the doors to their house in Whitewater were generally locked. Jarrell was surprised when Miriam answered that they never locked them. The same went for the downstairs door where Josh went into the house.

Asked why they didn't lock the doors, Miriam said, "Alan didn't think it was necessary."

Incredulous, Jarrell said, "He didn't think it was necessary!" In light of what had happened, maybe it was necessary.

But Miriam added, "He didn't even know we had keys to the house until a couple of months ago. We never had any trouble out there."

Moving to a different topic, Jarrell said, "Tell me about Alan. Did he have any enemies? Did he have any problems with the contracting that was going on?"

Miriam shook her head no.

So Jarrell asked, "Would he share that with you if he did?"

Miriam responded, "I think so. He shared a lot with me. I didn't really understand the business end of a lot of things. He was trying to help me understand it. Not that I knew everything he was up to."

Jarrell turned to Detective Norris, who was off camera. He said to Miriam, "Speak about his land projects and distributing water. Any neighbors have any problems with him developing that land? Any neighbors have problems with him and the water?"

Miriam said that she didn't think so. "He hadn't gone through the process far enough to even tell them about it. But I hadn't actually kept up with it all."

"How did he get along with the neighbors?"

Miriam replied that everything with them was fine. The only neighbors they really knew were a young couple that had a play set in the front yard. Otherwise, they didn't socialize in the neighborhood. Then Miriam said that Alan was kind of a hermit and he didn't even know for sure if he wanted to develop the property in front of their house and have anyone live that close to them.

Detective Jarrell spoke up and said, "Why does that not surprise me? The way you talk about things in your relationship."

This elicited a small smile from Miriam, who agreed with her.

Jarrell asked, "Any firearms in the house?"

Miriam thought for a while and said, "I know he's got a rifle. I think it's a twenty-two. He used it when we had prairie dog problems. He's got a shotgun. And a box with a handgun in it."

"Do you know the caliber of the handgun?"

"No."

"Is it like a small derringer? Or is it a larger gun?"

Miriam said that it was small and could fit in the palm of a person's hand. "He put it on the back shelf in a closet. And he has bullets there. He had his rifle out the other day, and he thought I should learn how to use the pistol. He showed me how it fired, and how to pull the handle back on it, which I didn't do. I told him I don't do guns. So he put it back where I wouldn't see it."

Detective Jarrell wanted to know what Miriam meant by "handle." They finally agreed that she meant a slide on the small handgun, which opened the breach where a bullet could be placed into the firing chamber.

Detective Norris spoke up again. "The prenup—did he have a lot of assets, where this is an issue with his family?"

Miriam appeared as though confused by this statement. She lifted back her head in thought. Finally she said, "You know, I don't know if it's been an issue with them or not."

Norris asked, "Is he a wealthy person?"

Miriam replied, "It's all in dirt." (By this she meant that it was all tied up in real estate and planned projects.) "He had a title company in Delta and he sold that, like, two months ago. And he had two hundred forty acres in Delta County, but it's just dirt. He'd been looking into whether he could run electricity and water to it before he could sell it. That was kind of offset by money he owed to investors and the bank."

Bev Jarrell responded, "Did that ever concern him, financially?"

Miriam answered, "He never let on if he had any financial problems. There was a time when he told me to tighten my belt, but I didn't handle the money, anyway. He did."

"Any depression going on with him about his financial dealings? It sounds like he had a lot of money tied up in investments?"

Miriam said, "If he did have any [depression], he didn't tell me about it. Sometimes he'd tell me stuff. Sometimes he doesn't." Then she corrected herself. "*Didn't.* I kind of liked it that I didn't have to worry about the bills, that he handled all the finances. We had a wonderful life together and did so much together."

Moving on, Detective Jarrell asked, "Did anyone else know where he kept his firearms?"

Miriam said, "No, not that I know of."

Jarrell then wanted to know if Miriam stayed home most of the time. She said that she and Alan usually traveled around together, unless he was doing business. But if it was just for running errands around the area, they usually did that together.

"How about the landscaper? Would that person come to the house?"

"Yep." And then she gave the company name. Miriam said that there had been a beef between Alan and that company. Miriam added, "Alan was kind of upset with them because our sprinkler system was not working. They were supposed to have installed it two years ago, but it broke. And they wouldn't come out to fix it. Alan was on him and on him and on him. Finally he did fix it, but it was too late for the plants. We used to have nice plants in front, but they died because of the lack of water."

Jarrell wondered if any words had been exchanged between Alan and the landscaper. Miriam replied, "I don't know, because Alan has always handled that."

Asked if there was anyone else that Alan had problems with, she said that Alan tried to keep his business dealings separate from the house. And he had an attorney for the business end of things—a man named Bill Coleman. As far as an attorney for his will, Miriam said it was a different attorney, and she didn't know that person's name.

Jarrell asked, "Who did your prenup agreement?"

Miriam said, "Alan wrote it up and I signed it. I don't know who handled it after that. There's probably a copy of it in his desk drawer."

Danny Norris spoke up and asked, "Did he have prescription drugs for medical problems?"

Miriam responded, "Um, he quit smoking cold turkey last year. He ended up having to go to the doctor because his blood pressure shot up. And they also put him on Wellbutrin, because he had emotional issues with that. (The blood pressure going up.) But he wasn't taking that lately."

"You mentioned three daughters. Does he have a son?"

For the first time, Miriam brought up the fact that he did. "Alan Jr.," she said. "I think he lives in Alaska now. Um, Alan wasn't really on good terms with Alan Jr. He was supposed to be coming to Denver to meet Kristy (at the airport) and they were coming here."

According to Miriam, Alan was only going to allow Alan Jr. to stay with them for a few nights, because there were problems between him and his son. And everything said about Alan Jr. now came through Miriam's perspective. A lot of the things she had to say about him were fairly negative.

All of this was important, and Jarrell asked with surprise, "Why didn't you tell me this earlier?"

Miriam replied, "Because Alan didn't like to talk about it. Alan tried to keep Alan Jr. at arm's distance, because there was always a fight or something going on when he was there."

Obviously, the mention of a fight and problems was disconcerting to the detectives. Jarrell asked, "When did Alan last talk to Alan Jr.?"

Miriam said that had been about a week and a half before, so Jarrell followed up with, "When was Alan Jr. supposed to arrive?"

Miriam thought he would be flying to Denver and would then make arrangements with Kristy. Kristy was supposedly going to fly to Denver, rent a car and they both would come out to Whitewater.

As far as where Alan Jr. was presently living, Miriam said, "He just went up to Alaska and no one really knows where he's living at." When asked how long ago he had moved up there, Miriam replied, "Three or four months ago."

Jarrell wondered, "What was the relationship like between Alan and Alan Jr. three or four months ago?"

Miriam responded, "The same. It's been that way for many years."

"Did Alan Jr. know where you guys lived now?"

"Yes, he did."

Jarrell wanted to know how old Alan Jr. was. Miriam didn't know an actual age, but thought that he was in his early forties. Then Jarrell asked if Miriam had ever witnessed any fights between Alan and Alan Jr.

Miriam said, "No. He was on his best behavior at home."

Detective Jarrell took a long time digesting all of this. While she did, Detective Norris asked, "How was Alan Jr. to get from Alaska to Denver?"

Miriam said, "I don't know for sure. That never came up. I know that every time Alan Jr. called, Alan would get kind of prickled."

"Prickled?"

"Not mad, but very cautious. Kind of like the hair goes up on the back of your neck."

"Did Alan ever talk about any concerns about Alan Jr.? About him showing up unexpectedly?"

Miriam replied, "Oh, yeah. I think he told him in the past not to show up unexpectedly. Because Alan really didn't want him to know where we lived. And Alan Jr. would say to Alan, 'All I want to do is go fishing with you.' But Alan would reply, 'No, you want something else.' Alan tried to be real guarded about his son, but he prickled up pretty good every time Alan Jr. called."

"Did Alan ever express any concerns about his daughters' well-being around Alan Jr., as well as his own?"

Miriam replied, "He never really expressed it. But he did tell me, 'If Alan Jr. ever shows up, call the cops.' That's when I realized, this was an area where I shouldn't step."

Of course all the statements about Alan Jr. were from Miriam's perspective of the situation.

While Miriam had been talking about Alan Jr., both detectives had been busy writing down notes. In light of Alan being murdered only hours before, this information was being taken very seriously.

CHAPTER 6

"LIFE STRESSORS"

Moving to a different subject, Detective Norris said, "You brought up about Alan's daughter or granddaughter taking riding lessons."

Miriam said that Portia's daughter took riding lessons at the ranch in Whitewater. Then Miriam said that this granddaughter lived in Delta, with Portia. Concerning how often Miriam saw Portia, she said about once a week, and she talked to her on the phone almost daily.

Detective Jarrell excused herself at this point and exited the room. Norris continued wanting to know about Alan keeping his work away from the home, and wondered if he had an office somewhere. Miriam said that he had an office in Delta, or at least he did until about six weeks before when he sold his interest in a title company there. From that point on, he did most of his work at home. In fact, he did it near the spot where he had been murdered. Miriam didn't know of anything that Alan was working on, for which someone might want to kill him.

As far as the liquor cabinet went, Miriam said that she might have a glass of wine once in a while, and Alan only had a few drinks at the end of the day. He preferred Crown on the rocks or Jack Daniel's.

Norris asked, "Did he get intoxicated every night?" Miriam said no, but that he would once in a while. And when he did, as she put it, "he was a happy drunk."

Norris wondered if Alan had any "life stressors. Any financial problems with work?" Miriam said those weren't really stressors. "He always had to have a project going. I know that he had a note due at the bank. I don't know any more about it than that."

In relation to having dogs at the house, they had two but neither of them was a watchdog. They were friendly dogs that weren't aggressive at all, Miriam said. Then she added about the dogs that day, "They were outside. Alan doesn't like to leave them in the house when I'm gone."

Getting back to the wallet, Miriam recalled that Alan usually kept it on his desk. And when he traveled, he just laid it out on the car seat or truck seat until he had to exit the vehicle. Then he stuffed the wallet in a pants pocket, since it was cloth.

Norris asked, "Does he normally keep a cell phone on him?"

Miriam responded, "Mm-hmm" (meaning yes). Then she laughed, and said, "It's pink."

Norris was surprised, and said, "It's pink?"

She laughed again and explained, "He liked the color pink."

Norris wanted to know if she or Alan had seen anyone strange around the property in the last week. Miriam answered, "In front of our property, there is an open space, where people walk. Sometimes we see people out there. But no one was out of place or any problems."

Getting back to Alan Jr., Norris questioned, "You said that Alan supported the mom on the adoption of Alan Jr.'s daughter. In what way did he support it?"

Miriam answered, "I think he went to Denver or wrote a

letter to the judge. He told the judge that his son, Alan Jr., had no business being a father."

"Do you know if any threats or problems came from that?"

Miriam heaved a big sigh. Then she said, "I don't know. Alan didn't really say. I just know that he said that his son still blamed him for it."

"How long ago was that?"

"About two years ago."

"Have things calmed down since then?"

Miriam replied, "I've never actually seen them at odds. Well, really, Alan didn't give him much of a chance to argue over anything because he doesn't want to get into it. Alan Jr. stayed with Portia for a while, but Alan told him to leave."

"Anything we haven't asked you about that you can think would be important for us to know?"

Miriam thought awhile and answered, "I can't think of anything."

CHAPTER 7

"WHO WOULD WANT TO HURT ALAN?"

Both Detective Norris and Miriam sat quietly until Bev Jarrell returned. Once again, she sat down across from Miriam at a small table. Detective Jarrell said, "I'm not clear about your relationship with Josh and his relationship with Portia."

Miriam responded, "He's very quiet. Very private. From what I know of his relationship with Portia—it's fine. I know a while back Alan was on Josh to get a job. Josh got a job with Halliburton as, I think, some kind of truck driver. And the rules are—he's on call and has to be within twenty minutes of their office in Grand Junction. So that's why he's been staying with us."

Jarrell wanted to know when the last time was that Josh worked. Miriam said that Josh had probably gotten up around six in the morning, and he was already gone by the time that she and Alan got up. Asked when he was expected home, Miriam thought that would be about 4:30 P.M.

Jarrell asked how Josh accessed the house, and Miriam replied that he used a downstairs door, and he practically had his own apartment down there. She didn't see him very often in the main part of the house. Sometimes she would see him in the evening when she and Alan fed the horses. Asked if Josh had any firearms, Miriam said that she didn't know. And as far as laundry went, she said that Josh did his own laundry and would use the upstairs laundry room for that. Then Miriam joked, "I don't do his laundry, and I don't do Alan's."

Caught off guard for a moment, Jarrell said, "Oh, I'm okay with that."

Miriam added, "That was one of our agreements."

Getting back to Josh, Miriam thought the last time he had done his laundry was on the previous Thursday night. And she said that Alan had told Josh to be more careful about not dropping lint on the floor. Alan wanted Josh to pick it up and put it in a garbage can.

Miriam said that she hadn't seen Josh on Friday, Saturday, Sunday, or Monday morning. She had called Portia to see if Josh was all right. Portia told her that Josh had some time off from work and had been in Delta with her.

After nearly an hour and a half of an interview, Detective Jarrell said, "I know we've asked you a lot of questions. So let me ask you this, who would want to hurt Alan?"

Miriam sighed and responded, "I don't know. Um, I don't know how stressed he got with the sprinkler guy. They had done some work at the house. And they had asked for half payment up front. Alan always wanted a bill in writing. And they never provided that. So he didn't write the check. Finally around April [2008], they came over to talk to Alan about the second part of the payment and finally produced a bill. This thing had been going on, back and forth, for nearly a year. So maybe that was an issue."

Jarrell wanted to know how much of a bill it was. Miriam answered, "I don't know. Alan never discussed the whole thing."

Jarrell said, "Ranking people you found Alan to be contentious with—who would be at the top of that list?"

Without any hesitation, Miriam replied, "His son. I don't know of anyone else he dealt with professionally that he was . . ." Miriam's thoughts trailed off at this point.

Detective Norris asked, "What vehicles are supposed to be at the house right now?" (It was 3:04 P.M.)

Miriam said, "The little maroon Dodge farm truck, his silver Chevrolet truck, the Oldsmobile"—the vehicle she had been driving—"One vehicle is in the shop. It's a pink Buick Roadmaster."

"What vehicles did the landscapers come in?"

Miriam thought for a while and said, "The sprinkler system guy came in a white pickup with maybe a camper-type top. His assistant has a little black pickup truck."

Norris wanted to know, "How many bank accounts are there?"

Miriam replied, "There's a bank account at American National Bank. And a bank account for Dance Junction. I have a dance studio downtown."

Detective Jarrell was surprised by this and said, "Oh, ballroom dancing?"

Miriam responded, "Yes. It's more than we can handle."

For some reason, either the mention of bank accounts or Dance Junction made Miriam agitated. She began rocking back and forth in her chair. At one point, it almost looked as if she was ready to stand up.

Norris continued, "Is that a joint account?"

Miriam answered, "No, just in Alan's name."

Jarrell questioned, "Did you have any financial documents in the house? Something where someone could steal personal information?"

Miriam said, "No. He tried to keep it bare bones at home. He didn't like to manage too many accounts." And once again, she said that their money was in "dirt."

Norris asked, "The credit cards were just in his name?"

"Yes. And I was very happy with that. He took very good

care of me." Miriam looked directly at Bev Jarrell when she said this, although Norris had asked the question. Miriam added, "I'm gonna start taking quarters out of the car, because all the money was in his name."

Jarrell wanted to know, "Even though you had a prenup, you guys didn't think of taking out a life insurance policy?"

Miriam answered, "No. We didn't expect anything to happen. All we had was health insurance." And then Miriam said that there was a life insurance policy, but that was only to pay off creditors, should Alan die unexpectedly. Miriam related, "He was going to get another life insurance policy, but his blood pressure would never come down. He had to wait for his blood pressure to come down, or at his age he would have had to pay astronomically for that policy."

Regarding the one insurance policy Alan had, Miriam reiterated, "I think it was for one hundred thousand dollars and that's to pay off creditors and anything like that." Then she seemed to know a little more about his business expenses than she first indicated. Miriam told the detectives that Alan owed $275,000 to investors on one set of loans, and $140,000 on a bank note. As far as how much money he had in the bank, she thought he had $100,000.

Jarrell said, "Describe the little firearm you talked about earlier."

Miriam responded, "Um, he had it in a little bag."

"Did you ever handle it?"

"I did. But I never could pull the little . . ." She didn't know the word.

Jarrell added, "Did it have a slide on it?"

That was the word Miriam was looking for. She said, "Yes."

Jarrell stated, "Understand, Miriam, we're looking for things out of place."

Detective Jarrell had Miriam go over the timeline of her travels once again. Once she was done with that, Norris asked, "We talked briefly about what you first saw. You need to be very detailed about this."

As Miriam related what she had seen, she became more and more teary in her conversation. Often it was punctuated by small sobs. Miriam said, "I saw him on the floor and thought he had a heart attack or stroke or something. I put my hands on his chest to kind of shake him and wake him up. I patted him on the side of the face. I saw that he had blood coming out of his nose. I got my phone and called 911." At this point, Miriam broke down crying. When she could speak again, she said, "The operator told me to give him CPR. Empty his mouth and nose and do chest compressions. I turned his head . . . and . . ." Miriam completely broke down then.

Jarrell asked, "Are you going to be sick? Do you want me to get a trash can that you can use?"

Miriam nodded her head that she did.

Jarrell brought a wastepaper basket into the room and placed it near Miriam's chair. Miriam lowered her head and retched for a while, but did not actually throw up. When she was through retching, Miriam continued, "His mouth had bloody liquid in it. The operator told me I had to do chest compressions four hundred times. I kept doing it. And I could hear the emergency person on the phone, but it wouldn't work."

Norris jumped in and said, "Did you notice any injuries on him beside what you've mentioned?" Miriam answered that Alan's left eye was black-and-blue. Asked if she had washed anything besides her hands since she had left the house, Miriam said no.

Norris added, "Okay, because I'm preparing you. We're going to have to do a test on your hands. It's just for residue, if you were around where a gun was shot."

Miriam nodded her head that she understood. Norris continued, "Also, I need to prepare you for . . . Well, I noticed there's some blood on your clothing. So we'll have to give you a change of clothing."

Miriam looked down at her blouse and, with surprise, noticed blood there as well. She let out an "Oh!" but said she would hand over her clothes.

Jarrell said, "It sounds like Alan kept you pretty much at bay when it came to family, finances, and everything."

Miriam replied, "He pretty much let me know what he thought I should know."

Jarrell asked, "Were you okay with that?"

Miriam responded that she had been and added, "The only thing I did for him financially, well, he got the flu for a couple of weeks. And I called his engineer."

Jarrell wanted to know if they ever went on trips together. Miriam answered that they went to Lake Powell, where Alan had a cabin cruiser. "Two weekends ago, we were down there with some friends."

"These friends—did you have a good relationship with them?"

Miriam said the relationship was fine, so Jarrell asked, "Who are they?"

Miriam replied, "Bob Isom and his wife, Peggy. They're from Delta. There was another couple, but I only knew their first names. Bob was a good friend of Alan."

"Would Alan confide in him if there was a problem?"

Miriam answered, "Probably not."

Jarrell asked, "If Alan were to confide in anybody, who would he confide in?"

"I don't know. He's very private. Kind of hermit-y. He was very comfortable just sitting on the porch, enjoying the view. I had to talk him into going to Lake Powell with those couples. We hadn't planned on meeting up with them. We went, possibly knowing they would be there. So I had him drive around the marina, and we found them. There was an open slip, and I had him move into that one so we could socialize."

Jarrell asked if it was "painful for Alan to socialize." Miriam said no, but that he just liked to be by himself when not working. Then she added, "I kind of wanted to get to know Peggy a little bit more. Alan has been really good friends with Bob Isom since high school. I never really did know his wife."

Asked about who the other couple was, Miriam only knew their first names, Phil and Christy.

After a long pause, Jarrell asked, "What questions do you have for us?"

Miriam thought and then said, "I was wondering when I get to go home?"

Jarrell replied that it wouldn't be for a while. The house had to be thoroughly investigated for evidence. The sheriff's office would call Miriam when she could go back inside.

Miriam responded, "I didn't drive here. I don't have a vehicle. I don't know where to go."

Jarrell asked if Portia would come and get her. Miriam replied that someone would have to tell Portia about her father being dead. And then Miriam said that she didn't think that Portia should be driving under those conditions. Asked if John Robert "Bob" Isom could drive her somewhere, Miriam thought that he would. But now it was a matter of where she could go. She didn't know that many people in the area very well.

Finally Miriam said that perhaps she could be taken to Alan's sister's house. She lived in Grand Junction, and Miriam got along well with this woman. But once again Miriam could not think of the woman's last name. "I know her name is Merredith, but I don't know her last name. I'm bad with names." All Miriam could come up with was that Merredith lived on Texas Street in Grand Junction. Jarrell said that they would try and find out where this Merredith lived and contact her.

CHAPTER 8

"SOMEBODY TRIED TO TORCH OUR CAR."

At 3:35 P.M., it seemed that the meeting was about to break up, when Miriam said, "You asked me a bunch of questions about where I was this morning. I have a bunch of receipts in my pants pocket. Would that help you?"

Detective Jarrell said yes, and Miriam pulled a wad of receipts out of her pocket and laid them on the table. Miriam also pulled out a wad of cash and said that was what was left of the money that Alan had given her that morning. Jarrell had Miriam leave the money on the table because Miriam's clothing was soon going to be taken.

Then Jarrell said to Miriam to hold out her hands. Miriam did so and was embarrassed by her dirty fingernails.

Detective Jarrell said, "I understand. I grew up on a farm." Then Jarrell pointed at one of Miriam's fingers and asked, "That's an old injury?"

Miriam said that it was.

"How did you get that?"

Miriam responded that she had injured her finger at Lake Powell.

At that moment, another woman who worked in the sheriff's office came into the room to find out what size clothing Miriam wore. At that point, Detective Norris sat down next to Miriam. A test for gunshot reside (GSR) was just about to be performed upon her.

Before actually starting the GSR test, Detective Norris told Miriam, "We do this whenever a weapon's involved." He opened the kit, removed some latex gloves, and put them on. Miriam, meanwhile, looked relaxed, as if she wasn't worried at all that GSR would be found anywhere on her.

Norris had Miriam hold up her right hand and dabbed all over it with a "rod," which looked somewhat like a large Q-tip. He did this on the right hand, and then the left hand. Then he did it to her face and neck.

Miriam spoke up and said, "I picked up and held his twenty-two rifle this last weekend. Would that show traces?"

"Not if you washed your hands since then," Norris replied.

Miriam assured him that she had washed her hands since then.

Norris asked, "Were you around a firearm that was fired today?"

Miriam said no.

Norris added, "When a weapon is shot, the powder and all sorts of chemicals go out into the air. This test picks that up."

There was a knock at the door, and Detective Jarrell soon entered once again. Jarrell asked, "Do we need her bra and panties?"

Norris answered, "No, she can keep those."

After he was done collecting all the swabs and placing them into the kit, Norris left the room. For the first time, Miriam was in there all alone.

Miriam sat in the interview room at the small table while the hidden camera filmed everything. She heaved a big sigh; then she put her hand to her mouth and began crying. At first, she was fairly quiet, but then she began sobbing. Her upper body rocked back and forth as she sobbed. About one minute into this, Miriam said under her breath, "Damn it!" She used some Kleenex to wipe her nose, and then the sobs quieted down until she was only sniffling.

After nearly five minutes, Detective Jarrell came back into the room. By this point, Miriam had composed herself once again. Jarrell asked how Miriam was, and she replied, "Tired."

Jarrell agreed. "Yes, this is very draining."

Bev Jarrell wanted to know if Miriam had changed her last name from Giles to Helmick when she got married. Miriam said that she had done so. This would show up on her driver's license, but that was in her purse back at the house.

"You made mention that Alan's first wife died. Did you know her?"

Miriam said that she had not. When asked what Alan's first wife's name was, Miriam answered, "Sharon." Then she added, "After I'd met him, he had the girls come over to the house where we lived in Delta to divide up the things that had belonged to their mother, Sharon. And that's when I first met Wendy."

Jarrell asked, "How did you meet Alan?"

Miriam responded, "I taught him to dance."

Surprised, Jarrell said, "Oh, really!" Then she added, "Oh, you had the ballroom dance studio. That's a lost art, isn't it?"

Miriam agreed that it was. And then she said something that was odd. "I didn't like Alan initially."

Taken aback, Jarrell replied, "Really?"

Miriam didn't elaborate why she didn't like him. She just said, "He was taking dance lessons from me. Then he grew on me."

"Where'd you guys get married?"

"We had a big party at the Two Rivers Convention Center."

Detective Jarrell was impressed. This was the largest convention center in Grand Junction. Jarrell said, "Oh, wow."

Miriam added, "He had a lot of family and friends there."

Jarrell asked, "Was your marriage good?"

Miriam said that it was and remarked, "He was a good person."

"Sounds like it. But it sounds like he was very tight to the vest with some of his information, though. I guess I would find that frustrating in my world."

Miriam said, "I figured if he really had issues, he'd let me know. He never wanted me to worry about anything."

Detective Jarrell said, "You've been very open and honest about things. I assume you've never had any contact with law enforcement in an investigation before. Or have you?"

Miriam put her hand to her chin and answered, "The only contact I've had was in Delta. Somebody tried to torch our car. And they (the police) thought I did it because I was the only one with Alan at the time."

Detective Jarrell let out a gasp of genuine surprise. "Oh, really!"

The interview was just about to go into a whole new and unexpected direction.

After letting out this revelation about the car fire, Miriam quickly relayed, "Nothing ever came of it. We never were contacted back by the Delta Police."

Jarrell asked, "So it actually got torched in Delta?" Obviously, she knew nothing about this incident.

Miriam said that the car had been in front of the title insurance company that Alan had owned in part in Delta. She recounted, "This occurred on April 30, [2008], and I was with him. His car has a back gas tank, where it fills up from the back and not the side. I had just bought gasoline a few days before, so it was a full tank. And we went to Delta and he closed the thing (meaning a deal) and I was having stomach issues pretty badly. I went back inside. He was in the car and smelled something. He turned off the ignition, but it got worse. He popped open the trunk, went around to the back of the car, and the rubber lining back there was burning. It looked to him like somebody had done something."

"Wow!" Jarrell declared. "I guess we covered about Alan having problems with anyone here, but how about in Delta County? That car fire seems pretty significant."

Miriam replied, "Well, the police said there were surveillance cameras up there. They were supposed to call us back and say what they'd seen. They had told me, 'We've got surveillance from across the street. What do you hope we'll find?' And I said, 'Well, I hope you find who did it.' It was very strange. Alan had just closed a deal he had in selling his share of the title company for one hundred twenty thousand dollars. And he had the check in his pocket. And somebody would wanna burn it up? Or I'd wanna burn it up? I don't think so."

Jarrell asked, "There was a surveillance camera at . . ."

Miriam responded, "From across the street."

Once again, Jarrell asked, "Can you think of anybody in Delta who had any problems with Alan?"

Miriam said, "Nobody knew we were going to be there. Alan did say he saw a teenager going through the parking lot. He thought it might have been a random-type deal."

Jarrell queried, "Did they have to take the cap off of the gas tank?"

Miriam answered, "Um, there was a big restaurant-style skewer that was wrapped with like gauze or something. And then they stuck it down in the gas tank and lit it. But because the gas tank was full, it didn't do anything except catch the rubber on the outside of the trunk on fire."

Jarrell replied again, "Wow! That's significant!"

Miriam said, "Alan called the Delta PD a couple of times, but they never called us back."

"Huh." Jarrell turned to Detective Norris, who had returned to the interview room, and said, "We have to follow up on this."

Detective Jarrell was exasperated that all of this was coming up so late in the interview. She said, "What did Alan think about that situation?"

Miriam replied, "Oh, he talked about it. And at first it was scary. Because if I had not gone into the bathroom when I did, we would have driven down the road and things would have been a lot worse. After a while, Alan said he couldn't think of anything. It had to be random because—"

Before she finished, Jarrell asked, "How much damage was done?"

Miriam said, "It wasn't too much."

"You said you were the only ones who knew you were going there. Did anyone in his family know you were going there?"

"I don't know."

Detective Norris took down Miriam's date of birth, January 26, 1957, and he looked at her hands again. Jarrell asked, "Any other suspicious incidents?" Miriam said no. When asked about Alan's will, Miriam answered that she didn't know all the details about it, and would have to contact Alan's lawyer. Then Miriam added, "Where things stand today, I don't have enough money to make the next house payment."

Jarrell wanted to know how much that was, and Miriam said that it was $3,200 per month. Jarrell replied, "Wow, that's a pretty substantial house payment." Then she paused and wanted to know, "Who do you think has the most to gain from all of this?"

Miriam thought for a while and then said, "Probably Alan Jr." And then Miriam dropped another bombshell late in the proceedings. She said about daughter Wendy's ex-husband, "He (Alan) threatened to kill him one time."

Jarrell was flabbergasted that this was only being revealed now. The list of possible suspects seemed to keep growing and growing. Miriam added, "Wendy was at a Red Lobster restaurant and saw her husband there with his girlfriend. She threw a big scene. At least that's what Alan told me. Wendy came to live with Alan for a while. And the Grand Junction police had her stay away from her ex-husband. Alan told them she could go wherever she wanted to go. Then he said, 'If her ex-husband ever turns up dead, you can come looking for me!'"

Jarrell's head must have been spinning at this point. But obviously the car fire incident in Delta had grabbed most of her attention. She asked, "Had you ever seen that skewer before, or the gauze, or whatever?"

Miriam replied, "No. It looked like something that might have come out of a hurricane lamp."

"The wick?"

"Yes."

Finally, after two hours and forty-five minutes, the interview was over. Detectives Jarrell and Norris exited the room, and a female employee entered with a bag of clothing for Miriam to put on once she gave up her own clothing. This woman asked Miriam, "You okay?"

Miriam replied, "I'm getting there. What time is it?"

The woman answered that it was 4:20 P.M. To this, Miriam said, "Oh, I have to feed the horses sometime tonight. Could you call them?" (She was referring to the officers who were still at the Helmick residence in Whitewater.)

The woman said that she would, and then asked where Miriam intended to stay the night. Miriam replied that she was going to go over to Alan's sister's residence in Grand Junction. Then she said that she didn't want Alan's kids to find out about their father by some news report.

Perhaps to lighten the mood, the woman said to Miriam, "Well, I hope I color coordinated the clothes okay."

Miriam chuckled and replied, "The clothes, well, they're good enough to get me out of here." Then she joked, "They're not orange, are they?" This might have been in reference to orange jumpsuits that jail inmates wore.

The woman laughed and said, "No."

Miriam was given a pair of jeans, a T-shirt, and red clogs. Then she exited the room to exchange her clothing, and the long interview was over.

CHAPTER 9

"THEIR ACTIONS WITH EACH OTHER WERE VERY STRANGE."

Dr. Robert Kurtzman, a forensic pathologist who worked at Community Hospital in Grand Junction, arrived at the Helmick residence around 3:00 P.M., June 10, 2008. Several law enforcement investigators were there, and the scene was under the control of MCSO investigator Jim Hebenstreit.

Dr. Kurtzman had graduated from medical school at the Des Moines University College of Osteopathic Medicine and Surgery. He later interned at Cranston General Hospital in Rhode Island. Since then, Kurtzman had become a medical examiner (ME), first in Wayne County, Indiana, and later in Grand Junction, Colorado.

As Kurtzman later said, causes of death could be broken down into several categories: "A heart attack, for instance, is typically regarded as a natural disease process, and so 'natural' would be the cause of death. If somebody walked down the street and they fell and sustained a head injury and died, that would be an accident. If somebody takes a gun and shoots somebody, that's a homicide. And if the person uses the gun on themselves, that's a suicide.

"As far as forensic pathology goes, it's the analysis of injury patterns. We're looking at the mechanism by which an injury is produced. It's helpful for me to see where the individual is located to see characteristics of flooring, the bloodstains, things of that sort."

When Dr. Kurtzman came on the scene, there were already bags on Alan Helmick's hands to ensure that any transfer evidence or evidence under his fingernails stayed in place. It very quickly became obvious to Dr. Kurtzman that Alan Helmick had sustained a gunshot wound to the back of the head. There didn't seem to be any transfer blood patterns around Alan. Kurtzman believed that as soon as Alan was shot, he ended up in the position where he now lay. No one had shot him elsewhere and then dragged his body to that position.

Multiple law enforcement individuals took many photographs, and finally Alan Helmick's body was loaded into a body bag and removed from the residence. Several investigators stayed behind, going over the whole house and taking literally hundreds of photos of everything they thought might be significant.

On June 11, around 3:15 P.M., Dr. Kurtzman began his autopsy of Alan Helmick. Blood that had accumulated at the back of Alan's head was washed away and a portion of the hair was shaved. When that was done, Kurtzman noted a "defect" six and a half inches from the top of the head and an inch and a half from midline. That defect was where a bullet had entered into the back of Alan's head.

From lack of stippling and soot on the skin, Dr. Kurtzman determined that the shooter was at least two feet away from Alan, but not at a great distance. The actual bullet was recovered from the right side of the front of Alan's brain. Such a wound would have caused Alan's death within seconds or up to about a minute. He would have been instantly incapacitated.

Kurtzman also determined the trajectory of the bullet's path would most likely have made Alan fall to where his body had been found. Kurtzman added that a bump on the back of Alan's head was consistent with being struck by a bullet and falling onto the floor. "In this case, a broad diffuse appearance, typical of falling onto a surface such as the floor of his residence."

Kurtzman noted that Alan did not have any defensive wounds on his hands. There were no needle marks or other signs of illicit drug use. Alan did have two black eyes, but that was not from being punched in that area by a fist or some object. Instead, as Dr. Kurtzman later explained, "The bullet was like a speedboat through calm water. It would create a huge wake. So, when a bullet strikes the brain and it's traveling so fast, it actually displaces the brain tissue and creates a temporary cavity. The bullet in this case was traveling from back to front, and recovered from near the forehead. Because bones near there were fractured, they produced bleeding around the eyes. So it looked like black eyes, like somebody had punched him."

As far as toxicology went, Alan had caffeine in his system and cotinine, which was a by-product of smoking. He did not have alcohol in his system. With all the factors weighed in, Dr. Kurtzman determined that Alan Helmick had died a few hours before the first officers had arrived on the scene. Official cause of death was a gunshot wound to the head.

The Mesa County Coroner's Office (MCCO) released a short press statement on June 11, 2008. It noted that a sixty-two-year-old resident in Whitewater had been identified as Alan Helmick: *A postmortem examination was performed at the Mesa County Coroner's Office and a gunshot wound to the head was determined to be the cause of death. The manner of death has been classified as a homicide. No addi-*

tional information is currently available from this office. The release was signed by Robert Kurtzman, Forensic Pathologist. All further inquiries were directed to the Mesa County Sheriff's Office.

One of the first things the MCSO investigators did was transcribe phone messages that had been received on Alan Helmick's cell phone. Besides the messages left by Miriam on the morning of June 10, there were others as well. At 9:29 A.M., Alan's daughter Portia called him, but he did not respond. She left a voice message, saying, "Hi, Dad. I hate to bother you so much. It's just I haven't been able to talk to you, so things are piling up. I have a verification that I need for you to fill out. Call me and let me know [about this]. That would be great. Thanks. Bye."

Another phone message came in that day, from one of the Helmicks' neighbors, who did not know that Alan was dead. The phone message came in at 2:22 P.M.: "Hey, Alan. This is your neighbor Joe. My daughter just called and said there's investigators and police going all over your property. They came up to our house and asked us questions about your whereabouts. I'm just calling you to touch base in case you weren't aware of this. I hope you're okay. Give me a call. And then I can call them (the police) and lay to rest . . . um, put their mind at ease, is what I'm trying to say."

Another message was left on Alan's cell phone, even though it was directed to Miriam. It was from Miriam's friend, Penny Lyons, at six thirty-nine on the morning after Alan's murder. Penny was crying on the phone: "Miriam, if you get this message, this is Penny. Please call me if you get this. I love you sweetie. Bye."

Another message was left on June 11, at 7:58 A.M. "Hi, this is Trish. I read in the paper about the robbery at your house. Just making sure you guys are okay. Please call me back and let me know."

And at 8:56 A.M., a man named David left a message for Alan that was clearly related to the horses. David apparently didn't know that Alan was already dead. "Alan, this is David. I need to talk to you about the hay and see if you want it or not. And where to stick it. Please give me a call."

Then at 9:29 A.M., June 11, there was a very short message: "Accounts payable department. Please give me a call." The person did not identify himself, but the caller did leave a phone number. It was the last phone message Alan ever received.

The initial articles about the murder on Siminoe Road in Whitewater were very sketchy as to details. The *Grand Junction Free Press* related that MCSO deputies responding to a robbery call found an adult's dead body: *Sheriff's spokeswoman Heather Benjamin said it was too early to say whether investigators had a homicide or suicide, instead labeling it a suspicious death investigation.*

Then the article noted: *According to 911 dispatch radio traffic, someone at the home was attempting to resuscitate an injured subject as deputies were on route to the scene. The adult—authorities confirmed little about the individual—was dead when law enforcement and fire personnel arrived.*

Digging into the Mesa County Assessor's Office records, the reporter discovered that the property in question was owned by Alan Helmick. The reporter also learned that Alan owned Creek Ranch Sporthorses LLC and several other businesses.

By the next day, the *Grand Junction Free Press* knew about Alan Helmick's other businesses and also about the Mesa County Coroner's ruling as to Alan's death. According to the *Grand Junction Free Press, Mesa County Coroner's Pathologist Dr. Robert Kurtzman said Helmick died of a gunshot wound to the head. The ruling was a homicide.* The newspaper also reported that all thirteen investigators at MCSO were now looking into this murder.

Not getting much more from MCSO spokesperson Heather Benjamin, a reporter for the newspaper went out to Whitewater and talked to the Helmicks' neighbors. One neighbor said, "The whole thing is just bizarre. They (the Helmicks) pretty much kept to themselves." Then this person related that Colorado Bureau of Investigation (CBI) agents and MCSO investigators had canvassed the neighborhood asking if anyone had seen any suspicious vehicles or people in the area during the previous week. Apparently, no one had.

Looking into Alan Helmick's business records, the reporter noted that he lived on Siminoe Road with his second wife, Miriam. Alan's sixty-acre property was valued at around $500,000. Alan also owned the sports horse facility, a dance studio in Grand Junction, and had an interest in various subdivision housing and lots in the area. Alan had owned the Helmick Mortgage Company in Delta, Colorado, until giving ownership to his daughter, Portia Vigil, in the previous year.

Grand Junction and Delta city planners confirmed Alan's involvement in two recent subdivision business ventures. One was the Crista Lee subdivision in Orchard Mesa for twenty-one single-family lots on six acres. The other was a twenty-three-home subdivision in the city of Delta.

Allan Laurel, a dance instructor at Dance Junction, which Alan owned, and which his wife, Miriam, managed, told the reporter, "We're shocked! They're good people."

And Melody Sebesta, of Grand Junction, who had known Alan since childhood, declared, "Within the community, he's somebody everybody knew."

The reporter also phoned Portia Vigil's home, and an unidentified person there told him, "The family has no comment at this time."

What really piqued the reporter's interest was information

he picked up in the city of Delta. He learned that a vehicle owned by Alan Helmick had suspiciously caught fire in April. Delta PD chief Robert Thomas said that the incident "was suspicious in nature." Both Alan and Miriam Helmick had spoken with an investigator about it, and Thomas related, "There are no suspects."

Penny Lyons, Miriam's friend from the Dance Junction days, had also learned about Alan's murder. Penny said later, "Luda Miller called me one evening and asked if I remembered what Alan and Miriam's address was. She had heard a report on the news that a gentleman had been killed in his home. And I said, 'Of course, the address is right here.' So I looked it up, and then she said, 'I think that's the same one.' And when I checked online, that was their home.

"The night that I found out about Alan's murder, I tried all their phones, and no message, of course, could go through. But I called the police station that night because I was very concerned that Miriam might be alone and I was very worried about her. The detective told me that they couldn't say anything. But I spoke with the police the next day and they let me know she was staying at Alan's sister's place. So that comforted me."

While local reporters were trying to find out as much as they could about the murder of Alan Helmick and about his businesses in general, there was a lot going on behind the scenes that they knew nothing about. MCSO investigators were fanning out all across the region, digging up information about the Helmicks and why someone would want to murder Alan.

Jim Hebenstreit was the lead investigator on the case for the Mesa County Sheriff's Office. Hebenstreit had years of experience with the sheriff's office and had investigated many homicides. He'd taken refresher courses on many aspects related to homicides and knew that everything the detectives gathered now would be very important if an arrest was to be made in the murder of Alan Helmick. Hebenstreit wasn't working alone on this case. In fact, the majority of the MCSO detectives were looking into various aspects of Alan's murder.

One of the many people MCSO investigators would eventually talk to was Patricia "Trish" Erikson, who had known Alan Helmick for quite a few years. As Erikson later related, "I lived in Delta for twenty-five years, and cleaned houses in Delta, Cedaredge, and Eckert. I originally met Alan Helmick and his (first) wife, Sharon, when I used to wait tables. In about 2004, I was also cleaning houses and he or his secretary called and asked if I wanted to clean his office building. I started doing that.

"Later his secretary called me and asked me if I was interested in cleaning Alan's house in Delta. I was, and went over there and met him. That was in 2005. I cleaned the house every Friday.

"In 2006, he moved to a home in Whitewater. I went back and forth to clean that house once a month. It was usually about the last Monday of the month. I met Miriam there. They were in and out a lot. They would go take care of the horses or run to town or take care of business."

Trish happened to be at the Helmicks' Whitewater home on June 9, 2008, the day before Alan was murdered. She usually saw Alan and Miriam when she first arrived. But on June 9, Alan and Miriam were out doing something when she got there. The door was not locked, however, as was generally the case, and Trish went to work cleaning the house.

Later she recalled, "I went into the house about ten A.M. It would normally take me between four and five hours to clean the house. I would start with the living room, then go to the dining room, the kitchen, the office, and then the bedroom. They also had a bathroom off to the side of the office and I would clean that. And from there, I would go downstairs to clean.

"When Alan was home, he would chitchat with me. He would always say something to me, and Miriam, too. I was in the master bedroom when they came home that day. Alan did not say hello to me. Miriam came rushing in and asked me if I was okay, and I said yes. And then she apologized for not being there, but they'd had some business to take care of.

"Alan was sitting at a desk near the patio, and I asked him if he was okay, because he hadn't said 'hi' to me or anything. He said that he was. I asked him another question, and I didn't really understand what he said. It didn't appear that he wanted to talk to me at all."

Erikson thought Alan's conduct was very strange. He had always been talkative and friendly with her. Now he wouldn't even look at her. Trish added, "At that point, he got up, walked past the back of Miriam's chair, came down the hallway, where I was, and started to go toward the living room. Miriam was sitting at her desk at the time. He went past Miriam, and she had an awful look on her face.

"Alan accidentally knocked down a board that they used to block off the downstairs, so that the dogs wouldn't go through there. Miriam said something to him, and at first I don't think he even heard her. So she said it again. He started to pick up the board, but I told him don't bother, because I was going downstairs, anyway.

"Their actions with each other were very strange from the moment they came in the door. Later I saw Miriam and she was going to fill out the check that was for me. Usually, it was Alan who gave me the check, and if he didn't, he would just leave me an unsigned check and I would fill it out and leave the information for him. The last time I saw Alan alive, he was heading for the bedroom."

* * *

Investigator Lissah Norcross, of MCSO, began looking into phone records and data about any calls coming in for Alan Helmick that might have been threatening or considered as stalking. When Norcross gave her findings to Hebenstreit, he noted in a report: *Investigator Norcross did not discover any information leading to a person or persons with a motive to kill Alan Helmick. She also did not find any information to support that Alan was being stalked, harassed, or threatened by anyone.*

So then the investigators began looking into phone calls left on the Helmicks' answering machine on the morning of June 10, 2008. The first message on the machine came in at 9:03 A.M. In the message, Miriam said, "Hi, Alan. Love you," and then she began chatting about going to Walmart and City Market. Miriam asked if Alan wanted her to pick up salad and also if he was going to meet her for lunch. Miriam added that she didn't want Mexican food that day, and asked if he could meet her at a Chinese restaurant in Grand Junction.

Obviously, it was a very innocuous-sounding call from Miriam dealing with shopping and lunch. The second phone call from Miriam came in at 9:57 A.M. and sounded much the same way. "Hi, Alan. Haven't heard from you yet, but I have a question." Miriam asked if they could exchange a bit for a horse after they had lunch at the Chinese restaurant.

The tone of the messages began changing with the next phone call. Miriam said at 10:27 A.M.: "Hey, Alan! You need to turn your phone on. Question for you—I went to pick up your prescription and they said that you hadn't been by yet. So, are we still gonna be able to meet for lunch? If not, well, it's not like you not to call me, so give me a holler. Thanks. Bye."

The next message from Miriam had an even more concerned tone. It came at 11:15 A.M.: "Hey, Alan. This isn't funny anymore. I've been sitting here in front of the Chinese Dragon, or the Chinese place, for fifteen minutes. And you're never late. So, would you call me? I'm gonna go ahead and go home 'cause I think maybe you're caught up somewhere. Just thought I'd let you know so that you don't come over here looking for me. I will see you when you get home. Love you. Bye."

That was the last phone message from Miriam to Alan that morning. Of course, when she returned home, she found that Alan had been shot to death.

While MCSO detectives were conducting their investigation, Miriam Helmick sat down with Channel 11 news reporter Kieran Wilson, of Grand Junction. Wilson asked Miriam about her mentioning of a burglary on the 911 call. Miriam responded, "They took a lot of things, so I won't really know what's missing until they (the investigators) tell me what they have."

Wilson wanted to know if Miriam had been scared that the person who had shot Alan would come back. Miriam replied, "I don't know. Yes and no. I don't want to leave because I'm closer to him there. But I still keep things buttoned up pretty tight." Then she added, "I want the sheriff's office to find out who did it and what they possibly did it for."

MCSO investigators were certainly doing that. Investigator Chuck Warner was directed to conduct a background investigation of Miriam Giles Helmick. Using Accurint, which was a computer Internet program, Warner discovered that Miriam had lived in Jacksonville, Florida. While living there, Miriam had been married to Jack C. Giles, who had committed suicide on March 15, 2002. Before that, their daughter, Amy Giles, age twenty-three, had died on August 29, 2000. Amy had died of an accidental prescription drug overdose.

Warner found that Miriam had two liens and judgments against her. The first was a federal tax lien of more than

$20,000 from the year 2007. The second was a civil lien in the state of Georgia for $9,731.

Warner pulled up other data on Miriam and noted that she had lived in homes around Jacksonville, Florida, during the 1990s until 2004. In 2003 and 2004, a number of court actions had taken place concerning Miriam. Conseco Finance Company sued her, and in the judgment Miriam had to turn over a boat, a boat motor and trailer to them. American Express filed a suit against Miriam and Jack Giles for $68,189. Miriam seemed to have sold her home on Landmark Circle to help defray these costs. Then Miriam moved in with her father and stepmother in the Jacksonville area after the death of her husband.

CHAPTER 10

"I'm Better Off with Him Alive Than Dead."

On June 11, 2008, Investigator Lissah Norcross interviewed Portia Vigil, thirty-seven, Alan Helmick's daughter who lived in Delta, Colorado. Portia told Investigator Norcross that she didn't know of anyone who might want to harm her father. She said he had always been fair and even-handed in his business practices. Most people who met her father liked him.

Portia added that Alan's first wife, and her mother, Sharon Helmick, died unexpectedly about four years previously. This had been from a sudden heart attack. It had been a very difficult situation for everyone in the family, including her sister, Wendy, who lived near Denver, Colorado, sister, Kristy, who lived in Seattle, Washington, and her brother, Alan Jr., who also lived out of state, in Alaska.

Portia related that her father, Alan, had run Helmick Mortgage in the area since 1986. She stated that he had always been an honest but stern businessman, and that everyone in Delta knew him. Portia also said that, in 2002, her father had gotten out of the mortgage business and moved into land development through his business Crista Lee. Portia mentioned that he owned land in Delta, Garnet Mesa, Fruita, and Clifton. Portia also related that she now ran the Helmick Mortgage business in Delta.

Portia didn't know if her father had a specific attorney or if he had a will, but she had talked with him about getting a will after her mother had died. Portia related that her father had always been the type to be very active in his finances and to keep on top of his business transactions.

Portia told Investigator Norcross that after her mother's death, her father said he was going to take ballroom dancing lessons because it was something his deceased wife had always wanted to do. Miriam was working at a dance studio and she became Alan Helmick's dance instructor. The couple had been living together first in Delta, and then got married in June 2006 and bought a home in Whitewater, where they had lived up until the point of Alan's murder.

Portia said that Miriam was very different from her mother, and it was hard for her and her siblings to get to know the woman. Then Portia added that before his marriage to Miriam, she could always call her father, leave a message, and he would get back to her in a short period of time. Portia stated that during that period, she spoke with her father on the phone at least twice a week.

Portia reported that everything had started changing when her father married Miriam. And over the past six months, he had become harder and harder to reach by phone. Portia began getting only voice mail; and even when she called him back, he did not return the call. In frustration Portia started calling Miriam's cell phone number, asking that her father call her back. Even then, he did so only infrequently.

Portia told Investigator Norcross that her father had been very sick between January 2008 and the end of April 2008. He was so sick, in fact, that there were many days he couldn't get out of bed. Alan said he felt dizzy, his legs hurt, and he was always tired. Portia didn't know what was making her father so sick, but there were a few times he had to check into the hospital in Grand Junction. It got so bad that her father told her at one point that he had bedsores, and Miriam was only giving him Gatorade to drink.

Portia told Norcross that she found this scenario very suspicious, because her father had always been a healthy man before meeting Miriam. Portia became so concerned about her father that she started showing up at his home unannounced. Around May 1, she did see that her father was feeling better. He seemed to be his old self, happier and more vibrant.

And then Portia switched subjects. She told Investigator Norcross that when Miriam moved in with her father, they started owning horses. Portia thought this was strange, because up until that point, her father had never shown any interest in animals at all. Going further into this horse-owning business, Portia said that she knew her father had fired a horse trainer named Stephanie because he thought she had lied to him about how many hours she had worked during one period. Alan and Miriam then hired another woman, whose name she thought was Julie, as the horse trainer, but Portia didn't know Julie's last name.

Another thing struck Portia as strange. When Investigator Norcross told Portia that Miriam had phoned Alan several times on the morning he was killed, Portia said that things were not usually like that. Portia related that her father and Miriam almost always went to town together. And it was not like Miriam to be phoning her father and leaving him messages about where she was and what she was doing. Miriam did not go out on her own very often.

Portia also said that recently she had been receiving odd phone calls about her father's finances. That was completely out of character for him. On June 4, 2008, she received a call from American National Bank. They were calling her about a loan that her father had with the bank; and even after numerous phone calls to him, he had never called them back. Alan Watkins, the man at the bank, knew that her father had been sick for a prolonged period of time, and Watkins wanted to make sure her father was okay. Then Watkins told Portia that he needed to talk to her father about his account right away.

Portia tried calling her father about this situation, but once again got no answer, just a recorded message. Around that same time, Portia received a phone call from a woman named Savanna at the State Farm Insurance Agency in Delta. Savanna told Portia they were closing Alan's policy due to a lack of payment. This was completely out of character for her father, Portia said.

Portia told Norcross that between June 4 and June 9, she had called her father three times per day, with no response. Miriam did call Portia back on June 5 and said to her that on May 29, 2008, while on the way to Lake Powell, Alan had told her to call the bank and lie to them. The lie was supposed to be that Alan was in Denver receiving electrolyte treatment, and to ask the bank to let Miriam cash a check for him. Then Miriam added that this was information she would not even tell her best friends. Portia thought this comment was very odd, since she and Miriam were not close, and the so-called information Miriam had just provided did not make sense. Portia related that she did not believe her father would ever ask anyone to lie. In fact, Portia adamantly stated, "To my knowledge, he does not lie, and, to the contrary, dislikes people who do lie in business."

Portia told Norcross that Miriam had made arrangements for Portia's nine-year-old daughter to have riding lessons at the Helmicks' Whitewater home every Tuesday at noon. Portia's daughter had her first lesson on June 3, 2008, and all went well. Alan and Miriam had picked up the girl the night before, and the girl spent Monday night there in Whitewater. The next day, Portia's daughter had her riding lesson at noon, as scheduled, and then she was driven back to Portia's home after the riding lesson.

But on June 9, 2008, Portia had tried calling her father to ask if he was picking up her daughter for the next lesson, which was scheduled for June 10. Portia could not get through to him, so she left a message on his cell phone. Portia next called Miriam's cell phone and also left a message on it. Miriam later called Portia back and said that the new horse trainer was having a problem with a horse named Billy, which her daughter rode. Miriam then added that she wanted to cancel the ride slated for June 10 and reschedule it for Friday, June 13.

Norcross made a note about this horse trainer, Julie, but actually found out later that the horse trainer was named Sue Boulware. Portia added that when she got Miriam's message, she was very upset, but she said it was okay to do the new plan for June 13. Portia also said that she wanted to speak with her father right then. Miriam replied that Alan had gone to an appointment in the town of Montrose at 2:00 P.M. and planned to stop off at Portia's home on the way back. Portia now told Norcross that this was also strange, since her father almost never popped in unannounced.

Alan Helmick did not stop off at Portia's house on June 9, and Portia phoned Miriam once again. Miriam said this time that she had told Alan to phone Portia. That phone call never came, nor did Alan stop by Portia's home by five o'clock, as Miriam indicated he would do. Concerned about this, Portia phoned her husband, Josh Vigil, since she knew Josh had plans to spend the night at the Helmick residence after his workday with Halliburton. Once Josh got there, he said that this whole scenario was strange. He phoned Portia from the Helmick residence in Whitewater and said that from where he stood he could see both Miriam and Alan out by the barn.

Miriam phoned Portia later that same night and told her that Alan had stopped by the Elks Lodge in Delta to pay his dues on his way home. Then, according to Miriam, Alan had arrived home "really drunk," so she put him to bed. Portia said that this was unlikely. She had never known her father to drink to excess and drive.

Portia did not question Miriam at the time, but she did phone Josh once again. Josh said that Alan did not appear to be drunk when he saw him by the barn. Portia did not pursue this matter because all the kids were planning to visit Alan on Thursday, June 12, and have their riding lesson the next day. Portia related that she would talk in person with her father on that occasion. Of course, by then, he was already dead.

Portia tried calling her father on the morning of June 10, but as usual, the call went immediately to voice mail. Portia next phoned Miriam's cell phone and spoke directly with her, telling Miriam that she needed to speak with her father right away. There was some important business he needed to attend to. Miriam responded that she was at Walmart and Alan was not with her. Then Miriam said that Alan was picking up a car and they were supposed to meet and have lunch at a Mexican restaurant later that day. Portia told Norcross that was the last time she spoke with Miriam before she heard about the murder of her father.

Portia Vigil learned about a murder in Whitewater and got online on a computer to see what it was all about. There was mention of a robbery out at her father's house and that a male had been found deceased inside the home. Portia immediately phoned her husband, Josh, who answered and said that he was just pulling into the Helmicks' driveway. Portia phoned her father-in-law, her sisters, and then her husband once again.

Portia told Investigator Norcross that Miriam had two small dogs, and she was certain they would have barked if there had been an intruder in the house. To a question about cell phones, Portia said that her father's phone was pink and Miriam's phone was black. Portia had even joked to her father that it wasn't very masculine to have a pink cell phone. Her father had joked back that he was comfortable with his masculinity and didn't worry about having a pink mobile phone.

During the interview, Portia said that Bob Isom was her father's closest friend. Isom had stopped by her home upon hearing the news about Alan. Bob told Portia that he had spoken to Alan on the previous afternoon about a golf game they had scheduled for the morning of June 10. Bob said that Alan canceled the golf game because Portia's daughter was coming over to the Whitewater residence for her riding lessons. Portia told Bob that Miriam had canceled the riding lesson. This made no sense to Bob, since Alan had canceled the golf game so he could attend his granddaughter's riding lesson.

Regarding the Helmick home in Whitewater, Portia said to Norcross that she didn't think the home had ever been locked. It was in a supposedly safe area, and people just didn't lock their doors out there. But Miriam had told Portia that two months previously she had found some house keys that had been missing. And Miriam added that they were going to start locking the doors because the area was becoming unsafe. Portia said the area was not unsafe; and despite Miriam's statement, the doors at the home had remained unlocked during the time period of April, May, and early June 2008.

Portia also told Norcross that her father and Miriam had gone to Portia's daughter's dance recital on May 10. It was there that Portia heard about her father's vehicle being on fire in Delta. The strangest part of all this was that Miriam told Portia at the dance recital that the police in Delta suspected Miriam of being involved in the car fire. Then Miriam added that this was ridiculous and that she and Alan had a prenuptial agreement. If anything happened to him, Miriam was not going to benefit from an insurance policy on his life. According to Miriam, everything that Alan owned, and all assets before he and Miriam got married, were to be split among his children after his death. For her to kill him would have left her destitute.

Miriam related to Portia that she had told Delta investigators she had no policy taken out on Alan's life, and she added, "I'm better off with him alive than dead." And Portia knew that even though her father had a $275,000 life insurance policy, the benefactors were his business partners and not Miriam.

Delving more deeply into the vehicle fire in Delta, Investigator Norcross learned from Portia that she and her father had a cell phone conversation about it right after the incident, which had occurred on April 30, 2008. Portia related that the Delta police had called her, because they could not get in contact with her father after the car fire. Portia called Miriam and said she needed to speak to her father immediately. Miriam responded by saying that Alan was busy and would get back to her. But Portia wouldn't be put off. She told Miriam that the Delta police had just called her about her father, and she wanted to speak with him now, not later. At that point, Miriam handed the phone over to Alan.

Portia said that she could hear her father ask Miriam where his cell phone was, and he also asked if she had turned it off. Portia added that after that point she began to believe Miriam was hiding her father's cell phone and turning it off whenever she could get away with it.

CHAPTER 11

A MATTER OF POISON

Based on the information that Portia Vigil had given Investigator Norcross, MCSO investigator Chuck Warner called the Delta Elks Lodge about whether Alan Helmick had become intoxicated there on June 9, 2008. Warner talked to Chris Ranker, the Elks Lodge bartender, who had worked the bar that evening. Ranker said that she had known Alan Helmick for years, and she was sure he was not at the bar in the lodge on June 9. In fact, Ranker said she had not seen Alan or Miriam Helmick at the club for four or five months.

On June 12, Investigator Pete Burg interviewed Bob Isom at the Mesa County Sheriff's Office. Isom stated that he had known Alan Helmick for forty-five years and they had gone to school together. They had been friends for a long, long time, and even neighbors at one point. Bob also stated that he and Alan were members of the Elks and that they used to boat on Lake Powell together. Those trips, according to Bob, ended when Miriam came on the scene, except for one trip to Lake Powell. That had been on May 30, 2008, to June 1, 2008, when he, his wife, Peggy, Alan, and Miriam had been there.

Isom told Investigator Burg that Miriam had been hard to

get to know, but on that particular trip to Lake Powell, she was more relaxed and talkative than usual. Bob added, "My wife, Peggy, even thought it was kind of funny how nice Miriam was being to all of them." Bob did admit that he didn't notice any problems between Alan and Miriam on that trip.

Bob related that the last time he saw Alan Helmick alive was on Monday, June 9, 2008, at around 1:30 P.M. Isom had driven to the Helmick residence and invited Alan to play golf the next morning at nine-ten. Alan told Bob that he had a horse-riding lesson scheduled for his granddaughter, but he would see if he could move that to a different date. He promised to call Bob back about the golf game.

Bob Isom told Investigator Burg that at that meeting, "Alan looked like his old self. He looked super." After Isom left, Alan phoned him about four hours later and said that he could not make the golf game on the following day. Alan said he had to do the "grandbaby thing"—meaning he had to be there when his granddaughter took her riding lesson.

Isom did go to the golf course on the morning of June 10 and played a round of golf. When Bob returned home that evening, his wife, Peggy, immediately told him that Miriam had called earlier and said, "There was a robbery and Alan has gotten shot, and he's dead." Then Peggy told Bob that Miriam wanted him to go and be with Alan's daughter, Portia, because Portia would be distraught.

Isom did go over to Portia's house, and it was there that he first learned from Portia that Miriam had canceled the riding lesson. Isom told Investigator Burg, "This made no sense! Alan had canceled the golf game because of that riding lesson! He would have gone golfing, if not for that riding lesson."

Investigator Hebenstreit went to see Dr. Robert Kurtzman, who had done the postmortem on Alan Helmick. Hebenstreit told Dr. Kurtzman that some of Alan Helmick's family and friends were suspicious that Miriam might have been poisoning Alan before his murder. This was based on Alan's long period of illness, where at times he could not even get out of bed.

Dr. Kurtzman told Hebenstreit that he had found no evidence of poisoning, but Alan did have serious heart disease. Kurtzman said this would have caused Alan intolerance to physical activity, fatigue, and gastrointestinal (GI) symptoms, such as heartburn.

Hebenstreit said that several people mentioned that Alan had looked and acted better one week before his death. Hebenstreit wanted to know if that was consistent with heart disease. Dr. Kurtzman said yes, and all things considered, family and friends might have mistaken legitimate health issues for poisoning.

On June 12, 2008, Detective Beverly Jarrell interviewed Sue Boulware by phone. Boulware said that she had first been contacted by Miriam Helmick in February 2008 to train the Helmicks' horses. Boulware's duties as a trainer were dressage training and an evaluation of the equestrian sport property. Sue said she did not know much about the personal lives of Alan and Miriam, and she didn't ask. In fact, she had never been to the Helmick residence in Whitewater. The training had taken place at a location in Loma.

Boulware related that on June 9, 2008, the day before Alan was murdered, both Alan and Miriam arrived at the training center in Loma to take one of the horses to Dr. Harris for medical treatment. Sue said that Alan and Miriam were in a hurry, but that was nothing unusual. The Helmicks got the horse into the trailer and then transported it to the vet. Boulware added that everything seemed normal between Alan and Miriam that day, and they returned a few hours later with the horse.

Boulware told Jarrell that she received a phone call at eight forty-three in the morning on June 10. Sue believed that Miriam was calling her on a cell phone while driving, because at one point near the end, Miriam said she was at a store. During the phone call, Miriam said that she would be canceling the noon appointment for the riding lesson for Alan's granddaughter. Miriam added that they had not made it to Delta on the previous night to pick up the granddaughter as scheduled. This was news to Jarrell. Miriam had told Portia Vigil that it was Sue Boulware who had canceled the riding lesson, because the horse, Billy, was having problems.

Boulware related that at the end of the cell phone conversation on June 10, Miriam had offered to drive to Loma and pay her for the missed lesson. Sue told Miriam that it was too far to drive, and just to send her a check, instead.

Oddly, even after such traumatic events on June 10, Miriam phoned Sue Boulware the very night of Alan's murder to tell her that the check would be late. The reason for the late check, Miriam said, was that there had been a robbery at the house and Alan had been killed. Then Miriam told Sue that they never locked their doors. Miriam even went out of her way to tell Boulware that all the assets that Alan had were in a trust fund, and she didn't know how her finances were going to be for a while. Sue was stunned that Miriam was phoning her after such a devastating event.

Boulware told Investigator Jarrell that the Helmicks were nice people and she never had any trouble with them. Then she added that Alan was intelligent, business smart, and financially oriented; he was reasonable to get along with. It was Alan who had been more involved with the business side of the horse training center. Miriam had been more involved on a day-to-day basis, but Boulware thought that both had been enthusiastic about it.

* * *

That same day, Bev Jarrell also met with Stephanie Soule and her husband, Brian, at the MCSO headquarters. Stephanie told Jarrell that she had been approached by the Helmicks in March 2007 regarding horse-riding lessons. Miriam had been the first to take the riding lessons on one of the Soules' horses. As the lessons continued, Miriam had talked about having her own business venture in horse training. She wanted to use land that Alan owned for riding lessons, horse training, and also the selling of horses.

The original scheme was to divide some of the White-water property and make it into a "horse subdivision." All of these initial plans had come from Miriam, but Stephanie added that all of the horse-riding lessons were being paid for by Alan Helmick.

When the plan went into reality, it was Stephanie Soule's job to set up the facility, to arrange schedules, equipment, and diet for the horses. The trainer said she was there about five days a week, but there were occasions that the Helmicks would cancel because of Alan's other business operations.

Stephanie then said that Miriam lied to Alan regarding the financial issues of the equestrian-training center. And she became concerned when Miriam asked her to put down more time than she had done on the actual training. Miriam told her, "That's to prepare Alan for the future." The trainer told Miriam that she was not comfortable with falsifying records.

Stephanie related that initially Alan had been very nice with her. But over time, he seemed more irritated and questioned her about discrepancies. And Miriam made an odd comment to her: "I don't maintain any type of financial records because of something that happened to me during my first marriage. Alan has been trying to help me out of this financial problem." Just what that problem was, the trainer didn't know.

Stephanie said that Miriam would often make excuses for not training or riding when Stephanie was under contract for payment. And even though Stephanie was going by the contract, Alan started becoming angry with her for writing down on her training log times that he knew Miriam had not ridden or trained horses. It got so bad that there were times that she had to go to Miriam in order to get paid for services she had rendered.

Both Stephanie and her husband, Brian Soule, said that things only got worse in relation to the Helmicks. Brian described Alan questioning his wife's training time; and when Miriam tried to intervene, "he would shut her down." Brian added, "Alan became irrational at the end of 2007. He cursed Stephanie around Christmas, 2007, and said that this was his business and she could not tell him what to do!"

December 30, 2007, was the last time Stephanie Soule contacted the Helmicks in person at their Whitewater home.

On June 13, Investigator Lissah Norcross interviewed another of Alan's daughters, thirty-two-year-old Wendy. Just like Portia, Wendy said that it had been very hard to get in touch with her father over the past several months. Wendy declared that Miriam had been keeping Alan's phone and not turning it on. This wasn't a secret, however, since even her father had stated that Miriam was keeping his phone for him. To Wendy, it seemed more like Miriam was keeping the phone *from* him.

Wendy had lived with Miriam and her father at the Whitewater residence from May 2006 until June 2007. While she lived with Miriam and Alan, everything seemed to be fine between her father and his new girlfriend. However, Miriam did over time "start confiscating" her father's cell phone and turning it off. Wendy didn't say anything at the time because she was trying not to be "a burden to my father and Miriam," as she put it.

Between the time Wendy moved out of the Whitewater

residence, and until she moved to Denver in March 2008, she only saw her father twice. She did phone the residence on occasion, but she only spoke with her father in very few instances. Wendy added that she would ask her father why he didn't phone her back, as she had left a message. Alan often replied that he hadn't received any message.

As to Miriam's statement that she had tried phoning Alan several times on the morning he was killed, Wendy said that made no sense. Wendy claimed, "Miriam always had my father's phone and kept it turned off." Alan had even told Wendy that Miriam kept his cell phone in her purse.

Then Wendy wondered why Miriam had gone out so early on June 10. Wendy told Investigator Norcross, "Miriam is not a morning person. While I lived there, I never saw Miriam get up first and go out by herself somewhere. My father was a morning person, but Miriam wouldn't get up until ten A.M. and start moving around."

When Wendy had lived with her father and Miriam, she fed the horses in the morning or her father did. Miriam never fed the horses in the morning at all. Not once while living there, had she seen her father and Miriam leave the house before ten o'clock in the morning.

In a later interview with Wendy, Investigator Norcross brought up the aspect of a will that her father had made. Wendy said that in 2007, while her father and Miriam were living together before being married, her father had shown Wendy a handwritten document. Her father had not let her read the document, but he had only said that it concerned his children. Alan did say that the children didn't have to worry if he died, because Miriam was not to get any of the assets that Alan had amassed previous to her arrival. That was the bulk of the property and money involved. Alan did say that Miriam would receive assets from the period after they were married, which basically concerned the new house and property in Whitewater. Wendy didn't know where this document was, but she believed it was probably in a filing cabinet, where he kept all his important papers.

On June 13 as well, Lissah Norcross interviewed Alan Helmick's youngest daughter, Kristy Helmick-Burd, who was thirty. Kristy lived in Seattle, but she had returned to Colorado because of her father's death. In fact, Kristy stated that she and her husband had planned to visit her father in the current week, and then they suddenly found out that he had been murdered. This, of course, had required that they go to Colorado even earlier than planned.

Kristy related that she and her husband had lived in several places, but they had moved back to Delta in August 2004 to November 2004, when her mother had died. They had done so to help her father during that period. Kristy said that her father had been very depressed after his first wife died. Just before Kristy and her husband moved to Seattle, she did meet Miriam. She said that her father and Miriam were "like newlyweds."

Kristy had last spoken with her father on Sunday, June 1; for the next nine days, she had tried to reach him on his cell phone. Kristy was unable to do so. She learned of his unexpected death on June 10. The aspect of not being able to reach him for those nine days greatly concerned her. Kristy said that before the advent of Miriam on the scene, she had always been able to reach her father by phone. In total frustration during that nine-day period, Kristy finally called Miriam's cell phone and asked Miriam to have Alan phone her back because she had to make travel plans. Kristy wanted her father to call her back immediately. To this, Miriam replied, "Well, he's in one of those financial moods. Kind of being a jackass."

Kristy told Investigator Norcross that she didn't know what Miriam meant by that. Alan had not been in that "kind of mood" before, especially with his children. Kristy added that despite her request for Miriam to tell her father to call her back, he never did. Kristy stated that she didn't know of her father having any problems or of anyone who would want to hurt him. She did say, "He was kind of a hard-ass in business, but always fair." Then Kristy related about the phone situation, "Miriam always had my father's phone as a way of gradual isolation and manipulation."

Investigator Norcross asked Kristy if her father had ever asked her to forge his signature. Kristy said no, and she added that she could not imagine him ever asking anyone to do that. Her father had fired people for lying before, and he would not tolerate lying or cheating. As to the vehicle fire, Kristy said that Miriam had spoken to her about that. Miriam had stated at the time that if Alan died, she (Miriam) would not get anything because of the prenuptial agreement. About this prenup, Miriam even said, "I didn't want him to be so infatuated with me that he forgot you girls." And Miriam made it a point that it was she who had insisted upon the prenuptial agreement before she and Alan got married. Kristy now told Norcross how these comments were very odd at that time of the vehicle fire. Instead of reducing her suspicions about Miriam, they only increased them.

CHAPTER 12

A FUNERAL AND A SHOCK

On June 15, 2008, Investigator Jim Hebenstreit was notified at the sheriff's office to phone J. P. Morgan. This J. P. Morgan was not the financial institution, but rather a patrol officer with the Duval County, Florida, Sheriff's Office. Hebenstreit phoned Officer Morgan, who told Hebenstreit that Miriam was his half sister. Morgan said that he hadn't seen or spoken with Miriam in five or six years. And then Morgan dropped a bombshell. He said that Miriam had stolen $120,000 from their parents, who lived in Jacksonville, Florida.

That wasn't all. Morgan related that Miriam's first husband, Jack Giles, had died in a violent manner. This was the first time MCSO investigators heard anything about this. Morgan believed, because of the investigation, that Jack's death was a legitimate suicide. Morgan added that Jack and Miriam had been married for twenty-three or twenty-four years, when Jack pulled out a pistol and shot himself in the head while both he and Miriam were in bed. Apparently, Jack had been distraught about the death of his daughter on his birthday, two years after the young woman had died.

Officer Morgan added that Jack Giles was a "gun nut." According to Morgan, Jack had even persuaded Miriam to always carry a loaded .38 handgun with her. Morgan also said that Miriam was a good shot. As to Investigator Hebenstreit's question of whether Morgan ever knew Miriam to own a .25-caliber gun, Morgan didn't know. It had been determined by now that Alan Helmick had died from a .25-caliber bullet to the brain.

A few days later, MCSO investigator Chuck Warner interviewed Sergeant Lewis, who was with the Jacksonville Police Department (Jacksonville PD) in Florida. Lewis had investigated the death of Miriam's first husband, Jack Giles, on April 15, 2002. Lewis, not unlike Morgan, said that Jack had been in bed with Miriam when he shot himself. After Jack had shot himself, his thumb was found in the trigger guard. That was unusual, but Sergeant Lewis said that Jack had been depressed over the death of his daughter and committed suicide because of it. The death of Jack Giles was officially ruled a suicide.

Investigator Warner received photos connected to the death of Jack Giles and a report about gunshot residue testing. GSR was not found to have been on samples taken from Miriam. However, GSR testing had not been done on Jack Giles's hands and clothing to see if he had, in fact, fired the pistol.

Investigator Warner later received copies of two reports from the Jacksonville PD concerning the death of Jack Giles. In looking through these reports, Warner noted that Miriam had been investigated for depositing counterfeit checks in January 2004. The total amount had been $6,800. The report went on to state that Miriam eventually admitted to depositing and cashing the counterfeit checks.

Investigator Warner also checked on the time Miriam

had spent in Gulfport, Mississippi, before she had come to Colorado. While living there, Miriam had gone under the name of Francehssea (her unique spelling) Miriam Giles. Warner contacted the Gulfport courts and found that there were three inactive court cases involving Miriam from 2005.

Investigator Hebenstreit later received court documents from Gulfport noting that in two cases Miriam had been charged with embezzlement and the third charge was for petty larceny. The date of all the charges was November 12, 2004. According to the documents, Miriam was found not guilty on all the charges. But it seemed to be "not guilty" because the charges had never gone forward. A big part of the reason was that Hurricane Katrina had ripped apart Gulfport, Mississippi, around that time, and these charges were of little concern in the wider scope of that disaster.

Investigator Warner received Gulfport Police Department (Gulfport PD) charges on the incidents and learned that Miriam had been investigated for taking monies belonging to Barbara Watts, who owned a dance studio there. Miriam left Gulfport for Colorado before she was arrested; but then for some reason, she went back to Gulfport on March 15, 2005. Barbara Watts saw Miriam there, and Miriam was arrested and eventually had her court date. And, of course, because of Hurricane Katrina, the charges were eventually dropped.

The funeral services for Alan Helmick didn't occur until June 17 in Delta. Alan had a wide group of friends and family from all over who attended the services. An important person who would later speak with investigators after the funeral about what occurred there was Mike Pruett. Pruett was Alan Helmick's former brother-in-law, having been Sharon Helmick's brother. Pruett recalled of the funeral, "After the cemetery, we came back to the church, and there was a dinner there. There were a lot of people, and at some point Miriam came over and sat down where I was. And we began to speak to each other.

"She came over and said that Alan had mentioned that when he passed on, Sharon's ashes would be spread at his grave. Apparently, the ashes had never been distributed anywhere, and Alan had been in control of them.

"She and I sat face-to-face at a table. We just pulled our chairs out more or less and faced each other. There was no one else involved in the conversation. From time to time throughout our conversation, people would come and say, 'It's good to see you again, Mike,' and they'd say, 'We're sorry for you, Miriam.' Just exchanging pleasantries and moving on, but no one else entered into our conversation.

"I asked how she was doing, and she responded, 'I'm the number one suspect.'

"And I said, 'Well, that's probably to be understood. That's just the way it is. I think everyone's a suspect until you're eliminated, so it doesn't surprise me that you're a suspect.'

"I asked her if she thought Alan might have known the shooter. And she said that she didn't know. Then she talked about the day that it happened. She said she had laid out some clothes for him on the bed that morning, but then she said he didn't pick those clothes. He apparently didn't like what she had picked out.

"She also talked about somebody that had worked for her at one point in time at the dance studio. Alan had a real dislike for that guy for some reason. She said there was a beef between this guy and Alan. She may have said that the ex-employee had been stealing from them."

And then Miriam said something about the ex-employee that caught Pruett completely by surprise. According to Pruett, Miriam declared about the man, "He'd better have a fucking good alibi!"

Pruett said later, "I was taken off guard. I asked her, 'What did you say?' So she repeated it. 'He'd better have a fucking good alibi!'

"I asked her if she had given that information to her attorney so that it could be passed on to law enforcement. And she said that she had not done so yet. Then she mentioned something about a prenuptial agreement. My belief was at the time that Alan probably had some kind of provision for her in some way, while the bulk of his estate would go to his family.

"We were concluding our conversation, and I asked her, 'Well, where do you go from here?' And she said, 'I'm going back to the house.'

"I found it troubling that she would go back to the house with an unknown shooter out there somewhere. It was like, 'Why would you go back and put yourself in harm's way?'"

Penny Lyons, who was also at the funeral, recalled, "When I saw Miriam at the funeral, she was sitting up front with the family. And I felt really compelled to let her know that I was there for her. So I went up just to let her know I was there.

"After the funeral, she asked if I could come to the meal afterward, but I couldn't. I had to get back to work. We had to open the clinic that afternoon. So I told her that I would come by after work, and I did. I went straight out to her house after seven P.M. I stayed until close to midnight. It was just me and Miriam there. We sat in the living room for a while and Miriam smoked. Then we spent the rest of the time in the garage, because she didn't like to smoke in the house.

"I did not enter the kitchen. I walked past it. There were some towels placed on the floor in a T shape that I assumed was covering bloodstains that were there. I didn't want to look at it. I was just there to comfort my friend. I was really surprised that stains were still there. That they wouldn't have been cleaned up already.

"Most of our conversation, I just let her talk. She did

mention that when she first walked in from the utility room to the house, she saw Alan's feet first and didn't realize something was wrong right away. This was odd, though, because it seemed to be in direct contrast to the way the towels were laid out. I simply chose to shine that on at the time and let it go. I just wanted to be there for her, so I didn't think any more about it."

Housekeeper Patricia Erikson also attended the memorial service. Later she recalled, "I walked up to Miriam and apologized for telling the police that I was there the day before, and I apologized for telling them how I felt about that day. I said, 'I had to tell them how I felt that day.'" (She was speaking about her interview with the police.)

Miriam didn't seem to be too upset by Patricia's words. In fact, Miriam was basically telling various people that she was being investigated by the authorities, and she realized that was all very routine in a murder case like this.

The day after the funeral, the *Delta County Independent* ran an article about Alan Helmick entitled FORMER RESIDENT MURDERED. The reporter spoke with various people who had known Alan over the years, including his friend, John Taylor. John spoke of both of them loving to hunt, fish, golf, and play cards. He relayed, "He'll be missed. He would bend over backward to put you in the home you wanted with a mortgage you could handle."

Another friend, Les Mitchell, had known Alan since 1974, when Alan had been hired as the golf pro at Cottonwood Golf Course. Les recalled, "We played a lot of golf together. We took fishing trips to Canada and to Mexico. Our families spent time together as our children grew up. He was big on his kids."

The article went on to note that Alan had sold his mortgage business to daughter Portia in the previous year, and he'd currently been pursuing land development projects. One of those was before the Delta Planning Commission for town houses between Sixth and Seventh Streets in the city of Delta at the time of Alan's death.

The article revealed one more thing: *The Delta Police Department had forwarded information on an investigation into a fire which damaged a vehicle owned by Alan Helmick. The incident, which occurred at the end of April, was labeled suspicious, according to DPD spokesman Jamie Head.*

CHAPTER 13

"She Wasn't Going to Miss Him at All."

Detective Beverly Jarrell interviewed Jeri Yarbrough, who was an equestrian trainer and lived in Fort Lupton, Colorado. Fort Lupton was a town hundreds of miles away from Mesa County, just northeast of Denver. Yarbrough had originally met Alan and Miriam Helmick through Stephanie Soule. Much later, Jeri recounted what had occurred when she began talking to investigators.

Jeri said, "Stephanie introduced me to the Helmicks and she told me that she was going to be working for this couple. They were interested in starting to buy young horses and maybe getting into the breeding of warmbloods. They came to look at my horses and at my facility. They bought a three-year-old gelding, Hollywood, and then they bought a mare that was in foal to my stallion, Presley. And they had an Arabian mare, Jasmine, that they also purchased to breed her.

"They put all the horses on Nationwide (a trucking company) and hauled them up to their ranch. Later, Miriam called me in December 2007 and said that Stephanie was not going to be working for them anymore. They had all these young horses and they were concerned about who they would get to train them. My friend, Shannon Dahmer, was training out of my barn at the time, and I suggested that Shannon could help her get her horses ridden, and they sent them down. They sent three horses, Hollywood, Pharaoh, and Vegas. They used Nationwide for that and it cost at least a thousand dollars.

"The horses were there from about February 2008 to May 2008. After May 2008, the horses were going back up to Miriam's place. She said that she missed them and she had found a trainer named Sue Boulware, that I knew of. Sue would be taking over the training and that way they'd be able to see them more.

"I had a lot of contact with Miriam Helmick right around then. The mare I had sold them, Sadie, had just foaled. Miriam called me and said the foal was doing really well. She'd call about horse stuff. Things like how the horses were doing, 'cause I care about all my horses, and like to know that they're doing well and that they're being taken care of.

"I actually went to a stock show with the Helmicks. Alan wasn't feeling very well and Miriam came down and was watching a lot of horse events. She asked if I'd like to come and watch the grand prix jumping, and I said sure. I met her there. She said Alan had been sick a lot with stomach flu, and hadn't been feeling well. And right about then, when the horses were being boarded and trained at my facility, we didn't receive some of the payments.

"So I called her to say we didn't receive the board money and training money. And she said they had been out vacationing on their boat and the payments were in the mail. I called a week later and said the payments never came. Miriam said the payments probably got sent to Alan's daughter by mistake. She added Alan had taken an overdose of blood pressure medication and he had been misplacing stuff.

"I tried calling Alan once, but only got through to his voice mail. When I finally got a check, it was written on checks from the dance studio. Even then, the checks didn't clear. My boyfriend called back to see why they didn't clear. And there was supposed to be two signatures on the checks, but there was only one. From what I understood, Alan was a pretty good businessman. I couldn't understand why he would write a check, knowing that it required two signatures. That didn't make sense to me."

Moving on in time, Investigator Jarrell wanted to know when Jeri Yarbrough first learned about Alan Helmick's murder. Jeri said, "My friend Stephanie Soule called me and left me a voice mail. I called Miriam and said how sorry I was, and if there was anything I could do to help her, and my thoughts were with her. On Thursday night, a couple of days after he had been shot, Miriam called me.

"She just started talking about what happened and I just said how sorry I was. I asked how she was doing, and had concerns for her safety. She said she was doing fine, but that she was pretty upset because she couldn't go back home because the police were there. She said it was because they had to do those kind of things. She said they had talked to her for a long time, interrogated her and stuff. And I said, 'Well, that's probably normal.'

"She told me that originally on the day he was killed, they were supposed to go out and do some errands together. But Alan decided not to go, and she went off to do the errands. After that, they were supposed to meet for lunch. Alan didn't show up, and she started trying to call him and he didn't answer. So she went back home and found him. She said he was lying on the floor and that he was gone. He was cold to the touch, and she called 911 and they instructed her to do CPR, which she did, but she said that she knew he was gone.

"She thought it was a home burglary, but she also thought the police were focusing on her. And I said that that was kinda normal. 'They always look at a spouse first. Just answer the questions and let the police do the work so they'll be able to figure everything out.' She said her hands had been tested for gun residue and that her clothes had been taken. And they were also testing for high-velocity blood spatter.

"She said she didn't know who could have done it. She didn't know whether it was related to one of Alan's businesses or not. She said she didn't know about his businesses. All the money was in his name. He controlled the checking accounts and money. It was strange—she was pretty matter-of-fact about the whole thing. I mean, I was surprised that she wasn't more upset about finding her husband killed so tragically. I just thought that maybe she handles things a little bit different than I react to stuff.

"She was just talking and said that she and Alan hadn't been getting along for the last few weeks. She said they had been fighting and not getting along, and that he'd been a real asshole the last couple of weeks. They had been at a business, and she went into a restroom and their car started on fire while she was in the bathroom. And she made a strange comment, 'I didn't know that a car won't explode if it has a full tank of gas.' And then she laughed."

Detective Jarrell wanted to know more about Miriam's attitude regarding law enforcement and what she had done. Jeri related that Miriam had told her that the police had looked for traces of gunpowder residue on her hands. Police had also taken her clothing, looking for traces of blood spatter. Miriam had added to Jeri, "Of course, they had to look for evidence, and told me to be up front so that they could try and learn who had done this."

During the phone call to Jeri Yarbrough on June 12, Miriam told her that she didn't have any money. She wondered if Jeri could buy back some horses at the purchase price. Miriam then told Jeri that the horses were hers and she could do anything she wanted with them. However, Jeri did not want to get into a dispute over property and legal entanglements after Alan Helmick's murder, so she declined.

Jeri Yarbrough once again told the investigator that she was not a close friend of Miriam's, and that some of the things Miriam was saying made her very uncomfortable. She wondered why Miriam was going into such details about what Jeri considered to be private matters.

Miriam spoke about Alan's children, and how the daughters were already asking for property, such as the boat and other items. Miriam told Jeri that there was a will, but that she was not mentioned in any of Alan's life insurance policies or checking accounts.

In a later conversation with Jeri Yarbrough, Bev Jarrell learned that Jeri had not told her everything that had occurred between herself and Miriam during the phone conversation of June 12. Jeri said that she did not want to betray Miriam in any way, if she was not the one who had been responsible for Alan's death. During this conversation, Jeri told Jarrell, "Miriam told me that maybe there was a person at the dance studio that had taken money, and maybe Alan had found out about it. [The killing] might have been a vendetta against Alan. I told her she had to contact the police and be honest with them about everything. I don't remember what her answer was to that."

Jarrell wanted to know if Miriam used the words "murdered" or "killed" when speaking about Alan. Jeri said that Miriam hadn't used either one. She only used words such as "died, gone, or dead," according to the horse breeder.

"Alan was an asshole to me for the last couple of weeks," Miriam had told Jeri. "I had to hide money at the dance studio so that I had some money at all." Then in a sarcastic tone, Miriam added, "Sure am going to miss him!"

Jeri observed, "And then she laughed. The feeling I got was that she wasn't going to miss him at all."

CHAPTER 14

"I Just Froze Like a Prairie Dog."

Trying to get a handle on Alan Helmick's financial dealings, Investigator Jim Hebenstreit went to see Bob Cucchetti on June 18, 2008. Cucchetti was an accountant with the firm of Cucchetti Baldwin and Co CPAs. Cucchetti told Hebenstreit that Alan had been his customer for almost twenty years. Cucchetti said he didn't know Miriam very well, but he did know that the first year that Alan and Miriam were married, they didn't file a joint return. According to Cucchetti, it was because Miriam had "problems with the IRS from a pervious marriage or something."

Cucchetti related that Alan and Miriam had filed jointly for their 2006 Internal Revenue Service (IRS) tax returns, but they had not yet done so for the tax year 2007. Asked if this was unusual, Cucchetti said no; Alan routinely asked for a time extension.

Investigator Hebenstreit asked Cucchetti about Alan's financial ventures into a dance studio and horse-training facility. Cucchetti answered, "Alan was always optimistic, but I told him he was going to lose his ass on those businesses. And he did. As far as the dance studio went, Alan financed it, but

Miriam ran it. Both the dance studio and horse business were financial losers."

All in all, Alan had financial interests in the Title Company of Delta, A. Hughes LLC, Dance Junction LLC, Creek Ranch Sporthorses, Helmick Mortgage Corporation, and Crista Lee LLC. Miriam Helmick was only listed as co-owner of Dance Junction and Creek Ranch Sporthorses. And even with those, she was only a 5 percent owner of each, while Alan was a 95 percent owner. Cucchetti didn't know if the Helmicks had a prenuptial agreement or any estate planning. That was not part of his business dealings with Alan Helmick.

Investigator Hebenstreit looked further into Alan Helmick's financials and noted that Alan had accounts with American National Bank and Wells Fargo. Hebenstreit obtained Alan's bank statements, copies of canceled checks, tax records, personal financial statements, and real estate information. Among the documents Hebenstreit received from American National Bank was a personal financial statement completed by Alan and dated November 27, 2007. This was part of a statement by Alan to request a maturity date on two financial loans.

On that financial statement, Alan had documented his total assets as $3,487,650. This included $1,300,000 in real estate and $2,120,350 in marketable securities.

Hebenstreit noted that all of the businesses were in Alan's name, and Miriam had none in hers. In fact, she did not have a checking account or even a credit card in her name. All she had was a 5 percent interest in the dance studio and a 5 percent interest in the horse-training facility. Whatever money she had, Alan apparently doled out to her.

Hebenstreit spoke with a loan officer at American National Bank named Alan Watkins, who had some very interesting things to say. Watkins told the investigator that when he first learned of Alan Helmick's death, he wondered if it had anything to do with a letter the bank had just sent Helmick. Watkins said that for the previous three or four months, he had been trying to contact Alan Helmick concerning problems with his accounts. Watkins added that he had sent letters to Alan, left voice messages, and had even gone by the Helmick residence. Not once, however, did Alan respond to these messages. Watkins said that had not been the pattern with Alan Helmick until the previous three or four months. Watkins even wondered if Alan had committed suicide because of these financial situations.

On June 19, Penny Lyons went over to Miriam's house in Whitewater. As Penny recalled, "Miriam had a cleaning van out front, and I assumed it was to clean up the bloodstains in the kitchen. I met Miriam in the garage, and I didn't want to go into the kitchen because of the cleaning. We got into her car a while later, and she mentioned that she'd forgotten her purse in the house. I said I'd go get it. So I went into the house, and when I opened the door from the utility room to the kitchen, I didn't realize that the towels were already picked up from the floor.

"I froze when I went in. I just froze like a prairie dog. I couldn't take my eyes off it! There were still bloodstains on the floor."

Penny said later that she realized that law enforcement had allowed Miriam to be back in her home a few days after Alan's murder. She couldn't understand why Miriam hadn't already cleaned up the bloodstains.

Penny continued, "We went to a Walmart on North Avenue in Grand Junction, and I told Miriam I'd buy her a cell phone. She was extremely concerned about her son, Chris, and she had no way to reach him because the police had taken all her phones. So I bought her a phone with so many minutes on it. It wasn't like Verizon or BlackBerry or something like that.

"She was having a lot of trouble because she didn't have

any money. She didn't have access to any money, and that made even just basic living very difficult. She didn't have money for feeding the horses, groceries, or gas. So I purchased that phone for her."

Another person law enforcement investigators spoke with was a woman named Laegan McGee. Laegan took dance lessons at Amour Danzar in Grand Junction in 2004 and 2005. Laegan said later that she began dating a dance instructor there named David Griffin. David was going to move to another city; and around that time, Laegan was introduced to a new dance instructor, who called herself Francehssea. Later, Laegan learned that the woman's real name was Miriam.

Laegan recalled about Miriam, "She told me she was looking to start a dance studio with her former professional partner. I don't remember his name. She said they had been on the pro circuit together. She indicated that he had been her boyfriend at one time. She also said that they had been looking around for a place to start, and that was when an offer came in from Barbara Watts, who owned Amour Danzar to be a manager there. Miriam thought Grand Junction was a great place to start, because it was somewhere that had a low cost of living and didn't have a high-quality dance studio."

One night in the spring or summer of 2005, Laegan and her boyfriend, David Griffin, went to a bar/restaurant on Main Street in Grand Junction called Boomers. She recalled of this particular night, "Miriam was with a gentleman there. I did not know who the man was, but David did. David pointed him out to me and said that the man had been a student of his at the dance studio.

"David and I were seated about three-quarters into Boomers, and they were back in toward one of the pillars in a darkened area. David said to me, 'Don't look.' So, of course, I looked. I saw Miriam, and she had her hand under the table, on the man's right leg. And when she saw me, I tried to turn away quickly, because I wasn't supposed to look.

"But she caught my eye and did one of those kind of waves like you do when you accidentally pull out in front of somebody in your car. Kind of like, 'Oops.' Ten or fifteen minutes later, she came over by herself. She kind of singsonged, 'You know, I hear wedding bells.'

"I was kind of disoriented because David hadn't filled me in about information of who the man was she was sitting with. I said to Miriam, 'Your boyfriend in Florida?' That's because that person had been with her approximately a month before. And she said no. 'It's Alan over there. Do you want to go meet him?'

"And then she said, 'He's going to buy me a house. He's going to buy me horses. He's going to build me my own dance studio.' And she was ticking those things off on her fingers. I said, 'Wow, that's really fast.' She didn't really respond to that.

"When David and I were getting up to leave, David knew Alan (Helmick) from having taught him previously. And Alan and Miriam came over, because David waved them over. And we were standing there talking. And David and Alan kind of talked briefly, like have you seen so-and-so. And Miriam told me that he owned several businesses. I was still kind of shocked by the suddenness of all of this. I was still trying to put the pieces of the puzzle together. I was going to wait for David to fill me in on who was what, and what and where."

Since it was now known that Miriam had managed a dance studio in Grand Junction for a woman named Barbara Watts, before opening up her own dance studio, Investigator Chuck Warner contacted the Harrison County Sheriff's Office (HCSO) in Gulfport, Mississippi, where Watts lived. The Harrison County Sheriff's Office gave Warner information as to how he could contact Watts. Until contacting HCSO, Warner had tried on thirty different occasions to reach Barbara Watts by phone, and he had received no return calls.

An officer for HCSO eventually contacted Barbara Watts and put her on the phone with Investigator Warner. Warner asked what Miriam's relationship had been with Watts, and she said that she had hired Miriam after Miriam had come to Mississippi from Florida. Miriam had told the dance studio owner that she needed a new start in life because her husband had recently shot himself in the head. Two years before that, her daughter had died from taking aspirin while having an ulcer.

Miriam started attending the dance school, Amour Danzar, and wanted to work there. Watts told Investigator Warner that Miriam was very good, and got even better under training. Miriam started teaching on her own, and she also did book work in the office.

Miriam wanted a man named Anthony Keith Coppage, who went by the name Keith, to come teach at the school as well. Watts said that when Keith arrived, he showed up in a wrinkled shirt that looked as if it hadn't been pressed for days. He didn't have dance shoes or even good clothes, but Watts added that Keith did a fine job once he was properly outfitted. He was a good dance instructor.

Later, after Keith left, Watts noticed that the money collected from a Friday-night dance party was missing. Miriam generally collected that money and put it into a safe after the parties. Miriam, who was living in a cottage in back of the dance studio, told Watts that she had no idea where the money had gone. The studio owner assumed Keith had stolen it before taking off. Later she would think otherwise.

As well as the dance studio in Gulfport, Barbara Watts owned a dance studio in Grand Junction, Colorado, and the woman who managed the place was going to quit soon. Miriam asked if she could manage that studio, and Watts agreed that she could. Just before Miriam left, there was a

Christmas party and Watts decided to pay for it by a credit card rather than cash. While they were at an Outback Steakhouse, Watts noticed Miriam looking at the wad of money she had not used for the party. At that point, Watts told Investigator Warner, "I knew something was up with her."

On the way home from the party, Watts and Miriam sat in the front seat of Watts's car. The employer recalled placing a checkbook on the front seat between them. Later on, she could not find the checkbook. Even though this concerned her about Miriam, she couldn't prove it and decided to send her to Grand Junction, Colorado, anyway. As a safeguard, however, she wanted all the clients to pay by check and not with cash.

Watts and Miriam flew to Colorado, where they stayed in a hotel. At one point, Watts left the room to get some ice, leaving the door ajar, since she was already suspicious about Miriam. When Watts was gone from the room, she heard the door shut. She said that she returned with the ice and stood outside the door, listening. She thought she heard Miriam rummaging through suitcases. Watts told the investigator that she believed a lot of her money was gone when she returned to the room; but once again, she could not say for sure if this was so.

Despite this, Barbara Watts still let Miriam stay on as manager of the dance studio in Grand Junction. Watts even left Miriam with a credit card for business expenses. After a while, Watts started getting charged for things on the credit card that were not related to business. And Miriam would not return Watts's phone calls. When she finally reached Miriam, she demanded the credit card back. Within a few days, she got it.

Time passed, and Watts was going through her canceled bank checks and noticed that some bank statements seemed off. She contacted her bank, and they faxed her copies of canceled checks. She noted that some of the check signatures were not in her handwriting.

Soon she went to her other bank and found that the same thing was occurring there. Watts was sure by now that Miriam had stolen some of her checks in Gulfport and was forging them. She wanted Miriam returned to Mississippi so that she could be arrested.

On top of that, Watts heard that Miriam was trying to set up her own dance studio in Grand Junction and was "stealing" Watts's dance students right out from under her nose. One of those students was Alan Helmick. In a bold move, Watts faxed Alan documents about Miriam and warned him about her.

Then, in a clever ruse, Watts contacted Miriam and told her to come back to Gulfport, Mississippi, for more dance training. Surprisingly, Miriam complied. As soon as she did, she was arrested.

Apparently, Miriam was able to raise bail. Once she did, she got in her car and left Gulfport. In response, Watts said, she faxed Alan Helmick every damaging thing she could about Miriam that same day. "Like bank statements and such. I warned him and told him not to let it happen to him," she said.

Around that same time, Watts went to the cottage, where Miriam had been staying, to retrieve a computer that was there. She found two envelopes. One of them was marked *Personal,* and the other had no writing on it. The envelopes were pasted shut, but when she held them up to the light, she could see that they contained her altered bank statements.

Then, in an incredible set of circumstances, Barbara Watts flew out to Colorado and tried contacting Alan while she was there. Instead, Miriam answered the phone and wanted to know if she was fired. The employer said that Miriam was not fired—just why Watts did not fire Miriam at that point is not clear. Perhaps she wanted Miriam to do some new illegal activity where she could be arrested in Colorado.

Once back in Mississippi, Watts found a diary with Miriam's handwriting. In one portion was a very strange notation. Miriam had written that she was in love with Keith and would do anything for him. She would even "die for him," according to the diary.

Also, while cleaning out the cottage, she found a garment bag with a lot of documents inside. They concerned Miriam's father and stepmother and some kind of fraud that Miriam had perpetrated upon them.

A short time later, Miriam wanted this garment bag sent to Colorado. When Watts did not send it right away, Miriam sued her. Not long after that, Watts was able to contact Miriam's parents in Florida. In a new twist to all of this, Miriam's father contacted Miriam. He said if she continued the lawsuit against Barbara Watts, he would come to Colorado and testify on Watts's behalf. Miriam did not want that to happen, so she dropped the lawsuit.

Meanwhile, Barbara Watts countersued about all the shady business deals that Miriam had been involved in with the dance studio in Grand Junction. This was eventually settled out of court. Even then, Watts said she was so concerned about Miriam, she bought a gun for protection.

Barbara Watts told Chuck Warner, "Miriam said to me, 'I'm looking for a sugar daddy to take care of me.' I even told Alan Helmick about this statement. I warned him over and over about her! I think she is capable of a lot of things."

Watts added that when Miriam first met her, Miriam went by the name Francehssea Giles. Watts believed that Miriam had a document stating that she had come from Salt Lake City, Utah. Apparently, Miriam had never been there and certainly had not been born there. How Miriam had obtained this document remained a mystery.

The dance school proprietor said that she no longer had Miriam's diary. It had been lost during Hurricane Katrina. A few of the comments she could remember were about Keith and the way Miriam was in love with him.

Miriam had written, *I will do anything to keep us together. . . . I can mesmerize anybody.*

Asked by Investigator Warner if she thought that Miriam was involved in Alan's murder, she said yes. "If I had gotten a good attorney in Mississippi, Miriam would have gone to jail and would not have married him." Then Barbara Watts said she felt partially responsible for Alan's death for not having warned him in even stronger terms about Miriam Giles.

CHAPTER 15

48 HOURS

Stories about what the investigators were discovering seeped into the local newspapers in bits and pieces. Stymied by the lack of information he was getting from MCSO, reporter Paul Shockley, of the *Grand Junction Free Press,* was able to interview Miriam Helmick at her residence in Whitewater. Miriam had, of course, returned to live there after the police had allowed her to do so. Miriam told Shockley, "I feel real close to Alan here. All of this was our project."

Miriam wanted to send some photos of her and Alan together to Shockley's newspaper, but she said that she couldn't because they were on the computers. The MCSO investigators had seized all the computers after Alan's murder.

Miriam related that she had printed one of Alan's favorite sayings on his funeral program: *"I wonder what the poor people are doing?"* She quickly added that he didn't mean money. "What he meant was, smelling the roses. Enjoying themselves." Alan had often remarked upon that when he took a boating trip to Lake Powell. It was about using one's money to enjoy life and not just storing it away in a bank somewhere.

Then Miriam told Shockley about her first husband,

Jack Giles. She said that Jack Calloway Giles had committed suicide only six years before. This had happened in the home that Miriam and Jack shared in Jacksonville, Florida. According to Miriam, Jack had shot himself while they were in bed together. He had done so because of the accidental death of their daughter, Amy, who was only twenty-three years old.

Miriam said, "He couldn't handle it. He sat there on his birthday, before he killed himself, and waited for her phone call. Of course, she could no longer call him." After the death of Alan, Miriam told Shockley, "I thought that kind of life was over." What she apparently meant was the violent death of a husband.

Asked why she had moved to Colorado after the death of her first husband, Miriam told Shockley that a dance studio where she was working in Mississippi had indicated a new dance studio was opening up in Grand Junction. Miriam not only wanted a change of scenery, but the chance to manage a dance studio as well.

After her transfer to Colorado, Miriam related, one new student who came in for lessons was a recent widower who had always wanted to try ballroom dancing. Miriam said, "I usually don't associate or fraternize with students. I guess he (Alan) sort of grew on me. Such a gentleman and very sweet." Miriam didn't speak of moving in with Alan, but she did say they got married in June 2006.

Speaking of Alan's business ventures, Miriam told Shockley that Alan was hard-pressed to find the time to enjoy one of his biggest passions, golf. She also said that he was the big decision maker in their family, and that he was more logical than she was. Miriam added that she was more of the artist in the relationship. Miriam commented, "I never saw a business situation where he couldn't pull a rabbit out of a hat."

Asked about the suspicious car fire in Delta in April, Miriam said that she had been with Alan that day. She was inside a building where he was selling a business. When Alan started the car, there was an immediate fire coming from the gas tank area. She also said that there was a full tank of gas that day, because she had recently filled up the car. Asked if this incident was somehow related to Alan's murder, Miriam replied, "I don't know. It very well could be related. I know he thought it was random."

Shockley wanted to know who would want to harm Alan. Miriam said she didn't know, but it was part of the ongoing investigation. Then she said that once the investigators had researched that angle, they would let her know.

As to what she had done and where she had been when Alan was murdered, Miriam said that she had gone on a shopping trip into Grand Junction. She had left the house about eight-thirty in the morning. Miriam added that everything had been fine when she left the house. Alan was supposed to meet her later at a Chinese restaurant on North Avenue in Grand Junction for lunch. Worried when he didn't show up, she kept calling him. After a few calls, she left the restaurant and returned home to find out why he hadn't returned her calls. Miriam said, "That's when I found him, and it all went downhill from there."

Shockley wanted to know if Miriam had noticed items missing from the home, or if it looked as if it had been ransacked. She declined to elaborate, except to say that she hadn't looked around at the condition of the house. "My first concern was him," she responded.

By now, even CBS's national program *48 Hours* thought something fishy was going on concerning the Alan Helmick murder. The *Grand Junction Free Press* learned that *48 Hours* was doing preliminary research on the case. And the reason why was because of Melody Sebesta's words in print and online. Sebesta had been a friend of Alan Helmick since high school, and she had been quoted in newspapers and was posted on the Internet. A staffer for *48 Hours* contacted Sebesta about the case and wanted to know more details.

Looking into this angle further, the *Free Press* learned that MCSO spokesperson Heather Benjamin was scheduled to meet with a producer of that television show. Benjamin told the reporter, "I really don't have anything new to tell them that I haven't told locals."

The reporter also noted in his piece that if a segment on Alan Helmick aired, it would be the third time in recent years that *48 Hours* did a show about murder in the Grand Junction area. On June 10, 2008, only hours after the body of Alan Helmick had been discovered, a one-hour program about the case of a missing thirty-four-year-old mother, Paige Birgfeld, aired nationally on *48 Hours*. A few years before that, they ran a program about a man named Michael Blagg, who was convicted of murdering his wife, Jennifer, and his daughter, Abby. Jennifer's body was found buried in a landfill. Abby's body was never found.

CHAPTER 16

THE YELLOW ENVELOPE

On June 22, 2008, Miriam started telling Penny Lyons about strange things occurring at her home in Whitewater. Penny recalled, "She said the lights that she had never turned on were on, when she came home. Cabinet doors that she had never opened were left open. Doors that she had never touched were unlocked. She was scared, but I admired her courage for staying home. If someone was trying to scare her, then I admired her strength to stay. And besides, she didn't have anywhere to go."

A few more days passed, and on June 26, 2008, it seemed like any other day at Miriam's home on Siminoe Road in Whitewater after Alan's murder. As Penny Lyons recalled, "I was at work and Miriam phoned me. She had been out in the earlier part of the day, and she didn't want to go home by herself. So I told her that I only had about an hour's work left and why didn't she just go out to my house and relax for a while. Then I had a bunch of errands to do in the afternoon and she could come along with me.

"She came with me to an appointment I had with a lady in Palisade. I had a haircut there. Miriam and I had a pleasant afternoon. We got back to my house at about a quarter to six. When she was getting into her truck, I said that I would follow her out to her home. It took about fifteen minutes to get there.

"We pulled up to the garage doors, and she usually left the garage door partially open so that her dog, Cisco, could run in and out. She always went into the house through the garage doors, and not the front door. We just walked into the garage first. We kind of walked in side by side, and Miriam looked through the window in an easterly direction, where she could see the front door.

"She said that the police tape was off the door, and she hadn't removed it. She said that she didn't want to tear the stucco off when it was removed. And she never used the front door, anyway, so she just left it there. I went around the corner of the garage and I walked up toward the front door, with Miriam a ways behind me. I looked down and noticed a bright canary yellow envelope sticking out from the corner of the doormat.

"I reached down to pick it up. And handwritten on the front was 'To the greving [*sic*] widow.' I said, 'Miriam, it's addressed to you.' She came up behind me, and then we opened up the card and read it together. On the inside of the card, it said, 'Allen [*sic*] was first, your [*sic*] next. Run, run, run.'

"It really scared me. She started to shake and just seemed to tremble and kind of crumble. And I was terrified because I didn't know if someone was watching us or if they had been waiting all day for Miriam to be at her front door.

"I swore. I swore a lot. And I just threw the card down and grabbed her hand and said, 'Get in the car! Get in the car!' We both just started running for the car. And I wanted to make sure I had that envelope, so I ran back and threw it and the card into the backseat of the car. Then I took off down the road.

"I was terrified and Miriam looked scared to me. I started to phone 911 right away, and my cell phone did not work at their home. It never did. I had to go a little ways down the road to get a signal. I started to phone 911 again, and Miriam asked me not to call the police. I wanted to, but she said, 'Please, Penny, don't second-guess me. Please call my attorney. Just call my attorney.' So I called her attorney, Colleen Scissors.

"When we got home, the card and envelope were in the backseat of the car. And I put the card in the envelope and took both of them into the house. At first, Miriam just wanted to go back home because she wanted to get the truck so that she would have a vehicle to use. I didn't feel that we should go back there."

On Friday, June 27, 2008, Investigator Pete Burg spoke with Kirsten Turcotte, who had been a house sitter for the Helmicks on occasion when they were not at home. Kirsten, who was also known as Katie, told him that she had received a telephone call from Miriam at six fifty-three on the previous evening. Miriam told her that she had received a threatening letter, and she was leaving the area. Miriam did not say where she was going.

Then Kirsten related that Miriam had said, "This needs to stay between you and [me]. I have got to leave the house. I need for you to feed the horses for me tonight and tomorrow morning and don't go into the house." And then she added a strange addendum: "Don't go into the garage, either. I don't want you to leave your prints on anything."

Turcotte told Investigator Burg that the whole conversation had been "really weird." She related that she did not have a key to the Helmicks' house, but usually she could go straight into the home because the doors were always unlocked. Kirsten also said that while Miriam was making her phone call, she could hear another, unidentified female's voice in the background.

Miriam had told her, "Take the little truck to feed the horses." But as soon as she said it, Kirsten could hear the unidentified female say, "No, don't have her take the little truck in case there are fingerprints in it."

Asked by Investigator Burg what the threatening message was about, she said she didn't know, other than Miriam had said, "I got a threatening message and they said they were going to kill me."

Burg queried Turcotte if she had asked Miriam if she had gone to the police about this strange phone call. She had indeed asked her that question and Miriam had replied that she hadn't done so yet. In fact, Miriam said she was going to talk to a lawyer first about the matter. Then Miriam added that she knew someone had been in her house recently, but she could not prove it. Miriam claimed that on the previous Monday she had left the house. When she returned, she knew that some things inside the house had been moved around. Then on Tuesday, the same thing had happened. Miriam got back home that day to find things moved around in the kitchen. On Wednesday, she returned home to find the balcony door was unlocked, when she knew she had locked it. And one night, the dogs had been barking very loudly. When she shined a spotlight outside, she did not see anyone there.

Miriam told Kirsten that on Thursday afternoon, June 26, she had returned home to find lights on in two bathrooms, both unused medicine cabinet doors opened, and items moved around in the kitchen. Also, the yellow police tape, which had been attached to the door, was now gone. Miriam said that it was on Thursday evening that she and a female friend had approached the front door and Miriam spotted an envelope protruding from the front doormat.

About this doormat, Miriam had told her that a key had been under the mat until a year before, and then it disappeared. As to what was in the envelope, Miriam didn't tell her at that point. She did say, however, "I just want this to be over! I almost wish they'd come back and finish the job and just kill me, 'cause I'm sick of this!"

Turcotte was worried about this line of reasoning, but Miriam assured her that she wasn't suicidal, because she didn't want her son to lose another parent that way. Miriam then said she was going to go to the neighbors and ask if they had seen anything suspicious lately. And she also wanted the neighbors to write down any vehicle license plate numbers they saw in the area. Miriam added that two weeks previously she had seen taillights go past the lower driveway when she had been in one of the house's bathrooms. Miriam had then walked outside and saw a white Chevrolet truck. The driver must have spied her, because the truck suddenly "peeled off."

That same day, Friday, June 27, Investigator Jim Hebenstreit received a message from Colleen Scissors that Miriam Helmick wanted her to report suspicious activity at the Helmick residence. Scissors told Hebenstreit that Miriam believed someone had entered her residence on several occasions when she wasn't home.

Investigator Hebenstreit went by Colleen Scissors's office and retrieved the yellow envelope and card. It was a greeting card, and on the envelope was written in capital letters: *TO THE GREVING WIDOW.* On the inside of the greeting card was written, also in capital letters, *ALLEN WAS FIRST—YOUR NEXT! RUN RUN.* The name "Alan" had been misspelled as "Allen."

On the front of the card was an illustration of a woman sitting in a chair reading a book. Next to the illustration was a quote attributed to Albert Einstein: *"Insanity is doing the same thing over and over again but expecting different results."* Part of the card containing the UPC code had been cut out.

The investigation was going in a lot of directions now. Jim Hebenstreit spoke with Robin Cook at the Title Company of Delta. Cook told Hebenstreit that she had bought Alan Helmick's share of the title company in April 2008. Cook had first met Alan in 1987 and later went to work for him at Helmick Mortgage. Cook added that Alan had loaned her money to start the Title Company of Delta, and he was a 50 percent partner until April 2008. For thirteen years, Cook had given Alan 50 percent of the profits she had made.

Over the years, Alan had asked Cook if she wanted to buy him out. However, she didn't want to incur more debt and declined. Then in March 2008, Alan had told her that she could either buy his share out, or he would sell his share to someone else. Cook agreed to buy Alan's interest in the company for $125,000.

On the day of this transaction, April 30, 2008, Miriam and Alan came to Cook's office without calling first to set up an appointment time. Cook was distressed by this arrangement, because she was very busy. She told Hebenstreit that she wasn't happy about the circumstances or in a "visiting mood." Cook said she just wanted to give Alan his check and estimated the meeting lasted ten minutes. Then Cook added that she learned a short time later that same day that Alan's car had caught fire right outside her office building in the parking lot. Nothing like that had ever occurred there before.

CHAPTER 17

THE CARD

Investigator Robin Martin followed up about the greeting-card angle in the case. Investigator Martin found a Web site on the Internet concerning the greeting card, based on the creator's name being on the back of the card, which had been seized by law enforcement. Martin located several stores in the Grand Junction area that carried the creator's cards, and Martin was able to narrow down the particular card as being sold at City Market at a couple of locations in Grand Junction.

On June 30, Martin contacted Joe Vessels, who was a store-loss prevention officer with City Market, and asked if he could track the sale of the card. Vessels thought that he could track the card by the price of the card selling for $2.95, instead of $2.99. Obviously, the UPC code had been cut off on the card. Investigator Martin then asked Vessels to search the date range of June 10, 2008, to June 27, 2008.

Meanwhile, Investigator Jim Hebenstreit spoke with Miriam Helmick's friend, Penny Lyons, who confirmed that she had been the one who had been with Miriam on the day that Miriam found a card beneath the doormat. Hebenstreit asked

Penny to describe the events leading up to the discovery of the card. Penny recounted that Miriam had been out doing some errands and phoned her about 1:45 P.M. on Thursday, June 26. Penny told Miriam she had to work for about another hour and suggested that Miriam go to Lyons's house and relax. After that, Penny would come home, and Miriam could go with her as she ran a few errands.

The two women got together sometime after three in the afternoon, ran a couple of errands, and got back to Lyons's house around 5:45 P.M. During their driving around, Miriam told Penny that over the past three days she had noticed that several things in her residence had been moved around and some things didn't seem right. It was all mysterious and very frightening in light of what had happened to Alan.

Lyons told Hebenstreit about following Miriam to her home in Whitewater, and Miriam noticing the police tape had been removed from the front door. When they went to investigate, they noticed a yellow envelope sticking out from beneath the doormat. Penny said that the envelope was not sealed, and then she told Hebenstreit about the contents of the message. Penny added about hurrying out of there, and Miriam not wanting her to call the police, but rather her lawyer. Penny added that Miriam spent the night at her residence.

Investigator Hebenstreit asked Penny if Miriam recognized the handwriting on the card. She said that Miriam had not. Just who might have placed that envelope and card under the doormat, Penny didn't know.

The investigators also learned later that Miriam had told Jeri Yarbrough about the card. Jeri recalled, "Miriam said she had come home and she had found it at the front door. I told her she shouldn't handle it, that she should call the police about it and let them come over and fingerprint it, and find out who did this. I was concerned about who did this.

"She said she put some powder down on the floor and that one time she saw footprints in her house. I told her she needed to contact the police and get them over there. And that she shouldn't stay there because it wasn't safe. She said she was okay, that her dogs were there and she felt okay. I don't know if she ever did contact the police about this."

On June 30, service technician Christi Walker contacted Bob Dundas, who lived on Pronghorn Drive in Whitewater. Dundas lived near the Helmick residence, and he said that he had been outside his home when Miriam contacted him on June 27, 2008. Miriam asked him if he had seen any strange vehicles around the Helmick home. She also said to him, "There's been some issues over at the house." Dundas described her demeanor as being "weird" and that she appeared to be nervous. Then he added that his gut feeling was that Miriam wanted him to support her observation about strange vehicles in the area.

Investigator Jim Hebenstreit also looked into this issue of Miriam contacting neighbors about "strange vehicles" that might have been around the Helmick residence. Hebenstreit interviewed Josh Devries, who lived near the Helmick place. Miriam had gone to Devries's home on June 27 about noon. Josh was home that day with his two children when Miriam pulled into the driveway and came to the door.

Miriam asked Josh, "Have you seen anything strange going on next door? Cars or people who aren't normally there?"

He replied that he hadn't seen anything out of the ordinary. Then he added, "Unfortunately, we didn't see anything the day of the incident, either." (He was referencing the day that Alan Helmick was murdered.) Josh asked Miriam why she was asking him about this, and she responded it was because she had been finding things out of place in the home. She mentioned doors being left open and particularly mentioned two medicine cabinet doors left ajar. Miriam said there wasn't anything in those medicine cabinets, and she wondered if she was losing her mind.

Miriam added that she had seen a midsize white truck driving around the area lately and hadn't seen it before. She described opaque canisters being in the back of the truck. She had never caught a glimpse of its license plate. However, Miriam told her neighbor that she only saw the driver of the truck in silhouette and he had dark, curly hair.

Hebenstreit asked if Devries had seen a truck or a person like that around the area, and Josh said no. He then added that he could see the Helmick property from the front of his house.

Miriam had also told Josh about the card she had found beneath her doormat. When he asked her about it, "she started choking up a little bit and became teary." Then Miriam told him the contents of the note. "Alan was first, you're next. Run, run, run," as he put it. Miriam said she had given the note to her lawyer. Then Miriam added she had placed objects in front of her door to see if they had been moved around. Josh related that this was the longest conversation he had ever had with Miriam Helmick.

In the four years that he had lived there with his family, he had only spoken with Alan a few times, and with Miriam almost not at all. His wife had spoken with Miriam on occasion, but only briefly. Asked if he ever had prowlers around his place, or had anything suspicious occur, Josh said "zero" occurrences, and that it was "very quiet around here." So quiet, in fact, there were times that he and his family would be eating dinner and they would see a herd of antelope between his house and the Helmicks' house. Nothing, especially prowlers, had frightened those antelope.

CHAPTER 18

AN INCIDENCE OF FIRE

Investigator Michael "Mike" Piechota was an investigator for MCSO's Property Crime Unit. He was going to be an important part of the MCSO team of investigators to try and find a modus operandi (MO) for why Miriam might have murdered her husband. To reach his level of expertise, Piechota had taken intense and varied courses after becoming an investigator. In 2001, he'd attended the Computer Crimes Conference; a year later, he took part in an Advanced Crime Scene Investigation conference. In 2003, Piechota studied with the Colorado Bureau of Investigation on Bloodstain Pattern Recognition and Collection, as well as a conference on Death and Homicide Training.

Just as important, Piechota took a six-week course at the Federal Law Enforcement Training Center in 2006 and attended a Mortgage Fraud Conference in 2008. These two subjects were important elements of the Alan Helmick case. It was looking more and more that financial matters might have been a big part of the murder. As yet, however, MCSO couldn't say why.

Piechota faxed a request to Carol Hee, of CBI, about a

suspicious activity report (SAR). All of it had to do with Miriam Helmick, aka Miriam Giles, Francehssea Giles Miriam Giles, and Miriam Morgan. What came back to Piechota was the possibility that Miriam had defrauded her own parents at some point.

Francis Morgan, Miriam's father, had indeed filed the police report with the Jacksonville PD on October 11, 2004, and Piechota wanted to look into this matter. One SAR concerned the SouthTrust Bank; and early in 2004, a check of $2,500 was made payable to Showcase Dancewear. Miriam was involved with Showcase Dancewear, and it may have been a company name she created for herself. Soon thereafter, a $1,875 check was also made payable to this company.

Through a videotape at that bank branch, the suspect was described as a white adult female. A police officer reviewed the videotape, and the woman on the tape and the photo on Miriam Giles's driver's license were one in the same.

Another SAR was filed because MBNA suspected that Francis and Frankie Morgan had some of their checks stolen. Francis and Frankie said they had not written checks against a credit card account in 2004. However, $32,312 in checks had been used to obtain cash from that credit card account. Worst of all for the Morgans, MBNA was holding them responsible for the amount taken out as cash.

Following up on this information, Investigator Norcross contacted Frankie Morgan, Miriam's stepmother, in Jacksonville, Florida. Frankie Morgan told Norcross that for the past four years, she and her husband had been dealing with fraudulent debt incurred by Miriam.

Frankie said that Miriam had moved into their house after Miriam's first husband, Jack Giles, committed suicide. Miriam had told the Morgans that she couldn't stand living in the house where her husband had killed himself. Frankie estimated that Miriam lived with them for six to eight weeks.

Miriam's father was going through heart surgery and

Frankie was battling cancer at the time. Miriam said she would take care of the bills for them, which they thought was great. A short time later, Miriam bought her own home in the Jacksonville area. Frankie was with Miriam on the day she bought her home. She noted that Miriam paid cash when she moved in. Frankie was also with Miriam on a day that she bought new furniture for the house. She paid cash for that as well.

Frankie said that Miriam acted as if she didn't have to work full-time. About this circumstance, Miriam told Frankie that her deceased husband had a large 401(k) account and large life insurance policy. Frankie said she thought it was good that Miriam only needed a part-time job to help pay taxes and for incidental expenses.

Frankie told Investigator Lissah Norcross that after Miriam had her own home, she still came over almost every day to visit around noon. Frankie thought it was odd that she visited every day around the same time, but she didn't comment on it. She and Miriam's father thought it was wonderful that Miriam liked visiting them so often.

Investigator Norcross wanted to know about Jack Giles's suicide and possible financial problems, and Frankie related that Miriam had told her that part of the reason was that Jack had a child by another woman. Whether it was blackmail or some other reason, Jack ended up paying that woman $84,000 over time, and he bought her a new Mercedes as well. Frankie didn't know if this other child really existed, but she took Miriam at her word.

Miriam also brought up that Jack allegedly had not paid his taxes for years; and now after his death, she was being sued by the IRS to collect back taxes. This eventually got so bad, Miriam told Frankie, she had to sell her new house, which she had purchased so recently, just to pay back taxes to the IRS. Miriam was very bitter about this, and she had to rent a room in the area. Frankie even learned later from a housemate of Miriam's that Miriam sold very expensive furniture, which she had just purchased, for practically nothing at garage sales.

Frankie told Investigator Norcross that one day her husband received a phone call from his bank advising him that he owed $10,000. Frankie added that she and Miriam's father knew that there was no way they were that overdrawn. Nonetheless, Frankie's husband went to a credit union, pulled $10,000 out of there, and paid the bank. Around that same time, the bank manager showed Miriam's dad surveillance footage of Miriam making a withdrawal, and the manager asked if that was Francis's wife. He, of course, said no, that was his daughter.

Frankie related that at the time her husband thought it was no more than a mistake, but the bank manager showed Francis that his daughter had to use her driver's license to obtain the money. After that, Francis called Miriam at her new job and told her not to contact the bank, but rather to come over to his house, where they would discuss the matter. Instead, Miriam never showed up. Frankie and Francis found out later that right after the phone call, Miriam left her desk at work and went home to the room she rented. Miriam quickly collected her dogs, and enough items to get by, and simply vanished.

That wasn't the worst of it. The same night that Miriam disappeared, Francis and Frankie's home was set on fire. Frankie told Investigator Norcross that she thought it was too much of a coincidence that their house was set on fire the same night that Miriam disappeared. Frankie said that their house had a screened-in back porch, and much of it was constructed of wood. Her husband had some rags on the porch covered with oil, and someone had set those rags on fire during the night. It was obvious that the fire had been intentionally set.

Frankie noted that there was a large plant hanging in a plastic pot above where the fire had been set. The fire melted the plastic pot; luckily, the pot, which was full of water, fell on the fire and doused it. Frankie added that the police department was immediately called. They told the Morgans that it was arson.

The fire department also arrived quickly and firemen noted that the walls were still burning inside the wooden porch structure. Frankie told Norcross that the point of origin was directly opposite her bedroom wall and she had been home at the time. Frankie said that she suspected the fire was started by Miriam, because Frankie's dog, which barked at strangers, did not bark when the fire was set. At the time, Frankie and Francis did not know that Miriam had disappeared, but they found out the next day when Francis went to the place where Miriam rented a room.

It was on that morning when Francis went to his daughter's residence that he discovered many items of hers were missing and a large moving box in the room contained shredded bank statements and cut-up credit card statements. It was at that point that Francis knew for sure that Miriam had been taking out credit cards in his and his wife's name and running up huge amounts on them. Frankie told Norcross that they suspected Miriam had been obtaining their information from the mail. That was the reason why Miriam had always come over to their home around noon, about the time that the mail was delivered.

Frankie said that Miriam always sat in the kitchen, where she could see the mail lady when she arrived. And according to Frankie, Miriam was always the one who rushed out to get the mail first. Frankie asked Miriam why she always insisted on getting the mail, and Miriam replied that she liked to look through the "junk catalogs."

Frankie told Investigator Norcross that after Miriam disappeared, Miriam sent an e-mail to her and her father. Miriam claimed she was now in Maryland and would one day explain what had happened. Miriam added for them not to believe what others were saying about the matter and she would explain it all in time.

After some time had passed, Frankie learned that Miriam had not gone north to Maryland, as she had claimed, but rather west to Mobile, Alabama, where Miriam's mother lived. And Frankie somehow learned that Miriam had allegedly stolen $6,000 or $7,000 from her mother, before moving on to Gulfport, Mississippi.

Frankie also learned that Miriam met a woman in Gulfport named Barbara Watts, who owned a dance studio there. According to Watts, Miriam wanted to go into the business of designing dance costumes. Eventually, Barbara Watts hired Miriam as a bookkeeper and wanted Miriam to run a dance studio that she owned in Colorado.

A while later, Frankie said, Miriam started her own dance studio, Dance Junction, in Grand Junction "and stole Barbara's customers away from her." Frankie also related that Barbara found out that Miriam had written checks to herself, using Barbara's account. It was Barbara Watts who had actually first contacted the Morgans, because she found one of their checkbooks when Miriam left the Gulfport area.

After speaking with Frankie, Investigator Lissah Norcross spoke with Miriam's father, Francis Morgan. Francis reiterated what Frankie had said, and he added that he'd made a police report with the Jacksonville Police Department, which put out a warrant for Miriam's arrest. Eventually the district attorney (DA) got back to Francis about this and told him that it was going to be too difficult prosecuting a case that involved a father and daughter. Francis told Norcross that Miriam had, in essence, stolen about $80,000 from him and that he would probably never get it back.

Francis also mentioned that Miriam's biological mother was named Betty, and she lived in Mobile, Alabama, but he did not know her address or phone number. Francis added that Miriam's brother would know how to get in touch with Betty.

Norcross asked Francis how she could contact Miriam's son, Chris. Francis replied that he and his wife wanted to leave Chris out of the investigation and would not give that information. Francis added that Chris was in South America serving on a church mission and that Chris had nothing to do with any of this.

Francis did say that Miriam had phoned Chris and her brother, Wayne, recently. She told them what had happened to Alan Helmick. Miriam had told them that Alan had been murdered during a robbery of the home in Whitewater.

Later, Norcross spoke with Frankie Morgan again, and she related that she'd heard from Wayne that Miriam claimed she had an alibi for the time that Alan had been murdered. Miriam added that she had been caught on surveillance videotape at the time of the murder and was nowhere near the Whitewater residence.

Investigator Norcross asked if Miriam had experienced mental-health problems or had gone to a psychiatrist when she was in Florida. Frankie said that they had never known Miriam to have mental-health issues or to have gone to see a psychiatrist. It had come as a complete surprise to them when Miriam had ripped them off for so much money, and allegedly set fire to their house.

CHAPTER 19

FORGED CHECKS

Investigator Jim Hebenstreit again contacted Alan Watkins at American National Bank in Grand Junction. Watkins told Hebenstreit it appeared to him that Miriam had been signing some of Alan Helmick's checks, even though she was not authorized to do so. Watkins said that he had on numerous occasions tried to tell Alan Helmick that this practice needed to stop. Watkins phoned Alan several times about this issue, but he never got through to him. All he was able to do was leave voice messages, which were never returned.

Watkins had heard that Alan Helmick had been very sick. He had surmised that was the reason that Miriam had been signing the checks, and also why Alan Helmick had not returned his phone calls. Nonetheless, the practice had to stop, and Watkins planned to go and see Alan in person. Before he did so, Alan Helmick had been murdered.

Watkins added that he'd seen Alan Helmick at the courthouse in Grand Junction about two months before his death. Watkins said that he had spoken with Alan briefly then, and told how he had left at least twenty phone messages on Alan's cell phone. Alan Helmick replied that he had never heard any of those messages. Then Alan said, "Maybe Miriam got them and never told me about them."

Watkins related to Hebenstreit that when he first heard that Alan Helmick was dead, he assumed that Alan might have committed suicide because of his recent illness and possible adverse financial situations that had occurred.

Watkins also mentioned that after he had flagged Alan Helmick's account, a bank teller in an Orchard Mesa branch called him one day and told him that Miriam Helmick was in the branch, trying to cash one of Alan Helmick's checks. Watkins had the bank teller put Miriam on the phone, and Watkins explained the situation to her. Miriam replied that Alan had been very sick, but that she would tell him and have Alan talk to Watkins about the situation. Alan Helmick never did phone Watkins back.

Jim Hebenstreit next spoke with American National Bank president Scott Holzschuh. Holzschuh explained that Alan Helmick had personal and business bank accounts with American National Bank, and these were in Alan's name only. Miriam had a password, and could inquire about the accounts, but she was not supposed to sign any checks on that account.

The investigators later retrieved a letter from the Helmick residence from American National Bank. It was dated June 6, 2008, and stated in part that Alan had two accounts that were past due and numerous attempts to reach Alan had been unsuccessful. The letter related that $137,746.54 was now "set off" from Alan Helmick's deposit account to pay down the loans, leaving a current deposit account balance of zero. After applying the setoff amount, Alan still owed $15,564.35 on one account and $21,833.06 on the other account. They were to be paid immediately.

* * *

Following the money angle further, Jim Hebenstreit contacted Alan Watkins again. Investigator Hebenstreit discovered that Watkins had originally wanted to learn the status of two projects that Alan Helmick had going, after the bank had extended the maturity date on two loans in December 2007. Watkins kept trying to tell Alan that he needed to get a personal financial statement before the loans could be extended once again in May 2008. And Watkins added, the more that Alan didn't respond to the calls, the more the calls increased.

Watkins said, "It wasn't like Alan not to return the phone calls. Whenever a borrower stops returning calls, it's usually an avoidance tactic. This kind of tactic usually happens right before foreclosure or repossession."

And then Watkins told Hebenstreit, "Alan was not the type to use the avoidance tactic. We were worried about his mental health. Alan was looking at a situation—if he couldn't find an investor for his development project, he'd be looking at a situation where the bank might have to foreclose on two of his properties. The closer Alan's loans came to maturity, the more I tried to contact him. I even drove up to the Helmick residence on May 14, 2008."

As to what the land developments included, Watkins said that Alan had been trying to convert an approved single-family–zoned area in Delta to a multifamily development and was looking for investors. The bank's discussion back in December had been that they would not extend the loans again, unless Alan could show that the project was actually moving forward and he had lined up investors.

Watkins believed that he had first tried contacting Alan about all of this in March 2008. Watkins said the initial messages he left were just generic in nature, telling Alan to call him back. When Alan didn't call him back, the messages became more like, "looking for an update on the projects." Watkins related that he was still trying to be polite because Miriam had told him, "Alan is really sick."

Watkins then said, "By April, the messages were more like, 'Get ahold of me ASAP so we can discuss the status of the loans.'" Watkins described his tone as being "frustrated and firm."

On May 12, 2008, Watkins sent a letter to Alan about his accounts. The letter in part stated: *Please be advised that the loans mature May 28, 2008. At this time the loans are past due for the April 28, 2008 payment. On behalf of the bank I have made numerous attempts to contact you to discuss the status of these accounts and the options available upon maturity. Due to non-responsiveness on your behalf it is our intention to not renew these Notes and to pursue payment in full upon maturity. Please contact me immediately to set up a time to discuss this further.*

Investigator Hebenstreit noted that this letter was not found when a search of the Helmick residence was done after Alan Helmick's murder. And during the present interview with Alan Watkins, Hebenstreit viewed a document that authorized only Alan Helmick to be the one to sign his checks.

Things were looking very dicey as far as Miriam Helmick's actions went in relation to Alan Helmick during the previous few months. And they only got worse in the eyes of the investigators as they looked further into the matter. Jim Hebenstreit noted that both of Miriam Helmick's business operations had been losing money on a consistent basis. These were, of course, the dance studio and the horse-training center. Examples of forged checks included a check dated February 7, 2008, for $5,000 to Miriam Helmick and a check dated May 1, 2008, for $4,000 to Dance Junction. Just how poorly Dance Junction was doing as a business was reflected in bank statements. In June 2007, the profit/loss balance was –833.91 (negative $833.91). Without infusions of money, mostly via forged checks, the balance would have always been on the negative side.

With those facts in place, Investigator Hebenstreit wrote some very damning comments in a report: *Miriam Helmick was transferring funds from Alan Helmick's personal checking account to herself and the Dance Junction account without Alan Helmick's knowledge.* Hebenstreit added that she was also preventing Alan Watkins at American National Bank from contacting Alan Helmick concerning his loan accounts with the bank. Hebenstreit believed that Alan Helmick would have learned from Watkins that more than $139,000 had been transferred from his personal checking account by Miriam, leaving him with a zero balance in that bank account.

This was all bad enough for Miriam Helmick, but a lot worse was just about to happen.

CHAPTER 20

STRANGE ACTIONS

Perhaps to deflect some of the suspicions that were starting to swirl around her, Miriam went to the Mesa County Sheriff's Office on July 3, 2008. It was termed by the sheriff's office, "Consent to Provide Non-Testimonial Evidence," and Investigator Hebenstreit actually gave Miriam a form with that title to fill out. Miriam was asked to provide head hair, saliva, photographs, handwriting exemplars, and palm prints. Miriam read and signed the statement, and she allowed head hairs and saliva swabs to be taken from her.

Handwriting exemplars from Miriam were also obtained. Hebenstreit dictated things for Miriam to write down, such as "To the grieving widow" and "Alan was first, you're next." Miriam had to print these things, rather than do them in cursive style.

Perhaps Miriam thought she was being clever by slightly changing her printing style; but after she was gone, Hebenstreit noticed some similarities between the card that had been under the Helmicks' doormat and Miriam's exemplars. The most glaring similarity was the use of the word "your."

Instead of spelling "you're next," on both the card and in Miriam's exemplar, the word was written as "your."

These exemplars and checks from American National Bank, which were believed to have been forged by Miriam, were sent to the Colorado Bureau of Investigation. So were checks from Wells Fargo and First Equity.

Later, Investigator Hebenstreit received documents from the CBI. Agent Bryan Jordan related that he had compared the copy of the First Equity check with Miriam Helmick's handwriting exemplars. Agent Jordan stated, "It has been concluded that Miriam Helmick probably wrote item number one-seventeen."

Other items included check #5798 from American National Bank. Jordan noted that he believed that Alan did not write the signature on that check, nor did he do so for check #5800, and that Miriam most likely wrote the numbers and lettering on the body of the check. This also held true for check #5854. Agent Jordan could not determine if Alan or Miriam wrote the signature on a Wells Fargo check, #9356, but he believed that Alan Helmick did not write the body of the check.

Around this same time, Penny Lyons received a phone call from Miriam. Penny recalled later, "She told me that she had an offer from friends in Eagle to stay up there with them for about a week. They had offered her a home so she could just get away from everything for a while. And I thought that was a wonderful idea. The police had never said she couldn't go anywhere. I didn't know that she had friends in Eagle, but I thought it was a great idea. She said that she'd be gone about a week."

While Miriam was gone, an event occurred on July 15, 2008, that was absolutely devastating for her. Investigator Pete Burg spoke with Joe Vessels. Vessels was, of course, the main security officer for City Market. Vessels told Burg that he had found a record of three card purchases with the UPC of 7000063849 and associated video footage of those transactions. The first two transactions were from the Rood Avenue City Market on June 25 and June 26, 2008. The investigators did not recognize the people involved with those purchases. The third transaction had occurred at the Orchard Mesa store and Vessels didn't immediately have video footage of that transaction.

At around 12:30 P.M., on July 15, Joe Vessels obtained the video footage, and Investigator Robin Martin went to the Orchard Mesa store and met with Vessels again. They both sat down and Vessels told Investigator Martin that the card in question was sold at 2:06 P.M. on June 22, 2008. The purchase amount was $3.18, and had been purchased at the self-scan terminal. As Investigator Martin looked on, he immediately recognized the woman buying the card. It was Miriam Helmick.

Viewing the whole video footage of that time period, Investigator Martin noted that Miriam Helmick entered the south-facing doors of the Orchard Mesa City Market at 1:54 P.M. She entered alone and did not appear to be carrying a purse. A few minutes later, a surveillance video camera picked her up near the pharmacy area of the store. She went out of frame and was not seen again until 2:01 P.M. in the greeting-card aisle.

Due to the angle of the camera, the only portions of Miriam that could be seen were her black pants and distinctive striped shirt. Investigator Martin noted that the "Insanity" card, with the yellow envelope, was located at the eastern end of the aisle on the south side. And due to the quality of the tape, Miriam was not clearly seen again until 2:04 P.M. at the self-scan terminal. The camera angle only showed her head, as the terminal itself blocked the rest of the view. A minute later, Miriam was seen on video leaving the store holding a single City Market plastic bag. There wasn't video footage of Miriam actually scanning the card in question, but it was noted that the card was purchased at that time.

By now, there were multiple angles about Miriam Helmick that the investigators at MCSO were checking into. On July 17, 2008, Investigator Pete Burg spoke with Kirsten Turcotte, who had been caring for the animals on the Helmick property. Since early July, Miriam had asked Turcotte to do it; because according to Miriam, her son, Chris, had come to visit her from Florida, and Miriam told Kirsten that she was going to show Chris around the area, especially Grand Mesa and Colorado National Monument. Miriam was supposed to have returned on July 11, but she had not done so.

Burg asked if Miriam and Chris had planned to go to Denver. Kirsten said that Miriam hadn't mentioned anything about that. Miriam did phone Kirsten from a non-Denver area code on July 11 but said that she was in Denver with Chris. Then Miriam told Turcotte to keep feeding the animals until July 18, when she would be home. Miriam did not arrive home then or any day thereafter.

Kirsten added that no one had been able to reach Miriam directly since she had taken off. All the messages went directly to voice mail. She added that she had not seen any suspicious activity around the Helmick residence since Miriam had been gone.

That same day, Investigator Pete Burg talked by phone with Kevin Cooney, who had purchased a horse from Miriam Helmick about three weeks previously. Miriam had insisted upon cash, and Cooney had given her $1,250 for the horse. Kevin was interested in buying another horse as well, but

Miriam said that horse was part of Alan's estate and she couldn't sell it.

While Kevin was at the Helmick residence, she told him that she wanted to sell all the things that were not part of Alan's estate, including tack, buckets, stock panels, and other horse-related items. Miriam told him that her husband had recently died, but she did not go into details about it. Miriam did mention that there was some kind of prenuptial agreement and that she couldn't sell the house or property. Cooney ended up not only buying a horse, but farm equipment, too, which he paid for in cash.

Penny Lyons recalled later about Miriam's absence from Whitewater, "I tried continually, after seven days had passed, to call her. I never got in touch with her. And I went by her residence. I wanted to see if anyone was there. I left a note inside the garage in case anyone found it, to please just give me a call if they'd heard from Miriam.

"I went to the utility room door, off of the garage, and it was unlocked. And I stared into the house, but I did not have the courage to enter the house. One of Miriam's dogs was still at the house. Cisco, the Lab."

An MCSO investigator spoke again with Jeri Yarbrough, on July 23, 2008, and asked her if she knew what had become of Miriam's horses and if she had spoken to Miriam lately. Jeri said that she had spoken with Miriam almost daily, until July 6. And then Yarbrough added one very interesting comment: "During my last conversation with Miriam on July sixth, I got the feeling she was going to leave town and run."

Around that same time, reporter Paul Shockley of the *Grand Junction Free Press* was doing some investigation of his own. Shockley either contacted Jeri Yarbrough, or she contacted him. Whatever happened, she was speaking with Shockley only a day after she had spoken with an MCSO investigator. Yarbrough told Shockley about the investigator questioning her about whether she had seen Miriam lately. Jeri added, "I haven't heard a word from her, and nobody I'm aware of has talked to her. She and I last spoke on July sixth."

Jeri related that Miriam had given her a new cell phone number on July 6. She left messages twice on that number, but she never got a return call. Yarbrough related, "I figured if she wanted to get ahold of me, she would. She said her son had been visiting, and she might go to Florida later."

Paul Shockley next spoke with MCSO spokesperson Heather Benjamin about what Jeri Yarbrough had said. Shockley asked if MCSO knew where Miriam was. In reply, Benjamin said, "I'm not going to say. But her whereabouts are not a concern to us." That indicated one of two things: Either they didn't know where she was, and they weren't concerned about her. Or they did know where she was, and could reach her whenever they wanted.

In his article, Shockley noted that he had been out to the Helmick residence three times since July 16, and had found little activity there, other than three horses roaming around inside a fenced area. Shockley did speak with Kirsten Turcotte, whom Miriam had asked to keep an eye on the place. Kirsten told Shockley, "Miriam left a couple of weeks ago and was bound for Denver. Nobody can reach her. She gave me a cell phone number, and it's not working."

CHAPTER 21

STRANGE MEDICINE

Jeri Yarbrough's comment about Miriam possibly being "on the run" was more than just a hunch. Yarbrough knew that Miriam's son, Chris, had been in the Grand Junction area in early July, and Miriam kept saying that she wanted to leave Colorado and return to Jacksonville, Florida, where Chris lived.

Penny Lyons, of course, had also been worried about Miriam ever since she had last seen her sometime in early July. Then out of the blue, Miriam phoned Penny on July 25. Penny recalled, "I was at work, and I remember it was a Friday because the other lady in the office had gone home early that day. When Miriam called, I was up front with patients, so I couldn't talk with her right then. And it upset me very much, because she was crying and I wanted to help her. I couldn't have a long conversation.

"She said that she was on her way back from Colorado Springs. That was contrary to where she said she had been staying in Eagle. She was very despondent, and she didn't know what to do and she was scared. She was worried about her son, Chris. She said that she'd lost everything and felt like driving off the pass, but she couldn't do it because of her son."

Around that same time, Investigator Jim Hebenstreit spoke with Merredith Von Burg, Alan Helmick's sister. Hebenstreit asked if Merredith had heard from Miriam lately. Merredith said no, but she had heard from Miriam's friend, Penny Lyons, who had spoken by phone with Miriam on July 25. Penny had told her that Miriam indicated that she would be home in Whitewater in a few days, but that had not happened.

Merredith gave Hebenstreit four phone numbers that Miriam used to call in Florida in the past. All of these numbers were in the 904 area code, which included Jacksonville, Florida. Von Burg thought that two of the numbers were those of Miriam's son, Chris.

Merredith added the last time she had seen Miriam was on July 4, when Miriam and Chris had come over to watch fireworks. Then Miriam left with Chris on July 6; since then, Von Burg had phoned Miriam's attorney to see if she had heard from Miriam. Hebenstreit asked Merredith if Miriam had mentioned leaving the area with Chris. Merredith said no; all Miriam had said was that it would be fun to be with Chris for a while.

Merredith expanded upon her phone calling to include Kirsten Turcotte, who was keeping an eye on the Helmicks' house and feeding the animals. Kirsten had not heard from Miriam in a while. Von Burg went to the Helmick residence and found the garage door open and the door from the garage to the utility room unlocked. Merredith looked around the house for Miriam; not seeing her there, she went down to the barn to look there as well.

Merredith said that it was strange in the house, because all the doors were unlocked and Miriam had been insisting lately that she had been locking all of the doors. As to the reason for the locked doors, Merredith said, "Miriam thought that someone was trying to harm her." She added that Miriam told her that after Alan died, she didn't have any money, even for groceries or gas. Merredith gave Miriam $1,000 and was surprised when Miriam left the area. She wondered if Miriam was using that money for her trip.

Von Burg also told Hebenstreit that Miriam had related that her wedding ring, watch, and Alan's wedding ring were missing from the house. She asked Hebenstreit if the sheriff's office had those items, and he told her that they did not. Merredith said that Miriam had told her that she and Alan always took off their wedding rings before going out to care for the horses. She wondered if Miriam had found her watch and wedding ring later, and she described Miriam's wedding ring as containing a blue diamond.

One of the phone numbers that Merredith Von Burg had given to Investigator Hebenstreit did belong to Miriam's son, Chris. Jim Hebenstreit phoned the Florida number and contacted Chris. Hebenstreit told Chris that several of Miriam's friends were concerned about her, and Chris responded that his mother was now staying with him in Florida, and that she was fine. Hebenstreit asked if Miriam had indicated that she was returning to Colorado, or what her plans were. Chris said no to both questions. Then Hebenstreit asked if Miriam owned an Oldsmobile convertible, and he said yes.

This question about the Oldsmobile was important. Hebenstreit had recently learned from Portia Vigil that Miriam had taken a 1993 Oldsmobile Cutlass, which had been owned by Portia's mother, Sharon Helmick. Miriam was not supposed to have that car. Now Chris Giles indicated that Miriam had driven that car to Florida and was using it at the present time. Miriam had never brought up with Chris the fact that she might not be allowed to have that car in her possession.

Portia also told Hebenstreit that other items, listed in her father's estate, were missing. These included a 2006 Arctic Cat, valued at $5,000, a horse vacuum, valued at $2,500, tack worth $2,000, and a ring owned by Alan, which was valued at $4,200.

Portia knew about all of these items because she was the administrator of her father's estate. Back on July 17, 2008, Portia had been so concerned about Miriam removing items from the property that she began listing them in a court order. Paragraph 5 stated: *Assets of the estate of Alan Helmick are being removed from the decedent's residence and some assets have been sold.* Paragraph 6 noted that Portia had repeatedly tried contacting Miriam about this, and had not been able to reach her.

And so it went, in paragraph after paragraph. One paragraph noted that payments on Alan's debts were not being handled properly by Miriam. In fact, many checks written to Alan's creditors were being returned, due to insufficient funds in his bank accounts. Bank personnel had contacted Portia that there was a problem, but they could not legally discuss the deficient accounts with her.

In another document, Portia noted that even Alan's home in Whitewater was not being properly maintained, and Portia worried that things might become so bad that the house would not be suitable to be put up for sale.

Reporter Paul Shockley of the *Grand Junction Free Press* was always keeping an eye on developments, and he contacted Portia Vigil not long after her recent interview with Jim Hebenstreit. Shockley learned that Portia had been granted "emergency legal authority" over her father's financial matters. Shockley also learned that in her affidavit to the Mesa County Court, Portia wrote, *While I am not accusing any person of wrongdoing, the circumstances surrounding his death suggest that special care should be taken to preserve assets, property and records. At this time, no one knows what information might be helpful to the sheriff's investigators.*

Portia had also not been able to contact Miriam for a lengthy period of time. In fact, Portia wrote: *Despite repeated attempts, I have been unable to contact the spouse to be formally named as personal representative for Alan Helmick's estate.*

Shockley added a comment of his own to the article: *Sheriff's office remains tight-lipped about the murder and has named no suspects.*

All through August 2008, the investigators were busy with other sheriff's office matters, but they still took time to do more research about the Helmick case. And one of the main focuses was what Alan or Miriam Helmick had been looking at on the Internet. Investigator Mike Piechota examined the Helmick residence computers and sent a CD about "Online Medical Searches" to Investigator Jim Hebenstreit.

There had been twenty-eight searches on May 18, 2008, with the keywords "how to put a horse down." There had also been searches with such words as "horse euthanasia procedures," "barbiturate painkillers," "painkiller overdoses," "OxyContin," and "Halcion drug overdose." This was all very interesting in light of Portia Vigil's concerns that Miriam might have been poisoning Alan when he'd been so ill.

Someone had also looked at an article on the Helmick's computer that was titled, "More Drug Overdose Deaths from Painkillers than Cocaine or Heroin in the U.S." On May 19, 2008, there had been a visit to BestRXPharm.com, and the activity stated: Your cart contains two items—60 Ambien

10mg pills and 30 Ambien 10mg pills. The total order was $388, but there was no indication that the order had actually been purchased. There was a similar preliminary order for Triazolam and OxyContin at that Web site, but no indication that they had actually been purchased as well.

Someone had been particularly interested in Ambien. The person had searched on the Helmicks' computer for "Ambien overdose," "Ambien CR and alcohol," "Ambien death," "Heath Ledger's death linked to Ambien," and "Accidental death ruled in death of Joliet detective." The last search about the detective included the line: *Coroner has ruled the death of police detective Frank Miller last month was an accidental overdose of prescription medication.*

On May 27, 2008, someone had searched on the Helmicks' computer about "purple foxglove." Some of the sentences that came up read: *poisonous, the source of digitalis and liquid nicotine.* Another article described the death of a Phillip Morris scientist from drinking liquid nicotine.

As if that wasn't enough about medication overdoses, more Internet searches had been done through early June 2008. These included "Viagra overdose" and "Viagra overdose possible cause of death in Rome." Another Internet search was about Lisinopril. Investigator Hebenstreit noted that bottles of Ambien, Lisinopril, and Viagra had all been collected at the Helmicks' home after Alan's murder.

On August 19, 2008, Jim Hebenstreit spoke once again with Stephanie Soule about her dealings with the Helmicks. This conversation centered around the Internet searches Miriam had conducted concerning horse euthanasia and horse euthanasia drugs. Hebenstreit asked Stephanie if she was aware of any of the Helmicks' horses being ill or injured. The trainer said she wasn't aware of any.

Hebenstreit asked if the Helmicks had ever euthanized a

horse, and Stephanie said that just before she started working with them, she understood that they had euthanized a colt in 2007. Soule said the colt had a bowel problem and the Arrowhead Veterinary Services had put the colt down. Following this lead, Hebenstreit contacted Arrowhead Veterinary Services and asked about the colt. The secretary there said that the vet had indeed put a colt down, but the Helmicks had not complained of any horse problems in 2008.

Looking further into this horse euthanasia and drugs situation, Hebenstreit spoke with Portia Vigil. Portia told him that she thought the Helmicks' horse, Pharaoh, had a leg problem and had been seen by Harris Equine. Hebenstreit spoke with a vet there, who said that he had seen that horse on two occasions, and both times had been in June 2008. In fact, the second time had been on June 9, the day before Alan was murdered. Both Alan and Miriam had come to the "horse hospital" at about nine in the morning and stayed until noon. After some ultrasound tests, the vets recommended physical therapy exercises for Pharaoh. At no time had there been a discussion about euthanasia.

Horse euthanasia drugs and medication overdoses—someone in the Helmick household had been very interested in those matters in May and June 2008. And all during early 2008, Alan Helmick had shown signs of possibly suffering from misuse of medicine. If Miriam had been the person on the Internet looking at these things, it gave the idea of poisoning more validity.

CHAPTER 22

A MURDEROUS WEAPON

In the course of the investigation, Jim Hebenstreit learned that Alan Helmick had possibly owned a .25-caliber pistol, and this pistol had not been located after his murder. Hebenstreit began contacting Alan's friends and family members to ask if they recalled this pistol and any other weapons that Alan might have owned. Alan's daughter, Kristy Helmick-Burd, remembered seeing a handgun in her father's dresser drawer at his house in Delta. She thought she had seen it while putting laundry in the dresser drawer for him sometime between August and December 2004. Kristy described it as a small handgun—the type that a woman would put in her purse.

Kristy said this particular handgun had originally belonged to Gerald "Gerry" Wait, her mother's stepfather. When Gerry Wait died, Sharon had come into the possession of the pistol. And when her mom, Sharon, died, the gun passed to Alan.

Jacob Burd, Kristy's husband, had also seen this handgun. He described it as being silver in color, with white handgrips. The handgrips might have been mother-of-pearl. Jacob thought the caliber was .25, although he didn't know which company had manufactured the gun. Jacob believed it was a .25, because he had looked at a .25-caliber Bauer pistol around the time that he had seen that particular handgun.

This whole handgun business had an interesting side story to it. Investigator Hebenstreit contacted Mike Pruett, who was Sharon Helmick's brother-in-law. Pruett recalled an incident in Delta, Colorado, in the 1980s when a neighbor of Gerry Wait's had to wrestle a handgun away from him. In the struggle, Gerry Wait had a heart attack and died.

Jim Hebenstreit spoke with Sean Wells, of the Delta Police Department, about any incident from the 1980s that might match this. Jamie Head, of the Delta PD, got back to Hebenstreit concerning an attempted homicide by Gerald (Gerry) Wait on October 5, 1989. A .25-caliber Lorcin handgun had been recovered from the scene, and photographs were taken of it.

Looking at reports of that incident, Hebenstreit noted that Gerry Wait had gotten into an altercation on the 800 block of East Fourth Street in Delta. Gerry had actually fired a shot from the gun at his wife, Wanda, and neighbor Terri Helm. Gerry had been standing in the front yard when he fired at the women. Terri Helm's husband, Daniel Helm, ran over and tackled Gerry Wait and disarmed him. Gerry Wait subsequently had a heart attack and died.

From the report, Hebenstreit learned that the .25 Lorcin pistol, was a Model L25, and contained a magazine of six live rounds, and one spent .25-caliber shell casing. That casing was found in the driveway. The Lorcin pistol was silver-blue in color and had white handles. It seemed very possible that this pistol had been passed to Sharon Helmick and then to Alan Helmick when Sharon died. And there was a very good possibility that this very same pistol had been used to murder Alan Helmick.

* * *

During a conversation with Terri Helm, Jim Hebenstreit learned from her that the bullet fired by Gerry Wait went into the ground in the front lawn as she was running away from him. This was very interesting to Hebenstreit, and he asked Palisade police chief Carroll Quarles to assist him in searching the front lawn with a metal detector. During the search, Chief Quarles located a .25-caliber bullet from the east end of the lawn. The bullet was embedded in the soil under the grass, about an inch deep in the ground, and had been there for eighteen years.

Hebenstreit booked the bullet into evidence at the Mesa County Sheriff's Office as item JH-35. It was taken to the Colorado Bureau of Investigation for analysis to determine if that bullet and the bullet fired into the head of Alan Helmick had both been fired by the same gun.

The examination of the bullets was performed by CBI agent Sam Marso, who was a ballistics expert. Eventually Agent Marso got back to Hebenstreit and said that both bullets had similar characteristics and could have been fired by the same gun. But there was too much damage to the bullet recovered from the lawn to reach a positive conclusion. Both bullets, however, did have characteristics of being fired from the Lorcin brand pistol.

Hebenstreit contacted Brad Kolman, an attorney in Delta County, and faxed a copy of the report about the case involving Gerry Wait. Kolman looked through his files and noted that after her father's death, Sharon Helmick had asked for the pistol to be released to her custody. A letter was also in the file that indicated that the pistol had indeed been given over to the custody of Sharon Helmick.

There was even an audiotape from April 1991 by a secretary to Kolman. The audio part related, "Sharon wants pistol and tape recorder only of the items you got from the PD. Wants to sell to help out Wanda." Wanda was the wife of Gerald Wait. Eventually Sharon did receive a Lorcin .25-caliber semiautomatic pistol with six live rounds, a box of Remington .25-caliber ammunition (minus 7 rounds), and a GE voice-activated tape recorder.

This possible sale of the .25-caliber Lorcin pistol, of course, threw a wrinkle into the mix. Had Sharon ever sold the pistol to someone, or had she kept it? Hebenstreit didn't know at that point. Had that .25 Lorcin pistol eventually been retained by Alan Helmick, only to be used by Miriam to kill him on June 10, 2008? The investigators intended to find out.

CHAPTER 23

WHERE THERE'S SMOKE

Investigator Hebenstreit had continuously been intrigued by Miriam Helmick's comment in her conversation with several people about a car fire. In fact, Miriam had only brought up such an important incident very late in the interview, when asked directly by Detective Bev Jarrell if she had been involved with any other police matters. Miriam had mentioned that the authorities had found a wick-type item placed into the gas tank and ruled the fire as arson.

MCSO Investigator Chuck Warner contacted Sergeant Sean Wells, of the Delta Police Department, regarding the car fire of April 30, 2008. Sergeant Wells said that there had been a suspicious car fire on that date and the case was still under investigation. Wells faxed Investigator Warner a copy of the report about this car fire. The vehicle in question was a 1994 Buick Roadmaster registered to Alan and Sharon Helmick. The fire had occurred on the 700 block of Main Street in Delta, Colorado.

A short time later, Investigator Hebenstreit received a packet of material from the Delta PD related to the car fire. Included was an audio CD of Officer Summer Kirkpatrick's interview with Alan and Miriam Helmick about the incident. The interviews had been conducted on May 1, 2008. During the interview, Miriam Helmick said that a woman named Barbara Watts was the only person she could think of who might have wanted to start a car fire. Miriam added that she didn't know if Watts was in town.

When asked if she had any criminal history or was being investigated about anything, Miriam answered no. Miriam then said that she had put gasoline into the vehicle on Saturday, April 26, at the gas station connected with the Orchard Mesa City Market and Alan had not been with her at the time. Miriam also said that she usually drove Alan's Chevrolet truck and not the Buick Roadmaster.

Miriam stated, "We go so many places together. We're rarely apart." And she admitted that it was unusual for her to go shopping or to a gas station without Alan. Officer Kirkpatrick noted that Alan had a number of businesses and asked if Miriam was part of that. She answered no, but she added that Alan liked her to go with him on his business rounds so that she would know what was going on. Miriam related that she sometimes made business phone calls for Alan, but legally she was not involved. Miriam also stated, "Everything is in Alan's name—the house, bank account, credit cards. He gives me money and takes a draw from time to time from the dance studio I run. Life is wonderful."

Officer Kirkpatrick asked Miriam to detail her actions on the day right before the car fire. Miriam said she had to use a bathroom because she felt ill. "As I got out of the car, I had been in such a rush, I dumped my drink and purse on the ground. I had to pick that up after I came out of the restroom. I'd even hit my head on the car door while rushing to the bathroom and it still hurts. I kinda passed Robin Cook coming out with the trash and I know she stood there and talked to Alan for a good five minutes while I was inside."

At that point, Alan was back in the vehicle. Miriam

continued, "I came back out and it was so hot I asked Alan to pop the trunk so I could go get my sandals. But when I went outside to get them, I had to turn around and rush to the restroom again."

Officer Kirkpatrick asked, "So you did get your sandals out of the car?"

Miriam laughed and replied, "No . . . it's got the electric lock on it, so I kinda pushed it (the car-key locking system) back down and ran back into the bathroom. I never even got to the back of the car."

While Miriam was in the ladies' room the second time, she said, she heard Alan come into the building and say to someone that he needed a fire extinguisher. Miriam related that she didn't see any fire or smell anything while in the restroom. Then she added that the wind had been blowing hard that day, and it might have blown the smell in the opposite direction. In fact, it was so windy, when she dropped her water bottle, she had to chase it down the road later.

Miriam also said that Alan had asked for a cigarette when she was at the car, when she had been asking for her sandals. She gave him one just before running back into the restroom. Miriam related that she didn't retrieve her sandals until later after the car fire was put out.

Officer Kirkpatrick asked Miriam a very pointed question. Why did the bathroom Miriam had been in smell like lighter fluid when officers went in there? Miriam answered, "Because Alan gave me the wick after the car fire and told me to do something with it. So I threw it in a garbage can. Alan then told me to get it back out later, which I did."

Officer Kirkpatrick brought up the fact that Miriam had been looking for a pair of pliers after the car fire, and Kirkpatrick asked why. Miriam responded that Alan had seen a wick, but he couldn't get it by just using his fingers. Miriam related that most of the wick had been in the tank, with a small piece sticking out near the gas cap.

Officer Kirkpatrick then dropped a real surprise on Miriam. Kirkpatrick said that there was a surveillance camera across the street pointed in the direction of where the car fire had taken place. Kirkpatrick asked Miriam what she thought they would learn from that. Miriam said she didn't know.

In fact, this had been a ruse on Officer Kirkpatrick's part. There was no surveillance camera across the street. Kirkpatrick wanted to see Miriam's reaction to this statement.

Officer Kirkpatrick asked about life insurance policies and Miriam answered that Alan had life insurance, but all of it went directly to his estate, and those proceeds went to his children. Miriam added that Alan had been ill lately, but he was feeling much better now. And once again Miriam confirmed that Alan had been in the car at the time the fire started, and she had been in the restroom.

Summer Kirkpatrick next interviewed Alan, outside of Miriam's presence. Alan told Kirkpatrick that both he and Miriam had been previously married, and both had lost their spouses. Concerning a motive for the car fire, Alan said there were only two people who came to mind as possible suspects. One was the former vice president of the Olathe State Bank. This was a man named Don, who had done some prison time after an incident Alan had reported. Even with that, Alan said he couldn't imagine Don doing something like this.

The other person was Barbara Watts, whom Miriam had been involved with in the dance studio business. Alan said Barbara had once had Miriam arrested in Mississippi for bank fraud, stealing money from her checking accounts, and altering bank statements. Alan added that Miriam had been found not guilty in that case. Alan wondered if Barbara Watts was still angry about this and wanted to get even.

Alan then said that all of his money and assets were in

his name, and Miriam was only a minor shareholder in the dance studio and horse-training business.

"Miriam is dependent on me to make money," Alan claimed. The implication was that he was more valuable to her alive than dead.

Officer Kirkpatrick wondered why Miriam's name wasn't on everything, and Alan said they didn't want to put her name on everything because of the problems Miriam had in Mississippi. Another reason was Miriam's late husband's problems with the IRS. Alan told Miriam he loved her, and no matter what they'd make the best of the situation and he'd stand by her. In fact, he had even told her that if she was guilty of the crimes in Mississippi and had to serve out some time, he'd stand by her and take care of her. "I know that Miriam isn't a malicious person," Alan declared.

Alan continued, "Her first husband didn't leave her with anything. He was running around on her, pulling his money out of the bank to spend on other women." Of course, these were things based upon what Miriam had told Alan about her first marriage.

Alan did admit that Miriam came with some "baggage." He added, "I'm not saying she couldn't have done it. I'm not stupid. And if she comes with malicious baggage, I'll find out about it. You can always be wrong about people, and I didn't want her on anything for a while."

By those remarks, he meant he didn't want Miriam's name on his various business interests and in his will until he found out for sure about her. Then he added that he was worth several million dollars and he wanted the bulk of that money to go to his children and grandchildren when he died. Miriam seemed to be okay with that.

Alan added that he wanted the home in Whitewater to go to Miriam when he died. There was still a lot of debt on it, but he estimated that it had between $250,000 and $300,000 in equity. Alan said, "That's her home, because we acquired and developed that, and developed the equity after we were together."

Officer Kirkpatrick asked at what times the Buick had been unattended by either one of them in recent days. Alan said that Miriam told him she had gotten gas on Saturday, but she had a bad memory about specific dates. They had gone to the Texas Roadhouse on Sunday and it had been in the parking lot unattended at that time. Since then, it had not been out of their sight until it was at the parking lot on Main Street in Delta on April 30, the day of the car fire.

Alan said, "The car is in the garage ninety-five percent of the time."

As to the morning of April 30, Alan said that he got up at around seven and noticed about that time that one of their horses had escaped. Just what he did about this, he didn't say. Alan did say that he and Miriam went to the courthouse between nine and nine-thirty to pay taxes on two parcels in Delta County, and they parked between the library and jail. Both he and Miriam went into the courthouse together; then they drove to a parking space in a lot at the title business on the 700 block of Main Street.

Miriam followed him inside the building, and Alan went to the title office while Miriam went downstairs to the ladies' room. After that, Miriam came up to the title company and sat outside the door, because "she didn't want to be involved in the business."

After he finished his business at the title company, which was actually the selling of his half interest in it, Alan said that he and Miriam left and got back into the car. Miriam had "stomach troubles" and jumped out of the car after giving Alan her last cigarette and cigarette lighter. When asked if he always smoked, Alan said that he had quit cold turkey on November 15, 2007. Alan added that he didn't know it at the time, but his doctor told him later that quitting like that had been the worst thing for him. His body chemistry changed and his resistance to diseases went down. Alan related that he got the flu in January and kept getting sick off and on for months after that. Alan said that Miriam had made a deal with him that she would quit smoking when they went to Lake Powell on March 17, 2008. But they weren't able to make that date because Alan was sick again. Since November, Alan admitted, he now smoked off and on, and felt healthier.

Officer Kirkpatrick asked if Miriam had dropped anything on the ground as she ran back into the building to use the restroom. Alan replied that she hadn't, as far as he knew. He did say that Miriam's purse was in the car, because he put the cigarette lighter back into the purse after using it. (Miriam, of course, had said just the opposite—that she had dropped it on the ground while running to the restroom and had to pick it up on her way back to the car.)

Alan added that he was sitting in the car, which was running, and Robin Cook came out of the building. Alan began talking with Robin, who was carrying a live wasp in a container. It may have been in a wastepaper basket, since Miriam had spoken of Robin emptying the trash. Apparently, she didn't want to kill the wasp and let it go outside, instead. Alan and Robin spoke for about five minutes, until Miriam came out of the building after her first trip to the restroom. Before Miriam got into the car, she complained of being sick again. She rushed back into the building to use the restroom a second time.

While Miriam was gone that time, Alan sat in the car, listening to the radio, when he noticed a white plume of smoke coming from the back of the car. At first, he thought it was normal exhaust fumes and he turned the car off. But the white plume increased in intensity and volume, and he soon realized it was a fire coming from the car. Alan explained, "There were flames going everywhere!"

Alan stated that he rushed to the back of the car and then into the building looking for a fire extinguisher. As he searched the building, he met Miriam coming out of the restroom. He quickly told Miriam what was happening. She obtained a pitcher somewhere in the building, filled it with water, and ran outside, throwing the water on the car. She did this several times, running back and forth to collect more water.

Alan related that they called 911 immediately. Once he got the fire doused, he noticed what he thought was a piece of burned gas cap, but it turned out to be a "wick." Alan said he pulled the wick out of the gas tank just before the police and fire department arrived.

Officer Kirkpatrick asked Alan why Miriam would want to get into the trunk of the vehicle. Alan said that Miriam always kept various sets of shoes and boots in there, and she had been wearing tennis shoes with no socks that day. He assumed the tennis shoes were bothering her, and she told him, "Pop the trunk. I need to get a different pair of shoes." Alan thought this occurred just before he started talking to Robin.

Kirkpatrick asked if Miriam had changed her shoes to sandals, and he answered no, she hadn't changed shoes. Alan surmised this was because Miriam got sick again and ran back into the building to use the restroom before she could do so. Alan commented that Miriam was the only one near the back of the car, and he would have been able to see if anyone else had sneaked up and put a wick into the gas tank. As to Kirkpatrick's comment that it seemed that Miriam had been the one to start the fire, Alan responded, "But that can't be! I'm the one who had the cigarette lighter." And then he paused and was thoughtful.

Finally he added, "Of course, you can never be one hundred percent sure about anybody."

CHAPTER 24

"THAT WOULD BE TERRIBLE!"

Officer Kirkpatrick asked Alan how Miriam got money. Alan replied, "I give it to her when I want to. I always tell her if you need money, ask me. I'd even asked her if she wanted an allowance. She said no. 'You always give me what I need.'"

Alan related that Miriam was not a spendthrift. "She does make a little money at the dance studio, but it's minor. She pays the rent there. It's a low-key thing. It kind of pays its way. Once in a while, she might make one hundred, two hundred dollars."

The officer asked Alan if he thought it bothered Miriam to ask him for money, and he said it didn't seem to bother her. Alan even said that at one point he had looked Miriam in the eye to see if she "felt too dependent or too captured." He offered to give her a fixed income every month. She said she liked things the way they were. He had talked to her about cash flow and told her that sometimes they would have a good amount of money on hand, and at other times it was tied up in his business deals. The main part of that was money already tied up in real estate, and it would turn a good profit "down the road."

Dance instructor Miriam Helmick moved to Grand Junction, Colorado, to manage a dance studio. She arrived with $600, a dog, and two suitcases. *(Mug shot)*

Miriam became a popular dance instructor in the community and eventually opened up her own studio, Dance Junction. *(Courtesy of Mesa County District Attorney's Office)*

One of Miriam's students was local businessman Alan Helmick. Alan had recently been widowed.

(Courtesy of Penny Lyons)

Alan is depicted here with his daughter Portia, when she took over Alan's mortgage company. *(Courtesy of Delta County Independent)*

In high school, Alan was popular, very athletic, and a good musician. Even in later years as a businessman, he was spoken of as a "nice guy." *(Yearbook photo)*

Alan and Miriam moved into a new house that Alan had built in Whitewater, Colorado, essentially to please Miriam. She wanted a place where they could keep horses, which she loved to ride.
(Courtesy of Mesa County District Attorney's Office)

Besides paying the bills for Dance Junction, Alan also bought Miriam a horse-training business beneath the towering cliffs of Colorado National Monument. *(Author photo)*

During a visit to Alan's title company, Miriam wanted to put these sandals on. But before she did so, she complained of bad stomach problems and rushed off to the ladies' room in the building.
(Courtesy of Mesa County District Attorney's Office)

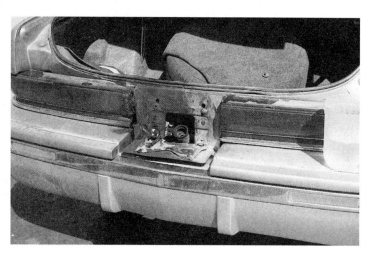

While sitting in the car and waiting for Miriam to return, Alan smelled smoke coming from the back of the car. He found that the rubber lining near the gas cap was burning. *(Courtesy of Mesa County District Attorney's Office)*

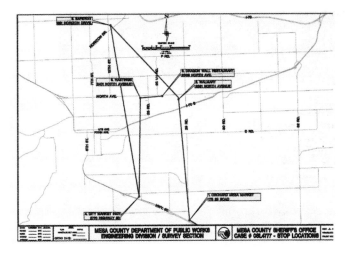

On the morning of June 10, 2008, Miriam ran errands all over town. This map was later constructed by the Mesa County Sheriff's Office to show her route. *(Courtesy of Mesa County Sheriff's Office)*

Miriam returned home around 11:30 AM. In her car trunk, she had several items she had purchased, including a large bag of carrots for her horses. *(Courtesy of Mesa County District Attorney's Office)*

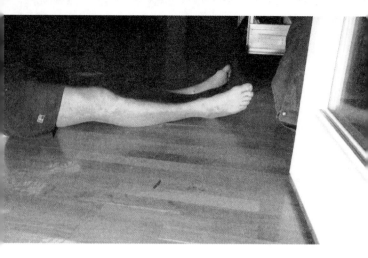

Miriam told a 911 operator that she found Alan lying on the floor and that he had blood on the back of his head. *(Courtesy of Mesa County District Attorney's Office)*

Although Miriam said that she gave Alan CPR, she told the 911 operator that it was not working. His hands had already turned blue.

(Courtesy of Mesa County District Attorney's Office)

Alan's wallet was discovered near his body. *(Courtesy of Mesa County District Attorney's Office)*

Investigators looked at receipts and papers in the Helmicks' home to determine if Alan's death had something to do with his businesses. *(Courtesy of Mesa County District Attorney's Office)*

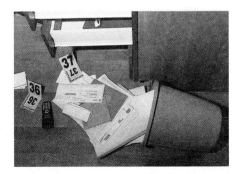

There was a trash can tipped over near Alan's desk as if someone had been going through the papers inside. *(Courtesy of Mesa County District Attorney's Office)*

Alan had been shot in the back of the head. Investigators looked at this handgun in the house. But its caliber did not match that of the bullet recovered from his body. *(Courtesy of Mesa County District Attorney's Office)*

A spent shell casing was discovered on the floor. It seemed to come from a .25 caliber handgun—the same size as the bullet found in Alan's body. *(Courtesy of Mesa County District Attorney's Office)*

Investigators wondered why a robber wouldn't take valuable items like this hunting rifle if Alan had been shot during a robbery. *(Courtesy of Mesa County District Attorney's Office)*

Keys were found in the ignition of one of Alan's vehicles in the driveway. Investigators wondered why a burglar would not steal this vehicle. *(Courtesy of Mesa County District Attorney's Office)*

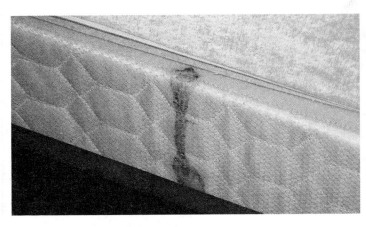

A blood stain was found on this mattress, although Alan's body was lying in the kitchen/work space area. *(Courtesy of Mesa County District Attorney's Office)*

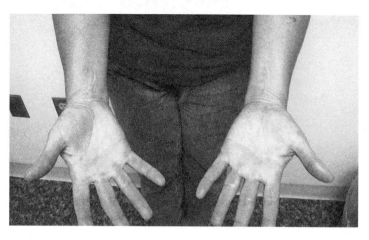

Miriam was tested for gunshot residue on the day that Alan's body was discovered. None was found on her hands, body or clothing. *(Courtesy of Mesa County Sheriff's Office)*

Miriam had left messages on Alan's cell phone about her morning's activities of June 10, 2008. *(Courtesy of Mesa County District Attorney's Office)*

Miriam's cell phone had numerous messages from Alan's daughters. In the week before his death, they called Miriam and asked why he was not responding to messages they left for him. *(Courtesy of Mesa County District Attorney's Office)*

Miriam and her friend Penny Lyons discovered a card under the Helmicks' front doormat on June 26, 2008. Part of the card had this message written on it. *(Courtesy of Mesa County District Attorney's Office)*

Another section of the card had this message. Alan's name was misspelled. *(Courtesy of Mesa County District Attorney's Office)*

Investigators were able to track down where the card had been sold. They also received a security video of Miriam buying that card at a store in Orchard Mesa. *(Courtesy of Mesa County District Attorney's Office)*

One of Miriam's errands on the morning of June 10, 2008, had been to buy carrots for the horses. But she already had carrots in this bucket in the barn. *(Courtesy of Mesa County District Attorney's Office)*

This small Derringer-type weapon was most likely the gun used to kill Alan Helmick. *(Courtesy of Mesa County District Attorney's Office)*

Miriam used this vehicle, which had belonged to Alan's first wife, Sharon, to drive away from Grand Junction in July 2008. Then she disappeared off the radar. *(Courtesy of Mesa County District Attorney's Office)*

Miriam was caught on surveillance video at a pawn shop in Jacksonville, Florida. She pawned jewelry that had belonged to Sharon Helmick. In fact, Miriam was passing herself off as Sharon Helmick. *(Courtesy of Mesa County District Attorney's Office)*

MIRIAM FRANCIS HELMICK

D.O.B. 01/26/1957

On December 8, 2008, Miriam Helmick was arrested in Jacksonville, Florida for the murder of Alan Helmick. *(Mug shot)*

Assistant D.A. Rich Tuttle questioned numerous witnesses in the case against Miriam Helmick. *(Courtesy of Rich Tuttle)*

Investigator Jim Hebenstreit collected many items connected to the murder of Alan Helmick and spoke with a long list of people who knew both Alan and Miriam. *(Courtesy of Mesa County Sheriff's Office)*

Miriam did not fight extradition to Colorado, believing that she would be found innocent. Even her lawyer had high hopes that Miriam would be acquitted. *(Mug shot)*

Miriam's trial for the murder of Alan Helmick took place at the Mesa County Courthouse in Grand Junction. *(Author photo)*

Alan thought that Miriam understood all of this, and she had never asked him for an exorbitant amount of money on anything. He even told Kirkpatrick if he just gave her a twenty-dollar bill, she understood that he was short on cash at the moment. Alan said, "She'd stretch that money forever."

Alan related that before they bought the property in Whitewater, he knew it was a kind of high-risk project with a big debt. Alan asked Miriam what she thought about it. Miriam said that she had been out there in Whitewater, and replied, "Let's make it work if we can." Alan added that in the long run it had been a smart investment, and they'd developed $250,000 to $300,00 equity on the property and house within two years.

Officer Kirkpatrick asked if Miriam had a debit card or credit card, and Alan said that she didn't. Kirkpatrick wanted to know how Miriam managed to do any shopping. Alan responded that for those times he either let her use a credit card that he had or gave her cash.

"Anything she wants, I give to her." Then Alan added, *"I'm more valuable alive to her than dead."*

The wick in the gas tank was obviously an important issue, and Officer Kirkpatrick wanted to know what had happened to it. Alan couldn't remember for sure and he thought he'd either laid it on the parking-lot surface or handed it to Miriam.

Officer Kirkpatrick asked, "She didn't take it away and then bring it back to you?"

Alan replied, "No, why would she do that?"

Officer Kirkpatrick responded, "Because that's what she said happened."

Alan was indeed surprised by that comment, saying, "Oh, she did?"

So Officer Kirkpatrick related that the bathroom in the office building had smelled of lighter fluid. Miriam had told Kirkpatrick that Alan had given her the wick to throw away, which she did by depositing it in the bathroom. And then

Miriam added that Alan had come into the restroom later and wanted the wick back.

After hearing that, Alan said that he wasn't sure if things had happened that way or not. His mind had been so focused on putting out the fire, perhaps he had done what Miriam said and couldn't remember it now. "I don't remember her taking it in there. I don't remember going in and asking for it. But I very well may have," Alan finally said.

Then Alan stated that Miriam had a very good memory and logic process. "I would have a tendency to think that Miriam was right about this, and I'm wrong. I don't remember events moment by moment, but I do remember being focused on putting out the fire."

Officer Kirkpatrick decided to use the ruse about the video surveillance camera across the street from the title company. Kirkpatrick said, "There is footage of Miriam starting the fire."

Alan replied, "Oh, God! No, I don't think that . . . That would be terrible! Why would she do that?"

Officer Kirkpatrick said that officers had watched the video, and Alan asked, "Is she on there?"

Kirkpatrick responded with a question: "What do you think?"

Alan replied, "No, but I could be wrong."

Officer Kirkpatrick then asked what Miriam would gain by Alan's death.

Alan replied, "I don't know what she would gain if she did it. What she would get was a mess because I have three land developments in different levels of process. They're worth nothing unless they're carried through. My name is the only one on all of them."

Officer Kirkpatrick asked him about the prenuptial agreement. Alan said, "She gets nothing that was created prior to the marriage. The only thing that was created after the marriage was the equity in the house in Whitewater."

Perhaps suspicious now, Alan asked about the video surveillance tape, and Officer Kirkpatrick admitted that it had not actually been checked. (It may not have existed at all.) At that point, Alan realized exactly what Officer Kirkpatrick was doing. Alan declared, "You only did that to get my reaction! Well, that's okay. I'm not sure if there is a videotape, but if it showed there was evidence of Miriam starting the fire, I'd be shocked. The first thing I would do is find out. I can't imagine her being malicious. What I could imagine is her being very sick. But I don't think she's sick."

Once again Alan said that he understood why Officer Kirkpatrick had used that ruse about the videotape. He said that Kirkpatrick wanted to find out where his "head was at about Miriam."

Alan added, "You know, anyone in the world could have done it. You could have done it, but I doubt it. I feel the same way about Miriam."

After getting the car fire report, Investigator Hebenstreit received another package of items connected to the Buick car fire from the Delta PD. Among the items was a photo they referred to as the "wick." Also in the package were photos of the scene, including some photos showing the filler cap of the gas tank, which was at the rear of the vehicle below the license plate.

Jim Hebenstreit went to the Delta Police Department headquarters and met with Sergeant Sean Wells. Hebenstreit viewed the wick, which he described as "a wooden skewer with a piece of fabric or rope attached at one end with what appeared to be glue."

The next day, Hebenstreit took a photo of the wick to show Josh and Portia Vigil at the Helmick residence in Whitewater. Since Portia was the executor of Alan's estate, she was there packing up items and cleaning the house. After looking at the photo, Josh said he had found a rope at the Helmick residence that looked similar to the one in the photo. It was a rope that appeared to have been glued to the "skewer" part of the wick.

Josh brought out a short, braided lead rope for use with horses, which was attached at one end to a brass snap. He told Hebenstreit he found the rope in the Helmicks' horse trailer. Hebenstreit collected the rope and contacted Sergeant Wells.

Wells met with Hebenstreit two days later, and he brought along items connected to the car fire. One of the items was the wooden skewer and rope, which had been termed as the wick. The rope on the wick and the lead rope found by Josh in the Helmicks' horse trailer appeared to be similar. Hebenstreit noted that to the human eye they had the same color and composition. It even appeared that the wick rope had been cut from the lead rope. Hebenstreit sent strands of rope from the wick rope and lead rope to the Colorado Bureau of Investigation.

All of this was just one more item in a chain of items and incidents that made Miriam Helmick's actions very suspicious.

CHAPTER 25

A KITTEN AND TIGER

While all of this was going on, it still remained a mystery as to where Miriam Helmick was, and what she was doing. And that remained a mystery until links started connecting her to her son, Chris.

Miriam's son, Chris, had flown out of Grand Junction to Denver in early July 2008, and then to Jacksonville, Florida, on July 6. He was back in Florida only a few days when he received a call from his mother, Miriam. She told him that she was on her way to Jacksonville; Chris was totally surprised by this.

He recalled, "I wanted to make sure everything was clear with the police in Grand Junction. I mean, if you're under investigation or whatever, sometimes it's not feasible to leave the area. She indicated to me that law enforcement knew she was on her way out to Florida.

"I kind of advised her to stop and try and find something, maybe a job or a place to stay for a little while in Savannah, Georgia. Kind of settle everything down. She was born and raised in that area. And she got there, but I got a couple of phone calls from her while she was there, saying that she couldn't find anything, so she was going to come on down to Florida."

Miriam arrived in Jacksonville near the end of July 2008. Apparently, she had stopped off in Savannah first. None of this was known to MCSO investigators until they received a phone call from Portia Vigil.

On October 16, 2008, Portia Vigil contacted Jim Hebenstreit and told him that she had recently received an e-mail from Miriam, who was now living in Florida. This e-mail was in response to a letter that one of Alan's attorneys, had sent Miriam. Portia forwarded the e-mail from Miriam to Hebenstreit. Within the text, Miriam had written about items she had sold since leaving Colorado.

Miriam indicated that she had sold ten used horse panels and a manure spreader for $1,000. Then Miriam listed four bills that she had paid before leaving Colorado. These included a barn and training bill of $2,700 to Sue Boulware and car insurance of $114.98 in May for all the Helmicks' vehicles. The list also included an April and May electric bill of $156 and new battery and electric repair of $120.

Then Miriam wrote that she was going to try and bring back the Buick Roadmaster herself, but she wanted to be reimbursed for the trip. Miriam added that before she left Colorado, the vehicle had 121,998 miles on the odometer. Since then, she had been careful not to drive it too often.

Miriam concluded the e-mail without asking any questions about the investigation or the status of Alan's estate. This obviously seemed strange to both Portia and Hebenstreit.

A few days later, Investigator Hebenstreit received an official document on Alan Helmick's estate. The main residence in Whitewater was valued at $620,000, with a first mortgage balance of $411,488 and a second mortgage of $57,873. Based on those figures, there was $150,639 of equity in the property. As things stood, eventually Miriam was to receive that money.

* * *

Meanwhile, concerning events that occurred in Florida, a man named Charles Kirkpatrick began searching on Internet dating sites for a woman who shared his tastes. Kirkpatrick was a wealthy man who owned a Fred Astaire ballroom dance studio and an Arthur Murray one as well. He also owned a human resources management company in Albany, Georgia.

Kirkpatrick began his Internet dating search on Seeking Arrangement.com and later on MillionaireMatch.com. That was because Charles fell into the multimillionaire category. He liked the MillionaireMatch.com site because they had an identity-verification feature. For his own profile, Charles stated that he lived in an expensive Florida high-rise building and made over $500,000 per year. Kirkpatrick's apartment in the high-rise was very spacious and overlooked a pool and Jacuzzi. Not only that, he had several expensive automobiles, including a BMW, a Mercedes, and a 1985 neo-classic Zimmer Golden Spirit, which he said looked like a 1930s Rolls-Royce.

A woman calling herself "Sharon Helmick" did contact Charles Kirkpatrick and he became interested in her. Her initial message to him stated: Saw your profile and loved it. I can dance any dance and I'm pretty good at it, too. I just haven't learned the West Coast Swing. Your profile requirements described me completely. She sent along a photo of herself on horseback, and described herself as a pretty lady with an impish smile.

Charles sent some more information about himself, including that he lived in Orlando, Florida. To this, Sharon sent a return e-mail: Honesty is the best policy. I'm sure you won't be disappointed. I'd love to come to Orlando. I will call you soon. Then she added that all the photos she posted were of her riding horses, but she would take another photo in the coming week. And she also stated, I can't wait to be a kitten and a tiger all in one day.

The woman calling herself "Sharon" said that she liked the finer things in life, and that she could participate in them with "elegance" and "finesse."

Apparently, Charles had made some comment about going from a "ballroom to a barroom." Sharon thought that was a clever remark. She said that she was very "sensual and sexual," and there were many things that they could explore.

After this exchange of e-mails, Charles and Sharon had a telephone conversation. He suggested that they meet in person within the next few days. Kirkpatrick didn't have to wait long; Sharon showed up in Orlando that same day. They went to a T.G.I. Friday's restaurant and stayed there until two in the morning. During that time, Sharon told him about her previous husband.

Charles recalled, "She told me that he had been dead about six to twelve months. Something like that. I commented that it was pretty soon to be out with someone, and was she okay with that?

"She said it was okay. She told me that he had died with some type of brain disease or something, and that he had been sick for three to four years prior to that. She said it wasn't like a sudden thing. She didn't show any emotion about her former husband. At the restaurant, she was excited and very up and positive. She even brought her dance shoes with her in case we could find a place to go dancing."

Kirkpatrick recalled that they had dinner and drinks and had hit it off. And then they went back to his place; and as he put it later, they had "intimate relationships."

Sharon stayed for the weekend. On Monday, Charles had to work. One thing that began to turn him off to her was that she said that she didn't have any close ties to Jacksonville, where she was now living. She wanted to move in with him right away. Charles relayed, "It was the manner in which she said it. It was repeated several times."

Kirkpatrick was suspicious about this urgency. He lied to her and said that he was going out of town to see his kids and grandkids in Georgia. Even though they exchanged e-mails again, he never saw her in person after that.

One of the few people back in Colorado who was contacted by Miriam during this time period was Jeri Yarbrough. Sometime in September 2008, Jeri received a phone call from Miriam, who was now residing in Florida. As part of a settlement for buying back the horses, Jeri said that she wanted part of the proceeds to go to Sue Boulware, to whom Miriam still owed money. After that was accomplished, Miriam would get the balance. Miriam told Jeri to go ahead and do that.

Jeri remarked about this transaction, "I paid the debt off to Sue Boulware, who actually had the horses at that time. I paid Sue two thousand five hundred and sixty dollars. Later I paid Miriam two thousand. And I asked Miriam how she was, and she said that she hadn't been good. She had been in an institution because she tried to commit suicide." (Law enforcement checked later on and could not find any evidence that this was true.)

"She called me again and said that she was trying to find a job in Florida. It was during this phone call that she said [of the alleged suicide attempt], 'I didn't try to shoot myself.' I couldn't understand how she really tried to kill herself. It was getting more crazy, as far as the stuff she said. The whole case was going bizarre. I wanted to handle the horse stuff, and strictly deal with that and keep all the other stuff to a minimum. When I asked where to send the money, she said to her son's account. She indicated that she was living with him in Florida."

CHAPTER 26

SPECIAL AGENT MORTON

Possibly because of their experience with the Michael Blagg case, which had elements of a staged robbery in the home, MCSO contacted Robert Morton, of the Federal Bureau of Investigation (FBI). Morton was an expert in this field, and he came with a lot of experience.

Morton began his FBI career in Chicago as a senior member of an evidence response team (ERT). During his tenure there, he investigated evidence in the Oklahoma City Bombing case and the Atlanta Olympics Bombing case. He also did work at the Pentagon when terrorists crashed a plane into it on September 11, 2001.

Later, Morton transferred to the National Center for the Analysis of Violent Crime (NCAVC), in Quantico, Virginia. As Morton noted later, "We worked on cases that are so unusual, they don't usually occur with normal policeman's experience level. We focus specifically on those types of crimes, and by doing so, we maintain an expertise in those kinds of crimes."

By the fall of 2008, Morton was certified by the International Association for Identification (IAI) as a senior crime analyst. In order to qualify, he needed a minimum of five years of experience supervising crime scene work and had to pass a four-hundred-question test.

Of the Helmick case in particular, Agent Morton would later recount that he came to Grand Junction to meet with members of the Mesa County Sheriff's Office. According to Morton, MCSO wanted his opinion on whether the crime scene at the Helmick home had been staged to look like a burglary gone bad.

Of such a crime scene in general, Morton said, "The whole purpose of doing so is because the offender feels they will be targeted by the police as a prime suspect. So they stage the crime scene to disguise the crime scene to make it appear as something else other than what it really is.

"Staging almost always, in my experience, reflects some type of relationship between the offender and the victim. If I'm a stranger, there's no connection between me and the victim. Therefore, I have no need to stage a crime scene. I can just walk away from whatever happened.

"In my experience, most of the crime scenes that are staged are done so by people who have very little familiarity with the offense they're attempting to portray. In other words, if I want to stage a crime scene as a robbery gone bad, but I've never been a robber, I don't actually know what happens in that scene. So I use instead my experience or exposure through the media, television, et cetera, to gain those experiences.

"Because police officers are exposed to real crime scenes on a daily basis, they understand the dynamics and the interactions that occur in those crimes. So when they come across a staged crime scene, it looks to be convoluted or made up to them because it doesn't have the necessary elements that they're used to seeing when they investigate certain types of crimes."

Agent Morton looked at various Helmick crime scene photographs that MCSO had taken right after the murder.

Morton commented later, "What was interesting in reviewing the scene and looking at the aerial shots was that it wasn't the first residence that you would come to. You would have to go past several other residences to target that house for a burglary.

"And there was a long driveway where you couldn't see the residence from the roadway. You'd almost have to know there was a residence back there to drive back there and find it. That would be a concern to a burglar. If I'm a burglar and I'm stealing property because I need money to do whatever I need to do with it, my concern is not being detected. Getting in as quickly as I can and exiting as quickly as I can. To limit myself to one way in and one way out—well, I can't even see if there's anybody at home. If I drive up there and there's somebody home, and I attempt to flee the residence, I'm basically pinning myself in a very difficult situation."

As far as two pickup trucks being parked in the driveway at the time of the crime, Morton stated, "Most daytime burglars are looking for an unoccupied house so they can go in and steal things. That there's vehicles parked in the driveway would almost indicate someone was there. There's better targets to choose than going into a house and taking a chance that somebody would be home."

About the photos taken by the sheriff's office of the interior of the Helmick home, Morton related, "The ransacking that took place in the residence did not appear as other burglaries I've seen. Burglars are interested in finding things quickly. They'll empty drawers out. There's no concern for neatness in how you open drawers or close drawers. When you looked at those photographs, the drawers were open, but it doesn't look like some of the contents were gone through other than there was a jewelry box in the bedroom on the dresser and its drawers were open. Even that was left on the dresser. It wasn't thrown on the bed and the drawers pulled out."

As far as the kitchen went, Morton observed, "The trash

can was knocked over. If I'm a burglar, there's no need for me to knock a trash can over and look through the trash can. People don't keep valuables there. Same thing with the home office. Valuables are kept, for the most part, in a master bedroom because it's the inner sanctum. That's where everybody keeps their valuables, guns, money, all those kinds of things."

When it came to drawers just being opened up and made to look as if they had been searched through, Morton said, "The whole idea for a real burglar is to get in and out as quickly as possible. So you search the areas where you know most people keep things that they can trade. In reviewing the crime scene report, I noticed that there was a handgun and several long guns that were not taken."

Morton noted that computers, a fax machine, and a laptop were not taken. These were all items most burglars wanted to get their hands on—especially the laptop. And as far as a pistol went, Morton stated, "It's a very good item for a burglar to steal, simply because you can sell it on the street with no strings attached. You can get a very quick turnover of money."

And when it came to the master bedroom, Morton said, "Other than the drawer on the nightstand being opened, and the jewelry box drawer being pulled out and some other drawers ajar, nothing seemed to be taken. The jewelry box was still in place on the dresser instead of drawers being pulled out and contents dumped. That was unique to me. If I was trying to steal things, what happened to those person's belongings were of no concern to me. I'm only concerned with taking things out of there and leaving as quickly as I can."

And there was the position of Alan Helmick's body as well. Morton stated, "From my experience and training, the position that he fell in . . . Well, most people, unlike on television, when you get shot, you fall in the direction of the shot. You don't get blown across a room and through windows, and all those other things they love to do. What happens is, especially with a shot like Mr. Helmick received, which would have been almost instantaneous in killing him, he falls directly back toward the direction of the shot. It would put the position of the person who did the shooting in very tight quarters near him. A very narrow position.

"The distance of the gunshot was not a contact shot, so the offender didn't have the gun at the back of his head when it was fired. For a stranger to shoot him in that position would be very unusual. It seemed to have occurred at about a two-foot range. If I was a burglar and I'm confronted by the home-owner, the easiest thing for me to do is run out the door and escape. And for the offender to literally target Mr. Helmick is not consistent with any kind of daytime burglar who's there to steal."

CHAPTER 27

AN ARREST

By the end of November 2008, investigators for MCSO had amassed an immense amount of material that put Miriam Helmick in a bad light concerning the murder of her husband, Alan. There wasn't a smoking gun found in Miriam's hands, or, for that matter, any GSR on her hands or clothing that could link her to the murder. But all the bits and pieces of evidence collected by the investigators kept pointing to only one viable suspect in Alan's death—Miriam Helmick.

On December 1, 2008, Investigator Jim Hebenstreit wrote up a probable cause warrant for the arrest of Miriam Helmick. The document was eighty-three pages long and contained incident after incident alleging the acts that Miriam Helmick had engaged in to murder her husband, Alan. The key lines at the end stated: *Based on the preceding, there is probable cause to believe that on June 10, 2008, in the county of Mesa and State of Colorado, Miriam Helmick (AKA Miriam Morgan Giles) committed the crime of Murder in the First Degree.*

Also based on the preceding, there is probable cause to believe that on April 30, 2008, in the County of Delta and

State of Colorado, Miriam Helmick committed the crime of Criminal Attempt to commit Murder in the First Degree.

As to this second charge, Hebenstreit noted that it had happened forty-one days before Alan Helmick was actually murdered. And he wrote, *Although the two crimes were committed in separate counties, they arise from the same continuing criminal episode.*

Investigator Hebenstreit wanted all of these acts charged, contending that Miriam Helmick had been trying to kill Alan all spring long to cover up the fact that she was stealing from him. She may have even tried to poison him, although that possibility was only alluded to in the document, and was not part of the charged acts.

The actual arrest of Miriam Helmick was carried out by MCSO investigators, Jacksonville Police Department (JPD) detectives, the Florida Department of Law Enforcement (FDLE), and the United States Marshals Service (USMS). It happened on December 8, 2008, in Jacksonville, Florida, and Miriam went under arrest quietly. She was taken to the Duval County Jail and was booked on first-degree murder and the other stated charges stemming from the car fire in Delta in April 2008.

In a short press release, MCSO announced, *Today, investigators with the Sheriff's Office in cooperation with the Florida Department of Law Enforcement and U.S. Marshals Service arrested Miriam Helmick for the murder of her husband, Alan Helmick. As with any on-going investigation, details which led to Miriam Helmick's arrest cannot be discussed or released at this time.*

That didn't mean that Colorado newspapers and television stations didn't try to find out as many details as possible. On December 9, the *Daily Sentinel* ran an article with the headline WOMAN ACCUSED OF KILLING HUSBAND. MCSO sheriff

Stan Hilkey wouldn't say much to the reporter other than sharing, "Miriam Helmick was a suspect right from the beginning. We're confident we've got the right person."

The reporter managed to contact Barbara Watts, and she said that she wasn't surprised when she heard about Miriam's arrest for the murder. Watts declared, "Miriam is a very, very powerful lady and she plans things very, very well and wisely. She was a dynamic woman and experienced dancer. I thought she was dynamite. She was after a hot sugar daddy. She wanted someone to take care of her."

Watts went on to say that she learned Miriam had stolen money from her, and she told Alan "watch your back." Watts added that Alan couldn't see the dark side of Miriam because he was so much in love with her.

The reporter contacted Miriam's attorney, Colleen Scissors, but Scissors made no comment. Duval County Sheriff's Office (DCSO) spokeswoman Melissa Bujeda, however, had a few things to say about the fact that Miriam's first husband had died from a gunshot wound to the head, just as Alan Helmick had. Bujeda revealed, "Mesa County Sheriff's Office investigators have discussed their case with our investigators."

Picking up on this story of Miriam's first husband being shot to death with a pistol, allegedly by his own hand, the *Florida Times-Union* ran a story headlined, TWO-TIME WIDOW HELD IN COLORADO KILLING: *Jacksonville homicide detectives reviewed the 2002 death of Miriam Helmick's first husband, Jack Giles, after learning several months ago that she was a possible suspect in a Colorado slaying. Chief Rick Graham, of the sheriff's office, will likely stay in touch with Colorado officials to see whether anything relevant to the local case turns up in their investigation.*

There were several interesting comments, in relation to this article, that readers posted on the *Florida Times-Union* Internet page. One person who had known Miriam before she had moved to Colorado commented: **Having been a former roommate of Miriam, it's not surprising at all. Always had a gut feeling she had a dark side.**

Another person wrote: **Miriam—the moll of the docks.**

The *Denver Post* ran an article, stating, *Miriam Helmick appeared in court, shackled, stooped and dressed in a high-security red jail jumpsuit.*

Even Jacksonville television station Channel 4 reported about the two dead husbands, and its news coverage noted that both men had been shot in the head. Miriam had claimed about Alan, "I came in and found him, and then it went from there. That's all I know."

Miriam soon had her first court appearance in a Florida court. Bail was set at $2 million, an amount she could not post. So she remained in jail, awaiting extradition to Colorado. And instead of fighting extradition, Miriam told the judge she looked forward to going back there to clear her name. Perhaps she was buoyed up by the fact that in all the charges brought against her in an earlier case by Barbara Watts, she had eventually been acquitted. Even the alleged burning down of her parents' house and stealing money from them had never gone to trial.

A few days later, the *Grand Junction Free Press* was still looking at the aspect of the car fire in Delta County. A reporter spoke with Mesa County assistant district attorney (ADA) Richard "Rich" Tuttle, who said, "We're alleging this [car fire] is part of the same criminal episode." Tuttle added that it didn't matter that the car fire incident had occurred in Delta County. Under Colorado law, it could be prosecuted in Mesa County, as long as it was part of the same criminal acts by Miriam Helmick to murder her husband, Alan. Tuttle contended that Miriam had been attempting to murder Alan Helmick since at least April 30, 2008. According to Tuttle, she had succeeded in doing that on June 10, 2008.

Following a different angle, the *Daily Sentinel* ran the headline DESIRE TO DANCE MAY HAVE COST MAN HIS LIFE. The article described Alan Helmick in the following way: *a natural athlete who played college baseball and had a solid golf game. Helmick was trying to get a new lease on life after his first wife, Sharon, died, said Dennis Edson, a longtime business associate and friend of Helmick in Grand Junction.*

In a prophetic turn of phrase, Edson said that one of the items on Alan's "bucket list" was to learn to dance. Of course, "bucket list" included things a person wanted to do before they "kicked the bucket."

The reporter also spoke with Barbara Watts again. Watts said, "Miriam Giles asked to be sent to Grand Junction. She begged me to send her. She was very persuasive." Barbara also said that during the time she knew Miriam in Gulfport, "I had told her not to fraternize with customers outside of class." Then she added, "It didn't take long for her to get her claws into Alan."

Another associate of Alan's had a very different take on the couple. Ken Rabideau said, "There was nothing at all to make you cast any suspicion or doubts about the relationship."

Even Dennis Edson agreed with this assessment by Rabideau. He declared, "It came as a great surprise when we found out he was murdered. He wasn't the type of guy I would have thought had enemies." In this case, the enemy wasn't someone he did business with, but rather the person who lived in his own home.

As good as her statement, Miriam Helmick did not fight extradition, and was back in a Mesa County, Colorado, courtroom by December 12, 2008. Miriam was clad in a red jail jumpsuit, which indicated that she was being held in a high-security pod at the Mesa County Jail.

In front of Judge Bruce Raaum, Miriam asked for a court-appointed defense lawyer, because she could no longer afford the services of Colleen Scissors. Miriam's bail was set once more at $2 million, which was an amount she could not raise. So Miriam stayed in the Mesa County Jail, awaiting trial.

CHAPTER 28

A WOMAN POSING AS SHARON

Even after the arrest of Miriam Helmick, the investigation against her did not cease. Investigator Jim Hebenstreit noted that he and FDLE agent Larry Perez learned that Miriam Helmick had been using identification with the name of Sharon Helmick, Alan's first wife. Searching this name at pawnshops around the Jacksonville area, Perez discovered a person claiming to be "Sharon Helmick" had pawned a necklace at Value Pawn and Jewelry on November 29, 2008. Of course, this was impossible, since Sharon Helmick had been dead for many years by then. It had to have been Miriam Helmick, using Sharon's name.

Hebenstreit and Agent Perez went to the pawnshop on Atlantic Boulevard in Jacksonville, and a transaction slip there showed a woman who had identified herself as Sharon Helmick, using a Florida driver's license. She had received $35 for a ten-karat necklace.

Looking more closely at the driver's license, Agent Perez said the numbers were not consistent with Florida driver's licenses. It had to be a fake. Later, Hebenstreit and Perez looked at surveillance video of the transaction. The woman purporting to be Sharon was actually Miriam.

The next day, Hebenstreit went with Florida agent Greg Holycross to A&B Marketing, which was a distributor of RainSoft water-conditioning products. Miriam had been working at A&B Marketing after leaving Colorado, but she was passing herself off as Sharon Helmick. Once Hebenstreit and Holycross arrived at the office, general manager Jay Toblin said that he assumed they were there to talk about Sharon. According to Toblin, several employees had seen a story in the local newspapers about the person they had known as Sharon Helmick.

The files on "Sharon Helmick" at A&B Marketing included copies of a birth certificate and Colorado driver's license. There was also a W-4 form, with the signature of Sharon Helmick. "Sharon" had written as her work history that from 1990 to 1999 she had been a receptionist/secretary for the East Slope Mortgage Company. As to why she had quit that job, she wrote: *My husband owned the business and passed away.* The application was dated September 8, 2008. The termination report at A&B Marketing was for November 21, 2008, and the reason was absenteeism/tardiness.

Investigator Hebenstreit spoke with Chris, Miriam's son, about this business enterprise. According to Chris, he thought Miriam had quit her job with A&B Marketing because she was going to move to Orlando, Florida, to work as an assistant for the company's owner, Michael Keck. Both Keck and Toblin said that was not true. In fact, they said that Miriam had not done a good job while she was employed with them at A&B Marketing. They certainly weren't going to hire her as an assistant in Orlando.

Asked by Investigator Hebenstreit if Miriam had made any friends while working at the company, Keck and Toblin said that she had often talked with a woman named Pamela Miller while on her breaks.

Meanwhile, Sergeant Henry Stoffel talked with Aline Lee, Miriam's next-door neighbor in Florida. Lee had plenty to say about Miriam. Later, Lee recalled, "Miriam was my neighbor back in 1988 when she was married to Jack Giles. She moved and I didn't see her again until August 2008. She called me out of the blue. I knew her son, Chris, and attended the same church he did. When Miriam came back, we met at a Chili's restaurant in Jacksonville.

"She told me about her husband in Colorado being murdered, and she was a widow. And she told me about the dance studio. She had moved out to Mississippi and she was in contact with someone there who set her up in a dance studio in Denver." (Lee had misunderstood and thought Miriam was in Denver, not in Grand Junction.)

"She started telling me about what she was doing on the day her husband was murdered. She said she had gone shopping and he was supposed to meet her for lunch. She kept calling him and he didn't show, so she decided to go home. And then she found him. She found him in the house. She said the house was all ransacked.

"She told me that when they were first married, how happy they were. A happy marriage. They did a lot of fun things together and had a lot in common. She said that at first she didn't date him because she didn't date students, but he pursued her. There were months before she agreed to go out on a date with him, and they just hit it off. They went sailing, liked horses, and they fell in love. She said he provided for her and took care of her. She was very, very happy. He lavished her with a nice, beautiful home and everything.

"One thing was strange when I met her at Chili's. Her hair color was black, and she'd had brown hair like mine. I'd never seen it that dark before. She just didn't look the same. She had lost a lot of weight. But it was mainly her hair color that stuck out.

"While at Chili's, I asked her point-blank if she had killed him. She said that she hadn't and there was a prenup.

Then she said that he'd been shot by a robber. She cried. Not hysterically, but she cried. She said she loved him. I thought it was all kind of strange telling me there at Chili's, but she acted like a grieving widow.

"She said that she was not allowed to live in the house after the murder. She said that the locks had been changed and the police wouldn't let her live in the house." (That, of course, was not true.) "Alan's children had changed the locks. That's what she said. She said she had been living out of her car until she got to Florida. She hadn't even been able to get any of her personal belongings out of the house. Her papers, birth certificate, or purse.

"She said that she had a driver's license and it was of Alan's previous wife. I told her, 'Miriam, you can't do that! You need to get your own driver's license.' But she said she couldn't because it was kept by the police. So I asked her, 'Were you a suspect and not supposed to leave?' And she said no. Later, at some other time, she said that she got a Georgia driver's license. She said that she didn't have to use a birth certificate there.

"Beforehand, she did say that she had a driver's license from someone who had her weight and hair color." (Actually, it was Sharon Helmick's driver's license. And that may have been why Miriam dyed her hair black upon returning to Florida.)

"Miriam said that Alan had given her a wad of money, so she had a little of that. Later I gave her money. I wrote her a check for a hundred dollars. The check was made to Chris, her son, because she had no way of cashing it. She said that the car she was driving was a gift from Alan, and that was one of the only things she had left from him.

"Miriam said that one of the daughters was causing trouble for her. They didn't get along. The daughter's name was like a car—Porsche." (The name was actually Portia, easily mistaken as the auto name by Aline.) "There was some kind of holdup with Alan's estate, and she was trying to get what belonged to her. She said that they (Portia and law enforcement) could reach her through her lawyer, and so forth. She did say that she was eventually cleared by the authorities in Colorado."

One thing that Aline thought was odd was that Miriam used a disposable cell phone. Aline recounted, "It was like a prepaid thing. It couldn't be traced. And I told her, 'Well, if they (Alan's daughters and law enforcement) tried to get ahold of you, how could they do it?' And she said that they knew she was in Florida and could contact her at her son's house. And she said she was also in contact with her lawyer."

As far as Miriam keeping up with the murder case, Aline related, "Miriam said she tried, but she couldn't get through to the authorities. That sounded odd to me."

And about Alan and his business practices, Aline recalled, "Miriam described him as an unusual businessman that didn't keep good records. She did talk about how rich he was. It was over a million dollars. But he was sick the last few months of his life. Miriam came here with just the clothes she wore. And she needed good clothes because of the job she was doing in Florida. A water softener–type thing.

"She was the size of my daughters, so I took her two big bags of clothing from them. I took 'em to Chris's house, where she was staying. And it was at that time that she was on a computer at the house. She started talking about being online with a dating service. I thought it was kind of strange, but she showed me the Web site. It was to meet someone online.

"She said she wanted a sexual partner, someone to have fun with. She said she needed a sugar daddy. She also said that she was horny and needed some sexual satisfaction and to be taken care of. She needed to let her hair down. Her exact words were that she was as 'horny as hell.'"

Aline said that Miriam showed her the ads that she was looking at. Aline observed, "She didn't have anything in common with some, and others didn't have enough money.

She wanted one with lots of money. A high income. She showed me one man from Orlando. His name was Kilpatrick." (Obviously, Aline was referencing Kirkpatrick.) "He liked horses, was a dancer, and had lots of money. He even owned a dance studio.

"She was excited about going and meeting him, but kind of nervous, too. I was very nervous for her because I didn't really think she should go there, because it's kind of scary the way the world is now. She had never met him in person, and she was going down there. To her son, she said she was going for a job interview. A personal assistant–type job.

"And I talked to her on the phone when she was actually at the restaurant with this man. He went to the bathroom, and Miriam told me that everything was great. He was awesome. He was a gentleman and everything was wonderful.

"I even talked to her on the phone a day later. To make sure she was all right. She was at his place, and said everything was fine. She said he was everything she dreamed of. She was very impressed with him."

Jim Hebenstreit did more investigation on Miriam Helmick while he was in Florida. Hebenstreit discovered that Miriam had the cell phone number of a man named Chuck. Hebenstreit contacted Chuck and asked if he knew a woman from Colorado who had run a dance studio and had a horse training center. The name Miriam didn't mean anything to Chuck, but the description of a dark-haired woman, answering to the name Sharon, did. She had contacted him on a Web site titled MillionaireMatch.com. In fact, "Chuck" was Charles Kirkpatrick.

Chuck said that he had met "Sharon," and she had even stayed at his apartment for a couple of days in December 2008. Chuck said that she made it clear that she was very interested in starting a relationship with him and wanted to relocate to Orlando. "She was pretty aggressive about this move, and that was a turnoff to me," Chuck said.

Hebenstreit asked if Sharon had mentioned a husband dying in Colorado. Chuck said that she had mentioned something about it. And Chuck could not remember Sharon ever telling him her last name. Asked about his financial situation, Chuck said that he was a business owner and had sold two companies in the previous year. One of the businesses he sold was an Arthur Murray dance studio, and he was well-off financially. After Sharon's insistence about moving to Orlando, he'd had little contact with her. They had only exchanged e-mails from that point forward.

The next day, Chuck phoned Investigator Hebenstreit and said he did remember on one occasion that Sharon told him that her husband had died. She told him that her spouse had died from a brain tumor. It was interesting to Hebenstreit that Sharon didn't say her husband had died from a heart attack, cancer, or something else. According to her, he had died from something to do with his head—the exact place where Alan had been shot.

Hebenstreit asked if Sharon had said how long in the past it had been that her husband had died. According to Chuck, Sharon said it was about six months previously. That would have put it in the summer of 2008, the time when Alan had died. Chuck asked Sharon if it was okay with her that she was out dating so soon, since not that much time had passed since her husband had died. She told him it was okay, because her husband had been sick for a long time before dying.

Hebenstreit asked Chuck, "Did you and Sharon have intimate relations when she spent the night?"

Chuck replied, "Yes, we did."

Meanwhile, back in Grand Junction, Colorado, Miriam and her defense lawyer, Steve Colvin, waived her right to a preliminary hearing within the next thirty days. And the local newspapers learned just exactly what the arrest warrant contained. One of the notations by an investigator was that even though Alan Helmick's body was lying on the kitchen floor next to a .25-caliber shell casing and a wallet, the residence was not greatly disturbed. There were a few desk drawers opened in an adjoining room and an overturned wastebasket. But as the investigator wrote, *None of the drawers were on the floor and nothing else appeared disturbed.* To the investigator, it was not the usual burglary scene, where many rooms are usually ransacked.

Mesa County pathologist Dr. Robert Kurtzman had also stated an opinion on this matter. He had told the investigators, "We should proceed under the assumption that this was a homicide, based on the scene and condition of the body." Kurtzman did not believe that it was a suicide.

The reporters were also able to track down an inconsistency in Miriam's statements. She had told investigators that Alan had been too drunk, after coming home from the Elks Lodge in Delta, to speak on the phone to his daughter, Portia, on the evening before his murder. Bartenders at the Elks Lodge stated that Alan hadn't been there in four or five months, and a toxicology report after Alan was deceased proved that there was no alcohol in his system.

The newspapers related further about Miriam forging Alan's checks and keeping all bank representatives from contacting him. They also went into the matter about the greeting card found under the doormat, which stated that Miriam had better run, or she would be next. And, of course, Miriam had bought that card at a local market.

There was a lot of circumstantial evidence against Miriam, but even the affidavit admitted that no gun had been found. Instead, there was a paragraph stating: *Alan Helmick likely owned a .25 caliber pistol which could have fired that bullet that killed him. A handgun hasn't been recovered in the investigation.*

CHAPTER 29

EXPERTISE

There was a lot of circumstantial evidence that Miriam had murdered Alan Helmick to cover up the fact that she had been forging his checks and raiding his bank accounts, but there was no concrete evidence that she had murdered him. No confession, no videotape of the act, no gunshot residue traced to her, not even a murder weapon. The prosecution was going to have to convince twelve jurors that she had committed first-degree murder for financial gain. And to do so, they were going to have to convince the same jurors that their list of expert witnesses knew exactly what they were talking about.

To this end, the prosecutors started collecting a list of some of the best in the business. They began with criminal investigator personnel, not unlike the types made so recognizable on the popular television show *CSI*. One of these was Cynthia Kramer, of the Colorado Department of Public Safety (CDPS). Her main discipline was forensic biology, which dealt with DNA and blood, and she was also a Combined DNA Index System (CODIS) administrator. On her path to being a Level II investigator, Kramer's education included a Bachelor of Science in biochemistry from Colorado State University in 1996, and graduate credits in molecular, cellular and developmental endocrinology from the University of Colorado in 1999.

Kramer's list of seminars and training had also been vast and varied: everything from Gene Mapper Training, to Shooting Scene Investigation and Reconstruction, to Bloodstain Pattern Analysis. She'd attended national conferences at the FBI on six occasions and had testified in more than a dozen major trials in Colorado.

Shawn West, of CDPS, was just as educated and trained in his field, which mainly dealt with controlled substances. West had received a Bachelor of Science at the University of Colorado and a Master of Science in forensic science–criminalistics from the University of Central Oklahoma. While his main area of expertise dealt with drugs, both legal and illegal, West also had attended various training conferences. These were as disparate as Fire Debris Analysis Training, Gunshot Residue Analysis, Microscopic Hair Analysis, and Fire Debris Analysis. He'd even taken a course called "How Not to Bomb in Court." In other words, how to stand up to grilling by a defense attorney.

Just as qualified was Barry Shearer, of CDPS. And Shearer was the most international of the lot. Shearer had received a Bachelor of Science in chemistry at the University of Leicester in England and a Master of Science at King's College London. Shearer's training had included everything from Secondary and Tertiary Glass Transfer to Use of Statistics in Forensic Science. Shearer had been an expert witness over thirty times in state and federal courts.

Covering the area of hair, fibers, and biological residue for CDPS would be Sheri Murphy. She had a Bachelor of Science from Phillips University and extensive training in Fiber Analysis, Gene Mapping, Hair Analysis and even something called Clandestine Labs Syntheses. For courtroom experience, she wrote down on her reference sheet: *Testified numerous times in several district courts in the states of Oklahoma, Kansas and Colorado in the areas of controlled dangerous substances, serology, hairs and fibers and trace evidence.*

The prosecution was going to be covering a lot of bases in the upcoming trial, not just with physical evidence but with psychological profiling as well. And one part of that angle was going to be Special Agent Robert Morton, of the National Center for the Analysis of Violent Crime. As Morton noted in his reference: *NCAVC serves as a resource for federal, state and local law enforcement officials in the investigation of bizarre, unusual and repetitive crimes, including serial murder, homicide cases, child abductions, kidnappings and terrorism.* Morton noted that he had been consulted by law enforcement agencies in hundreds of these types of cases.

Agent Morton stated that he was actively involved with research on serial murder and sexually motivated homicides. He was also the primary editor on the FBI Serial Murder Monograph. By 2009, he'd been a senior crime scene analyst for over ten years.

Even a criminal investigator from the United States Army Criminal Investigation Laboratory (USACIL) was going to be called upon. This was Shauna Steffan, who was a physical scientist with a Master of Science in forensic sciences from the University of New Haven, in Connecticut. Steffan was skilled in Evidence Photography, Crime Scene Reconstruction and Fingerprint Identification. She had even taught courses in Crime Scene Search and Preservation for the Colorado Bureau of Investigation.

The most exotic and specialized member of the group was Lieutenant Tracy Harpster, of the Moraine Police Department (Moraine PD) in Ohio. Harpster specialized in 911 homicide calls. In that capacity, Harpster taught courses to law enforcement agencies around the country about people calling 911 and reporting incidents as robberies and suicides— when, in actuality, the person calling in had committed homicide. And that is exactly what the prosecution was alleging with Miriam Helmick. Harpster had even been published on this subject, with titles such as "The Nature of 911 Homicide Calls to Identify Indicators of Innocence and Guilt" and "Is the Caller a Killer?"

MCSO had recently dealt with the Michael Blagg case, where Michael called a 911 operator about a supposed home invasion when he returned home from work and found his wife and daughter missing. As with Miriam's call to a 911 operator, Michael did not act like the usual person who was faced with similar circumstances. There were times he seemed to be acting.

And of the supposed robbery in the Blagg home, it was determined that Michael Blagg had pretended that a break-in had occurred and his wife and daughter ended up missing. Blagg, however, did not know how to stage a robbery to make it look convincing. As far as the prosecution in Miriam's case went, they believed the same thing had occurred at the Helmick residence in Whitewater. They conjectured that Miriam had opened a few drawers, got rid of a few pieces of jewelry, and knocked over a wastepaper basket.

Just what Miriam's state of mind was in 2009 as she went through the pretrial process was best ascertained by a recorded phone call she made. It was to her brother in Florida. A recorded voice came on the line stating, "Hello, this is a collect call from Miriam, an inmate at Mesa County Jail. This call is subject to recording and monitoring."

Miriam asked how her brother was, and he said he was doing fine. Then Miriam said that she was sorry it was so late at night, Florida time, but it was the only time she was able to make a phone call. Miriam began by saying, "I wanted to let you know that we had our pretrial hearing yesterday. And *48 Hours* was there. They're doing something on Sunday. It looks really, really, really bad [about me]. But it's not really bad (what's occurring in court). In fact, we're optimistic."

To all of Miriam's conversation, her brother barely said a word, except to say "Um-hmm," or "Okay." Miriam went on, "We're extremely optimistic because my attorney said something about me leaving here (jail) by Christmas. Our trial's not until November. We put it off to November because there's some work we have to do. The main thing that we did Friday was to do fact-finding, which we really did well. There's a lot to be desired from the sheriff's office here.

"I wanted you to see if you can call Chris and let him know there's nothing I can do about *48 Hours* doing this thing. It's ugly! And there's some stuff in there you would not believe! We're still trying to figure out . . . Well, it sounds worse than it is. And, um, we can't tip our hand.

"I can say, they (*48 Hours*) did ask the detective when they first started looking at me. And he pretty much said they never looked at anyone else. Part of the evidence—they (Miriam's defense team) are going to try to get thrown out. There were things that really made my attorney optimistic. He told me, 'Don't read the newspaper.' It will just depress me. 'I want you to stay focused. We have a lot of work to do. And, hopefully, you'll be out of here by Christmas.'"

Miriam wondered if the *48 Hours* segment would not be on until her brother and his family got out of church on Sunday evening. He thought it would still be on when they returned home.

Miriam continued, "The way they brought it (the story) out, well, because we didn't do objections, they were able to bring it out any way they wanted. I was furious. I wanted to jump up and down! But my lawyers told me to have a poker face the whole time."

Her brother said one of the people on Miriam's defense team had called him, and that it was a woman. Miriam replied, "Yeah, she's really a sweet lady. She's a good detective. She's the [attorney's] investigator. I'll put it this way. I can tell you that Portia got on the stand and lied." (This had happened at a pretrial hearing.)

Then Miriam was very excited about the next bit of news. "The gunshot residue test came back. Nothing! Absolutely nothing! So they can't place me there (at the murder scene). I'm only telling you stuff that can be verified. Our neighbor saw Alan out at the barn at eight A.M. I was gone by eight-thirty."

Her brother said he'd heard it was a weak case, and Miriam replied, "It's a very weak case. After Friday's hearing, I was walking on air. When the newspaper came out with a story—it still couldn't pull me down.

"I need to do more outside exercise. Keep my muscles in shape. When I leave here, I don't want to be an old woman. Anyway, I've decided I'm going to take advantage of this *48 Hours* thing. Whoever the highest bidder is, I'll give them an interview at the end, and that [money] will go to Mother and Daddy. And then I'll write whatever I need to write, book-wise or whatever. And that goes to paying back everybody that needs to be paid. And giving Chris school money."

Miriam then said, "They (the police) wouldn't give me back my ID. I couldn't apply for welfare or Social Security or even get an old 401(k). I couldn't get my driver's license."

And then switching gears very quickly, she declared, "They (Miriam's lawyers) are going to put me on the stand. Because they say a lot of the things have to be explained. And they figure I'm the one to explain them, because I'm the one who knows them best."

After that, her brother and Miriam talked for a while about his children. But Miriam really wanted to get back to what concerned her most, her present situation. "If Chris watches, or anybody watches . . . I'm really concerned about what he would see [on the show] and what he would say. I just want to get this over with."

Once again, her brother said that the Mesa County detective who came to Florida did not impress him. Miriam chimed in and said, "Well, they haven't impressed me, either."

Her brother added that a detective wanted to meet him at work to talk about Miriam. He finally said that they could meet for lunch near his place of work. He waited fifteen minutes there, at the appointed time, and then the detective said that he couldn't make it. The detective called and said he had been detained. Miriam's brother thought this attitude was very unprofessional.

Miriam replied, "I know what you're talking about. He's the one who . . . Well, we've had some interesting dealings with him."

Miriam's brother may not have been impressed with the MCSO detectives, and Miriam was unimpressed as well. They might have been more impressed, however, if they'd known just how hard the detectives had been working on the case, and how much information they already had.

CHAPTER 30

A MOVIE AND A CAR FIRE

By the time of Miriam's second phone call to her brother from the Mesa County Jail, she was not as optimistic as she had been on the first phone call. And once again, Miriam did most of the talking. She began by saying, "Sorry I didn't call earlier. Have you kept in touch with my attorney?"

Her brother replied that he hadn't talked to Steve Colvin in a while. Miriam continued, "Things are sort of happening here. We have a bunch of motions coming up and I wrote you about the Barbara Watts thing. And well . . . nobody has ever read me my rights. Not ever in Florida. So anything they got during that time can't be used." (This allegation of a Miranda violation was according to Miriam.)

"And, um, going back to the situation in Delta, the fibers they were trying to hang me on didn't match. Nothing of the tests they've done have come back their way. I didn't think they would." (Perhaps there had been some clothing fibers near the wick, which Miriam was referencing.)

Her brother said, "Well, you've got to jump through hoops."

Miriam agreed, and then replied, "The wheels of justice don't move fast like you see on TV. But my attorney seems to be very pleased with the motions. *Nightline* has been in contact with me. Because they're getting things they know are wrong. Delta didn't have a case (against me) because Alan told them I was with him the whole time. They conjured up their stuff.

"I'm starting my second novel. That's the honest truth." Miriam laughed aloud. "I've always wanted to write. When they didn't replace the books here after five months . . . I read every single one of them about four times. Finally I did what I should have done when I was younger. Sit down and write my own novel. I did it. And it was fun. I mean there's more to be done. Editing and things like that. It was written by hand, so it needs to be typed up.

"It kept me busy for a month. And I've got even more months before, well, dismissing this thing. Because when they arrested me . . . The minute they thought I was a suspect, and started digging through garbage cans . . . Well, that's why they considered me a suspect.

"Even when Chris was there, they lied to me and told me they wanted me to give them some stuff. The autopsy report showed Alan had such bad heart disease . . . but the family tried to get me for poisoning. The autopsy showed that his heart was so bad he shouldn't have been alive. But they arrested me on that one, anyway." (Miriam was referring to the poisoning charge.) "That was part of their arrest warrant. Smells fishy, doesn't it?"

Her brother asked, "If they did everything bogus, do you have the right to sue them?"

Miriam responded, "Oh, I've already got that started. I can use the attorneys here or I can use the ACLU. Because they held my driver's license, birth certificate, everything that I had that defined me as a citizen. They held those and wouldn't give them back to me, even after repeated requests.

"So I had to go to other means. When I went to Florida, I couldn't get a license. And I couldn't get a copy of my birth certificate because I didn't have any valid ID. And they were strict about it, because I wanted Chris to go get it. And I called them, and they said he couldn't. It had to be me, or it had to be an attorney who had a copy of my valid ID. Which wasn't happening!

"I went through all the boxes in the storage facility to see if I could find anything." (This was possibly in Jacksonville, Florida.) "And I was about to send off for a certified copy of my driver's license when they arrested me. There's a lot of fishy stuff!"

Then Miriam and her brother talked about his family for a while, especially his kids' activities, but she was clearly eager to get back to her current travails.

Miriam said, "My attorney told Chris if he ever had any messages for me to e-mail them, so I would get them. But he never did. But I'm glad he's doing okay. I just wanted to let you know what's going on here. Actually, I hardly know what's going on except what I read in the newspaper."

Her brother said, "I figure it will all work out okay."

Miriam laughed and said, "Well, you're not the one sittin' here."

He agreed about that.

Miriam added, "I wouldn't wish it on anybody, but I think it will be all right. I think that the biggest thing is, I never said a word to anybody about anything. The DA doesn't have enough stuff. They didn't even turn on Alan's computer to see that he didn't have Internet access for two months. He'd been using mine for everything." (This statement carried the implication that Alan had looked up about lethal doses of medication on the Internet.)

Miriam then asked, "Did you see Daddy?" Her brother said that he had done so the previous night. Miriam added, "Tell him . . . Well, don't tell him anything. I'm not allowed to communicate with him."

Truly surprised at this, her brother asked, "Why's that?"

Miriam answered, "Because he's on the DA's witness list."

"Oh, really!" her brother responded.

Miriam replied, "I found out about it through the newspaper here, but I don't know if it's true. Well, whether I get out of here or not, I want to write the book. Bye."

It wasn't until May 2009 that a preliminary hearing was held in the Mesa County District Court as to whether there was enough evidence to go to trial. ADA Rich Tuttle questioned witnesses, presented photos, financial statements, and CBI evidence. Miriam's defense lawyers cross-examined the witnesses, but they did not reveal what their upcoming arguments would be.

Outside the courtroom, Tuttle told a reporter for Channel 11 News, "It's really a kind of one-sided show, where the prosecution has the burden of making a standard, and that's what the judge will rule on is whether we have put on sufficient evidence for the case to go to a jury trial."

Most of the evidence Tuttle presented was already notated in investigators' reports, but a few new things did crop up. One was that an autopsy report showed that Alan Helmick died of a gunshot wound to the head sometime between 3:15 A.M. and 12:15 P.M. on June 10, 2008. If he had been murdered at any time before Miriam left the house, supposedly around eight in the morning, then, of course, she must have been the shooter. If it occurred after she left, then there must have been another gunman, as she and her attorneys claimed. That the autopsy report could not pin down the time in a more exact manner left this question wide open.

As far as the gunshot residue test went, there had been no GSR on Miriam's hands, body, or clothing, but there had been a small particle of GSR on the steering wheel of the car she had been driving on June 10, 2008. The prosecution declared this was proof that she had fired a gun on the morning of June 10.

The defense claimed anyone could have fired a gun and then touched the steering wheel of the car. Or Miriam could have fired a gun preceding Alan's death, and it would have nothing to do with his murder.

And for the first time, MCSO investigators revealed there had been one other suspect that they had looked at in the investigation. It was an individual who was an acquaintance of Miriam's who lived in Boulder, Colorado. Investigators testified that this person had an alibi and was cleared of being a suspect. Just who that person was, they did not say.

Another interesting twist to the case was a contention by MCSO investigators that someone in the Helmick home on April 26, 2008, had rented the movie *No Country for Old Men*. Tuttle stated, "The movie, rented via Dish Network, includes a scene in which actor Javier Bardem's character places an article of clothing in the gas tank of a car, lights it, and walks away into a pharmacy before the car explodes."

Then Tuttle pointed out that four days after that movie rental, a rope-type wick was placed into the gas tank of a car Alan Helmick was sitting in, and the wick was set on fire. That the car didn't explode was a miracle. And the main suspect in that car fire was Miriam Helmick. Less than two months after the car fire incident, Alan Helmick was shot to death in his own home.

In the end, district judge Valerie Robison ruled that there was enough evidence to go forward to a jury trial.

A few days later, Judge Robison was asked to make a ruling on whether evidence about the death of Miriam's first husband, Jack Giles, would be heard by jurors in the upcoming trial.

ADA Tuttle contended that the death of Jack Giles was not a suicide, but rather was an instance of where Miriam had shot him to death and then made it look like a suicide.

Hebenstreit noted that Jack Giles was left-handed, but he was found clutching a revolver in his right hand, with his arm lying across his chest. Jack's right thumb was in the gun's trigger guard.

Tuttle added to the judge, "According to law enforcement authorities who routinely investigate suicides, this is an extremely unorthodox, if not extremely difficult, way to commit suicide."

Judge Robison, however, responded, "Little, if anything, other than argument has been presented to indicate the defendant (Miriam Helmick) may have contributed to the death of Mr. Giles, or as asserted by the people that she murdered Jack Giles. Based upon all the evidence before the court, the court does not find by preponderance of the evidence that Mr. Giles was murdered and that the defendant committed the crime."

The jury in the upcoming trial for the murder of Alan Helmick would not hear anything about the death of Miriam's first husband, Jack.

By November 9, 2009, both the prosecution and the defense began questioning potential jurors. The parking lot across the street was filled with vehicles of the more than four hundred potential jurors who were going through voir dire. Security was tight, as court officers escorted the potential jurors through the security area and on to elevators to the actual courtroom. And as the *Daily Sentinel* noted, *Nearly all of the hundreds of jurors have heard at least snippets, either through news reports or gossipy chatter among neighbors, about the allegations against 52-year-old Miriam Helmick of Whitewater.*

The *Daily Sentinel* related that this was the area's biggest trial since Michael Blagg had been found guilty of murdering his wife, Jennifer, in 2004. Blagg had received a life sentence in that trial.

Some of the questions asked of potential jurors, who had made the first cut, were about whether they had heard anything new about the case over the previous week, and whether it would be too much of a hardship to sit on a jury for four to five weeks. Another question was whether they could put out of their minds anything they had heard or read about the case, and only base their decisions on what evidence was presented in an actual trial.

Steve Colvin, the office head of the Grand Junction branch of the Colorado State Public Defenders, asked one prospective juror about the fact that she'd heard about the death of Jack Giles. Could she put that out of her mind in basing decisions, because no evidence was going to be coming into trial about Jack Giles?

Another problem for both the prosecution and the defense was that the Grand Junction area still had a small-town feel to it, and many of the people either knew Alan Helmick, Miriam Helmick, or someone connected to the case. One prospective juror remembered Alan Helmick when he was a teenager. Another prospective juror worked at the Whitewater Post Office and heard all the talk about the murder case. Steve Colvin asked this prospective juror, "That (the murder) doesn't happen every day, right?" The person replied, "Not in Whitewater!"

Finally, by November 10, 2009, a jury was impaneled for the upcoming trial. The jury was made up of ten men and six women, four of them being alternates. And one more detail was learned. Judge Valerie Robison ruled that Miriam Helmick would *not* be wearing cosmetics during the trial. This was because the sheriff's office had noted that eyeliner pencils and cosmetics were considered to be contraband in the jail where Miriam resided.

CHAPTER 31

A PATH OF GREED AND LONELINESS

Chief Deputy District Attorney (DDA) Tammy Eret had been an important component in the Michael Blagg trial of 2004. Now she was once again in a murder trial that had some similar characteristics of one spouse allegedly killing another, and trying to make it look like a burglary gone bad.

Eret began opening statements by telling the jurors that at the end of 2007, Alan and Miriam Helmick sat down with a life insurance agent. Alan wasn't enthused about the idea, but in Eret's words, "Miriam was raring to go." Miriam later wanted the life insurance policy upped to a million dollars, but the limit for Alan was $250,000.

Wanting to implement that amount, the life insurance agent wrote and called Alan Helmick. Alan returned no messages, but Miriam did. She asked the agent, "Can we do this without him?" The agent said that would not be possible.

Alan Helmick eventually did take out a $25,000 life insurance policy, and Eret noted that six days after Alan's murder, Miriam called the agent and asked how she could cash in that amount. The agent told Miriam that she couldn't do so, because several monthly payments had been missed by Alan during the spring of 2008. And Eret contended that Alan missed those payments because Miriam was keeping all messages and mail from him.

Eret claimed that Miriam kept Alan isolated from friends and family for months, because she was raiding his bank accounts at an alarming rate. According to Eret, when Alan found out about this, Miriam murdered him and tried to make it look like a robbery gone bad. Eret declared, "When someone on the path to loneliness crosses paths with greed, the results are devastating!"

Eret also told the jurors that when Miriam's desk at her business, Dance Junction, was searched, stacks of bills addressed to Alan were inside a drawer there, unopened. "She kept his phone. She refused to pass on phone messages to him, and she did everything to cover up her theft and forgery."

Deputy public defender Jody McGuirk, of course, had a very different take about what had occurred in the Helmick household. McGuirk said that investigators ignored a series of leads, including a white pickup truck spotted on several occasions in the Helmicks' neighborhood. McGuirk also said that two individuals, dressed in black, were spotted in the area at 6:00 A.M. on June 10, 2008—the same morning that Alan Helmick was shot to death.

McGuirk said that none of the other leads mattered to the investigators, because they'd already made up their minds that Miriam had murdered her husband. "From the get-go, she was treated like a suspect and not a victim." In essence, McGuirk said, the investigators only collected evidence that would help what they believed had happened, and they ignored evidence if it veered off from that premise.

McGuirk did admit to the jurors that Miriam had made a "horrible error in judgment" when she purchased a greeting card and wrote on it: *Allen was first. Your next. Run, run, run.*

The deputy public defender said that Miriam had done so because no investigator was taking her seriously about mysterious things occurring at her home after Alan's murder. And no investigator would take her seriously about the white pickup truck. According to McGuirk, the reason they didn't was that they only wanted the pieces that fit into what they wanted to believe about Miriam being the prime suspect.

Actual testimony and admission of evidence began with the prosecution showing the jurors a series of photos of the crime scene at the Helmick home. Many of the photos were of Alan Helmick lying on the floor, with a pool of blood at the back of his head. Several drawers were open and a wastebasket was pushed over, but nothing else seemed to be disturbed. One photo after another depicted expensive items still untouched in the home.

Then the eighteen-minute 911 tape was played as Miriam spoke with the emergency operator. While the audiotape was played to jurors, Miriam sat at the defense table, dabbing her eyes with a tissue.

Deputy John Brownlee, the first law enforcement officer to arrive on scene on June 10, 2008, took the stand for the prosecution. On direct, he spoke of the things he had seen and how Miriam had acted when he got there. All of this went fairly smoothly until the subject of how Josh Vigil acted that day, as opposed to the reaction of Miriam Helmick, commenced. Steve Colvin asked Judge Robison for a sidebar, which was granted.

Out of the hearing of jurors, Colvin said, "I'm objecting to this witness (Brownlee) offering lay opinion testimony." In other words, Colvin was saying that Deputy Brownlee was not an expert witness on how someone should react when they found out that someone they knew had been murdered.

Tammy Eret responded, "I would say that this evidence is proper."

Judge Robison decided that the objection was overruled and Brownlee could state his opinion about how he viewed Josh Vigil's reaction and Miriam Helmick's reaction.

Eret questioned Brownlee, saying, "So Josh Vigil fell within the part of being very upset and crying?"

Brownlee responded, "Yes, ma'am."

"What about the defendant? Did she fall within either one of these categories?" (The two categories were considered to be visibly very upset or noticeably not responsive.)

Brownlee said, "No, she did not. It was strange to me that she wasn't like most people would react. When I asked her to leave the house, she went outside with Deputy Quigley. She didn't ask why or make any protest."

"Did she ask anything to you about whether you were going to do CPR or anything to save her husband?"

"No, ma'am. She never did."

Eret wanted to know more about people who were non-responsive during an incident like what had occurred at the Helmick residence.

Deputy Brownlee replied, "They just shut pretty much completely down. You have to help them up because they're not able to get up. They just kinda shut their bodies down."

"When you looked around, were there any types of rags or washcloths or towels around the body to help clean some blood off or anything like that?"

"Not that I saw."

Steve Colvin, on cross-examination, got Deputy Brownlee to admit that when he first entered the house, and saw a male lying on the kitchen floor, he knew there was a serious situation. And to be on the safe side, Brownlee searched the house until Deputy Pennay arrived. At that point, Brownlee returned to Miriam and Alan Helmick.

Colvin asked, "How long had you been in the house until you touched Alan Helmick to feel for a pulse?"

Brownlee answered, "It was about five minutes. He was cold to the touch and had no pulse."

Brownlee agreed with Colvin that, in his opinion, Alan Helmick was already dead. For that reason, neither he nor Deputy Pennay did not do any CPR. Colvin wondered why Miriam should have done any CPR on a dead man, since she had already told the 911 operator that Alan was dead. Brownlee said it was his understanding that Miriam had told the 911 operator that she was trying CPR.

Colvin asked, "And when you saw the bullet casing on the floor, you knew that it was a crime scene, correct?"

Brownlee said that was so. And he also agreed with Colvin that he'd stayed at the Helmicks' house for nearly six hours that day. Much of the time, he spent outside, maintaining security of the perimeter.

Colvin asked if Brownlee had put into his report of June 10, 2008, anything about his thoughts concerning the way Miriam Helmick had acted. Brownlee said that he had not. It wasn't until his next report, thirty-six hours after he first arrived on scene, that he noted how he felt Miriam Helmick's behavior was strange.

Colvin then asked how many death scenes he'd been to. Brownlee said about fifty. Wanting to know how many of those had been suicides, Brownlee answered ten to fifteen. Others had been accidents and natural deaths. When asked how many homicides Brownlee had been to, he admitted that the one at the Helmick house was his first.

Colvin queried, "Are you a trained psychologist?"

Brownlee replied, "No, I am not."

"Are you trained in grieving processes or post-traumatic stress disorder or any of those psychological processes?"

"We have some basic classes, but nothing classroom oriented or anything like that."

Brownlee did add that he'd taken training at the police academy and had follow-up courses on how to deal with people in traumatic situations. These included everything from traffic accidents to actual homicide.

Colvin asked, "You recall from training that the first thing they teach you about dealing with a traumatic event is that everyone acts differently, right?"

Brownlee answered that was true.

"When you first went there, she was not a suspect, right?"

"No, sir."

"She's a victim?"

"Yes, sir."

"Because if you thought of her as a suspect, you wouldn't have gone to clear the house and left her alone with Mr. Helmick, right?"

"Correct, sir."

"Certainly wouldn't have been turning your back on her, right?"

"Yes, sir."

"So, at what point did she shift out of that victim role for you?"

"It was later on in the investigation that it changed."

Colvin noted that Deputy Brownlee had testified on direct that he hadn't heard Miriam crying while he was clearing the house. Colvin asked, "How loud is it that spouses have to cry when you're not with them?"

Brownlee responded, "I'm not stating that they have to cry a certain amount. When I was nearby at the laundry room, I couldn't hear any crying."

"How many homicides have you investigated?"

"This was my first, sir."

"Of all the cases, when it's clear the person was deceased, someone always says to you, 'Did you get a pulse?'"

"Not always. But I did find it weird with the no sobbing and those kinds of things. So I put it into the report."

"She didn't ask a bunch of questions. She just did what she was told. That's suspicious?"

"In my training and experience, it was."

"Okay, so of those who are not catatonic, all of the rest of them ask questions?"

"I'd have to say probably ninety percent of them do."

"But again, you agree that you're not an expert in the field of grieving people?"

"Yes, sir."

Tammy Eret took her turn again on redirect. She asked Deputy Brownlee if he was taught to evaluate scenes and take notes about things that were out of the ordinary. He said that was so.

Asked about Miriam crying, Brownlee said that she was sobbing when he first made contact with her. However, when he searched the other parts of the house, he couldn't hear any more sobs. And that's why he put that in his report.

In a somewhat unusual circumstance, after the attorneys were done, Judge Robison related to Deputy Brownlee questions that jurors had written down. One such question: *Did a supervisor review your first report before you wrote your second report?*

Brownlee responded, "I'm not positive if it was reviewed before or after the second report. Most of the time, it would have been after the first."

Another juror question: *Based on your observations, was the defendant in shock?*

Brownlee answered, "I don't believe so. That's why I wrote the part about her not crying, and those sorts of things."

A third question: *Was she sent to the hospital?*

Brownlee replied, "No, she was not."

CHAPTER 32

TIME OF DEATH

Robert Kurtzman testified to what he had seen when he was at the Helmicks' residence on June 10, 2008, and what he had observed during the autopsy of Alan Helmick. One important question Richard Tuttle wanted to get at was Dr. Kurtzman's toxicology report. In it, Kurtzman had noted that there was no alcohol in Alan Helmick's system. This was at variance with Miriam Helmick claiming that Alan had come home drunk from the Elks Lodge in Delta, on the afternoon of June 9, 2008.

Tuttle asked, "If Mr. Helmick had been drunk the night before, let's say very intoxicated, would you expect to see some evidence of that in his urine as part of toxicology examination?"

Kurtzman replied, "There would be a good possibility. It would depend on the amount of alcohol in Mr. Helmick's system. If Mr. Helmick had consumed alcohol the night before, he would have to have had a level of alcohol sufficiently high enough to register."

Then Tuttle wanted to know about a very important question: Could a forensic pathologist nail down a very specific time when death had occurred? To this, Kurtzman said, "Unfortunately, no. On TV programs, they say when a person dies. But in reality, you can't do that unless a person happens to be hooked up on a monitor and you're evaluating the transition from life to death. We can only give general estimates."

Tuttle wanted to know what Kurtzman looked at in determining a time of death range. Kurtzman responded, "One of the things I look for is what's called lividity and rigidity. Lividity is the pooling of the blood that occurs after a person has passed away. When a person's heart stops beating, the blood doesn't circulate through the skin. When a person dies, the blood will gravitate toward the most dependent portions of the body—in the particular instance with Mr. Helmick toward the back.

"And the blood is liquid for a period of time. As that time gets longer, what happens is that there's water lost from the body, and different types of proteins in the blood congeal. When I evaluated Mr. Helmick at the residence at three-fifteen P.M. on June 10, 2008, his lividity was not fixed, so that typically would be in less than twelve hours.

"The other thing we look for is rigidity. Rigidity is the stiffening of the muscles after death. The muscles don't typically become fully stiffened throughout the body for about twelve hours. And when I evaluated Mr. Helmick at the scene, he did not have well-developed rigidity. The earliest time of his death would have been around three-fifteen A.M."

Tuttle asked, "If the first responding deputy arrived on the scene at around twelve noon and noted some rigidity in the body, how would that affect your assessment?"

Kurtzman responded, "Typically, rigidity takes a while to develop. It's usually a few hours before it becomes readily apparent."

"Eight o'clock A.M.?"

"Certainly."

"Eight-thirty A.M.?"

"Certainly."

Then Tuttle asked if Alan Helmick could have been killed around 10:00 A.M. Kurtzman said that was unlikely. As far as gunshot residue testing went, Dr. Kurtzman hadn't done the actual test. Law enforcement had done that, but he had collected samples of GSR from Alan Helmick.

When it came to Alan Helmick's heart condition, Kurtzman said, "He had severe coronary artery disease. He also had an older heart attack that had occurred weeks, possibly months, prior to the time that the death occurred." This may have been why Alan had been so sick and weak during the spring of 2008.

As far as Alan possibly being poisoned by Miriam in the months preceding his death, Dr. Kurtzman stated, "I feel confident that Mr. Helmick was not poisoned. It was actually remarkable that Mr. Helmick was even alive with his heart condition at the time he sustained the gunshot wound. The vast majority of individuals who had the severe coronary artery disease and heart attack, [which] he had, typically would have perished long before."

This was a new wrinkle. If Miriam Helmick had not shot Alan in the back of the head on June 10, 2008, as the prosecution contended—and she had been patient, instead—another heart attack might have ended Alan's life.

Perhaps this was not the way Tuttle wished things were going in reference to the poisoning. He said, "Are you positive that if the poisoning had taken place, to whatever degree, several months earlier that it would have dissipated entirely, or would you still see evidence of it, even if it was months earlier?"

Kurtzman replied, "It would just depend on what type of poison. When you talk poison, there's lots and lots of different compounds that can be used as poisons. If we were looking at heavy metal poisons, like arsenic, lead, mercury, or Valium, things of that sort, those are very, very toxic compounds and they will lead to physical findings or symptoms in some way. Therapeutic drugs or illicit drugs that can be administered to a person, those types of drugs have a half-life. In other words, a time period [in] which the body eliminates them if the person survives. In theory, they may be completely eliminated if the person doesn't succumb to their effects. So it is possible that he was administered some drugs or something with the intent of taking his life. It's possible. Would I detect anything or everything that could have been used? No, I wouldn't."

Now Tuttle had the answer he wanted to hear, and said, "No more questions."

Steve Colvin had plenty of questions, however. And the main thing he wanted to blow out of the water was the theory about Alan Helmick being poisoned. Dr. Kurtzman agreed with Colvin that Alan had severe blockage of his arteries, and that in January and February 2008, he probably would have been feeling sick and weak.

Colvin asked if Dr. Kurtzman had seen any type of poison in Alan's system that could have caused a heart attack. Kurtzman responded, "I didn't see anything that would be causing a heart attack."

"Other than Big Macs, cigarettes, and illness?"

"Right. There are plenty of drugs that can cause heart attacks. Methamphetamine, cocaine, others, stress the heart. But, again, I didn't see anything in the toxicology that was unusual."

Law enforcement had even asked Dr. Kurtzman to run tests looking specifically for signs of poisoning. About this, Colvin asked, "You informed law enforcement July first of last year that you thought additional tests were unnecessary because poisoning was improbable. Is that correct?"

"That's correct."

And as to time of death, Colvin said, "Assuming the rigidity or rigor was found at noon by someone, fair to say that nine thirty-seven A.M., for instance, would be perfectly consistent with rigidity found at noon?"

"Sure."

This was important. Miriam could prove she was not at home at 9:37 A.M., June 10, 2008, because she had a sales receipt proving that fact.

Dr. Kurtzman said because of the amount of rigidity he saw at 3:15 P.M., he thought Alan Helmick had died in the early-morning hours. Kurtzman could not narrow it down any further than that.

Asked if Dr. Kurtzman could tell by the trajectory of the bullet where the gunman had been standing, Kurtzman said no. "If you take a look at the injury, I don't know what position Mr. Helmick had his head at, [at] the time he sustained the gunshot wound. So if he had his head turned to the left, that would place the shooter farther to the right. If he had his head to the right, then it would place the shooter far to the left. If the head was tipped down, then it would line up with somebody being higher in the room. If it was tipped back, then it would be somebody lower in the room."

On redirect, Richard Tuttle once again questioned Dr. Kurtzman. Tuttle asked, "In general terms, the bullet path as it entered Mr. Helmick's body tells you very little about his relationship to the shooter. Is that correct?"

Kurtzman replied, "Correct. The only thing that I would say is that he's got a gunshot wound entrance, and there's no evidence of close-range fire on skin around the wound of entry."

Once again, the jurors had some questions, which Judge Robison read out loud to Dr. Kurtzman. One of the jury queries: *How much alcohol could Mr. Helmick have ingested the night before without any being detected in his urine?*

Kurtzman answered, "There's a number of variables. Mr. Helmick may have voided first thing in the morning when he got up. If he did so, then he would completely empty his bladder. In order for Mr. Helmick to have a detectable blood alcohol level at eight o'clock in the morning from eight o'clock the night before, he would have had to have an alcohol level equal to or greater than .24 at eight the night before. That would have been equivalent to twelve beers the night before. It's a hard question to answer, not knowing the starting point and ending point. He would have had to have a lot of drinks the night before for it to show up."

On this same topic, another juror questioned: *Is there any way to know if Alan Helmick could have been drunk the night before?*

Dr. Kurtzman replied, "Not from the information I have."

A third juror's question asked: *Did it look like someone had cleaned the mouth and nose area?* (This alluded to giving CPR.)

Kurtzman answered, "Not that I recall."

The judge asked if the prosecution or defense had any more questions. Steve Colvin did, and asked, "Can you say definitively that a layperson, untrained in performing CPR, could not have attempted CPR in a poor fashion?"

Kurtzman said, "I wouldn't be able to say definitively. But when somebody performs CPR, they're pressing on the chest. In an individual the age of Mr. Helmick, it's not uncommon that you'll see rib fractures associated with CPR. And normally to do CPR, you have to turn the head. Mr. Helmick's body was resting in the position I believe he fell. In my opinion, I would say no CPR was performed."

"But you can't say for certain that nobody tried to perform

chest compressions. You can say for certain they didn't do so with a lot of force, correct?"

"That's correct."

In the end, both the prosecution and defense had scored points from Dr. Kurtzman's testimony. Kurtzman had just said that he didn't believe Miriam had done any CPR on Alan, so she had lied about that to the 911 operator and police. On the other hand, Kurtzman didn't believe Alan had been poisoned, and he gave a window for the time of death that encompassed when Miriam had not been at home.

CHAPTER 33

A LOOK OF HATRED

When Alan's former housekeeper, Patricia "Trish" Erikson, testified, she told of the tension in the Helmick household on June 9, 2008, the day before Alan was murdered. Trish stated, "The atmosphere from the time they walked in the door—I could feel the tension mounting. You could cut through the tension with a knife."

Tammy Eret asked, "You told a police officer, when you talked about Miriam—you indicated that she had a look that was kind of hard to describe. Is that correct?"

The witness replied, "Very hard to describe."

Eret continued, "When you were interviewed recently, do you remember talking to Jim (Hebenstreit) and describing it as if she had a look of hate or anger?"

"Yes. I hate using that word, but that's what it looked like."

Steve Colvin wasn't going to let that last remark go unchallenged. He started off his cross-examination by asking Trish Erikson if she had liked Alan Helmick. Trish said that she had. Colvin continued, "And because you believe he was a good man and he treated you well, this was a big event in your life when he was killed?"

The housekeeper stated, "Yes, it was."

"And you paid attention to all the newspaper stories and all the media that came out about it because it affected you directly. Isn't that true?"

The witness could see where this was leading. She answered, "But that isn't why I feel the way I feel!"

Colvin retorted, "That's not what I asked you, ma'am. I asked you if you paid attention to all the newspaper stories and all the media attention about this."

Erikson agreed that she had.

So Colvin said that the first time Trish Erikson had spoken with an investigator, it was with Investigator Robin Martin, back in June 2008. And since then, Colvin asked if she had seen a lot more stories about the murder. She agreed to that as well.

Colvin now struck with the point he wanted to make. "You didn't tell Investigator Martin that Ms. Helmick had a look of anger and hatred on her face, did you?"

Trish replied, "If I didn't, I should have."

"Well, Ms. Erikson, we're talking about a look that you thought was horrible. Even if the police officer didn't ask you about it, you would have volunteered about that look, right?"

"I don't know," she answered.

"When you talked to Investigator Martin, you indicated that you and Ms. Helmick had chatted about a vacuum cleaner and grooming the dogs. But those aren't the things you told Investigator Hebenstreit just two weeks ago, right?"

"Right."

"Two weeks ago, what you remembered was a look of hatred and coldness?"

"That's right."

"Don't you think that your memory was probably better

seven days after [the death of Alan Helmick] than after watching all the media?"

Trish Erikson replied, "No."

Colvin looked at her for a while, and then just said, "Okay."

Tammy Eret questioned Patricia Erikson, once again, on redirect. "When you were interviewed by Investigator Robin Martin on June 16, 2008, do you recall stating that you got the overall feeling that something was not right? Isn't that what you told Robin Martin?"

"Yes."

"What you saw going on that day was not right compared to all the other times you had been there?"

"Right."

"You told law enforcement (in June 2008), you felt that they were having a spat?"

"Something was really wrong."

"So when you said to Jim (Hebenstreit) that she had a look of hate and anger versus what you said that day, you still get the same overall feeling?"

"I do."

The next trial day, the 911 tape was played for the jurors, and it showed that Miriam had remained fairly calm during the eighteen-minute tape. She had spelled out the name of Siminoe for the dispatcher, and had given him directions as to how to get to the residence.

The prosecution tried to show this calmness as proof that Miriam was not concerned, because she already knew that Alan was dead. In fact, it was their contention she knew because she had shot him to death.

The defense, on the other hand, told jurors that Miriam

spelled out the name of Siminoe and gave directions, because the dispatcher was having such a hard time in locating the Helmick residence. Miriam was relatively calm, because she had to be.

When Barbara Watts was called to the stand, she basically reiterated her contention that Miriam had stolen money from her in Gulfport, Mississippi, and then stole students from her dance studio in Grand Junction, when Miriam opened her own studio. Watts also said that Miriam broke policy rules when she started dating Alan Helmick. And once again, Barbara Watts said that Miriam was "looking for a sugar daddy to take care of her." She found that sugar daddy in Alan Helmick.

The witness went on to say, "It ended up being a joke around the dance school. She said she wanted to find a rich man, and it didn't matter if he had one foot in the grave. She just wanted someone to take care of her like she was used to."

Even more damaging to Miriam Helmick was CBI agent Carol Crowe, who testified that even though no GSR was found on Miriam's hands, body, or clothes, GSR showed up elsewhere. A few particles were found on the clogs that Miriam had worn that day and also on the steering wheel of the car she had been driving around the area while doing errands. Crowe explained that Miriam could have gotten rid of GSR from her hands by washing them, and from her body by showering. And she could have simply gotten rid of the clothes she had been wearing, if she had shot Alan to death.

On cross-examination, Crowe did say that it could not be determined how long GSR particles had been on the steering wheel or on Miriam's clogs. Miriam could have been around a gun that was fired on June 9, when Alan was still alive.

* * *

Investigator Lissah Norcross testified about Alan not receiving his voice mail messages. The prosecution contended that he never got those messages because Miriam Helmick was hiding his cell phone. And the reason in their estimation was because Miriam was forging checks and didn't want Alan to know about it. Norcross spoke of all of Alan's daughters saying that it was very hard for them to contact their father in the spring of 2008. They all believed that Miriam was hiding their dad's cell phone from him.

Steve Colvin, however, got Investigator Norcross to admit that she couldn't say why Miriam was keeping Alan's cell phone. It could have been for any number of reasons, and not just because she was cashing his checks.

On the other hand, Norcross was good for the prosecution, on redirect, stating that in the months before Alan's murder, Miriam had only left four voice mail messages on his cell phone. Then on the morning of June 10, 2008, she left four messages all within a few hours. The reasoning was, according to law enforcement, for Miriam to set up an alibi of where she was traveling that morning. They contended that she had already shot him to death, and was only pretending to leave messages for a man she already knew was dead.

Investigator Michael Piechota told the jurors about all the searches on Miriam's Gateway computer about overdoses from medicine and horse euthanasia as well. These included articles about various people dying from prescription drug overdoses.

The defense did have Piechota admit that it couldn't be proven who had searched those Web sites. It could have been Alan, using Miriam's computer. But unlike Miriam's contention that Alan's laptop was not working well with the Internet,

Piechota said he found no problems with it. Piechota would not budge from his assessment that Alan's computer worked just fine.

Piechota added one more damaging thing. He said that when he went back to the Helmick residence on June 19, Alan's blood on the kitchen floor had not been cleaned up. All that had been done was that Miriam had thrown a couple of beach towels over the bloodstains. This was amazing to Piechota in light of the fact that Miriam had said that Alan Helmick was the love of her life.

The next day, Kirsten Turcotte, the longtime house sitter for the Helmicks, testified that she had received a series of phone calls from Miriam about someone prowling around through her house when she wasn't there. On June 23, 2008, Miriam said things had been moved around. On June 24, Miriam stated that doors she knew she had locked were now unlocked. On June 25, a door leading to the balcony was found open. On June 26, she returned home to find lights on in the master bedroom.

Kirsten also testified that Miriam told her that she had placed objects around the house to see if they had been moved. Miriam said that she had put powder down on the floor to see if anyone left footprints there.

Kirsten also had some damaging things to say about Miriam's demeanor after Alan was dead. On one occasion, she and Miriam had been in the Helmicks' garage. Miriam laughed, saying she was worried that the carrots in the back of the Oldsmobile that she had been driving would spoil, since law enforcement still had that car in their possession. She did not seem very upset about Alan's murder.

Even worse, she said that Miriam told her, "They (law enforcement) are not going to want to go up against me."

* * *

Merredith Von Burg, Alan's sister, testified that Miriam had stayed with her for three days after Alan's death. During that time, Miriam had supposedly told Merredith that one of her rings, one of Alan's rings, and one of Alan's watches were missing from the Helmick home. The point was, how could Miriam know this if she hadn't gone any farther than the spot where Alan lay in the kitchen? Miriam told investigators she had not been in any other part of the house. And she had not been back in the house when she made those comments to Von Burg.

Merredith also testified that while Miriam was staying with her, Miriam shared some very disturbing news. Merredith stated, "She said she could have done it at Lake Powell two weeks earlier and that Alan was not a great swimmer. She had to rescue him once before." This declaration on Miriam's part did not allay Merredith's growing suspicions about her, but rather only increased them.

On direct testimony, Portia Vigil said that weeks after her father had been murdered, she found a folded-up piece of paper tucked away in a desk drawer at the Helmick home in Whitewater. It turned out to be the prenuptial agreement, which Miriam had been talking about. However, Portia said the paper did not mention what should happen for the distribution of items after Alan's death. Miriam had been contending that she was allowed to take all property that had been accumulated after she and Alan got married. According to Portia, none of these items were mentioned in the prenuptial agreement.

Portia also spoke about how hard it was when her mother, Sharon, had suddenly died of a heart attack. And she admitted it was hard for her to accept Miriam into the household. Portia did agree it would have been hard to accept anyone, and not just Miriam, under the circumstances. Asked if she treated Miriam badly, Portia said, "No." And she also said that Wendy and Kristy had treated Miriam well.

As far as not being able to contact her father throughout much of the spring of 2008, Portia testified, "The phone calls went straight to his voice mail or to Miriam."

There was one other big bit of news that same day. Tammy Eret, who was so much a part of the prosecution team, let it be known that she was leaving the DA's office. Part of her reasoning was "My kids don't get to do things, such as sleep-overs, just because of the things I've seen and my position. You have to be very guarded."

In fact, over the last few years with the DA's office, Eret had been a big part of the prosecution team on major homicide cases, sexual assaults, and other felony crimes. All of that took its toll on the mother of four.

After Miriam Helmick's trial was over, Eret would be moving on to be in private practice. She admitted that some of the cases she'd worked on had been "haunting." She added that the change would be good for her and her family. Alan Helmick's case certainly fell into the "haunting" category for Eret.

CHAPTER 34

"A LOVER AND A PLAYMATE"

Miriam's son, Chris Giles, was not comfortable being a witness in his mother's trial, but nonetheless, he was a witness for the prosecution. Tammy Eret had Chris speak about when he had first met Alan Helmick, and that had been when Miriam and Alan got married. Chris had been on a church mission in Ecuador when Alan was murdered. Then in early July 2008, Chris flew out to Colorado and spent a few days with his mother.

About that period of time, Chris testified, "I didn't stay at a hotel. I stayed at the residence (in Whitewater). We went to visit one of Alan's family, just to kind of get out, on the evening of July fourth."

Eret wanted to know if Miriam had told Chris what had happened to Alan Helmick. Chris replied, "She basically told me that Alan had been shot, and it was a home invasion. That was the gist of it. I was just kinda there to listen and help her out."

Eret asked who had brought up the fact that Miriam might move to Florida. Chris answered, "I had discussed it with her. I said that once everything got wrapped up, she could come

down and work some things out [about] what her next step
would be. But I advised her that she needed to remain in Colorado and make sure everything was taken care of here first."

Asked if Miriam had spoken about not having any identi-
fication, Chris responded, "She referred to everything being
confiscated in the house. Her ID card and all that was taken.
And she proceeded to tell me that she had copies of Sharon
Helmick's ID. I advised her that wasn't a good course to do.
It's not right, and it's not legal."

Jody McGuirk was worried about this line of questioning
and asked to approach the judge. The request was granted.
McGuirk said to Judge Robison, "This is the point where we
would like to ask for a limiting instruction in regard to the use
of Sharon Helmick's ID. It's so that can't be used as proof to
a prior crime."

Tammy Eret responded, "I'm not sure. I think it was
okayed by you."

All of this was because Charles Kirkpatrick was going to
be called as the next witness concerning Sharon Helmick's
ID, as well as other things. Judge Robison agreed with
McGuirk, and said to the jurors, "Ladies and gentlemen, certain evidence may be admitted for a particular purpose only,
and for no other. You're about to hear evidence relating to the
alleged use of Sharon Helmick's identity by Miriam Helmick.
This evidence is offered for the purpose of showing motive,
plan, and intent as to the charge of first-degree murder only,
and you should consider it as evidence for no other purpose."

Chris next spoke about Miriam supposedly going to
somewhere around Denver to see a family friend, and the next
thing he knew she was in the Southeast, possibly Savannah,
Georgia, and wanted to come stay with him in Florida. Accord-

ing to Chris, this occurred about two weeks after he returned home from Colorado, making it mid to late July 2008.

Chris was concerned about this request by his mother, and he wanted to make sure that Miriam had cleared up all things in Colorado with the investigators concerning the death of Alan Helmick. Chris testified that Miriam told him that the investigators knew that she was going to Florida. That, in fact, was not the case.

Chris added that sometime in August or September, he received a phone call from Jim Hebenstreit. Hebenstreit asked if Chris knew where Miriam was, and Chris told Hebenstreit that she was staying with him.

Tammy Eret asked, "Did you indicate to your mother that you told Investigator Hebenstreit where she was?"

"Yes, ma'am."

"And how did she appear to react to that?"

"She wasn't very happy."

"Did you know at the time that she was residing with you that she was actually using the name of Sharon Helmick?"

"I did not."

"Did she indicate to you what she thought she would get from Alan's estate?"

"She indicated to me, under Colorado law, that she was entitled to half of everything after they got married."

Surprisingly, the defense had only one question to ask Chris. Jody McGuirk said, "Your mom, Miriam—she seemed happy when she was with Alan?"

Chris replied, "Yes, ma'am."

McGuirk responded, "That's it. No further questions."

Charles Kirkpatrick reiterated to the prosecution what he had already told investigators about Miriam Helmick, a woman he had known as "Sharon." He spoke of being on a singles Web site called MillionaireMatch.com. He also spoke of having a

1,800-square-foot luxury apartment in Orlando, Florida, and owning several automobiles, including a 1985 neo-classic Zimmer Golden Spirit.

As Kirkpatrick kept listing all the expensive items he owned, Jody McGuirk objected. In a sidebar, she said to Judge Robison, "I don't see what the relevance of this testimony is. He's already spoken about income. You're (Tuttle) just randomly asking him how expensive some items are."

Richard Tuttle shot back, "It's certainly relevant to what we're offering. It goes to show Miriam's plan in the wake of murdering her husband, to hook up with another person with assets. And the whole relationship again belies her true love and motivation toward Alan Helmick. We'll be laying a foundation that she actually met Kirkpatrick in his Mercedes. And they went back to his apartment, which is very nicely appointed."

Steve Colvin chimed in, "You're also gonna elicit that she spent time in the Golden Spirit, when she was actually in the Mercedes? How's the value of this relevant to anything?"

Judge Robison sustained the objection, and the questioning by Tuttle moved to another area. This question concerned Miriam's posting about herself on MillionaireMatch.com: Saw your profile and I loved it. I can dance any dance and I'm pretty good at it, too.... Your profile requirements described me completely.

Charles testified about Miriam meeting him at a T.G.I. Friday's, where she mentioned about her former husband being deceased. Charles said, "She told me she was a widow. He had died about six to twelve months before from some type of brain disease or something, that he had been sick for three to four years prior to that."

Tuttle asked, "Did she talk about having time over those three to four years to prepare for his death?"

The witness responded, "Yeah. She said that it wasn't like it was a sudden thing."

* * *

Jody McGuirk asked Kirkpatrick what his posting had been on MillionaireMatch.com. Charles answered, "It specifically read that I was looking for a lover and a playmate."

"You were concerned that she mentioned she'd like to relocate to Orlando?"

"Yes. She mentioned it a lot of times."

"Her asking . . . This was kind of a needy type of behavior that was a turnoff to you?"

"Yes, it was."

"You mentioned that you lied to [Miriam] and told her that you were going to visit your grandchildren or something?"

"Yes. She had asked to stay over another day."

"So this woman that you found needy, that you slept with . . . you then lied to her to get rid of her?"

"No, it wasn't to get rid of her. It was because I didn't feel comfortable with the way she approached me about staying."

CHAPTER 35

"I Hear Wedding Bells."

There was nothing much new in Penny Lyons's testimony that differed from everything she had already told investigators earlier. The only real contentious part of her testimony was an objection from Steve Colvin about why Penny or Miriam did not phone the police after discovering the envelope under the front porch's doormat.

Colvin told the judge in a sidebar, "I'm trying to object before the evidence is elicited. She's going to talk about the fact that she did not wind up calling law enforcement because Ms. Helmick said she wanted to talk to a lawyer. I'm objecting preemptively to that evidence coming in because it's a comment on Miriam Helmick's Sixth and Fifth Amendment right to counsel. The evidence is being offered to show guilty knowledge because Ms. Helmick wants to talk to a lawyer. It's our position that it's improper to assume guilty knowledge simply from contacting an attorney."

Tammy Eret responded, "Miriam Helmick was not in custody. This has nothing to do with law enforcement. This is a statement that she made to a third party. It does show guilty knowledge. None of her rights are in play—because law enforcement is not involved."

Judge Robison overruled the objection, and Eret asked Penny Lyons, "Did you call 911?"

Penny responded, "I started to call, and Miriam asked me not to."

"Did she tell you why?"

"She said, 'Penny, please don't second-guess me now. Please call my attorney.' So I called her attorney."

Later in the questioning, Eret asked, "You were a good friend of hers?"

Penny replied, "I felt that I was, yes."

On cross-examination, Steve Colvin got to this subject of friendship. He asked Penny, "Fair to say that you feel as to the card that you found, and Ms. Helmick's behavior when the card was found and afterward, that you feel like your friendship was taken advantage of?"

Penny answered, "That would be true, yes."

Colvin continued, "Assuming that she took advantage of your friendship as to the card, that doesn't mean that she took advantage of your friendship as to her not having any money. Is that fair?"

"I never had an issue with giving her the money."

"And she really didn't have any financial resources at that point. Is that correct?"

"No, she did not."

"It really did appear that she lost everything when Alan was murdered?"

"That was my perception, yes."

Not unlike Penny Lyons, the tougher questions for Laegan McGee came during cross-examination. Steve Colvin asked her if she saw Miriam sitting and holding hands at one point with Alan Helmick. The witness said that she did. Then Colvin asked, "You thought she made an apology wave to you?" Laegan said that was correct.

So Colvin wanted to know if the witness thought Miriam at Boomers had something to apologize about. She answered, "She looked embarrassed."

Colvin continued, "You made a point of mentioning she'd had someone who'd been a boyfriend previously four weeks before. You made a point of mentioning that you thought this was pretty fast. Sound like you don't think it was appropriate that she held hands with Mr. Helmick."

"No, I felt that Miriam felt embarrassed, and that was how she felt. But I don't know what was in her head."

"And she said on that day, 'I hear wedding bells,' in a singsongy voice. So she clearly thought this relationship was leading somewhere serious?"

"Yes."

The testimony of Jeri Yarbrough, who had sold horses to Miriam Helmick and then bought the same horses back, basically followed the things that she had told investigators. One section of Jeri's testimony did bring an objection from Jody McGuirk.

Tammy Eret had just asked Jeri, "Did Miriam talk to you about whether or not she was nervous about the interview with law enforcement?" (The prosecutor was alluding to the June 10 interview.)

Jeri replied, "She didn't say that she was nervous. She said that she had been down that road before."

McGuirk objected immediately, and there was a conference at the judge's bench. McGuirk told Judge Robison that specific area had already been ruled as inadmissible for the jury to hear.

Eret countered, "The Delta incident, when she was questioned by law enforcement—that has not been excluded, and that is what she (Jeri Yarbrough) will talk about. I mean, what other things would she be talking about?"

McGuirk said, "Well, from discovery, it seems like she made that comment in reference to other things." (The other things probably related to the death of Miriam's first husband, Jack Giles, and that was off-limits.)

It was finally determined that Jeri could talk about the Delta car fire incident and not the death of Jack Giles.

On cross-examination, Steve Colvin had Jeri Yarbrough agree that she'd probably had fifteen separate conversations with Miriam Helmick before she left Colorado on July 15. And of those conversations, it was hard for Jeri to pin down when certain things had been spoken by Miriam to her over the phone.

Colvin said, "You don't have a word-for-word memory of what happened in each conversation, correct?" Jeri said that was so.

And Colvin wanted to get to an important point. The point was that Jeri Yarbrough might have acted differently than Miriam did when she first discovered Alan on the kitchen floor. Colvin said, "You had a pretty crazy conversation on Thursday night, two days after the murder. Crazy enough that when you get the phone conversation, you're thinking to yourself, that's not how I would behave if my husband was killed, right?"

Jeri answered, "That's correct."

"That had to be concerning to you, didn't it?"

"Very concerning."

"In fact, you're thinking to yourself, this lady's husband got killed, and she's not even upset about it, right?"

"I was shocked that she had called me and was being so frank, and stuff."

"Ms. Yarbrough, in testimony you just described it as suspicious. Was it suspicious?"

"It's suspicious, yeah. You're taken aback by it. It didn't put her in a good light."

"So you have suspicious conversations with someone regarding a first-degree murder and you immediately call law enforcement to report your suspicions, didn't you?"

"No, I did not."

"You did not call law enforcement. In fact, you never talked to law enforcement until they called you, correct?"

"That's correct."

And then Colvin got to the part where Miriam had supposedly laughed after relating that a tank filled with gas would not explode. Colvin asked, "Was it kind of a sinister, evil-person, movie laugh?"

"No."

"What kind of laugh?"

"Just kind of like, 'I didn't know a car wouldn't blow up' laugh. Not a sinister, movie laugh."

"Okay, so you took that statement as a confession that she tried to murder her husband by blowing up his car?"

"No."

"You didn't take it as that, because clearly that's not how she intended it, right?"

"Right."

"But you didn't make clear to law enforcement—'By the way, I didn't think she was trying to confess to a murder'?"

"They didn't ask me that question. I don't know what they assumed. That's up to the police what their thought processes are, not mine."

"And Miriam Helmick clearly expressed to you that they (law enforcement) were looking at her to the exclusion of anybody else. Isn't that true?"

"She thought she was the prime suspect, yes."

"She thought she was their only suspect, didn't she?"

"She said *prime* suspect. That's what she told me."

CHAPTER 36

HORNY AS HELL

Charles Reams was an attorney who specialized in probate and civil litigation. He explained that simply put, probate "is when the court determines that a document is a person's last will and testament after they die. It can include estates and assets."

Reams said that sometimes people who died had not drawn up a will. In that case, Reams would often be called in as a neutral party by people who were arguing over who should get what after a person died. Reams acted as a neutral party in dividing the estate.

Richard Tuttle showed Reams a handwritten document, allegedly penned by Alan Helmick, and asked Reams, "Are handwritten wills valid in Colorado?"

Reams answered, "Yes, they are."

"Do you have to prove that the person who died, actually authored the document?"

"Yes. That's the problem with them." Reams then spoke of lawyer-drafted wills, which didn't have problems. And there were also "holographic wills" supposedly written up by the person who had died. For holographic wills, it had to be proven that the person who signed it was actually the person who had died.

Tuttle asked if a handwritten will, dated November 2, 2004, concerned Alan and Miriam Helmick. Reams said that it did. Then Tuttle asked, "In Colorado, can a person cut a surviving spouse completely out of an estate?"

Reams answered no. Then he said for one hundred years, Colorado had ruled that a surviving spouse could not be completely cut out of an estate, no matter what the person who had died had written. A spouse always got $26,000 right off the top, no matter what, and up to $24,000 just to help meet expenses for up to a year while the estate was being settled.

On top of that, Miriam was going to receive $25,000 from a life insurance policy that Alan had taken out. There was also something called an intestate share. Reams said, "In this case, the surviving spouse would receive theoretically the first one hundred thousand." So Miriam was not going to be destitute, as she had claimed. Nor was the "prenuptial agreement," which she was always talking about, valid in cutting her off from the money mentioned by Reams.

Tuttle asked, "Why is this prenuptial agreement not valid?"

Reams replied, "First of all, the legislature has spelled out protections for the spouse. In any prenuptial marital agreement, there must be a fair and reasonable disclosure of the assets." Reams added that Miriam could waive her right to receive money and property from Alan's estate, but she had not done that.

Tuttle then questioned, "If Alan Helmick and Miriam Giles bought things after their marriage in June 2006, it's not affected by this prenuptial agreement?"

Reams responded, "It doesn't seem to address it. According to probate law, it's assumed that they're held in joint tenancy."

Tuttle also asked, "Bottom line, what would Miriam Helmick be entitled to in the wake of her husband's death?"

Reams answered, "She would receive, at minimum, one

hundred thousand dollars. And there is another legal right she has. It's a complicated formula, but she has a right, as the surviving spouse, from five to fifty percent of assets, depending upon the years they were married. You take into account the joint tenancies, life insurance, assets the spouse owned before the marriage, even assets given away two years prior to death."

Once again, it was not quite true that Alan was worth more to Miriam alive than dead. She was in line to receive a substantial amount of money, compared to the six hundred dollars that she had when she first arrived in Grand Junction in 2004.

Steve Colvin, on the other hand, tried to prove that the estate had to pay creditors first, and that was going to be a substantial amount of money. Not only that, it could take up to a year to do that. So for the first year after Alan Helmick's death, Miriam was going to receive very little money, if any at all.

During the year, from June 2008 to June 2009, Miriam hadn't even asked for an allowance out of the estate. Colvin questioned if Miriam had ever applied for something called an "elective share," to help her pay her expenses.

Charles Reams replied, "Not to my knowledge."

In fact, Colvin contended that Miriam didn't even know about money that was owed to her as a surviving spouse, because she was not a trained lawyer. Colvin said, "If you're not a probate lawyer, it's certainly possible you wouldn't know anything about intestate shares and elective shares and all that stuff?"

Reams answered, "That's highly likely you would not know it."

Colvin also asked if anyone, including Miriam, had ever challenged the prenuptial agreement. Reams said that no one had.

Colvin queried, "Is it fair to say that laypeople may well

think that in a prenuptial agreement, whatever you had before the marriage is yours, period, end of story?"

"Yes."

"And if she thought the prenuptial agreement was valid, there was no reason to make claims on the estate, correct?"

"Correct."

"Has any claim been made by Ms. Helmick against the estate, to your knowledge?"

"To my knowledge, which is somewhat limited, I'm not aware of one."

"And is it your understanding that everything in the estate was in Mr. Helmick's name and that there was not joint tenancy of any property?"

Reams replied, "As far as title in joint tenancy, I'm not aware of any."

Colvin's whole line of questioning tended to bolster the assumption that Alan Helmick was more valuable to Miriam alive than dead. In fact, the moment Alan died, it left Miriam virtually penniless.

The things Charles Reams had been talking about were so complicated, even Judge Robison asked him a few questions.

One question was "Can the time limit to claim any and all inheritance for any of the situations be put on hold due to a criminal case?" In other words, could Miriam have an extension on deadlines, as the criminal case went forward, and then make claims on the estate if she was acquitted of murdering Alan?

Reams answered, "I'm not aware of an exception concerning the criminal case. There are situations, however, where the court can extend the time limit for the elective share."

As with most witnesses, Aline Lee testified in a manner that was consistent with her previous statements to police. On cross-examination by Steve Colvin, she often seemed uncomfortable and distressed. Aline agreed with Colvin that her memory of exact dates was not good when it came to remembering when certain conversations with Miriam had taken place.

Colvin asked, "When you first talked to her, you told us that you asked her point-blank, 'Did you murder him,' right?"

Aline answered, "Yes."

"And when you did that, you looked her right in the eyes, right?"

"Yes."

"And it was after she answered that question, you went ahead and you loaned stuff to her, right? Money and jewelry."

"Yes, over the period of time."

"And you wouldn't have done that if you thought she murdered him?"

"No."

Later in the testimony, Colvin wanted to know when Miriam had made the statement that she was "hornier than hell."

Aline said it was just before she went down to meet the man in Orlando.

Colvin added, "Now that statement, you didn't even want to say it here in court today, right?"

"No."

"Because it embarrasses you, I gather?"

"Yeah, a little bit."

"And I gather you thought it was inappropriate to say it?"

"Yeah. For a grieving widow."

"At some point after her husband is murdered, is it okay for her to be as horny as hell?"

"Yeah, probably so, but I don't know what time that is for anybody. You know, everybody grieves differently."

"You didn't think it was acceptable for Miriam to feel that way?"

"I just thought it was unusual."

Perhaps facetiously, Colvin asked, "So, normally, when you talk to grieving widows whose husbands have been murdered, when do they say they're hornier than hell?"

The witness responded, "I've talked to a lot of people that lost husbands and I've never heard anyone saying anything like that behavior."

Colvin got the witness to admit that Alan had been murdered in June of 2008, and Miriam did not make her comment about being horny as hell until later October or November of 2008. In fact, Colvin contended that Aline Lee had not even told Sergeant Henry Stoffel about this incident during his first interview with her. She had only mentioned it just before the present trial.

And then he got to the point that Aline Lee had a problem not only with Miriam Helmick, but with her defense team as well. Colvin asked, "You were told that my investigator Barbara Bullock, with the public defender's office, wanted to talk to you. And you never called us, but you did talk to law enforcement, right?"

All Aline said to that was "um," which was taken for a yes.

Colvin added, "Between the time that Sergeant Stoffel came to your house and talked to you, and the time you called him about that statement, you had gone on the Internet and looked up about Ms. Helmick's case, right?"

Aline agreed that she had done that because she was curious. So Colvin asked if she had then called up law enforcement right after she had gone online. What ensued was an exchange over whether she had done so right away or much later.

One of her answers was very disjointed. "I don't know when they . . . of when I got on first to . . . you know, check into about if it was true that she . . . you know, so if it was true of some of the things . . ."

Finally Colvin butted in and asked, "The answer is you don't know, right?"

She finally replied, "I don't really know."

Another comment that came up in testimony was what Aline Lee had told Investigator Stoffel on December 9, 2008: "Miriam had to get rid of her lawyer (probably Colleen Scissors) 'cause she couldn't afford to pay her anymore."

Colvin continued, "She was real excited, kinda impressed, by this Kilpatrick guy, right?" (He meant Charles Kirkpatrick.)

"Yes."

And Colvin got her to agree that Miriam was not only excited because "Kilpatrick" had money, but that he liked dancing and horses as well. She agreed and said, "I don't think it was just the money."

Tammy Eret got a chance to redirect questions to Aline Lee, and Eret asked why she had such a hard time recalling specific dates during that period of time when Miriam was back in Florida.

Aline said, "Well, I just lost my mother, who I had been taking care of for twelve years. It's a very hard thing. So I wasn't very good with dates."

Just before Eret ended her redirect, she said, "Initially, before Mr. Colvin started his cross-examination, you got teary-eyed. Did you consider Miriam Helmick a friend of yours?"

Now the witness was more than just teary-eyed. She began crying on the stand.

Steve Colvin looked upon this as a cheap trick, so he objected. When the lawyers approached the bench, Colvin told Judge Robison, "This is an appeal to the passions of the jury by pointing out her emotional state, thereby bolstering her credibility. I'm objecting on that ground."

Eret countered, "I'm just asking her if it's difficult to provide information. She started crying. I can't help that she started crying."

Judge Robison overruled the objection, and Eret asked once again, "Did you consider her to be a friend of yours?"

The answer: "In the past, yes."

CHAPTER 37

A "JUVENILE" STAGED CRIME SCENE

On direct testimony, Mike Pruett, Alan Helmick's former brother-in-law, mostly talked about his conversation with Miriam at the dinner after the funeral. Once again, Mike, the brother of Alan's first wife, spoke of how jarring it was to hear Miriam pronounce about a Dance Junction ex-employee: "He'd better hope he has a fucking alibi!"

Tammy Eret asked if Miriam indicated that she had a suspicion about who the shooter was. Mike answered that she didn't know for sure. And then he began to say, "Knowing Alan the way I did—"

Before he finished his sentence, Steve Colvin quickly objected. In a sidebar out of the hearing of the jurors, Colvin told Judge Robison, "I anticipate the witness is going to testify that knowing Alan as well as he did, he knows that Alan would never have turned his back on a stranger in his house. Therefore, Alan had to have known the shooter. That's complete speculation, and it's improper. We're asking the court to not allow the answer that's about to come out."

Eret responded, "Well, it's habit evidence. And if he can testify that he's known Alan Helmick since 1967, and knows him well—knows him to always confront people and never shy away and turn his back on somebody, and is very cognizant of strangers, that's a habit that is allowed in."

Colvin retorted, "They haven't laid the foundation for habit. He (Pruett) hasn't testified to his observations of Alan when he was in the presence of a stranger in his house. How can you get a habit without laying observations that he's seen before?"

In the end, Judge Robison sided with Colvin and said that the question could not be answered because it was speculation.

Later, on direct, Mike Pruett spoke of what he knew about the car fire in Delta. Eret asked him, "Do you remember telling law enforcement that Miriam was giving you the impression that Alan was going to cover for her in that incident?"

He began to say, "I remember getting the feeling that if you're sitting in the car by yourself, and the person you're with comes to the—"

Before he could finish his statement, Colvin anticipated that he was going to say that Miriam went to the back of the car, and it must have been she who put the wick in the gas tank and lit it. Colvin objected, saying, "This isn't testimony. It's speculation and opinion."

Judge Robison sustained that objection as well.

When Steve Colvin got his turn, he got Mike Pruett to admit that he'd contacted Portia Vigil after the funeral and told her that he might have some things that would be of interest to law enforcement. Mike also admitted that he wasn't surprised when an investigator contacted him.

Colvin got into the fact that Mike had personally investigated three burglaries dealing with his own property, and two of these had led to convictions. Colvin asked if Pruett considered himself a "bit of a criminal investigator." He replied that he asked a lot of questions in those cases.

Colvin then spoke of Mike being surprised when Miriam had pronounced at the dinner after the funeral about an ex-employee: "He'd better have a fucking good alibi!"

Colvin queried, "What surprised you? The fact that she was indicating that this guy better have a good alibi, or that she was using profanity?"

Sharon's brother answered, "The profanity. It caught me off guard in the realm of the environment that we were in."

Colvin then said, "Fair to say, you've never been at a funeral of a murdered spouse, right?"

"Never have," he replied.

An important part of the prosecution's case was the fact that they contended that the so-called robbery scene at the Helmick home on June 10, 2008, had been staged. To lend weight to the prosecution's argument, they called Special Agent Robert Morton to the stand.

Before his testimony went very far, however, Steve Colvin wanted to voir dire Morton because Colvin did not buy the argument that Morton was an expert witness when it came to staged crime scenes. Judge Robison gave Colvin his wish.

Colvin began by asking if Morton considered himself to be an expert in the staging of crime scenes.

Morton replied, "I have an expertise in that. Yes, sir."

Colvin next wanted to know how Morton had supposedly gained the expertise he claimed to have. Morton continued, "It comes from experience in looking at thousands of cases."

Colvin continued, "So you look at a crime scene and you decide whether or not it's staged, right?"

Morton responded, "After examining all the evidence and discussing it with law enforcement officers, and reviewing all the material that goes along with that, yes."

Colvin wanted to know who validated his decision as to whether the crime scene was staged or not.

Morton stated, "It's validated through other people that I work with."

Colvin retorted, "Ultimately, in the end, the truth of the matter is nobody knows for sure whether it's staged or not. They just know whether they agree with you or not. Fair?"

Morton responded, "Other than it being a professional opinion, yes."

After the voir dire of Robert Morton, Richard Tuttle argued to Judge Robison on whether Agent Morton was an expert witness: "I think there's sufficient foundation laid. An expert can be judged as an expert in terms of experience, education, and training. I think he's laid the sufficient foundation, having seen over a hundred staged crime scenes."

Judge Robison ruled in favor of Tuttle, saying, "Mr. Morton is presenting expert testimony based on his experience, and the foundation that has been laid is appropriate and adequate for him rendering expert testimony."

Tuttle's questioning of Morton continued, and Morton spoke of the information that had been given to him by MCSO investigators. Morton added, "In the FBI's uniform crime reports, which are published every year, there's a section where they examine murder, robbery, burglary, rape, et cetera. Under murder, there's a section that talks about murder by circumstance. For example, during a robbery. In 2007, there were approximately 2.2 million burglaries in the United States. There were approximately 14,189 murders in the United States in 2008. In 2008, there were eighty-seven murders in conjunction with a burglary. That is about .005 percent. A very small number."

As a reference point, Tuttle asked how many people were struck by lightning and died in the United States in the same year. The number of people killed by lightning was much higher than those killed during a burglary.

As far as the staging of the robbery/murder at the Helmick home, Tuttle asked what degree of sophistication had been present.

Morton replied, "The staging was very unsophisticated for the reasons I talked about earlier. Obviously, it was done by someone who does not have a lot of criminal experience, particularly as a burglar. It was almost juvenile in its nature of staging."

During his cross-examination, things became very heated between Special Agent Robert Morton and defense counsel Steve Colvin. Colvin knew this testimony was important as to whether the jurors believed that Miriam Helmick had killed Alan and then staged a robbery scene, or whether a real burglar had surprised Alan and murdered him.

Colvin asked if to be successful at staging a robbery/murder, someone would have to be a good burglar or a police officer who knew about such things.

Morton answered, "Not necessarily. Burglars usually don't kill people, so a burglar wouldn't know how to stage a murder."

Colvin said that was not his question, and he tried again. "To convince you that it wasn't staged, they would have to be someone who's really skilled in either burglaries or a police officer. Is that right?"

Morton replied, "They would have to be extremely skilled, yes."

Colvin then asked if Morton had ever made mistakes in his assessments of whether a crime scene had been staged or not.

Morton testified, "I try to minimize errors, like anybody else does. I try to look at the entire thing in totality, as well as the circumstances. Using that barometer, measure the fact that the crime scene is very consistent with being staged and not consistent with a burglary gone bad. Have I ever made an error in describing a crime scene as being staged, and afterward found out it was not? No, I have not."

Colvin wouldn't give up on this point. He asked, "Had you made a mistake, you wouldn't know it. Let's say the jury acquits Ms. Helmick. That doesn't prove that you're wrong, because, according to you, they would be wrong, correct?"

Morton answered, "The jury isn't *only* determining whether the fact that I described the crime scene as staged. It's just one aspect of it."

Now things got even more contentious. Colvin questioned, "Even if the jury disagrees with your expert opinion, you still are going to maintain that you are correct because you don't make mistakes on this issue?"

Morton shot back, "That's an overly simplistic statement, sir!"

Colvin wouldn't give up, however. He said, "So you agree, then, that if the jury acquits Ms. Helmick, you will have your first time that you've ever been wrong on a staged crime scene?"

Morton responded, "No, sir. That's not what I said!"

"Do you know if Mr. Helmick is one of the 14,189 murders? Because you don't even know if Mr. Helmick got counted, right?"

Morton answered, "The way the Uniform Crime Reports work is that the department is mandated by federal law to report murder cases. There's a means that they use to compile data and send it in. Exactly which case out of those—well, I'm sure [the Helmick case] is in there. I can't tell you which one without asking somebody from Mesa County who actually submits that data."

Colvin pushed on: "So the answer to my question is, you don't know whether or not there's really 14,190, because you don't know if Mesa County counted this as a murder?"

Morton replied emphatically, "I know that there's been 14,189 murders reported in the UCR in 2008."

"And you don't know if this one was reported, right?"

"That's correct."

"And you certainly don't know if this was reported as a homicide in conjunction with a burglary, right?"

"No."

"So you don't know if it fits in that eighty-seven or not?"

"No, I don't."

Moving on, Colvin got Morton to agree that people were killed by lightning every year in the United States. It was a small number compared to the entire population of the country, but it did happen. Then Colvin asked, "Do you still think some people get killed in a burglary gone bad?"

Morton responded, "Yes, it does happen."

Colvin asked if Morton had been given any more discovery material on the Helmick case since October 30, 2008. Morton said that he hadn't received any new material since then. At that point, Colvin asked, "So your assessment could change, were you given additional investigative resources, additional discovery?"

Morton stated, "Depending on the nature of the information."

"And based as part of your professional opinion, you say this was a staged crime scene, but you can't say who staged it?"

Morton answered, "For purposes of this testimony, the only thing I'm allowed to say is that the crime scene was staged. And in the majority of staging cases, there's a relationship between the offender and victim."

"Hypothetically, if someone knows that Mr. Helmick and Mrs. Helmick travel together frequently, and sees a vehicle leaving from the Helmick house, they certainly would have reason to think there was no one there. Would you agree?"

"That could be possible."

"And if someone saw them leave and went into the house,

even though there were still vehicles parked there—if they had reason to think Mr. and Mrs. Helmick were always together, they would go ahead and go in. Would you agree?"

"Yes. If the offender is specifically targeting the Helmick house."

"If a burglar was in the house, was confronted by or saw Mr. Helmick, was startled and shot him, is it reasonable to say they might want to leave at that point?"

"In the context you said it, yes. But that's not what the crime scene reveals to me."

"Well, would you agree with that if somebody shoots somebody, their first thought may be 'I better get out of here.' Not that 'I should rummage through the china cabinet'?"

"If that was the sequence of events."

"Your professional opinion arrived at was based upon a review of the crime scene photographs and videos. It's not based upon any interviews of witnesses. Do I understand that correctly?"

Morton responded, "That's correct."

Richard Tuttle had one more crack at FBI agent Morton on this important issue of a possible staged robbery/murder scene. Tuttle asked, "Did you see any evidence in your review of the crime scene photos, crime scene video, and all that information that would suggest to you, or support the idea, that Mr. Helmick, who was shot in the back of the head, was ever confronted by a burglar?"

Robert Morton answered, "My opinion is that he was not confronted by a burglar. He had no defensive wounds. The position of where he was shot, and the circumstances in the location where he was shot, indicated to me that there was not a confrontation."

CHAPTER 38

IN HER OWN DEFENSE

The most dramatic part of the trial was, of course, the presence of Miriam Helmick on the stand. Her defense was taking a huge gamble that the jurors would find Miriam's testimony compelling. It was her one chance to try and explain all of the "coincidences" that pointed to her having murdered her husband. If she could explain them in a rational manner, it would take her a long way toward ensuring a verdict of not guilty. But if she came off as arrogant or evasive, the effect could be devastating for her.

Because this was so important, even before Miriam testified, the prosecution wrote up a memo for Judge Robison. Its title was "People's Motion Regarding Defendant's Anticipated Testimony." The motion read in part: *The People are particularly concerned with alleged statements attributed to Alan Helmick which are directly offered to negate the eleven counts of check forgery in this case. It is clear that the defense will argue that the defendant had the permission of Alan Helmick to write the checks at issue.*

This was a huge part of the prosecution's contention that Miriam had killed Alan Helmick because he found out that she was forging his checks. And the prosecution was worried that Miriam was going to get up on the stand and testify that Alan knew she was making out the amounts on those checks and signing them—in essence, forging his signature because he told her it was okay to do so. If that was true, then what did Miriam gain by killing him? She obviously had been strapped for cash after he was dead. Even Alan had told the investigating officer after the car fire, he was worth more to Miriam alive than dead.

In its motion, the prosecution related that if Miriam Helmick testified in that manner, the jurors should hear that these statements were not facts. Rather, they were the "worst kind of hearsay," because Alan was deceased and could not refute what Miriam was saying on the stand.

In the end, Judge Robison wrote on the motion: *Denied in part and granted in part.* In other words, she would take up these issues one by one, depending upon what Miriam Helmick actually did say during testimony.

Jody McGuirk began by asking Miriam Helmick how and why she had moved to Grand Junction, and Miriam retold that story. Then McGuirk asked Miriam about her first impressions of Alan Helmick.

Miriam said, "I really didn't have much of an impression of him at first. He was different. Very businesslike. He wanted to make sure that I could teach him, and teach him well. He only wanted to take ten lessons at first. Alan had dance lessons twice a week. He was very analytical. You couldn't just tell him to turn right or left. He wanted to know how many degrees."

McGuirk asked Miriam about her first dates with Alan and how her attitude changed over time about him. Miriam said that she began to realize that she and Alan had so much in common. And he was fun to be around, once he loosened up.

Then Miriam spoke about living in a room underneath Alan's main house in Delta, in the beginning. Asked how this situation changed, Miriam said, "I was standing on the back porch waiting on him to walk across the street. I had just come home from teaching a dance lesson. He walked up and told me that he thought I looked wonderful standing there, that I belonged with him. If he had only one day, one week, one month, with me, he felt blessed to have been with me at all." After that, Miriam said that she moved in with Alan into the main part of the house.

McGuirk wanted to know about one incident that had come in during Laegan McGee's testimony. It concerned a time when Laegan, Alan, and Miriam were at Boomers restaurant. McGuirk said, "You heard Laegan McGee testify in court earlier about seeing you at Boomers with Alan and that you waved to her in an embarrassed way, and that you came up to her and you talked to her about Alan buying you a house and horses. Did you ever see Laegan McGee at Boomers?"

Miriam said that she recalled seeing her at Boomers, but that she had never been embarrassed about being with Alan. Then Miriam added, "He made me feel like a queen. Wonderful." And Miriam said that she never spoke to Laegan McGee about Keith Coppage having been a boyfriend of hers.

As far as Alan "buying a house for her," Miriam said that it was a mutual decision to get a new house in Whitewater. "He had actually started looking at a house before he met me. He was trying for a fresh start. He'd been in the house in Delta for many, many years, and there were a lot of reminders of his wife there. We thought it was best to get a place in Whitewater. Halfway between his office in Delta and the dance studio in Grand Junction.

"It was twenty-seven miles away from Delta, so it was different than living there. In Delta, we could run over to the Elks Lodge and play pool and have a good time on the weekends. When we moved to Whitewater, he put in his own pool table, because we didn't want to drive that far away. We did see less people out there, but Alan wasn't bothered by that."

McGuirk asked about the day that she and Alan got married, and why Alan had thrown money at her after the ceremony. Miriam responded, "It was because he had written a poem, and in this poem—well, he brought out a wheelbarrow and buckets and horse manure, pitchforks and all kinds of things. It was to show we would be doing all those things in the new house. It was to show that money would have to be spent and I'd have to be doing all those kinds of things after we were married."

The contention from the prosecution and law enforcement, of course, was that Miriam had cajoled Alan into buying Dance Junction for her, and it lost a lot of money. Miriam now testified that Alan's reasons were very different. She said, "When I met him, he was paying a lot of money out of pocket each month to the IRS. And he said that he believed that if he was going to give money to the IRS, he'd rather put it into something he could enjoy than just giving it away. He enjoyed Dance Junction. I taught the teachers there, got them prepared, taught couples, group lessons, and I would figure the payroll. He did all the financial things. The hiring of managers, the setting up accounts, talking to creditors. He took care of the business end of it."

Miriam said that Dance Junction actually suffered financially when Alan quit going there as often as he used to do. Miriam testified, "My ladies loved dancing with him on Friday nights and at the groups. And you have more ladies than you have men in those, and they missed him. When he quit showing up, they didn't show." Miriam agreed that Dance Junction had never been a profitable business, and then she added that it never was supposed to be. According to Miriam, Alan was content with it being a loss; otherwise, he would have had to pay even more taxes to the IRS than he already was paying.

McGuirk wanted to know why Keith Coppage was at Dance Junction. Miriam answered, "Alan hired him. He was a previous dance instructor of mine. Alan hired him because Keith had had his own dance studio at one time, and he knew how to run one."

As to Miriam's relationship with Keith Coppage, McGuirk asked, "Did you ever date him?"

Miriam said, "No, I did not."

"Did you ever want to date Keith Coppage?"

"No, I did not."

"Was Keith Coppage a good manager?"

"Yes and no."

"Okay. In what ways was he a good manager?"

"He was good at getting people moving, motivated. He was very positive in that respect."

"In what ways wasn't he a good manager?"

"He wasn't always on the level with Alan. He didn't want to abide by the contract."

"In what ways?"

"On the contract, there was a specific amount that Keith got for dance lessons that he taught. And then he started having students make out a check to him instead of Dance Junction. Alan tried to nail him down on this. Once they got through that, Alan was going to extend Keith's contract, but Keith backed out completely and wouldn't communicate with Alan anymore."

"So, did their relationship end on good terms or—"

"No. It was very angry."

McGuirk wanted to know if Keith Coppage no longer being a part of Dance Junction hurt the business, and Miriam said that it did. "As manager, he had taught most of the women there. And the last thing that you want in a dance studio is animosity. People come there to have fun and enjoy themselves, and not get into the middle of other people's problems. So we hired another manager, named Cody. It brought some of the ladies back that had left because they all loved Cody."

As far as day-to-day finances at Dance Junction, Miriam said that she handled petty cash there, and on occasion wrote out checks when Alan instructed her to do so. These checks were signed by Miriam on Alan's instructions, and that's why there was so much confusion on law enforcement's part. They were trying to say she had done so without Alan's knowledge. At least that was what Miriam was contending now.

Moving on to the sports horse facility, Miriam said the business was also a joint effort by her and Alan. She responded that it wasn't just because she wanted the business, but Alan had been interested in it as well.

McGuirk asked, "Did you know why Alan wanted to go into the sports horse business?"

Miriam replied, "We were looking to buy a dressage horse for me. And we were surprised by the cost—anywhere from twenty-five thousand to forty-five thousand. And he thought that it would be a great business to be in. It would be something you could enjoy, even though it was a lot of work. I was basically chief flunkey. I got to clean stalls and move horses around and brush them down, tack them up, et cetera. I did all the heavy work."

"Did you ride horses as part of your job?"

"Only in lesson. I didn't ride them as part of a job."

"Alan was the one who ran the business?"

"He watched over everything. He handled the finances."

"Did you like the sports horse business?"

"Yes and no. I mean, I wanted to take lessons, but it was a lot of work. You had to get down and feed and move the horses and clean the stalls before they started training. I had to stay down there till one or two o'clock every day. And then turn around and go to the dance studio at four or five o'clock in the afternoon. I wouldn't get home until ten o'clock at night. So I was pretty busy."

"Okay, you heard Stephanie Soule testify that you told her to fudge her pay so Alan would get used to the expense of the sport business. Do you remember that?"

Miriam replied, "When she would submit hours, it would be like ten minutes or eight minutes, or whatever, for the time she spent with a horse. I wanted her to round it up to the quarter hour so that it would be easier to calculate."

"Why did you care if it was easier to calculate?"

"That's what Alan had asked for."

"Jeri Yarbrough testified that she received bounced checks from Alan for work that she did for the business. Did you write those checks to her?"

"No, I did not."

"Did you know anything about those checks when you got the call?"

"No, I did not."

"Were you surprised when she called you?"

"Very. It's embarrassing when anybody calls to say there are bounced checks. All I could do was forward the message to Alan."

Jody McGuirk then started asking questions about what kind of relationship Miriam Helmick had had with Alan's daughters. During the course of the questioning, Miriam replied, "I thought I had a good relationship with Wendy and Kristy. We (Alan and Miriam) were still working on building a better relationship with Portia. I just wasn't very close with her. I always felt like she kept me at arm's distance the whole time. It wasn't much communication, and I wanted to bridge that gap a little more."

Asked what kind of relationship Miriam and Alan had, she testified, "A wonderful relationship. He was a wonderful human being. He just treated me well. He had a saying, 'Have fun like hell.' That's what his life was like. We enjoyed each other very much. We built things in common along the way. Like the horses, the dancing. We enjoyed sitting on the back porch and looking over everything that we'd accomplished. I always told Alan he reminded me of the John Wayne movie when he sat up on the hill watching his entire little ranch every afternoon.

"We took trips together and just had fun. We had found out that by digging down from six to twelve feet that we had water underground at our place in Whitewater. So he wanted to tap into that and put in grass and make it into a really nice horse property. If he split up the property, then it would basically pay for the mortgage on the house, and he could pay the house off. He'd do that by selling off the front of the property."

Asked to tell more about the trips they'd taken together, Miriam said, "We went to Denver to visit his sister before Christmas. Then we went to Lake Tahoe for Christmas. We went to a stock show in January for my birthday. We went to Lake Powell twice, once in April and once in May. We went to Mesquite, Nevada, for a golf trip for him and a gambling trip there."

McGuirk asked if Miriam took messages for Alan, answered his cell phone, and kept appointments for him. She said she did all those things when he wanted her to. And, according to Miriam, he had wanted that a lot during the time he had been sick from the winter of 2007 through the spring of 2008.

McGuirk wondered why Miriam didn't make sure that Alan called back everyone who had left a message. Miriam answered, "That wasn't my job."

Then McGuirk asked, "When you were calling Elizabeth Callister about the insurance policy, why did you call her?"

Miriam replied, "Alan asked me to call her."

This brought an immediate objection from Richard Tuttle, who said, "That asks for an answer based on hearsay."

McGuirk replied, "Your Honor, this isn't being offered for the truth of the matter asserted. It's being offered for the effect on the listener, what she did in reaction to him telling her what to do."

What followed was a long sidebar, out of the hearing of the jury. The judge was just about to decide what the jurors were going to hear on the important matter of why Miriam Helmick had allegedly called Elizabeth Callister about a large insurance policy on Alan's life, not long before he was murdered.

CHAPTER 39

DEADLY DRUGS

The first real argument between the prosecution and defense during Miriam's testimony came over this issue of a life insurance policy for Alan Helmick. Richard Tuttle told the judge, "This is clearly hearsay. If the court's going to admit it, I'd ask that the jury be instructed that it's not being offered for the truth, just for the effect on the listener. And I would argue that the defense not argue that it's the truth in closing."

Jody McGuirk replied, "It's not hearsay, because we're offering it for the effect it had on Miriam."

Tammy Eret joined in on this, saying, "If they bring it up in closing argument, we'll never hear again that the only reason why that insurance policy was purchased was because Alan wanted it."

McGuirk shot back, "I'm not saying that at all. I'm not saying anything about purchasing the policy. I'm saying why did she call her (Callister) that one time."

Eret wasn't backing down. "This is so sidestepping hearsay."

Soon Steve Colvin was in the argument as well. "I would

just add that the prosecution has elicited several times statements that were offered for the effect on the listener and we've never asked for a limiting instruction. So I think that at this time for the court to start issuing limiting instructions would unfairly highlight the fact that some statements are elicited that are not offered for the truth of the matter asserted. I think to avoid unduly and unfairly highlighting, we need to go back and find every statement that's been admitted and do a limiting instruction for all of them. Otherwise, this is unfairly saying only Ms. Helmick's testimony needs to be looked at with caution."

If Steve Colvin got his way, this would be a major headache. It would mean that every witness so far—who the defense thought was bringing in hearsay testimony—would need the testimony explained to the jurors. And the judge would have to remind the jurors that those statements had to be looked at with caution.

Tuttle wasn't buying any of this and said, "For Mr. Colvin, who didn't take advantage of that—it doesn't make sense now! Every situation is judged on its own merits."

Colvin responded, "The prosecution wants you to preclude Ms. Helmick from explaining why she did something that they are saying is evidence of guilt. That flies in the face of everything that you have a right to do. If we can't explain why she did it, they can't be allowed to say that it's evidence of guilt."

Judge Robison responded, "I do find that it is the effect on listener that is being elicited—why she made the phone call." Then Robison asked the prosecution what kind of limiting instruction they wanted to be given to the jurors.

Tuttle replied, "I'd ask for the same language I proposed. 'Why did you (Miriam) call Elizabeth Callister?'"

Eret added, "When we go to do closing arguments, and I say Miriam was looking to take out an insurance policy, then they're gonna stand up and say, 'No, she wasn't. She only called because Alan told her to,' and they offer that for the truth. You can't do that, because it's hearsay."

Judge Robison wanted to get into this more in depth, so she excused the jurors and told them to take a break. Once they were out of the courtroom, Robison put together an instruction that read: *You have heard the defendant testify to statements allegedly made by the victim in this case, Alan Helmick. These statements have only been allowed to show the effect on the listener and cannot be considered by you for the truth of the statements.* In other words, Miriam supposedly heard those words coming from Alan's mouth, and she acted upon what she thought she heard. Therefore, what she thought she heard could never be determined to have been what Alan actually had said. Alan was obviously no longer around to verify that.

As far as limiting instructions being used now, and not earlier when the prosecution had been eliciting testimony, Judge Robison said, "I don't feel that it is unduly prejudicial to Ms. Helmick. The simple fact is, that if limiting instructions had been requested during testimony earlier, the court would have considered that and determined whether or not it would be appropriate to give it. No such request was made." Since neither Jody McGuirk or Steve Colvin had asked for limiting instructions, that was their decision and no one else's, as far as Judge Robison was concerned.

When the jurors came back in, Judge Robison gave them the limiting instructions. Jody McGuirk asked Miriam, "When you called Elizabeth Callister about the health insurance policy, why did you call her?"

Miriam replied, "Alan asked me to."

McGuirk wanted to know about Alan Helmick and his phone calls and messages. Miriam said, "He just threw his phone in my purse when he didn't want to carry it. He didn't like carrying it around in his pockets while he walked around."

"Did you ever keep Alan's phone from him?"

"No, I did not."

"Did you ever hide his phone from him?"

"No, I did not."

"Did he ever use your phone?"

"Yes. He used my phone because he liked to put it on a speakerphone, especially if we were driving. My speaker was clearer than his."

Getting back to Elizabeth Callister, McGuirk said that Callister had testified earlier that Miriam had phoned her and asked if she could set up a life insurance policy on Alan without his knowledge.

Miriam answered that she had not used those exact words. Miriam stated now, "I asked her because of the size of the policy if he had to have the nurse or whoever came in to do blood pressure and all of that. And she said yes, we needed to have that done. He wanted an insurance policy, but he couldn't get it at the time. His blood pressure was up and he started smoking again."

The topic soon turned to the car fire incident. Miriam told her version of the car fire incident and stressed that she'd never made it to the trunk of the car. She said that she'd gotten sick to her stomach and had to rush to the restroom in the building. When Alan first alerted her to the fact there was a car fire, Miriam testified, "I was walking out toward the other stairs to the front door, and Alan came in and said that the car was on fire, that he needed an extinguisher or some water. I didn't see an extinguisher, and I had a Pepsi bottle in my hand, so I handed it to him." (This was different from searching for a pitcher of water in the building, which had been mentioned previously.)

As far as the "wick" went, and the smell of gasoline in the restroom, Miriam testified, "He pried the stick with cotton out of the tank and looked at it, and then handed it to me. I went to get some water and I took it with me. I was upset about the car, so I wasn't really paying attention. I put it in the garbage can in the ladies' room. I took water back outside and he was calling 911. Somewhere along the line, he asked me to go get it (the wick), so I got it. I just don't remember the timing on it."

McGuirk asked, "Do you know why Alan wanted it?"

Miriam answered, "To have it for the police."

Asked how Alan had responded to the whole car fire incident, Miriam said, "He was very calm. I thought it was kind of unusual. I was not so calm."

After the lunch break, Jody McGuirk wondered if Alan Helmick sometimes used Miriam in a "secretarial role," and she said yes. She would take phone messages for him and sometimes return calls. She added, "I called more when he was sick. He asked me to do it more often."

Asked about when they got up in the morning, Miriam said she usually got up between nine and ten in the morning. As for Alan, it could be any time. He did not sleep well, and he might get up between two and seven in the morning. And then Miriam spoke of Alan sleepwalking. She said, "I came out to the garage one time. He was in the car asleep at the wheel with the keys in his hand. One time he was trying to find something to eat, and he had all the Tupperware out, looking, I guess. I finally got him back to bed, but when I put my hand on a cereal bowl to take out the next morning for him, it had oatmeal in it, so I knew he was up. Another time we were in Las Vegas. I heard a real loud banging on the door, and when I opened the door, he was standing there naked in the hallway. So he had awakened somewhere in the hall."

McGuirk asked about Alan being sick a lot, and Miriam said, "He was very tired. Flu-y. He would be that way for a little while, for a few days, and then he'd be fine for a few days, and it would just go back and forth. He had back issues during the whole year. With his back, he had two swollen disks, where he had to get an MRI, and he was going to the chiropractor twice a week. When he was sick, he normally didn't want to talk to anybody. He didn't want to have to think about things. He just liked to be left alone."

McGuirk wanted to know if this included Alan's children. To this, Miriam said Alan didn't want to talk to them, and at times he didn't even want to talk to her. And that was the reason she began answering his phone messages. She said she passed the information on to him; but whether he called people back, she didn't know.

As far as home computers went, Miriam stated that she used the Gateway computer and Alan had an Acer notebook computer. But according to Miriam, he started having problems with it, so he also used the Gateway computer more and more often.

Now came the important questions about whether Miriam had ever signed any of Alan's checks. To this, she said yes. McGuirk showed her one check after another that she had signed; and to each, when asked why she had signed those checks, Miriam said, "Because Alan asked me to." Most of these were to Dance Junction, and Miriam could, of course, cash Alan's checks going to that business.

Questioning also came up as to why Alan supposedly didn't want to talk to Alan Watkins concerning bank accounts. Miriam replied that she thought this was strange and it upset her. She added, "I got angry at Alan because I didn't know what was happening. I didn't like being put on the spot. He said not to worry about it, that he would take care of it. He was keeping me at arm's distance on things."

Back to computers, McGuirk asked about Internet searches on the computers regarding various medicines. Miriam said, "He'd been ill, and I brought it to his attention that he couldn't keep his blood pressure down. We didn't know if it was a combination of the medications he was taking or what was wrong."

McGuirk asked, "Did you look up articles about horse euthanasia?"

"No, that would have been Alan, not me."

"What about articles concerning the death of Heath Ledger?"

"I don't know if he did."

"What about an article concerning death by liquid nicotine? Did you look that one up?"

"No."

"Some of the searches were done at odd times. One o'clock in the morning. Two o'clock in the morning."

"That was probably when Alan was up."

"Would you be looking at the Internet at that time?"

"No."

"Why not?"

"I was asleep."

CHAPTER 40

"HE WAS JUST GONE."

Questions came up by Jody McGuirk about the day before Alan was murdered, and Trish Erikson's testimony that he and Miriam had been arguing that day. When McGuirk asked about this, Miriam said, "We hadn't been fighting. He had errands to run, and he was not really in a very good mood. He was just real, real grumpy."

As far as the riding lesson for Alan's granddaughter being canceled, Miriam testified, "Alan decided that he wasn't sure that he wanted to pick up the grandkids. He wasn't in a great mood. Originally, he had planned to go to Montrose. He didn't like having the girls over at the house if he couldn't give one hundred percent of his undivided attention. I had wanted to pick the girls up. I had started developing a relationship with the granddaughters and was enjoying their company. It was upsetting to me."

McGuirk wanted to know why Alan hadn't called Portia, instead of Miriam having to call her. Miriam said, "I don't think he wanted to get into an argument with her. He told me what to say to Portia."

Miriam added about how Alan spent the day of June 9,

2008: "I don't know exactly where he went. He was gone for an hour and fifteen minutes. He was still in a bad mood when he got back. He had me call Portia again and say he had a little too much to drink. That's what he asked me to tell her."

Now came questions about the crucial morning of June 10, the day that Alan was murdered. Miriam said, "He woke me up around seven. I'm not sure exactly when. He had the coffee going and thought it was time I got up. He wanted to go feed the horses. We went to the back porch and had a cup of coffee. We talked about doing errands. He thought if I went with him, I'd be sitting in the car a lot. I didn't want to sit in the car everywhere, because he planned on going to Clifton Water (a company) and a couple of other places.

"I had things I wanted to do, and I was out of shirts, the kind I'd use in the barn. I knew there was a sale going on, so I thought I'd take that in. After coffee we went down to the barn. He did most of the feeding. I couldn't lift or carry anything at the time. I could do a little cleaning of the barn, but I wasn't supposed to do any lifting. I'd had an ATV accident and I had broken a rib and injured my arm at the same time. We kind of got the ATV in a hole and he turned it the wrong way, and we dumped over. My arm got bruised and one rib was broken."

Getting back to the morning of June 10, Miriam continued, "After feeding the horses, we went back to the house. While he took a shower, I laid out a shirt and pants for him. Then I laid out a couple of things for him to take in the truck. I left about eight-fifteen. I went to the Orchard Mesa City Market, and I called Sue Boulware from there. That was to reschedule the horse lesson to Friday. I went into the Orchard Mesa City Market to pick up cigarettes and a drink. Then I went to Walmart to get the shirts I'd use in the barn."

From Walmart, Miriam said she went to Safeway on Horizon Avenue to get a large bag of carrots, which she was going to feed to the horses. Then it was on to Hastings Bookstore to pick up coloring books for Alan's grandkids. And finally she drove to the Chinese restaurant around 11:00 A.M. Miriam said she phoned Alan from there, got no answer, and finally returned home.

Now came the questioning of exactly what happened next. Miriam said, "When I pulled into the driveway, everything looked normal. Alan's truck was there. I grabbed my bags and purse and went inside. I went through the garage door, through the washroom into the hallway and to the kitchen. I saw Alan on the floor, near the back door. I dropped my bags and went to him. I knelt down beside him, by his left side. He was cold and gray. He didn't have a pulse. I just saw a little blood under his neck. For a while, I just sat there with him. I didn't know what had happened to him. I held his hand for a few minutes and tried to make some sense of it all.

"I finally called 911. I noticed that there were some drawers open. The 911 operator told me to do CPR. And I tried. It was hard. I was trying to do the chest compressions, but I could only do it with one hand. I didn't have the strength from my right arm, because I was still recovering from the rib injury. I pinched his nose together. And I turned his head sideways. He had saliva in his mouth and a little blood ran out of his nose. I tried to blow in his mouth, but he was already gone. He was just gone."

When the first officers arrived, Miriam said that they made her go outside. "I wasn't really thinking at that point. I was just numb. I talked with an officer, who was out there. He wanted to know if the dogs barked. I said I'm sure they did if someone came around."

Miriam also said that she wanted to get her purse from the house, but the officers wouldn't let her back inside. She waited around outside for quite a while, and then officers asked her to come down to the sheriff's office. Miriam recalled that Detective Jarrell and Detective Norris asked her a lot of questions and took the clothes she was wearing. As far as the questions that were asked, she said, "I can't remember them. It was all a blur."

After being questioned by the police, she went to Merredith Von Burg's house, because, as she put it, "that was the only place I knew of to go at that moment. I had a good, cordial relationship with Merredith. I stayed at her house for two to three days. While I was there, I worried about what was going on—getting the funeral process started, and things like that."

Asked if she was concerned about money at that time, Miriam answered that she was very concerned. She only had $180 with her, and no credit cards. She didn't even have her purse with her driver's license inside it. The police had that. As far as the funeral went, she said that she started the process and Alan's daughters took it from there. Miriam added, "It was hard. There was a private viewing. I don't really know how long it was. The funeral was wonderful, in that everyone had things to say about Alan."

Asked if she had a hard time recalling the day of the funeral, Miriam replied that she did. One line of questioning was interesting. McGuirk asked if she had spoken with a man named Mike Pruett on the day of the funeral: "He mentioned that you told him that you said an ex-employee could have killed Alan. Do you remember saying this?"

Miriam replied, "I don't remember, but I could have."

"Who were you talking about when you said that?"

"About Keith Coppage."

"Why were you talking about it there?"

"Cody, a man who worked at the dance studio, had brought it to my attention earlier that day. I think he told me the authorities were already aware of it."

In essence, Miriam was now saying that Keith Coppage might have murdered Alan because of their dispute at Dance Junction. The same Keith Coppage whom Barbara Watts indicated Miriam loved. Also, according to Watts, Miriam had written in a journal that Miriam would do anything for Keith, even die for him.

As to why Miriam went back to her Whitewater home at all, after Alan's murder, if she was afraid of a killer on the loose, Miriam said that she had responsibilities there. "I had to feed the horses and the dogs. It was too expensive to stay in town and run back and forth there. I didn't have the money for that. I spent my days mostly sitting in the garage. Alan's blood was still on the kitchen floor. It seemed different than I remembered. It was everywhere. It was not what I had seen that day. I tried to clean it up, but I couldn't. Portia finally came over and cleaned it up."

Miriam said that she tried getting her purse and driver's license back from the police, but they didn't hand it over to her. She added that this was devastating. "I needed my driver's license to go down and apply for public assistance, and I couldn't do that. You can't really do anything without your driver's license. And I couldn't get my birth certificate without a valid driver's license. I was caught between a rock and a hard place. I was only able to pay the light bill. I couldn't make the house payment."

As far as the money that Merredith Von Burg loaned her, Miriam said she used that to buy groceries, food for the animals, and some gasoline for the car. And Miriam said that she didn't sell any property that did not directly belong to her.

CHAPTER 41

"I LOVED HIM."

Now came time for the very important issue of the yellow greeting card under the doormat. Jody McGuirk asked, "Did you leave that greeting card for Penny Lyons to find that day?"

Miriam replied, "Yes."

"Why did you do that?"

"Up until that point, nobody had done anything about the truck I had seen and called in about. I'd seen it again, and there were other things that were happening."

"What were you hoping to do with the card?"

"I hoped the police would actually take it seriously and maybe watch the road."

"And did they do that?"

"No, they did not."

Miriam said that it had been the wrong thing to do, but she was in a panic at the time. "I used Penny badly. She's a friend of mine, and I shouldn't have done that. It didn't accomplish anything. I thought the police might listen to her, since they weren't listening to me. I feel very badly about using her now, but I had seen that white truck and the way it had behaved. It was driving around the side of the house and I saw it from the master bathroom window. I went down to the garage, because I thought it was maybe someone that I knew. And when I opened the garage door, it drove by slowly, and then they just kicked it into gear and spun gravel and left."

McGuirk asked if Miriam saw who was driving the truck. She responded, "It was a white male, with kind of light, curly hair. I called law enforcement about it. I called Mr. Hebenstreit. I didn't hear anything back from him about it. Then I saw the truck again, a week later. I heard the horses running around at night, and I went out and checked and shined a light down there and saw the truck again. As soon as I shined the light, it moved off."

Asked if she phoned law enforcement about it this time, Miriam said that she hadn't. As to why, she replied that they hadn't done anything about it after her first call. McGuirk wanted to know why Miriam stayed in the house if she was scared. Miriam replied, "I still had animals to feed. I didn't have money to go anywhere, and I didn't want somebody pushing me out of my own house. I didn't have family in the area, and Alan's family had changed."

McGuirk said, "Was anything else happening around your property?"

Miriam answered, "I would come home and there would be a back door open. Just little things. At first, I thought I was going nuts. Then I started putting it together."

McGuirk wanted to know how law enforcement had treated Miriam. She replied, "The day they came to measure the house, I was sitting in the garage, and when the gentleman left (Mike Piechota), he told me they really needed to talk to me. He said it in a way that was very mean. I felt like he was treating me as a suspect. I had asked for my driver's license back and they wouldn't give it to me."

As for how Alan's daughters began treating her, Miriam said, "I believe it was three days after the funeral, Kristy called me and told me they were going to sue me for everything.

I knew their attitudes had definitely changed. I knew they were treating me like a suspect at that point. And Alan's friends—it was strange. When something like this happens, you usually reach out, and nobody reached out to me. I felt like I was drowning the whole time. I couldn't seem to get ahead. I didn't know where my next income was coming from."

Miriam said that she just wanted to leave Grand Junction to be closer to her son, Chris. She added, "It wasn't until I put him on the plane that I decided to go. He was there (in the Grand Junction area) for several days and I felt secure while he was there. And when I put him on the plane and he left, it just started all over again. Like I was alone. I drove all the way through to Brunswick, Georgia."

Asked if she had law enforcement's permission to go, Miriam said, "I didn't ask. No one said I couldn't go."

"Were you running from law enforcement?"

"No."

"Your son, Chris, testified that you acted mad when he told you that he spoke to law enforcement and told them that you were staying with him. Were you mad about that?"

Miriam responded, "I wasn't mad about that. He had spoken with them, and he didn't tell me about it right away. He told me about a week later. I wasn't happy about that. If I had wanted someone not to find me, I wouldn't have gone to see my son."

McGuirk next wanted to know why Miriam had used Sharon Helmick's identification. Miriam said, "After all the things the police took from the house, that's actually the one thing they left. They had my driver's license and birth certificate. Her ID was in a drawer all by itself. You can't even get a hotel room without a license. I hadn't planned on using it in any other way."

Miriam had also done possible ID searches on her son's computer when she was in Florida; McGuirk asked about that. Miriam responded, "It was kind of a last-ditch effort to find an ID that I could actually send in to get my birth certificate and get a Florida driver's license."

As to why she didn't call any of Alan's family when she got to Florida, Miriam said that she wanted to put all of the bad memories of Alan's murder behind her. "I was not in a good state to call anybody. I needed to put my head under a pillow for several weeks."

This led into questioning about going on Internet dating sites, and Miriam said, "It was for communication, something that was lively and interesting, so that I could laugh a little bit again. A little intelligent conversation. I joined those sites to chat with someone. I wasn't looking for anyone in particular. I did it as an escape from always feeling bad. I had been drowning most of the time. I couldn't get out from underneath it."

McGuirk asked why Miriam used Sharon Helmick's name when she joined the computer sites. Miriam responded, "It was hard enough using one name. There would have been confusion of going back and forth between 'Sharon' and 'Miriam.' So I just used it."

As far as meeting Charles Kirkpatrick, Miriam said, "It was a fling. I didn't see him again after that. I wasn't interested."

After a long period of questioning, Jody McGuirk began to wrap things up. She asked, "Were you keeping Alan from his family?"

"No, I was not."

"Were you writing checks on his accounts without his permission?"

"No, I was not."

"Did you set his car on fire in Delta?"

"No, I did not."

"Did you shoot your husband?"

"No, I did not."

"Do you know who did?"

"No, I do not."

"Do you miss him?"

"Yes."

"Could you have done anything to hurt him?"

"No."

"Why not?"

"I loved him."

For Miriam Helmick, the direct examination had been the easy part. Now she was about to be questioned by the prosecution, and Richard Tuttle had believed almost nothing of what she had just said.

CHAPTER 42

A BATTLE OF WILLS

Richard Tuttle began by asking, "You described Alan as the love of your life in 2005?"

Miriam answered, "Yes."

"Was he the love of your life in June 2008?"

"Yes."

"But you said in January 2005 that you really didn't like him. Do you remember saying that?"

"Yes."

"And Barbara Watts testified that by Valentine's Day, you were in love with him and living in his house. You went in the course of a month from the El Rio Rancho Motel to living with him. Can you describe the El Rio Rancho Motel?"

"It's just a weekly-stay motel."

"Would you describe it as a cheap motel?"

"Yes."

"And how much did it cost to stay there?"

"One hundred seventy dollars per week."

"And at the time you came to Grand Junction, what did you have with you?"

"Clothes, a couple of suitcases, and I brought my dogs with me."

Tuttle asserted that Miriam Giles had come to Grand Junction with very little; and within a month, she was living with a wealthy man in Delta. Tuttle added that Miriam's lifestyle changed dramatically once she moved in with Alan Helmick; Miriam agreed. Then Tuttle retold the story of Laegan McGee coming over to her at Boomers in 2005, and Miriam saying to McGee in a singsongy voice, "I hear wedding bells."

Tuttle asked, "At that time, Laegan McGee talked about how you actually labeled off on your fingers, 'He's gonna buy me a studio. He's gonna buy me a house in Whitewater. He's gonna buy me horses.' Do you recall saying that?"

"I recall her saying that. Those conversations happened over the course of a year. We hadn't even decided to buy a house in Whitewater at that point. We hadn't talked about horses at that time. Wedding bells maybe, but not the rest of it."

Tuttle asserted that Laegan McGee was surprised about Alan Helmick, since she thought that Miriam Giles and Keith Coppage were a couple.

Miriam replied, "I didn't have a boyfriend. I had dated a fellow in Mississippi, but that was it."

Tuttle was very dubious that Alan Helmick wanted to buy a dance studio because it would help him pay less to the Internal Revenue Service. But Miriam responded, "He knew that I liked to teach. He wanted a tax break. So together, it worked out. I certainly wouldn't have done it on my own."

"So, in the course of two months of meeting you, he's now a big dance aficionado and this is his dream, not yours."

"I don't know if you'd call it a dream. I mean, that's just the way Alan did things. When he decided to do something, he moved on it, and he moved on it very fast. He enjoyed dancing."

"What about horses? Whose passion was that?"

Miriam replied, "He had this list of things to do over the next ten years. He wanted to trail ride up to a lake on the Mesa, where he could camp and go fishing, places where you couldn't go by car or truck."

But Tuttle got Miriam to agree that a trail horse and a dressage horse-training business were a lot different. And Tuttle got Miriam to agree that Alan never did take dressage lessons, only she did.

Changing subjects, Richard Tuttle asked if her relationship with Charles Kirkpatrick had moved along just as quickly as her relationship had with Alan Helmick. Miriam said that her time with Kirkpatrick was not a relationship. She described it as a fling.

Tuttle rejoined, "You were exchanging e-mails with him on MillionaireMatch-dot-com. And you saw how many assets he had, correct?"

Miriam replied, "I actually didn't look at his assets."

Tuttle responded with mock surprise. "Oh, you didn't look at his assets?"

"No, I was looking at more of what we had in common. His income wasn't actually all that important. He liked to dance and do those kind of things."

Now Tuttle was very scornful. "So his income was inconsequential to you?"

Miriam said, "That's correct."

"But, in fact, you were trying to build yourself up to fit the profile. There was that [admission that] you were a 2007 Western Colorado Dressage Champion?"

Miriam replied, "Actually, Shadow was a 2006 Grand Valley Dressage Horse of the Year."

"You talked about working for three CFOs of three Fortune 500 companies, correct? That wasn't true?"

Miriam answered, "I did work for CFOs of Fortune 500

companies. Regency Centers, a real estate investment trust, [and] for a publicly traded railroad, and the Southeastern Development Company." Miriam said that she worked as an assistant to the president of that company, but she could only recall his last name as being Morgan.

Tuttle was skeptical of this, and also skeptical when Miriam said that she had been a chef at one time. Tuttle asked, "You didn't actually work as a chef, did you?"

Miriam replied, "My dad taught me how to cook. My dad was a chef in the military." And then Miriam finally admitted that she hadn't worked as a chef.

Tuttle asked if her story now was that she had not been interested in Charles Kirkpatrick. Miriam answered that she hadn't been. So Tuttle asked why she had spent several days with him in Orlando if she wasn't interested. Miriam answered that she had only spent two days with Kirkpatrick.

Tuttle wouldn't let her off on this. "He didn't hold you prisoner there. Would you agree with me that shows quite a bit of interest in somebody that you just met for the first time?"

Miriam said in her mind that it did not. So Tuttle asked, "You weren't interested in his money?" Miriam replied that she wasn't. Sarcastically Tuttle replied, "Well, he's not exactly Brad Pitt. Would you agree with that?" Miriam did agree.

Getting back to the unattended house in Whitewater, Colorado, Tuttle questioned if Miriam was so worried about someone sneaking into the house, why had she abandoned it so that someone could go in there at any time. Miriam replied that Katie Turcotte was keeping an eye on the house.

Shifting gears, Rich Tuttle asked, "Do you recall telling Jeri Yarbrough two days after Alan was murdered—well, actually joking—about how you didn't know a full tank of gas would not blow up?"

Miriam responded, "I wasn't joking, but I do remember saying that."

"Do you remember telling her that Alan was being an ass-hole for the last two weeks?"

"Yes, I do."

"This is the love of your life who just had been murdered?"

"Yes."

"Pretty harsh words two days after he was murdered. Would you agree with that?"

Miriam replied, "It was just responding to a question that she asked in the conversation. I wouldn't have just blurted it out."

Getting back to the house, Tuttle asked why Miriam had lived there for six days after the murder: "With blood all over the kitchen floor?"

Miriam answered, "I didn't think it would be that way when I came home, because that's not how it was when I left."

"Well, everybody else seems to have been shocked by that blood on the floor, except you. Would you agree with that?"

Miriam said that she had been shocked by the blood on the floor, and that's why she hadn't cleaned it up. It was too traumatic for her to do so, Miriam claimed. Tuttle wanted to know why she hadn't expressed that to others. Miriam asked a question of her own. She wanted to know what "others" Tuttle was talking about. So Tuttle listed them: "Merredith Von Burg, Katie Turcotte, Penny Lyons."

Miriam didn't reply directly to this, but she answered that she had tried to clean up the blood. So Tuttle asked how she had done that. Miriam answered that she had tried getting down on her hands and knees to clean it up. Then she added, "I couldn't stay around it. I tried not going into that room as much as possible. If anyone came to the house, I asked them not to go into the kitchen."

CHAPTER 43

THE SPARKS BEGIN TO FLY

Turning to bills and checks, ADA Rich Tuttle questioned Miriam as to why she had never told anyone in law enforcement that on occasion she wrote out checks for Alan Helmick. In fact, she had stated early on to an investigator, "He writes all the bills. He pays everything and just gives me a little bit of money. Everything's in his name and he takes care of everything." Tuttle now queried, "You never told them that in the past year you had written eleven separate checks for over forty thousand on his accounts?"

Miriam replied, "I didn't think that was very important at the time. We were talking about his death."

Tuttle wouldn't let her off the hook about Alan's checks. He said, "Would you agree that it's rather unusual when you're taking a check out of a check register to pull out the stub as well?"

Miriam answered that it had been Alan who had done that, and then he handed her the checks.

Tuttle was extremely skeptical about that explanation and said, "So he took the check stub out so he couldn't keep track of what happened to the check?"

This brought an immediate objection from Jody McGuirk; a sidebar ensued. Outside the hearing of the jury, McGuirk said, "It's speculation because you're asking her to explain why Alan took the stubs out."

Tuttle countered with, "I just asked if she would consider it unusual to take the check stubs out. That's a perfectly legitimate question."

Judge Robison replied, "Well, the question that I recall is why Alan would have taken the check stubs out. What I'm going to do at this point is sustain the objection and ask you to rephrase your question."

When that was over, Tuttle did rephrase his question and asked, "Ms. Helmick, you've testified that Alan gave you permission to write each of these eleven checks. Is that correct?" Miriam said that was true, so Tuttle continued his questioning. "Did Alan also give you an explanation as to why he was giving you not only the check, but the check stubs as well?"

Miriam responded, "No. I mean, I took them down to the studio, separated them, and put them in an envelope so that we'd have them down there."

Tuttle wasn't buying this explanation, either, and said, "Would you agree that looks like somebody who is trying to write checks on another person's account and hide it by taking out the check stub?"

Not surprisingly, Miriam answered, "No."

"Do you know why Alan, or yourself, would take checks out of the middle of a checkbook?"

Miriam replied, "I don't know why he did it. He just handed me the checks."

"And Alan's not with us anymore, correct?"

"Correct."

"And he can't come in here and dispute anything you say that he said. Is that correct?"

"No, he cannot."

* * *

Moving on to the dance studio, Rich Tuttle said that Dance Junction was a very unprofitable business and Miriam agreed. But once again, she added that Alan had purchased the business to be a tax write-off, and because he knew how much she liked to dance. There was no sense of Dance Junction being financially successful, according to Miriam, if Alan Helmick wanted to use it as a tax write-off.

Tuttle responded, "Well, that's a pretty big thing to do for tax purposes. He lost fifty-seven thousand dollars on Dance Junction in 2005. And he lost another twenty-one thousand in 2006." Miriam agreed with those figures.

The horse business had been a losing proposition for Alan Helmick as well. Miriam testified that just three horses cost $18,000, and the riding arena cost $15,000. On top of that, Stephanie Soule was being paid about $2,000 every month. Tuttle wanted to know why Alan was spending so much money on all of this, if he just wanted a horse to ride into the backcountry to go camping.

Miriam replied, "Actually, all I wanted was a horse to ride and some lessons, and he took it from there. There was a lot of work involved, and he told me he would do it with me. He negotiated everything."

Tuttle asked if Miriam knew that the dance studio and the horse-training center were losing businesses that were running Alan into the ground. She answered by saying, "I knew that he made no profit from them."

So Tuttle said, "You knew that things were not going well financially in the Helmick residence at the time of his death, correct?"

Miriam responded, "That is not correct."

"Let's get this straight! Arvin Eby comes over on a Thursday or Friday, June fifth or sixth, with the first delivery of two loads of hay, where he was paid forty-eight hundred dollars. He was given a check. And he went to the bank, and the bank wouldn't accept it. And according to Arvin Eby, you later told him that there were stolen or forged checks on that account, and that was the problem. Do you remember saying that?"

Miriam replied, "I didn't say it quite like that. Alan told him that he had lost some checks and that there was a hold on the account. That's all I knew at that point."

Moving on to the insurance policy, Tuttle said, "Twenty-five thousand dollars to a person who came to town in 2005 with a couple of suitcases, two small dogs, and very little money—[that] is quite a bit of money. Would you agree with that?"

Miriam didn't agree. So Tuttle asked her, "How much did you have in your pocket when you hit town in 2005?"

Miriam replied, "Probably about six hundred dollars."

"And so twenty-five thousand is quite a bit of money compared to six hundred. Would you agree with that?"

Miriam answered, "Compared to six hundred dollars, yes."

"You never mentioned that twenty-five thousand to the detectives?"

"When we first talked about taking out the insurance policy, I didn't realize it was even there."

"Well, in fact, you were calling the insurance agent before Alan was even buried. Isn't that correct?"

"That's correct."

"You called the agent on June 16, 2008, the day before the funeral?"

Miriam responded, "I had found paperwork in Alan's drawer."

Once again, Tuttle wanted to know why insurance agent Elizabeth Callister had said that Miriam had phoned her about getting a million-dollar life insurance policy on Alan. Tuttle added, "You testified, 'She ultimately told me that he was too old to get a million-dollar policy and that we had to settle for getting a twenty-five thousand dollar policy.' Do you remember that?"

Miriam said that she didn't recall those words. Tuttle responded, "You heard Elizabeth Callister very clearly say that you wanted to do it without Alan's knowledge." Miriam responded that she had not said those exact words.

Miriam claimed now that she was trying to get the life insurance policy because one of Alan's investors wanted a policy, just in case something should happen to Alan. Miriam said that the person who requested it would be the beneficiary, and not her, if Alan died.

Tuttle countered, "Alan threw a lot of money at your interests and hobbies, didn't he? Things like dancing, horses, that sort of thing."

Miriam replied, "He didn't throw it at me. He gave it when he felt like it."

"Okay, he gave it for your benefit, and that was all coming to an end, wasn't it?"

"I didn't know that at the time."

Rich Tuttle wanted to know why Miriam testified that it was Alan who had searched about medicines and poisons on the Internet. Miriam responded that she didn't know why he did those things, and she added, "I don't know what he did in the wee hours of the morning. I know that we discussed looking up his medications."

As to why Alan would be looking on the Internet about euthanasia procedures on a horse, since they weren't planning to put one down at that time, Miriam said, "The only thing I can think of is he questioned some of the things on a bill about a horse."

Tuttle then asked a very pointed question. Why would Alan Helmick be looking up painkiller overdoses on Miriam's computer? And, as usual, Miriam had an answer for everything. She said that Alan was having problems with his computer connecting to the Internet.

Tuttle countered, "Mike Piechota testified there was no evidence that the Internet was problematic on Alan's computer during this time period. Mike Piechota's just wrong?"

Miriam answered, "I don't know. I'm not saying Mike Piechota's wrong. What I'm saying is that Alan couldn't pull up his Internet at all. His wireless wasn't working. He couldn't even get the front page when you get on."

Tuttle was very skeptical that Alan had been searching on Miriam's computer about overdoses from Halcion, Ambien CR, and Lisinopril. Miriam stuck to her guns, however, and said that he must have, because she hadn't done so.

Tuttle exclaimed, "So it's just a coincidence that those drug overdose searches are sandwiched between the car fire on April thirtieth and his murder on June tenth!"

Miriam answered, "I can't tell you that."

CHAPTER 44

"A Cat-and-Mouse Game"

Richard Tuttle moved on to why Miriam started passing herself off as Sharon Helmick after moving out of Colorado and heading back to Florida. Once again, Miriam claimed that it was because she couldn't get her purse from the sheriff's office to retrieve her driver's license. And without a driver's license, she couldn't get a copy of her birth certificate.

Tuttle replied, "You didn't just use her name. You assumed her entire identity. Isn't that correct?"

Miriam said, "What was on her license, yes."

"On your employment application, you said you went to Delta High School, correct?"

"I may have. I don't remember."

"Okay, so it wasn't just her name. You were living as Sharon Helmick, correct?"

"Okay. Yes."

"And you pawned at least one item of jewelry under the name Sharon Helmick, correct?"

"Yes."

"Even when you went on these dating Web sites, you were Sharon. You weren't Miriam. Correct?"

"Correct."

"Where were you born?"

"Jacksonville, Florida."

"What efforts did you make to get a duplicate driver's license?" (ADA Tuttle meant with the name of Miriam.)

Miriam said she had tried in Colorado, so Tuttle said, "At no other time, you asked for your driver's license back after June 2008?"

Miriam responded, "How many times did I need to ask for it?"

Moving on from that topic, Richard Tuttle asked, "You didn't disclose to the detectives [that] there had been an arson attempt on your husband's life, until they asked whether you had any prior law enforcement contacts, did you? You didn't blurt out, 'Somebody tried to kill him just forty days ago!' What was the story behind that?"

Miriam claimed, "I don't remember most of the conversations they asked me about. That was a hard day. I wasn't thinking normally."

"Well, Ms. Helmick, you seemed to be tracking their questions pretty well that day. Would you agree with that?"

"I really don't know. I don't think so. I mean, I answered their questions. Obviously, I didn't answer them the way you wanted me to answer them."

"Is it still your statement that you never actually got back to the back of the trunk?" (Tuttle was referring to the car fire incident.)

"No, I didn't."

"So, in the time that you asked him to pop the trunk and then left to run back inside the building to use the restroom, somebody else came to the back of the car, stuck a wick there, lit it, and tried to blow him up?"

"I have no clue when it was."

"So, in a matter of just a few minutes, some arsonist is out there waiting for you to go into the ladies' room and they seize those few minutes of time, go to the back of the popped-up trunk area, put a wick that's burning into a gas tank, and try to blow him up? That's your story?"

"I didn't say that."

"Okay. Well, does that make sense to you?"

"No, it doesn't."

"In fact, you were a suspect in that case from the very get-go, correct?"

"No, I wasn't."

Miriam, who had countered all of Tuttle's questions with quick replies, now seemed to be staggering from the on-slaught. She was like a boxer who had taken numerous punches, and was just trying to stay in the ring.

Tuttle wanted to know if the smell of gasoline on Miriam's hand had anything to do with the fact that she had just watched the movie *No Country for Old Men.* In that movie, a character had placed a wick into a gas tank and blew up a car. Miriam once again said that she had not watched that movie; Alan must have done so.

Tuttle wasn't buying Miriam's answer, and questioned, "Do you think it's just a coincidence that you're in the exact same position as the villain in *No Country for Old Men,* a movie that was rented in your house four days before this arson attempt?"

"I didn't watch the movie. I didn't do it."

"So it's just a coincidence?"

"It would have to be."

And now, Richard Tuttle got to the important aspect of the greeting card under the doormat at the Helmicks' residence in Whitewater. The prosecutor had Miriam agree that she had purchased a greeting card on June 22, 2008. She would have had a hard time denying it, since she was caught on store security videotape.

Tuttle asked, "That's the day you planned this whole thing to pull a ruse on the sheriff's department that somebody was out to get you and they had planted a card at your door. You started on June twenty-second by purchasing the card, correct?"

Miriam answered, "Yes."

"And the murder was on June tenth. That's a passage of just twelve days. What about the police interview of June nineteenth at your house?"

Miriam answered that an officer there had been "mean to her." So Tuttle asked what she meant by this, and Miriam said, "He spoke to me in a very mean-spirited way."

Tuttle countered, "You know that, that conversation was recorded?"

Miriam said that she hadn't known that, and then she added that the officer had spoken that way after he had left the house, so he probably hadn't had the tape recorder on at that time.

Asked about housekeeper Trish Erikson's testimony, Tuttle wanted to know why Erikson would say that Miriam and Alan had had an argument on the day before he died. Miriam disagreed with Trish's comments and said that she had not had a spat with Alan that day. She added, "I was just irritated with the way he wanted things done. I didn't argue with him over it."

Tuttle countered, "Ms. Erikson indicated that she had never been in the house when it was like that before."

"Well, she only comes in the house once a month. She doesn't see me enough."

As far as canceling the horseback-riding lesson for Portia Vigil's daughter, Tuttle said, "You told her a falsehood, correct?"

Miriam answered, "I told her what Alan asked me to tell her."

"What about that he went to the Delta Elks Lodge, instead of stopping to see Portia, he got drunk, drove home, and had you put him to bed early. That was his creation?"

"That was his creation. But I didn't say he got drunk. I said he had a bit too much to drink."

"Would you agree, Ms. Helmick, that's a pretty elaborate lie for him to concoct on his own?"

Miriam responded by asking a question: "Why couldn't he do it on his own?"

"Well, it's a pretty elaborate lie. And this is a man who was sick a large part of the year. Why didn't he just say to Portia, 'I'm sick,' if he wanted to pull something over on her?"

"I have no clue."

"In fact, at the time you told Portia that, you didn't know that we would be able to talk to Chris Ranker and confirm that Alan never went to the Delta Elks Lodge that day, right?"

"I mean, I would have no . . . Why?"

"Would you agree that you were caught in a number of mistruths on what was going on in the afternoon and evening of June 9, 2008?"

"I just repeated what he asked me to say. I wasn't happy about it."

"You didn't communicate to law enforcement on June 10, 2008, this whole elaborate set of mistruths that Alan supposedly directed you to say. You didn't think it was important on June tenth after he was murdered?"

"There was a lot going on that day for me to remember everything."

Richard Tuttle's questioning of Miriam Helmick had been very pointed and unrelenting on December 3, and it only intensified the next day of testimony on December 4, 2009.

Right off the bat, he questioned Miriam's testimony that she only had contacted one person about dating in Florida, Charles Kirkpatrick. Tuttle now asked if she had actually contacted another man, named David Benables. (There was some confusion as to whether the last name was Benables or Venables.) Tuttle contended that she had contacted David by phone.

Miriam said she didn't recall that name, and Tuttle countered it should have been easy to do so. David was rich, and had an English accent. Once again, Miriam said that the only man she remembered talking to on the phone was Charles Kirkpatrick.

Tuttle once again zeroed in on the greeting card placed under the doormat, and he wanted to know why Miriam had placed it there. Miriam responded, "The reason was that I didn't think that they (law enforcement) were paying attention to me, especially after I reported the white truck the first time. Nobody bothered to ask me about it, come out and check on it, and I didn't think they would believe me a second time. So I did the note to see if it would call their attention to the property."

Tuttle related that law enforcement couldn't respond directly to her, because she had already asked that everything go through her lawyer. And Investigator Jim Hebenstreit had even contacted the lawyer about this so-called white truck that was prowling around the Helmick home. Miriam said, "She didn't tell me that they had done anything about it."

Tuttle continued that Miriam had the opportunity to talk to Investigator Mike Piechota about the white truck on June 19, when he was out at the Helmick residence, and she hadn't done so. Miriam claimed that on that occasion her lawyer had told her not to have a conversation with anyone associated with the investigation team.

Now Tuttle tried tripping Miriam up on her description of the driver of the white truck. She had testified on direct that the man had light-colored, curly hair. But when she spoke with her neighbor Josh Devries, she said the driver had curly black hair. Miriam responded that Devries must have heard wrong and that she always claimed the driver had light-colored, curly hair.

As far as being afraid of this driver, Katie Turcotte had testified earlier that Miriam told her that she was putting powder down on floors, to see if anyone disturbed the powder. Miriam testified now that Turcotte had gotten this wrong. Miriam had only talked about doing that, but she had never actually carried out the plan.

Tuttle was very skeptical about what he called a "cat-and-mouse game" between the supposed "real killer" and Miriam. Tuttle wanted to know if anything was stolen from the house when the person was supposedly coming inside the home after Alan's murder and disturbing things there. Miriam answered that she didn't notice anything that was stolen.

Tuttle asked her about some comments she had made at the time that she wished the killer would just come in and kill her as well. Miriam answered, "Half the time I wished that he did come back. I was having a tough time surviving. If he had come back, I probably wouldn't have cared."

CHAPTER 45

"THERE'S A ROGUE KILLER LURKING OUT THERE?"

Soon it was back to the greeting card, and Richard Tuttle asked, "When you told Penny Lyons, Colleen Scissors, Josh Devries, Merredith Von Burg, and Katie Turcotte about the greeting card, you were just acting at the time, weren't you?"

Miriam responded, "Yes."

"You were an actress?"

"Just briefly."

"So you were acting when it comes to the greeting card, but you're not acting when it comes to the suspicious white vehicle?"

"No. At the time, I was under the impression that nobody really cared, that nobody was going to come out and check anything. My attorney didn't talk with me about it. Nobody called me back on it. I was out there all by myself, not knowing what to do. I'd never been in a situation like this before."

"Okay, so you took the very dramatic step of buying a greeting card at City Market, writing out this threatening message to the grieving widow, 'Alan was first, you're next.

Run, run, run.' Planting it under your doormat, and pulling a big ruse on everybody, correct?"

"Yes."

"How did you expect this to turn law enforcement in the direction of finding your husband's killer?"

Miriam replied, "I thought that maybe they might monitor the road or come out and watch the property."

"But the entire time you lived there, from Alan's death until you skedaddled out of town in July, nobody actually harmed you in any way, shape, or form, did they?"

"No."

As far as any security measures that Miriam did while she was there, she said she left the police tape on the door. Tuttle was incredulous about this and asked, "The tape wasn't really going to stop a suspect from entering the house, correct?"

Miriam answered, "No, but you hear it rip off."

"So, in the middle of the night when you're in your bedroom, you would hear the tape on the front door rip off?"

Miriam replied, "I slept on the couch in the living room. I didn't sleep in the bedroom."

Sarcastically Tuttle said, "Well, that's convenient! Why were you sleeping on the couch in the living room?"

Miriam responded, "Because I didn't want to sleep in the bedroom. I didn't want to be in there alone. The living room was in a central part of the house where I felt comfortable."

Tuttle asked, "Is it safe to say that during this time frame, you were afraid you could be knocked off, whether you were in the house or down by the horses or anywhere, because it's an isolated property, correct?"

"That's correct."

"Regardless of the ruse you pulled with the greeting card, you were afraid of this person in the white truck. And yet you asked Katie Turcotte to come out that same night and start feeding your horses, correct?"

Miriam answered, "I did. But she wouldn't have been at the house."

Tuttle queried, "But she would be down at the barn by herself, and you were exposing her to danger, weren't you?"

Miriam disagreed and said, "I felt like somebody was after Alan and me. I didn't think they would go after Katie."

Tuttle didn't take that for an answer, and he added, "So she'd be safe, even though there's a rogue killer lurking out there? Coming by your property, going into the house, playing this cat-and-mouse game, and you thought she would be safe?"

"Well, I figured that she probably wasn't a target."

Moving to a different area of questioning, ADA Richard Tuttle wanted to know about all the traveling that Miriam said she did on the morning of June 10, 2008. Tuttle asked if she would agree that she made it known pretty quickly to the 911 operator and first deputy on the scene that she had been gone all morning and had arrived home to find Alan Helmick dead on the kitchen floor. Miriam agreed with that assessment.

Tuttle asked if it was correct that Alan was supposed to have gone to the Clifton Water offices to pay a bill that morning, and then he was going to take a truck in for servicing at a place called Shiners, on Highway 50. After that, they were supposed to meet for lunch, but there was no set time. Miriam disagreed with the last part, and she said that they had settled on a time of 11:00 A.M. at a Mexican restaurant named Dos Hombres. Later she had called him, because she wanted to change the restaurant to a Chinese place in Grand Junction.

Tuttle was very skeptical of Miriam's explanation of why she had gone so many different places on the morning of June 10, with gasoline rates being so high at that time. He said she had gone to Walmart, and then clear across town to a Safeway, located on Horizon Avenue, just to buy a bag of carrots.

Then she said she went back to a City Market at a different location in town to check on Alan's prescriptions, and then backtracked eastward to a Hastings Bookstore to buy some coloring books for Alan's granddaughters. Tuttle wanted to know why Miriam couldn't have bought all those things at one location, at the Walmart store.

Miriam replied that she traveled to all of those locations, because the best items were at those establishments. She didn't mind traveling around, since she wasn't going to meet Alan for lunch until after eleven o'clock.

As far as lunch went, Tuttle wondered why Alan wasn't calling her back, if she left so many voice messages for him. She said she thought it was because he had been upset with her the day before. So Tuttle wanted to know what he was upset about, and Miriam said, "He was keeping me at arm's distance and didn't really want to talk about things. When we talked about him doing errands that morning, he basically made it sound like there was no way I'd want to go with him because I didn't want to sit in the truck all morning. It's like he wanted to do it by himself. I was trying to understand what he wanted."

If there had been friction between Alan and Miriam that morning, then Tuttle wanted to know why there was nothing in Miriam's voice messages that indicated tension. Miriam answered, "I'm not the type of person to drag out anything like that. I supported him in whatever he did. So if he was having a tough time of it, I wanted to support him."

"Well, if he didn't want to be bugged by you, why did you keep leaving him voice messages?"

Miriam seemed to be breaking down more and more by this point. She replied, "I—I—I can't . . . I don't know how to explain why people do what they do."

"So you're really not getting along. He doesn't want to talk with you, yet you leave him four voice mail messages spaced fairly evenly apart as you journey through town, telling him what's going on and what you're thinking about, and that sort of thing. You had just seen him forty-five minutes earlier when you left your first voice message?"

Before another question was asked, Miriam said, "Before he got to the shower, I gave him a hug and a kiss. And he went into the shower and I didn't have a chance to really talk to him very much. We had discussed over coffee what we were going to do for the day. I still wanted him to know that no matter what was going on, up in his head, that I still loved him. So when I left the first message, it was very sweet."

"Okay, so it wasn't like you were on that bad of speaking terms, according to your testimony. He was going to meet you for lunch that day, correct?"

Miriam said that was so, but she added, "He was very agitated, and I was trying to understand that. I could only do what I could do. I just wanted him to know he had support."

If Alan was so agitated, Tuttle asked, why was he willing to meet Miriam for lunch? Miriam answered that he wasn't so much agitated with her, as he was about his businesses and his bad health over the previous year.

Richard Tuttle got back to the germane point, that Miriam went to a lot of places that morning, because she wanted receipts that she could later show to officers. Miriam said that wasn't true. Tuttle then claimed that Miriam's plans had been disrupted when Sue Boulware told her not to drive out to Loma, because gasoline was too expensive.

Miriam replied that the price of gas didn't concern her, and said, "I could have driven out to Loma after lunch if I'd met with him."

Tuttle asked, "Isn't it fair to say, Ms. Helmick, that when Sue Boulware nixed your idea to go out there and pay the bill, you had to come up with a way to spend two or three hours wasting time?"

"No," Miriam replied.

Tuttle added, "You had to find a way to have documentation of where you had been?" (So that Miriam could prove to police she was not home when Alan Helmick was supposedly murdered by an intruder.)

"No. I actually enjoyed being out a little bit. I liked putting the window down. It was a very nice day. I enjoyed doing it, even though I didn't know some of the routes. This had nothing to do with whether I wanted to go to Loma or not."

Tuttle asked, "Why not just mail the check to Sue Boulware?"

Miriam replied that she was just trying to be nice, because Sue was concerned about being paid. According to Miriam, she wasn't trying to create alibis on June 10, 2008; she was just running a lot of errands on a nice day, and was enjoying driving around the area.

CHAPTER 46

"THAT GREETING CARD LED THEM TO THE *REAL KILLER*, DIDN'T IT?"

Richard Tuttle asked why Miriam had the receipts for all the items she bought that day so conveniently stuffed in a pocket, instead of her purse? So convenient, in fact, she could readily pull them out and show officers where she had been. Miriam said that she often just put her receipts in her pocket. She'd learned that when a woman went to a store parking lot and opened her purse to put receipts inside, she became a target for theft.

Tuttle didn't buy it. He responded, "You have a bunch of receipts in your purse from other shopping trips, yet these receipts on this day are in your pocket, and most of your cash is in your pocket, correct?"

Miriam claimed that her purse was overflowing with receipts, and that was the reason why she had stuffed those particular receipts in her pocket.

As far as the 911 call, Tuttle wanted to know why Miriam sounded so calm during it. He said, "You were pretty patient for having just come home and found your husband violently shot and bleeding to death on the kitchen floor. Would you agree with that?"

Miriam stated, "I didn't know he'd been shot."

"You knew something was desperately wrong with him, right?"

"Yes."

"It was a pretty horrific thing to walk in on. And yet you were pretty patient with this rookie dispatcher, who didn't even know where Whitewater was. Would you agree with that?"

Miriam answered, "I may have been patient on the outside, but it really kind of upset me when he couldn't get the address the first or second time. It was very annoying."

"You took the time to spell out S-I-M-I-N-O-E for him, correct?"

"Yes. He couldn't get it right. So I had to spell it for him."

When Tuttle said, "What I'm saying is, it's not really consistent with a wife who just came home, startled to find her husband shot dead on the floor."

Jody McGuirk objected, saying, "This is testifying."

Judge Robison disagreed and overruled the objection. Then Robison told the jurors, "Comments made by attorneys are not testimony. They can certainly ask questions, and they do so during the course of a trial." It may have been a polite way of telling Tuttle to actually ask a question of Miriam.

So Tuttle did this by asking, "Do you think that for the circumstance you found yourself in, this kind of patience was normal?"

Miriam replied, "I don't know, because I've not been in a circumstance like that."

Tuttle, no doubt, would have loved to point out that Miriam Helmick actually had been in a similar circumstance in 2002, when her first husband, Jack Giles, supposedly shot himself to death. But because of the rules laid down by the court on those circumstances, Tuttle did not go there. Instead, he wanted to know why Miriam had told police right off the bat that it looked as if the house had been robbed. Her exact words had been "There's stuff everywhere." In fact, there hadn't been stuff everywhere, but just a few drawers that were open.

To all of this, Miriam responded, "I was not rational during that time. I don't know what you expect of me! I mean, I called 911 because he was gone. I don't know how I should react."

Tuttle came back with, "All I'm expecting from you is the truth, correct?"

Miriam responded, "You're getting the truth!"

"Well, it's not like the place was ransacked. Like Agent Morton from the FBI was talking about in a real burglary scene, was it?"

"I didn't get up and look at everything. I just looked around me."

"Where did you look?"

"I was in the kitchen. I looked around at the drawers and things."

"Okay, do you remember telling Merredith Von Burg, Alan's sister, in the first three days after the murder that you saw Alan's ring, your ring, and watch, and they had been left by the bathroom sink." Obviously, Miriam couldn't have seen these if she had never gone past the area where Alan lay on the floor.

Miriam claimed she hadn't said that to Von Burg. So Tuttle asked, "She's dreamed that up?"

"Yes."

"Do you know any reason why she would have an animus or motive against you?"

Miriam answered, "I didn't say that! I think that with everything that went on, she probably just got it mixed up. I told her where my watch and ring were left before I left home that morning. I said by the sink. It was the bathroom sink."

Tuttle asked if Miriam had a chance to see what items had

been seized by law enforcement from the house on June 10. She said that she did. So Tuttle asked, after looking at that list, could she say with certainty what items were not on the list, and might have been stolen? Miriam answered that some jewelry was probably stolen.

Tuttle told her it was important to be exact about what items of jewelry had been stolen, because law enforcement could track those kinds of things through pawnshops. Miriam said that she had been as exact as she could have been.

Tuttle declared, "Most of the valuable items in your house were not taken. Would you agree with that?" Miriam said that she agreed. So then he listed those items: computers, four rifles, a handgun, items in a china cabinet. And then he said, "So from your perspective, it doesn't look like a real burglary, does it?"

Miriam replied, "I don't know. I'm not a professional."

Tuttle continued, "You walk in. You see your husband prone on the floor, blood around him. You dropped your bags. You're very startled. You go to him, and you kneel. And you're just sitting there. And on the cell phone call to the 911 operator, he asks, 'Is there anyone else there with you?' And you answer, 'No.' Do you agree with that?"

Miriam said that she did.

Tuttle continued, "And yet, you hadn't been anywhere else in the house?"

"I really wasn't looking to see if anybody was in the house. Alan was my main concern."

"Well, you knew some foul play had occurred, correct?"

"Yes."

"You said that the house had been robbed, and he's lying there in a pool of blood?"

"I wasn't putting everything all together, as somebody still being there in the house. I was concerned with Alan. I didn't know at first what had happened to him."

"Well, did you think the house had been robbed and then he died of natural causes?"

"I wasn't thinking like that."

"In fact, they asked you more than once if there was someone else in the house with you, and your answer was no. You hadn't gone anywhere else, and yet you knew for a certainty there was no one else in the house?"

"Well, I hadn't seen anybody else in the house. I was mainly directing my attention to Alan."

"There's been a robbery. Your husband's prone on the floor. Blood all over, and you're not scared for your own life, as well as your husband's life?"

"No."

"You weren't scared at all?"

"No. I was very upset. He'd just died. I really didn't care what was going on around me."

"Okay, let's talk what was going on around you. The dispatcher said you needed to place your hand on Alan's forehead and your hand under his neck, and then tilt his head back. And your response was 'He's all bloody.'"

"I was talking about his neck."

"Just his neck. That's all you were talking about?"

"That's all I saw."

So Tuttle got into the fact that Miriam said there had been blood also coming from Alan's nose and mouth. But when the first officer arrived, Tuttle noted, "There were no rags around or anything that you had even used as a rag to clean out his mouth, correct?"

"There wasn't blood in his mouth."

Tuttle shot back, "I wasn't trying to quibble over what was in his mouth. What I'm saying is, there wasn't any meaningful blood on your person or your clothes, correct?"

Miriam answered, "There was blood on my thumb from where I pinched his nose. That was all that was touched. I mean, he didn't have it all over his body."

"You testified that you had been injured." (The prosecutor was alluding to her earlier testimony about her rib being broken.) "But in your police interview, you never mentioned the fact that you had been injured, correct?"

Miriam replied that she didn't think that had anything to do with Alan dying.

"Well, on page sixty-four of the interview, you said, 'I put my hands on his chin and turned his head to the side.' You never told them you were trying to do this one-handed?"

Miriam responded that she had not told them that. She did testify, however, "I was trying to do the best I could. I wasn't dwelling on my problem when I was interested in Alan."

Focusing on another area, Rich Tuttle asked if Miriam had touched Alan Helmick's body and then gone back to the car. Miriam said she had not. So Tuttle asked why there would be a particle of gunshot residue on the steering wheel of the car she had been driving on the morning of June 10. Miriam said she did not know why that would appear there.

Tuttle then got to the phone calls Miriam had to her brother in Florida, when she had declared she would sell her story to the highest bidder on television programs. Tuttle asked, "You're looking to cash in on what's been happening, aren't you?"

Miriam replied, "It wasn't that. I was just frustrated over the whole thing."

"Well, you talked about staying in touch with *48 Hours* and with *Nightline*. And this was all over the love of your life being killed in a very violent manner. And you were willing to cash in on that?"

"No, that's not what it was about!"

"Was there ever a time you reached out to Jim Hebenstreit through your lawyer to ask about suspects they had developed in the case?"

"No. I figured that somebody would say something if they had."

"You weren't curious about who had killed the love of your life, Alan Helmick?"

"I was very curious. My job was not to do their work for them."

"Well, in fact, your job was to lead them astray. Is that correct?"

"At that point, yes, I did."

"When you say 'at that point,' we're talking about twelve days after the murder, correct?" (This was the incident of the card under the doormat.)

"I was very distraught. Very upset at the time. Very paranoid about what was going on. So yes, that's what I did."

"So you concocted a complete ruse to lead them on a wild-goose chase away from you and toward some phantom killer out there, correct?"

"I was hoping they would come out and keep an eye on the property and see who was coming onto the property."

"Well, their job really isn't supposed to be chasing phantom killers leaving hokey threatening cards on people's doorsteps, is it?"

"No. But if they had actually contacted me or done something about the white truck or listened, then maybe I wouldn't have been at that point."

"They spent hours tracking down the card. And they spent hours doing forensic testing it, fingerprinting it, DNA—and it all came back to you, correct?"

"Correct."

"It was all over this suspicious white vehicle that didn't scare you enough even to make you leave the residence?"

"I didn't have the money to leave the residence. When I got the money, then I did leave."

"You did what you thought was best for Miriam Helmick, not for the investigation, correct?"

"I did."

"And not to help them find the killer, but to lead them astray, correct?"

"It wasn't my intention to lead them astray. It was my intention to bring them out to watch the house."

"In fact, that greeting card led them to the *real killer,* didn't it, Ms. Helmick?"

"No, it did not!"

Richard Tuttle uttered three more words after Miriam's answer: "No further questions."

Just how well had Miriam Helmick done on the stand? Her testimony and her bearing were gauged by the press. Reporter Amy Hamilton, for the *Daily Sentinel,* noted that Miriam broke into tears when she had to describe her first vision of Alan lying on the kitchen floor with blood around his head. Journalist Paul Shockley noted what at times seemed more like a duel of wills, rather than just testimony between Richard Tuttle and Miriam Helmick. His headline stated: PROSECUTOR, HELMICK CLASH. And for Hamilton, Shockley, and everyone else who had been watching the trial, the question remained: who had won that battle of wills in the minds of the jurors?

CHAPTER 47

A VERDICT

On December 7, 2009, closing arguments began by Richard Tuttle telling jurors about all the things Miriam had done before and after the murder of Alan Helmick. According to Tuttle, the Helmick's housekeeper, Trish Erikson, had seen all the tension between Alan and Miriam on the day before he died. Tuttle contended that Alan had finally discovered that Miriam had been forging his checks, raiding his bank accounts, and keeping important business information from him. In fact, according to Tuttle, it was Miriam's actions that caused Alan to default on two major loans that were connected to his new business ventures.

In Tuttle's estimation, things reached a flash point between Miriam and Alan sometime in the early hours of June 10, 2008. While Alan was near his desk in the kitchen, Miriam walked up behind him and shot him once in the back of the head with a .25-caliber handgun. Then she tried to make it look like a burglary gone bad. But Special Agent Robert Morton had spoken of how shoddy the staging of this was. Morton had called it "juvenile," created by someone who didn't know what a real burglary scene looked like. Many valuable items were untouched in the Helmick home.

Tuttle also contended that a month before Miriam had killed Alan, she had tried to do so by sticking a wick in a car in which Alan had been sitting, in an attempt to blow him and the car to pieces. According to Tuttle, she had gotten the idea by watching the movie *No Country for Old Men* only days before. The only reason she hadn't succeeded was that the wick only smoldered, instead of catching on fire in the gasoline tank in the trunk area.

Tuttle also noted that Miriam never tried giving Alan CPR, as instructed by the 911 operator. And the reason she didn't was because she knew Alan was already dead. Tuttle asked what did Miriam do when she moved to Florida after Alan's death, and didn't tell anyone she was going there? She immediately started contacting rich men on dating sites. Not only that, but by that time she was pretending to be a person named Sharon Helmick. According to Tuttle, Miriam always lied when it suited her.

Tuttle said that Miriam claimed that she was better off with Alan alive than dead. What she hadn't mentioned was that she was entitled to a $25,000 insurance policy, and at least $100,000 from the estate, if not more. That was mandated by Colorado law, no matter what a prenuptial agreement might say. Tuttle insisted that for someone who had come to Grand Junction with $600 in her purse, that was a lot of money.

For his part, Steve Colvin refuted everything that Richard Tuttle had just told the jurors. Colvin stated that very early on, the investigators decided to zero in on Miriam as the killer of Alan Helmick. According to Colvin, they never seriously looked at anyone else as the killer, even though there were many leads that it could have been someone angry at Alan's business dealings, people who landscaped his yard, or even just a random act of burglary on the house that had gone bad.

Colvin noted that a murder weapon had never been found, and no gunshot residue had been found on Miriam's hands, body, or clothing. As far as the particle of GSR on the steering wheel of the car that Miriam had been driving that day, Colvin said that the vehicle had been driven to a police holding yard, and an officer could have inadvertently deposited GSR on the steering wheel from his own hands.

Colvin admitted that the greeting card under the doormat was a bad idea on Miriam's part. But he insisted it wasn't sinister, but rather a desperate act of last resort by Miriam to make the sheriff's office come out to the house and see a white pickup truck and its driver were lurking around the house.

As far as Miriam supposedly not being grief-stricken enough when she found Alan on the floor, Colvin said, "They thought she didn't cry enough? That's preposterous." And he said that law enforcement and the prosecution combined one minor thing after another, and they tried to make them seem like all parts of a guilty conscience: things such as not cleaning up Alan's blood for days after he was killed, or saying "I love you" too many times on her voice messages of June 10, 2008, or things even as minor as stuffing receipts into her jeans pockets rather than into her purse that day.

Colvin declared, "It's no wonder law enforcement focused on Miriam early in the investigation. Alan's family and friends never liked Miriam. They lined up to say she must have had something to do with his murder. She must have even poisoned him in the spring."

Colvin, however, noted that Dr. Kurtzman shot this idea down. Kurtzman had not found any indication that Alan had ever been poisoned. And Kurtzman said that Alan had suffered a heart attack sometime in February or March, and that's what made him so sick all spring. In fact, according to

Kurtzman, it was lucky that Alan was alive at all when he was
murdered, because his arteries were so clogged and his heart
so weak.

As far as gaining money from Alan's murder, Colvin
pointed out, that other than checking about the $25,000 insur-
ance policy, Miriam never tried to collect on anything else she
was entitled to. She had simply left the Grand Junction area
because she wanted to be near her son. No one in law enforcement had ever said that she could not leave the Grand Junction area.

And Colvin pointed out that Miriam didn't date anyone
new for several months after Alan's death. Colvin granted that
it was a mistake on Miriam's part to be using Sharon Helmick's name, but by that point she was desperate to have
some form of identification.

Colvin told the jurors, "Nothing suggests she benefited
from Alan's death. Your decision has to be based upon the
principles of law, beginning with the presumption of innocence. There has been a lack of evidence throughout this case,
and that's the basis for reasonable doubt. All their (the prosecution's) theories are based upon speculation."

Tammy Eret had the last say to the jurors. In some ways, it
was her last hurrah as a prosecutor for the Mesa County DA's
Office. She would soon be leaving that office to go into private practice.

Eret countered Colvin's arguments one by one, stating that
Miriam had plenty of motive to murder Alan Helmick. And
the main motive was that he'd found out that she was forging
his checks and keeping vital business information from him.

Eret also mocked Miriam Helmick's testimony, about how
she was right, and one person after another who testified with
damaging information against her were wrong. Eret said that

Miriam must be the "unluckiest person in the world" to have so many things misunderstood when it came to her.

Eret called Miriam a manipulative liar, who had come to Grand Junction, looking for a sugar daddy. Miriam had been so bold about this, she'd told many people at Barbara Watts's dance studio exactly what she was looking for.

And according to Eret, Miriam was such a liar, she even lied to her own son, Chris. Eret said, "She told him that she'd been cleared by Mesa County authorities. That was not true. If she tells her son a story, what are you to her? Who can believe her?"

When it was time for the jurors to convene their deliberations, Mother Nature intervened and almost made that impossible. A blizzard was blowing outside, and one of the jurors from Palisade, a nearby town, had to be driven to the courthouse by an MCSO deputy. The jurors deliberated for five hours; by three in the afternoon, they had their verdict.

A cordon of bailiffs and deputies stood near Miriam Helmick at the defense table, and by Alan's daughters in the gallery, as the jurors filed into the courtroom. When asked how they had found in the various charges against Miriam Helmick, the words poured out one after another: "Guilty." Guilty of first-degree murder. Guilty of attempted murder in the car fire incident. Guilty of forgery. Miriam was acquitted on only one minor incidence of forgery because of lack of evidence on that charge.

Miriam put a Kleenex to her face and started crying. Soon she was escorted from the courtroom by deputies. She was on her way to prison. Even though sentencing would come later, Judge Robison had no discretion in the matter. A guilty count on first-degree murder in Colorado carried a life sentence without the possibility of parole.

* * *

Outside the courtroom, Rich Tuttle praised the MCSO investigators, especially lead investigator Jim Hebenstreit. As far as Miriam Helmick went, Tuttle told a reporter, "I don't think she's mentally ill. I don't know what her issues are."

Wendy Helmick agreed, stating, "The things she says are beyond my understanding."

Even a few jurors spoke with reporters. They let it be known that within ten minutes of starting deliberation, they all agreed that Miriam Helmick was guilty of false reporting, and that concerned the greeting card under the doormat.

Soon one guilty charge after another came in—all except for a forgery count on a $5,000 check. As to why these jurors thought Miriam was guilty, four of them announced at the same time, "Liar!" One man named Tom elaborated and called Miriam a "psychopathic liar."

A man named Butch declared, "She's very scheming. Very manipulative. Her stories were not consistent."

In fact, the jurors, who talked to reporters, agreed that Miriam had actually hurt her cause by testifying in her own defense. A woman named Gale said that she was put off by Miriam's demeanor on the stand. Others called her "an actress."

Jurors also agreed that FBI agent Robert Morton had made a good case when he testified that Miriam had staged the crime scene. In fact, testimony was so compelling toward her being guilty on the murder and attempted murder counts, the jurors had spent most of their time deliberating about the forged checks.

CHAPTER 48

END OF THE LINE

Miriam was back in court on December 9, 2009, to learn what her sentencing would be. Up until her conviction, she'd always worn street clothes while sitting at the defense table. Now, clad in a jail jumpsuit, she also wore shackles as she sat by her attorney.

Chief Deputy District Attorney Tammy Eret asked Judge Valerie Robison for the maximum sentencing on all counts. Eret said that Miriam had "committed specific crimes on different days." Miriam already faced a mandatory life sentencing without parole on the first-degree murder count. Eret wanted the other charges also to carry sentencing to address the fact that Miriam had committed various crimes in her first attempt to kill Alan, and then in her successful attempt to murder him.

Miriam was given a chance to speak before sentencing. She chose not to, and instead stared at the wall with no expression on her face. Kristy Helmick-Burd, however, did give a statement, telling the judge that her father and all the girls trusted Miriam and tried to embrace her as Alan's second wife. And in return she had betrayed them all.

In the end, Judge Robison added 108 years for the other charges onto Miriam's life sentence. Robison said, "Whether it's symbolic or not, I think it's necessary."

After the verdict, defense attorney Steve Colvin told a reporter that he was disappointed in the sentencing. Then he added, "I do hope this brings some comfort to the family, but obviously Ms. Helmick has a constitutional right to an appeal."

After the trial, MCSO investigator Jim Hebenstreit was in Denver at the quarterly meeting of the Colorado Homicide Investigators Association. To Hebenstreit's surprise, he was awarded a plaque acknowledging him as Colorado's "Homicide Investigator of the Year" for his work on the Helmick case.

Complex Crimes Investigative Unit sergeant Henry Stoffel said of Hebenstreit, "I'm proud of Jim for getting this award, but his dedication to all cases and the pursuit of justice is his mission every time."

In a sense, Portia Vigil had the last word about Miriam Helmick. Portia told a reporter, "We are happy that she can't hurt anyone else, and this helps us to start healing. We have spent so much time and energy on Miriam, and this is the end. We will spend no more."

ACKNOWLEDGMENTS

I'd like to thank the Mesa County Sheriff's Office and Mesa County District Attorney's Office for their help on this book. I'd also like to thank my editor, Michaela Hamilton.